Goodbye Adulthood

CHLOE BANYARD

Copyright © 2024 Chloe Banyard

All rights reserved.

ISBN: 9798398114751

For friends lost and found

1

"You do know you're not a pop star any more?"

"Yes, thank you, I am aware," Sadie said, gritting her teeth.

Painfully aware.

"And they know we're not a band any more, right?" Cameron asked. "They don't think we're flogging it around the South West as a tragic three-piece, or something? *Funk Shui Minus Two.*"

"Well that's the whole point, isn't it?" Sadie said. "It's a reunion."

They'd been arguing about this for ten pointless minutes so far. As far as Sadie was concerned it wasn't something that required an argument. Debate the logistics, sure. Complain about how tricky it would be to get ten days off work at such short notice if you must. But whether they were going to say yes to a life-changing opportunity should not be in question. This was the most interesting thing that had happened to them for *years*. She couldn't believe they weren't all jumping for joy and hugging each other in a big circle right now.

"All I'm saying is that you can't define yourself by something that happened ten years ago." Cameron looked at her pointedly. "Or you shouldn't."

"It's nine years," Sadie muttered.

And how else was she supposed to define herself? As a shop assistant? As a serial renter with a flat full of IKEA furniture? As someone who never quite got it right when she bought clothes off eBay and who had never mastered that beachy wave before everyone stopped caring?

Perhaps Cameron would prefer her to define herself by her abject lack of achievement. By her aching dissatisfaction with life. By all the cute quirks and interesting hobbies that she'd failed to cultivate over the last nine years. Because, take your pick: there were plenty of things that she wasn't.

"It isn't who we are any more," he continued. "We've moved on. We've got grown-up lives. Why would we want to go back to all that?"

"Mia, *please* don't tell me you agree with this?" Sadie asked, watching the bright, shiny, opportunity of a lifetime fade before her eyes.

"Well, it's unusual, isn't it?" Mia said, frowning. "It's not something I've ever really thought about. What did the email say again?"

Sadie picked up her phone. "It says they've been trying to get in touch with us about a new TV show reuniting pop bands from our era. They're about to start filming and need to know if we want to be involved."

When pop ruled the world is what it actually said. And hadn't it ever.

"Hasn't this been done to death already?" Cameron asked.

"No!" Sadie said. "I mean, maybe with older pop bands but it says it's a *twist* on the classic reunion show. It's the same people who made *Village of the 90s*, so it won't be like those other shows."

"What kind of twist?" Mia asked.

"I don't know, it doesn't say."

"Is *Village of the 90s* that show where they made celebrities use landlines and play Game Boys?" Cameron asked, every sentence laced with distain.

"Celebrities from the 90s living together in a holiday village like it was actually the 90s," Sadie said.

She'd loved that show. *Loved* it. And now to be presented with the opportunity to not only be on a similar show, but as a *band* again, alongside all the other bands they'd spent so much time with back in the day? This was *it*: the moment she'd been waiting for where something amazing happened that changed everything.

As soon as she'd read the email her entire fleeting pop career had flashed before her eyes like she was looking into a zoetrope. Recording studios and Saturday morning television; awards ceremonies and promo trips. The band house. The tour bus. Every single glorious technicolour moment. She could almost feel the weight of the microphone in her hand. The heat of the stage lights. She'd felt dizzy; thought she might actually be sick. And then Cameron and Mia had pulled her right back down to earth with a crash.

"Another Sadie thing. Did you make this happen? Is this even real? Are we all just in your head right now?" Cameron said, smirking at how hilarious he was.

"It was a really great show," Sadie said, feeling more dejected with every minute this argument clocked up.

She knew what he saw: three ex-pop stars living out their sad little lives surrounded by people who neither remembered nor cared about the things they were doing nine years ago. Financially unstable. Out of shape. *Ordinary*. But she couldn't bear his contentment. The way he didn't ask for anything from his life and got back exactly nothing of note in return. The predictability of their crappy nine-to-five jobs where the highlight of the week was going for a drink on a Sunday evening. It made her feel itchy. Given the position she'd been in when she'd entered adulthood, Sadie had assumed that her late twenties would consist of slightly more than *this*.

"I just don't understand how this is the first we're hearing about it. *How* have they been trying to get in touch with us?" she asked.

"I can think of one person who wouldn't be inclined to pass on a message," Cameron said.

"You think they contacted *Jim*?"

He shrugged.

"But *we* don't even know where Jim is, how would *they* know?"

"Well that's another thing anyway, isn't it," Mia said. "It's not like we can do it as a four-piece."

Sadie's spirits sunk a little lower. Why did everything good have to come at a price, or with a catch? Considering it had also been nine years since any of them had spoken to Jim – or wanted to, for that matter – perhaps the odds of rounding up the stragglers and achieving a unanimous agreement from all five former band members were a little slim, but Sadie had never been able to shake the feeling that a part of her was still in that same spot where everything she loved had started to fall apart, sitting on the steps to the side of the stage with tears in her eyes and a microphone in her hand. It was as if life had fractured in two that day and she'd been left on the wrong side of everything, and she wasn't sure she could actually *bear* it any longer, living this wrong life.

"I think even a four-piece would be pushing it," Cameron scoffed. "Good luck getting Mr. Superstar involved."

"Ryan *might* do it," Sadie said, but even she knew that her words lacked conviction.

Would he do it? Maybe, if he wasn't in another band. Maybe, if he wasn't in a whole different country. Maybe, if wasn't busy enjoying the kind of success that saw him being played on Radio 1 and interviewed in *NME*.

She exhaled heavily.

"He's not going to have time to do some shit TV show," Cameron said. "Why would he want to?"

"Maybe because he's not boring?" Sadie suggested, but it went unnoticed.

Would Ryan return her calls if he weren't in L.A., in another band, being interviewed in *NME*? Too cool these days for the double blue tick, if it weren't for his fame would he reply to those one-sided messages that piled up to the point of it being embarrassing, or was it something else entirely? Did he even remember that boy and that girl who were once so inseparable that they spent their rare days off together, dragging duvets into the living room of the band house and lounging around with lattes and DVD box sets of American TV shows, feeling like the coolest people in the world? She'd thought a friendship like that was for keeps but all she'd been left with was a sad, hollow feeling. How could Ryan have changed so much while she felt like she'd stayed suspended in time? She didn't understand the formula that handed some people a wonderful life and left others by the side of the road.

"What would we *do*, anyway?" Cameron continued, on a roll now. "They don't want us to perform, do they? I can barely even remember any of our songs."

I can, Sadie thought. *Every dance move and every single word.*

"It says…" She scrolled through the email, trying to stay breezy in an attempt to defuse Cameron. "A chance to revisit your old songs with a live performance at the end of the ten days."

"You know we're the perfect case study to ridicule, right?" Cameron said. "Jim left the band and everything went to shit and the three of us who didn't have anything better to do washed up in the suburbs and went on to live unremarkable lives. Meanwhile Ryan is living it up in America, and who knows what Jim's doing but I'm sure it's something they can make a story out of."

"We don't have to live unremarkable lives," Sadie said.

"I *like* my unremarkable life. I'm just saying that's how they'll spin it. Make us look like losers."

"We *are* losers!" Sadie said, fed up with how this was going. "We're worse than people who never did anything at all with their lives! Literally nothing has come close to living up to what we did in the band, and now we've *finally* got the opportunity to have another go at it you are *ruining* it because you don't care about anything! This doesn't have to be all there is!"

Cameron and Mia were silent as she paused for breath, but then she found she didn't actually have anything else to add so she just let out an unintelligible growl instead.

"Wow, you genuinely believe that pop music made a terrible mistake all those years ago when it handed Beyoncé a solo career instead of you, don't you?" Cameron said.

Mia smacked him on the arm with the back of her hand.

"If you don't do this you are the worst friends in the entire history of the world," Sadie muttered crossly.

"I don't know, maybe it could be fun?" Mia said, raising an eyebrow at Cameron.

"Yeah, well, ten days off work is a long time. I can't just drop everything, you know," he said stubbornly.

"Maybe we won't even have to go back," Sadie said.

"What, like this is our big break? You don't really believe that?"

She just shrugged, wishing she'd kept that little slice of optimism to herself.

"I'm just imagining the stick I'm going to get at work when everyone finds out about the band," Cameron groaned. "I'd bet money on the fact that at some point someone will dig out those shots we did for *Attitude* magazine and plaster my desk with them."

"They don't know about Funk Shui?" Sadie asked, surprised.

"I must have forgotten to put it on my application form," Cameron said dryly. "Do you tell everyone you meet about your five minutes of fame, Mia?"

Mia shook her head as if she'd never even thought about it before and Sadie's frown deepened.

"Oh come on, no one even really knows *Ryan* was in the band, and he's got his own Wikipedia page," Cameron said.

Sadie felt the impact of his words as if he'd got up and shoved her.

"He doesn't tell people?" she asked, that sad, hollow feeling growing within her like a sinkhole.

While they might not all be clamouring to reform the band, Sadie had assumed they were at least *proud* of what they'd achieved in their teens. But to feel *ashamed* of their pop past? Even *Ryan*? Who were these people?

"No he doesn't bloody tell people. He's a guitarist in a *credible* band. He doesn't want that kind of attention," Cameron said.

Sadie shook her head. "Just shut up, okay? I don't care that you don't care. *I* care. We're doing this. I'm going to speak to Ryan and I'm going to find Jim. All right?"

Mia nodded but Cameron just rolled his eyes.

"How *do* we find Jim?" Mia asked.

"I don't know," Sadie said. "If I was Jim, where would I be?"

"On Facebook?" Mia suggested.

Sadie snapped her fingers at her. "Yes. Facebook."

She pulled up the app on her phone and typed in his name, scrolling through the handful of Jim Redwoods that didn't look anything like her Jim had ever looked.

She *would* recognise him though, wouldn't she? It had been a long time, but you didn't forget the face of someone you'd spent so much time with, did you? How much did people's faces change from being in their teens to their late twenties? Or would he be in his *thirties* now? Time was so weird.

She imagined the Jim Redwood who worked as an architect in London briskly descending the wrought iron staircase from his flat and hopping on a tube to Waterloo, meeting his friend and heading down to the river to catch a film at BFI Southbank. The stay-at-home dad Jim Redwood, laughing at something as his daughters stuck sequins on pieces of paper spread over the kitchen table. The Jim Redwood in Leeds, walking across the car park after another ordinary day and driving home to his two-bed semi to do nothing of note all evening. She wondered what the retired Jim Redwood in Cornwall did for fun. There was, in fact, a whole collection of Jim Redwoods on there, but none of them belonged to her.

Drawing a blank, she flicked back to WhatsApp and looked at the message she'd sent Ryan asking if he had time for a chat, as if she was some pathetic casual acquaintance. Every time he didn't reply to one of her messages, she imagined his entire phone screen filled with unread messages from people that he'd given his number to at some point. She imagined that he cared so little about whether they messaged him or not that it didn't even bother him to have that many unread messages. She imagined her message getting swallowed up in all of that: briefly pinging to the top of the list, soon to be pushed back down again. Maybe he even had a separate phone number for all the people he didn't care about, and his proper WhatsApp was full of messages from family and friends that he actually read and responded to. Or maybe when her message came through he expanded the notification window to read the message and then cleared the notification without actually having to register that he'd read it. Or maybe he just cleared the notification straight away when he saw it was from her.

Or maybe he didn't do any of that and he simply couldn't be bothered to reply. Whatever. It certainly wasn't keeping her up at night imagining where she was on Ryan's list of unread messages. Definitely not.

"We know he's not dead, right?" she asked. "Jim, I mean."

Cameron shrugged. "Who knows."

"I'm sure he's not dead," Mia said.

"But somebody did see him after he didn't turn up for that gig?" Sadie asked, looking at Mia and Cameron's blank expressions. "Or spoke to him? We checked he was okay?"

"Why would we have checked he was okay?" Cameron asked. "For someone who is so obsessed with the past you've got a really poor grasp of it."

Sadie tried to move the memory of four naïve teenagers standing three feet to the left of the expectant gaze of the nation onto what happened next, but she couldn't. There was nothing between that image and the four of them sitting behind a table as a sea of adults stared coolly at them.

"You do remember what happened after that gig?" Cameron asked.

"Yes! The press conference… I just can't remember the details."

Cameron glanced at Mia.

"It was a long time ago…" She said diplomatically.

"It *was* a long time ago, but she's the one who wants to drag all this up again and she can't even bloody remember it!" Cameron said.

"Did we go back to the house?" Sadie asked, still drawing a blank.

"They made us do the gig," Cameron said, looking incredulously at her.

"Without Jim?"

"They made us do *two more* TV appearances that week. You don't remember that?"

Sadie shook her head slowly, feeling uneasy.

"What is the matter with you?"

"Cameron, I'm not sure this is the right time to be having this conversation," Mia said.

"We bloody better be having this conversation," Cameron said. "Because she doesn't get it! She doesn't remember how horrible it was at the end! What they put us through! Why *would* we want to get involved with that again?"

"What are you talking about?" Sadie asked, unreasonable tears coming to her eyes. "I'm not remembering it wrong!"

"They told us Jim was ill and they made us keep working. Do you remember that?"

Sadie frowned. She did remember bits about the week before the press conference: a really sombre week where they weren't allowed out of the house and everyone looked more stressed than usual. But then her memory skipped straight to the press conference again, no matter how much she tried to slow it down.

"We had to answer question after question about where Jim was every time we were in public. The whole bloody world worked it out before we did. They took our laptops away, and our phones – I presume you don't remember that part either?"

Sadie shook her head.

"Well we're not *sure* what happened with that, are we?" Mia said. "I think things got a bit out of control at that point. They may have still been trying to work things out with Jim and didn't want us to hear any rumours in the meantime. We don't know. And actually, I don't think you're remembering all this wrong: I don't think you knew any of this was going on."

"But how could I not?" Sadie asked, her head feeling like it had curled up into a single tight swirl.

"You were very upset…" Mia said hesitantly. "I think Ryan was worried about you."

"Ryan?"

"Oh yeah," Cameron said. "Couldn't get anywhere near you without going through your personal bodyguard first."

"What do you mean?" Sadie asked.

"He practically kept you locked in your bedroom the entire week. You two went in a separate car when we had to work. He wouldn't let us see you."

"But why?" Sadie asked, feeling beyond weird now.

That's not how she remembered the dynamic of their friendship at all. But she *had* watched a lot of TV with Ryan the week they weren't allowed out…

"I do not understand why you are asking these questions when you were actually there," Cameron said, clearly frustrated.

"Well me neither!" Sadie exclaimed. "But how could I have known that I didn't remember any of this stuff?"

Was this some kind of post-traumatic stress thing?

"And you still want to do this show?" Cameron asked. "Look at what has already happened and we're not even being filmed yet!"

"Yes I do! Because from the sounds of it we all need to sit in a room together and talk about what actually happened!" Sadie said. "And do we even know *why* Jim left the band? I mean, if no one actually heard from him since? Do we know *why* he didn't turn up that day?"

"I think they said he was struggling with the fame…" Mia said.

"But what did *he* say?" Sadie asked.

Silence from the two musketeers.

"Right." Sadie nodded. "Well now I have two things to ask him when I find him."

2

It was like a bad maths problem.

If Band A has three members, and Band B has five members, which band is Mabel trying to avoid more?

It had become a bit of an obsession over the last month, trying to work out which bands were appearing on the show from the vague list the production company had sent over.

Band A – three members, two cabins.
Band B – five members, three cabins.
Band C – three members, three cabins.

It was the kind of obsession that also required wine, and downloading the Rightmove app, and looking at train tickets, as well as too many memories about things she liked to kid herself that she had managed to forget.

It was all anyone had talked about for weeks: bona fide celebrities, a whole busload of them, coming to their little holiday village in the middle of nowhere to film the next big TV show! Endless speculation about which bands it would be, and whether they'd get to meet them, and declaring how many times they'd seen their childhood heroes live, and did you know that once I *almost* got to meet one of them, and so on and so on. Anecdotes about sort of maybe seeing one of the band members in Tesco that were really scraping the bottom of the barrel. It was almost funny how Mabel had sat quietly in the office listening to her colleagues go on and on about it when she had real stories that would make their heads spin. Except it wasn't funny, and they were stories that she wouldn't be telling anyone.

"Don't you have a home to go to?"

Mabel jumped, coffee slopping down the side of the mug she was holding.

"Sorry," Greg said, grinning at her, tea towel in one hand. "You look like you were miles away."

"Mmm," Mabel said, mopping up coffee from the tabletop with a napkin.

"What are you doing here on a Sunday afternoon? I would have thought site managers had the power to opt out of weekend work."

"I'm just the assistant manager," Mabel corrected him. "And there's always something that needs doing."

And what was there to rush home to, anyway? A cold, empty house that wasn't even really hers? She couldn't remember the last time she'd actually been there. She much preferred it on this side of the wall, where everything was just slightly removed from reality: protected, sheltered. There was nothing that you could possibly need that they didn't have. Nothing that could happen to you that couldn't be made good. There was back-up plan upon back-up plan and someone was constantly making sure everything was okay. It was a perfect simulation of real life, if real life had a finite number of choices and outcomes. But out there you were on your own. A world of boundless, open-ended freedom, with no restrictions on the choices you could make and no guaranteed happy endings. How could you ever hope to get it right?

"I like being here on a Sunday, to be honest," Greg said, pulling out a chair and sitting down. "I like the end of the holiday vibe. Plus there are hardly any customers."

Mabel felt her body tense. Greg was nice: she knew he was nice because she heard him having nice conversations with other members of staff all the time, and occasionally she had nice thoughts about having nice conversations with him too. But nice was best avoided, so she generally ignored his nice smile and tried her hardest to avoid his nice conversations, and focus on drinking her nice coffee in peace. This wasn't why she came here, for small talk and Greg's knee too close to hers. She had work to do. Things to sort out. Lists to make as she tried to work out if this new life she'd constructed was about to come crashing down around her and whether she should cut her losses and just leave now.

"Are you working on the TV show thing?" he asked.

Mabel nodded stiffly.

"Big news, huh? Not that it means anything to me – it might not look it but I am actually in my very early twenties and far too young to remember any of these bands." He grinned again, and it was probably just friendly banter but Mabel couldn't do it, she couldn't; she needed to get out of there and just be alone.

She stood up abruptly, clumsily stuffing her notepad into her bag. She thought of the bottle of Rescue Remedy zipped inside one of the pockets and wished there was a more subtle way to take it. Like, intravenously. Constantly.

"I have to get back to the office actually. I need some, er, paperwork."

Greg looked surprised, but Mabel's urgent need to be away from all people was overriding any impulse to be polite.

"See you next week, then," he said, standing up too.

Mabel just nodded, already moving towards the door.

"Hey, do you think they'll come in here?" he called after her. "The celebs?"

She paused. "They're bringing their own catering team, so…"

"Maybe I won't change the things on the menu to a hilarious play on words using their band names, then. What do you think? Not worth it?"

She would have grinned, once upon a time; looked back over her shoulder and made some kind of flirty comment, that smile she used to give away so freely filling up her whole face and being reflected in his. It used to be so easy. But she didn't do that kind of thing any more. So her feet kept moving and, although she opened her mouth, nothing came out, and that was that. She burst out into the crisp air, the door banging too loudly behind her and goosebumps running up her arms.

"You are a stupid girl," she muttered as her heels echoed across the decking.

It was all fun and games, wasn't it, until the very people you'd moved across the country to get away from landed on your doorstep. How she was dreading coming face to face with those catastrophic blasts from the past. The ending had been so ugly and all the mistakes she'd made still haunted her nine years on, ghosts lingering in every corner no matter what she did. What would she even say to them now? *Long time no see! Sorry about ruining your life!* Somehow, sorry didn't really seem enough in this situation.

Of course she didn't know for definite that they would be on the show. If she was lucky, Prairie Dogs had made so little impact on the music industry that they'd be overlooked entirely. If she was even luckier, Granola Fantasy would be too proud to do it. But the queasy feeling at the pit of her stomach was dark and foreboding and it was telling her loud and clear that this was going to hurt, and there was next to nothing that she could do about it.

She was well aware that cowardice played a large part here: the fear of having to face the people she'd wronged and then run away from. But the very worst part was that in those awful moments of quiet in the middle of the night she found herself imagining an *alternate* reality, where the band had simply fizzled out – as they inevitably always did – and they found their way to this reunion with her still a part of it. And at that point she had to stop herself, because it was just too painful to think about how different things could have been if only she'd behaved like a decent human being. After all this time there was still the tiniest part of her that missed them all more deeply than she could ever bear to acknowledge. They had been the making of her, as well as her downfall, and what she wouldn't give to be able to talk to them as old friends: to tell them that she had tried so very hard to be a better person since she left; to be able to ask them how they were and what they'd been doing during those lost years. The regret that she would never be able to have that hurt much more than any other repercussion ever could.

But perhaps this was karma finally catching up with her, she thought as she walked around the lake, almost jumping out of her skin as a girl appeared on the path in front of her.

"Mabel!"

She tried to style it out, smoothing her shaking hands down her skirt. She'd been like this ever since she found out about the show: all the armour she'd spent years building up dissolving in the anxiety and the uncertainty of it all. She felt jittery all the time, like she was stumbling around where she had once been striding with confidence and purpose. She felt 18 again, she supposed, sitting alone on that bus: broken, shaken, nothing.

"Hi! I was looking for you!" Charlotte said, smiling widely.

Mabel had never been able to work out how old Charlotte, her least hard-working receptionist, was supposed to be. Her face suggested she couldn't be far off Mabel's age, but her attitude said younger. Perhaps that was just what you looked like when you hadn't messed up your entire life in your teens. That must be nice.

"Diane said I needed to talk to you about working during that TV show? I'm not too late, am I?"

Mabel shook her head. "It's fine, I'm doing the rota tomorrow."

Of course, it wasn't enough to merely grit her teeth through the circus that was about to descend on her nice quiet life: her job meant that she'd been in charge of organising and administrating the whole damn thing, and would have to continue to oversee it until the very last crew member had left the site.

"I just wanted to say that I am so keen to work 24 hours a day, if you need me. I can't *wait*," Charlotte said. "I was *the biggest* Granola Fantasy fan, I saw them, like, 100 times. I literally screamed when they announced it this morning."

And there it was. Confirmation, as if she needed it, jumping out at her from behind a tree and pulling a party popper in her face. This was not the way she wanted to find out. She wanted to be alone, with wine, and a blanket, where she could howl with the injustice of it all; of how she'd tried so hard to do the right thing and leave them all alone, and they'd found her all the same.

She swallowed hard and forced a tight smile.

"Granola Fantasy are one of the bands?"

"Yes! *Huge* news. Didn't you hear? It's been out there all day. Everyone's talking about it."

"Who else?" Mabel asked.

"Er… Kingpin, Polar Opposite… They said there's more, though. That was just the first announcement."

"When are they announcing the rest?"

She wasn't enjoying having this conversation with Charlotte, at all, but it was looking like her best option at the moment. The absolute last thing she wanted to be doing was putting anything to do with this into Google and trying to find out that way. That was the very slipperiest of slopes.

"Don't know." Charlotte shrugged. "Don't *you* know? Aren't you in charge of this whole thing?"

"I don't know anything," Mabel said. "I only know what facilities they need."

"Oh." Charlotte looked disappointed. "Do you think we'll get to meet them? The bands. When they arrive? Can I be front of house, or something? Like, in the middle of it all? I'm so excited. I bet Freddie Armstrong is still smoking hot."

"I'll see what I can do," Mabel said brusquely, feeling like she'd reached her limit of how much she could bear to talk about this today.

Why was everyone so obsessed with meeting these people, anyway? They were washed-up, has-beens, 30-something ordinary boring human beings!

Trust me, she wanted to say. *They're really not that great. No big deal. Nothing to write home about.*

But deep down she knew that couldn't be further from the truth.

3

"What happens when pop stars need petrol?" Kitty asked, watching how her nail varnish glittered in the daylight as she lifted the guitar case from the back of the van. "Like, on their day off, or something."

She put the case down just inside the double doors.

"Do they get their own petrol? Wait- do they *need* petrol? Are they allowed to drive their own cars?"

Olly glanced at her, hauling out a bass drum and setting it on the pavement.

"They must get their own petrol. Do you think?" she continued.

"Why do you think I would know the answer to any of these questions? Why are you asking anyone these questions?" he asked, bemused.

"Do you think you'd notice if a pop star was standing next to you at the petrol pump? Are petrol stations in London a lot bigger?" She picked up what looked like a flute case and passed it between her hands.

"You do realise that celebrities aren't a completely different species? They're just people. They look exactly like I do when I get petrol: bored of getting petrol," Olly said, swaying slightly under the weight of an amp. "Hey, do you know what pop stars use to pay for things? Pounds, just like us. Don't tell anyone."

Kitty rolled her eyes, taking two circular fabric cases from the van into the building.

"Stop staring at someone from Athlete," Olly said, brushing past her.

"I'm not," Kitty said, averting her gaze from where she had been taking in every detail of the "pop star" standing three metres from her.

Oh, the disappointment of having to play it cool around fame. As far as she was concerned, you shouldn't even be working in music if you didn't get goosebumps at the sight of a splitter van pulling up round the back of a venue.

"What do you mean *someone* from Athlete?" she asked.

"They literally all look the same to me. And to everyone else. How many of the men in their mid-thirties wearing casual shirts in this building are in the band? Maybe they don't even know."

"Chris knows."

"Chris makes an educated guess and often gets it right."

Chris was the one who got introduced to the band by name and was allowed to "pop into" the dressing room whenever he wanted. And he didn't seem to give a damn about any of it, as if dealing with famous musicians was nowhere near the most interesting aspect of his life. Kitty frequently wondered what on earth was wrong with the people she worked with.

"He always seems to know which one is the tour manager," she said.

"He just heads for the guy who looks the most annoyed and hopes for the best."

"Why would the tour manager be annoyed? That's got to be the coolest job."

"I am yet to see any evidence of a tour manager sharing that view," Olly said, dragging a rectangular flight case towards the edge of the van. "Are you actually going to be useful or are you just here for the minor fame aspect?"

"Athlete are famous!"

"Sure." Olly tilted his head towards the case. "A little help?"

"I'm just so busy moving all these wind instruments," Kitty said, grabbing the side of it. "*Are* they wind instruments? I'm not sure Athlete use wind instruments."

Olly heaved the case out of the van and Kitty tried not to grimace as the weight of the thing made itself apparent.

Loading in bands was like playing roulette. You could go for the small items all you liked but sooner or later you'd pick up something that weighed 500 tonnes and all you could do was style it out.

"What is *in this*?" she asked, trying not to trip on the kerb as they carried it around the corner.

"Keyboard?" Olly said, opening the swing doors with his shoulder. "If it's too heavy for you maybe you should sit out load-in next time."

"I could carry five at once," Kitty said, lowering her end of the case to the floor.

"You know, this isn't technically part of your job. Some might even say that it's a bit tragic how you loiter around in the hope of brushing shoulders with indie bands on the low-key comeback-slash-singles-album tour circuit."

"Just pulling my weight," she said, internally recoiling despite the fact that Olly was smiling.

And actually, it would be less depressing if this *was* as close as she ever got to celebrity. *Nothing* could be more irritating than standing two inches from it the majority of the time and having to pretend she wasn't.

"Sure you are," he said, gesturing towards the doors. "Shall we?"

"Yep," Kitty said, following him back towards the van, weaving past various band members (probably) and road crew.

The van was empty so she scanned the kit piled on the pavement, picking up a couple of cymbal cases as Olly commandeered a large square box on wheels.

"Thanks, guys." A man in his mid-thirties wearing a casual shirt and a beanie hat nodded at them as they passed.

"Is he in the band?" Kitty hissed.

"Probably," Olly said, miming tugging at a collar (of a casual shirt).

The stage curtain was pinned back now and the sound engineer was already darting between the stage and the sound desk at the back of the room. Always wearing shorts, regardless of the season. Kitty put the cymbals down, watching him joking with the tour manager as he ran cables along the floor. The tour manager didn't look very grumpy to her.

"Coming?" Olly asked, holding the door open. "Think we're done here."

She nodded reluctantly, feeling the quiet buzz of a venue coming to life ahead of a gig seep into her skin.

Could she work on a bit today? Was James expecting her home at a particular time? Aging indie band or not, there was nothing quite like the first strains of a sound check drifting into the office as the dusk gathered outside. It gave her a shiver every time and filled her up to the top with discontent.

"I bet I can name more Athlete singles than you," Kitty said, as Olly buzzed them into the staff quarters.

"I don't doubt it," he said, not taking the bait.

"Hey, are Athlete in?" Laura asked, bursting out of the door to the office as they approached it.

"Who knows," Olly said, drifting past her.

"We're not sure who's in the band," Kitty elaborated.

"I know, they all look the same, right?"

"There's a lot of casual shirts going on."

"I honestly hadn't even really heard of them until this morning."

"You hadn't heard of Athlete?" Kitty asked, surprised.

Surely everyone from the age of 20 upwards had heard of Athlete?

Laura shrugged. "Not really my era. Do you know where Chris is?"

"I actually don't."

Laura nodded. "Okay, cool, going to go see if I can do my interview," she said, holding up the video camera.

Kitty watched her go, wishing it had been her idea to start a YouTube channel for the venue. Laura was asking the bands all the wrong questions: Kitty would get inside their heads and under their skin; find out what it was like to *be* them. Find out what they did when they needed petrol. The story behind the songs she could take or leave.

She slunk back behind her desk, glancing at the open box of biscuits and focussing on the way the waistband of her skinny jeans dug into her stomach as she sat down. She scanned her emails and tried to remember what she'd been doing before she'd dropped everything and sprinted out of the office to help with loading the band in. Maybe she could tell James she was going to the gym after work, but stay on and listen to the sound check instead? She couldn't tell him the real reason – most days it seemed like he hated everything to do with music – but he'd buy a line about the gym…

"Hey, guys, what's your favourite Athlete song?" Kitty asked the room.

Silence.

"Anyone know any Athlete songs at all?"

"Errrrm…" Karen made a face. "Oh what was that one that used to get played on the radio all the time?"

"'Wires'?"

Karen shrugged. "I never really know song titles…"

Talk quickly turned to the latest M&S meal deal and Kitty switched off before she started grinding her teeth again. Did any of the people who worked in this arts centre even *like* culture? They certainly didn't seem to like music a great deal. Why was she the only person whose heart skipped a beat when Chris got a call on the radio to say a band had arrived? Why was it such a sin to find the fact that famous people were hanging out just down the corridor from them impossibly cool? She was the only person who cared and, for the most part, she couldn't get anywhere near the bands.

Stupid Laura and her stupid videos.

The rhythmic thud of the bass drum vibrated through the building and Kitty picked up her phone to send James a message saying she'd be home late. Her spirits sagged when she saw that he'd beaten her to it and had in fact messaged her half an hour ago asking what time she'd be home because he had something nice for tea.

If it turned out to be a M&S meal deal she'd cry.

She looked at her watch, the hum of the bass anchoring her to her seat.

Next time, she told herself, grudgingly formulating a reply that told James she was about to leave.

"Leaving so soon, groupie?" Olly asked as she stood up, smirking at her from the doorway.

"Places to be," Kitty said airily, sweeping her phone into her handbag and lifting her jacket from the back of the chair.

She overtook him in the corridor, pushing open the side door without a backwards glance and letting it swing shut behind her. She clattered down the metal steps and out onto the pavement, her thoughts returning to a familiar mantra as she strode along the deserted seafront.

Isn't it pretty; isn't it peaceful. Isn't it pretty; isn't it peaceful.

The boats clacked and clunked gently in the harbour, the whole town so quiet by dusk that you could sometimes still hear the push and pull of the sea from her doorstep. James loved that about the house, but Kitty found it menacing, oppressive, as if the sea was trying to reach across the houses using whispers and echoes, luring people in only to drag them under.

She turned onto her street, lined with cars even though no one ever seemed to go anywhere in them.

Isn't it nice to be able to walk to work, she'd thought, once upon a time.

One shiny black metal gate and three chunky steps and she was slotting her key into the front door, the stained glass panel reflecting the lazy glow of the spring sunshine as she swung it open.

Shoes off. Bag on the floor. Jacket slung over the end of the stairs.

Smelt like curry. Sounded like Mozart.

Kitty wrinkled her nose at both.

"That you?" James called from upstairs.

"Inevitably," Kitty muttered, the parquet flooring cold against her bare feet.

"Hey!" he said, appearing at the top of the stairs with a smile.

Kitty smiled back, involuntarily. Because, that face: it never failed to push a little shiver down her spine. He was so attractive, even with the very short hair and the stubble and the little hole above his chin which he hadn't put a stud in for ages.

"You never put your jacket on the coat stand," James said, reaching the bottom of the stairs and picking up Kitty's jacket.

Her smile faded and she shrugged. "I'm a rebel," she said, padding towards the kitchen.

"I found this great green curry recipe," James said, catching her up. "I got proper naan from the takeaway to go with it."

Calories, the voice in Kitty's head screamed, as she tried to work out how small a portion she could get away with having and then how long she'd have to spend in the gym for the rest of the week.

"Great," she said weakly. "Have you fed the cats?"

"Haven't seen them," James said, stirring his curry concoction with a wooden spoon.

"There you are," she murmured with a smile, sliding the patio doors open and picking up the kitten that was sprawled in front of them.

He let himself be lifted up, securing his claws in her top as he purred.

"So Sam finally got an offer on his house," James said. "I think Emily is practically camped outside the airport already."

"Mmm," Kitty offered disinterestedly.

"I don't think I could do that. Sell up and go travelling *now*. We're a bit old for that, really."

Speak for yourself, Kitty thought, nuzzling the cat before placing him on the floor next to his food bowl.

"Not looking forward to replacing him. He's such a great designer."

Kitty pulled the box of cat food out of a bottom cupboard and tipped some out.

"Was Tolstoy out there?" James asked.

"Nope. Just The Mask," Kitty said, putting the box back and sitting down again, poking at the newspaper that was lying on the side. "Can we go camping?" she asked.

"Right now?"

"Yes."

"For how long?"

"Forever," she said, watching him lift the spoon to his mouth to taste the curry.

"We'll just sack off work then, shall we?"

"Oh yes *please*."

James smiled but said nothing.

"Can we get a motorhome?" Kitty asked. "And fill it with all our friends and drive through the night on empty motorways while someone makes cups of tea in the back?"

"Where are we going in our motorhome full of people?" James asked, turning off the hob and getting two bowls out of a cupboard behind him.

"I don't know. Anywhere. Towards adventure," Kitty said.

James laughed. "You do realise you don't live in a young adult novel?"

She stood up, picking up The Mask again and draping him over her shoulder.

"Can we go and lie on the beach and get drunk?" she asked, wandering over to the dining table.

The Mask pawed at her hair as she sat down.

"You're on fast-forward," James said, kissing the top of her head and putting a bowl in front of her.

He put his own bowl down and then untangled The Mask from Kitty's hair, dropping him gently onto the floor.

"We could go camping next weekend, if you want?" he said, sitting down.

"Where to?" Kitty asked, picking around the rice.

"Anywhere you want," James said. "Maybe we could combine camping with location scouting?"

Kitty winced as her tooth caught the edge of her tongue.

"Ouch," she said, sticking it out and touching a finger to the sore spot.

"What do you think?" James asked.

Even out of the corner of her eye she could see how closely he was watching her.

"About what?" Kitty asked.

"About starting to look for where we might want to buy a house?"

She'd wondered how long it was going to be before he brought this up again. She saw him rehearsing the conversation in his head every time an advert for a property programme came on the TV.

"Well we have a house," Kitty said, pushing a large spoonful of food into her mouth.

"Yeah but this one is too small, long-term. And we didn't choose this one together. Remember we talked about it?"

Kitty nodded, still chewing.

"Oh!" she said, pointing to the patio doors as Tolstoy's tortoiseshell face popped into view.

Thank God.

She jumped up and let him in, getting the cat food out again and filling his bowl slowly.

"There you go, Toadstool," she said, stroking his back.

"That will never be his name," James said.

"It's a *better* name for him," she said. "Who calls their cat *Tolstoy*."

"Who calls their cat *The Mask*."

"You said *cultural*."

"Jim Carrey wasn't quite what I had in mind."

"It's a film," Kitty said, sitting back down, flow of conversation successfully interrupted. "Did you delete your Facebook profile? I was going to tag you in something and I couldn't find you."

James nodded, mouth full.

"Oh. Why?" Kitty asked.

"I don't know. Don't really use it," he said. "It seems a bit... *youth*."

Kitty curled her toes against the cold floor.

"Do you want a glass of wine?" James asked, getting up.

"Yes please," Kitty said.

Bring the bottle.

4

"Great set!"

"Hey, thanks, man," Adam said, grasping the hand of the *vaguely familiar* bearded man standing in front of him as the rest of the small crowd dispersed.

Hard to tell. So many beards these days.

"You should do it professionally."

Adam laughed, searching his face for signs that he was joking or taking the piss. It was unlikely, and he got it so rarely these days, but it had become habit to check, a throwback to when it had all been a little too raw.

"Nah, think I'll stick to the small-time," he ventured. "I just like playing."

And that was true, actually. Maybe the other guys in his old band hadn't felt the same, but he'd never been in it for anything else. Just the pure unadulterated love of playing music. Not even necessarily *his* music. Simply the magic of coaxing notes from an instrument. The way those notes could slot together to form a song, invisibly, out of nothing.

His bearded friend nodded. "I don't blame you. My mate works in the business. Sounds pretty cut-throat to me."

"So I hear," Adam said, hopefully giving off the air of someone who hadn't experienced that first hand.

And really, didn't everyone's mate work in the business these days?

"When's the next gig?"

"What- here? Or ours?"

"Yours."

"I don't think we've got anything for a couple of weeks now," Adam said, unplugging a cable and starting to wind it up. "We're playing at The Swan some time next month… Henry is your man for the facts and figures – think he's at the bar upstairs."

"Cool, I'll see if I can catch him. You look like you've been left to tidy up."

Adam laughed. "Yeah. Henry likes to make a dramatic exit."

"Need a hand?"

"Oh, no. It's only a couple of guitars. Cheers, though."

"Okay, mate. See you again."

"Yeah. Sure," Adam said, pushing the cable into the guitar case at his feet.

Despite Henry being instantly propelled towards the bar on a wave of compliments the second they finished playing, Adam kind of liked this part of the night. The vastness of the silence in a small dingy room after everyone else had left, their minds already on something else. That feeling of invincibility that followed a good performance; like nothing could possibly go wrong now, for at least an hour after the gig anyway. Henry lived for that feeling, trying to prolong it for as long as possible afterwards, with beer, sex, anything that hit the spot. But for Adam, these days it was enough just to exist in that buzzy contentment, letting it settle around him. You didn't get that opportunity once you broke out of the pub scene. It was all too exciting; too fast paced. Too many people winding up your cables for you and offering you ways to prolong the high. And who was to say he wouldn't have ended up in this very spot anyway? Yeah. Who was to say.

As he bent down, his eyes were drawn to a flash of bright blonde hair at the edge of the room. He stopped. His stomach lurched and he craned his neck to see better as she dipped in and out of view, obscured by a pillar and the hanging darkness. Even as his feet started to move forwards he knew it wasn't *her*. It was *never* her, and he should know that by now. He *did* know that by now. Really. And yet she was still that movement in the corner of his eye, the fleeting glimpse of familiarity swallowed up in the crowd.

She was every news story, every reality TV contestant and every radio phone-in. For a brief, heart-stopping moment, she was everyone.

"What are you doing?"

A voice from behind him; an arm slung across his back. Betsy on tiptoes, face pressed against his shoulder.

"I've been sent down to look for you," she said. "Henry's got three phone numbers already."

Adam blinked as the blonde girl – the girl who had been behind the bar all night – moved forward slightly, the dim glow of the red fairy lights illuminating her face just enough for Adam to see there was absolutely nothing familiar about her.

And he had *known* that. Really.

He sighed.

Idiot.

He hated that stupid disappointment. The way his heart held its breath for a second – hoping, hoping – and then exhaled all at once, thumping to the floor. Every single bloody time. What would he say to her, anyway? It had been so long now. If she'd wanted to be found he would have found her. If she'd wanted to find *him* she wouldn't have had to look very hard.

"Earth to Adam?"

He pushed a half-hearted smile in Betsy's direction. "Sorry. Nearly done."

"I don't know why you let Henry get all the girls," she said, hopping onto a stool as Adam retreated back to the stage. "No wait, actually I do know. But I still *don't*."

"Well, he's got the glasses, and the geek thing…" Adam said, skirting the question as he zipped his guitar case shut.

"You've got the geek thing," Betsy said. "And that isn't it, anyway."

She was swinging her legs and Adam couldn't look at her while she was doing that. It reminded him too much of worn armchairs and playful disagreements over Counting Crows.

"Can you- Is-" Adam shook his head at himself.

No.

"Can I what?" Betsy asked, but it was enough to make her stop swinging her legs.

"No, never mind. I'll be up in a minute if you want to go back."

"I'm helping you." She grinned.

"Are you really. I didn't notice."

"So this TV show…" Betsy said, watching as Adam coiled another cable into a circle.

"What TV show?"

"Your second shot at superstardom." She gestured dramatically. "Fame! Fortune! National humiliation!"

"Oh. That." Adam made a face. "Hopefully national humiliation is a bit strong."

"I think national humiliation is the only thing you can count on."

"Sounds so appealing."

"That's the point of these kind of shows! Especially *celebrity* humiliation."

"I think it's more about the music side of things," Adam said uncertainly,

Betsy's glee not exactly helping the growing feeling that sending Nat those contact details had been the top domino in a whole fresh run of mistakes.

A reunion show, his aunt had said. Bands dropping out at the last minute. Producers desperate to fill the slot. Maybe he could give them a call; get his old band back together.

Worth a shot.

And it hadn't seemed like the *worst* idea in the world. A bit of laugh. Everyone back together for old time's sake, enjoying the kind of hospitality they'd only had a brief taste of the first time round. Playing a few of the old tunes and getting a free holiday out of it. It wasn't like his fridge was bursting at the seams. Who *wouldn't* like a few free meals?

But then agreeing to go on tour with Granola Fantasy hadn't seemed like the *worst* idea in the world, and look how that had turned out. Digging all that up again certainly didn't sound like the *best* idea.

"When was the last time a show just about the *music* got all the ratings?" Betsy said.

"We might not even get on, anyway," Adam said, finding himself leaning more towards *not* getting on. "I don't know. It's not very cool putting your own band forward for this kind of thing, is it? Bit desperate."

"You'll *definitely* get on. The way it ended sounds like a total car crash. They love that."

"Who loves that?"

"The public! National humiliation," Betsy reminded him. "And the gossip magazines will be all over it. *Unknown band on the cusp of fame take down superstar pop act in their explosive descent.*"

Adam frowned. "We didn't take anyone *down* with us..."

How far could you fall from the bottom, anyway.

"*The scandalous love triangle that shattered the lives of these promising stars.*"

"She didn't-" Adam sighed. "Do you mind not making light of my past traumas?"

"Sorry, love," Betsy said, sliding off the stool and picking up a guitar case. "I could do with a famous friend, though."

Adam rolled his eyes and nudged her towards the exit.

"Time for a drink," he muttered.

"Maybe if it's really good it'll win an Oscar, or something," Betsy mused, as she made her way up the narrow stairs. "Or what are the telly ones? Something Television Awards? Do you think you'd get to go? *And here's the band that made it great.*"

"Do you have a responsible adult with you tonight?" Adam asked as they emerged into the hum of the upper bar.

He put the kit down to a smattering of applause from his friends.

"There you are!" Henry exclaimed, apparently on a break from gathering phone numbers.

"Oh here I am," Adam said dryly. "Can't imagine where I could have got to."

"So did you phone them?" Betsy asked.

"Who?"

"The TV people!"

"This again. No. I gave the number to Nat. He's better at that kind of thing," Adam said as he sat down, thinking about the ominous text message he'd got from Nat earlier in the day.

Work in progress, bro! Watch this space!

"Well, *I think*: might as well," Betsy announced decisively. "What else are you doing with your life, anyway?"

"Oh thanks very much!" Adam said, indignantly.

"What *are* you doing, though?"

"Drink?" Henry asked, leaning a heavy arm on Adam's shoulder and proffering a shot glass.

He took the glass from him and downed it without a word.

Slightly better.

"Hey, did you speak to that guy with the beard?" Henry asked.

"Yeah, he was asking about gigs," Adam said, sliding the empty glass along the table in front of him.

"I think he's stalking you," Henry grinned, eyes slightly glassy already.

"What!"

"Listen! He comes to every single gig we do. Haven't you noticed?"

Adam shrugged. "There are so many guys with beards at the moment. It's very hard to identify a specific beard. Maybe he's stalking *you*."

"I think he's stalking *you* and you should probably either call the police or take him to dinner," Henry said.

Adam laughed. "If you're going to set me up with a man, could it at least be one without a beard? I just feel like it would be distractingly *scratchy*."

"I'll set you up with a woman the day you stop lugging that massive great suitcase behind you."

Adam raised an eyebrow questioningly.

"B-a-g-g-a-g-e," Henry spelt, clicking his fingers.

Adam looked away. "I'm nowhere near drunk enough to discuss this with you," he muttered.

"So what happens to Henry when you go back to being a pop star?" Betsy asked.

"I don't think being a pop star of any description is on the cards," Adam said.

"I could be his sidekick!" Henry announced. "I could be your sidekick, right?"

"Guest rap?" Betsy suggested.

"*Yes*. That."

Adam rubbed at his eyes, feeling tiredness creep across his face.

"If I find myself with a vacancy for a sidekick I'll let you know," he said, sliding his phone out of his pocket and checking the time. "Actually, I think I might head off. I'm shattered."

"The night is so young," Henry said, raising his glass in the air.

"Want me to take your guitar?" Adam asked, slinging his own guitar over his shoulder.

Henry looked at the drink in his hand. "Probably best."

Adam nodded, looping his fingers through the handle of Henry's guitar case.

"It was a good one tonight," he said.

Henry nodded sagely. "I'd high-five you if you weren't carrying all our kit."

Adam smiled. "Later."

"We're going to talk about that suitcase!" Henry called after him.

"*No one* should still be talking about the bloody suitcase," Adam muttered, stepping out onto the street.

He thought about the money in his back pocket and briefly considered jumping in a taxi, but that wasn't really the point of getting paid for a gig and he probably should have given Henry some of it, anyway. Adjusting his grip on the handle he crossed the road instead, thoughts meandering towards the former bandmates he hadn't seen in too long.

It was fair to say that they'd drifted. Weddings, babies, proper jobs… Adam couldn't quite get his head around those three scruffy lads somehow morphing into responsible adults, especially when he was nowhere near any of that. He'd turned out to be pretty bloody good at frittering away entire years waiting to get round to whatever it was you were actually supposed to be doing in your late twenties, but the rest of it? Nope. At what point during adulthood did you start being able to manage your life in a successful and efficient fashion? When could he expect that to happen? When did it all click into place? He'd always thought it was an age thing, but maybe there was something else – or *someone* else – to it.

As he walked along streets that got less glossy the closer he got to home, Adam contemplated that he might need to get his drum kit out of his mum's garage and pick up the sticks again if they were going to reunite the band. If she hadn't already sold it on eBay, as she seemed to have done with quite a lot of his other things. Although it would perhaps be harder to pass off "losing" an entire drum kit. He'd never intended to leave it there for so long, but time passed, didn't it? And there wasn't an awful lot of space for a drum kit in a house share (which would probably be his mum's argument too).

Side-stepping the empty wheelie bins leftover from that morning, Adam let himself through the front door, putting Henry's guitar down on the floor and sliding his own off his back. This would all be over soon, as well. There was going to be considerably less room for a drum kit when he was living in his van. Denial, Betsy had called it, that he still hadn't found somewhere else to live after Simon had reluctantly given him two weeks' notice (nearly two weeks ago…) to move out so his girlfriend could move in. But it didn't really matter in the grand scheme of things. This wasn't home, just somewhere to stay for a while. He'd find somewhere else soon enough, even if it did mean spending a couple of nights on Betsy's sofa.

Only one place had ever felt like home, and it was less about the bricks and mortar and more about the girl that had radiated sunshine over everything. And she wasn't here, so he didn't need to be either.

5

Sadie tapped her fingers impatiently on the table. She'd never known time to pass so slowly. Where was he? There was a limit to how many old band interviews she could summon from the depths of the internet while she was waiting. She tipped the cold dregs of her latte into her mouth, adjusted her earphones and poked at the spilled sugar on the table top until her phone finally started vibrating with an incoming video call and Ryan's face brought her back to the present day.

"Hey, Paws," he said, smiling broadly at her.

"That's an old nickname," she said in surprise.

"Thought I might bring it back. Just in time for you to have to wear those awful gloves for the whole of the show."

Funny, somehow wearing fingerless gloves for an entire month in the middle of summer hadn't led to her becoming a style icon, as she'd assumed it would at the time.

"Don't you dare!" she hissed, her voice sounding too loud in this public space, despite the bustle of the café around her.

"Those bloody gloves." Ryan shook his head. "You see, this is the can of worms you're opening up here, I hope you're ready for this."

Despite his jovial tone, Sadie wasn't entirely sure he was joking. She couldn't even remember the last time she'd spoken to Ryan, or actually seen his face in real time. It was jarring how awkward she felt talking to him now, despite the lengthy WhatsApp conversations they'd had over the past 48 hours after her not so subtle *I NEED TO TALK TO YOU ABOUT JIM* message had eventually done the trick and got his attention.

"Where are you?" Ryan asked.

"In a coffee shop," Sadie said.

About a mile out of town, she didn't add.

There was almost no chance that Mia would pop home from work unexpectedly, but she hadn't wanted to take the risk. She was right by the motorway here, anyway. Whatever direction she ended up going in.

"Hiding from Mia?" Ryan asked.

"No," Sadie said, her smile betraying her lie.

Keeping secrets from Mia was about her least favourite thing, but unfortunately Mia didn't share her philosophy that the best approach to every opportunity was to say yes immediately and work out the rest from there, so there was very little to talk about in this case. There was absolutely no way Sadie was going to miss out on something this huge and that was that: the thought of having to watch *Village of Pop* on her sofa instead of actually *being* there made her feel like she was suffocating. She was prepared to do whatever it took to get her band on that show and everyone else was just going to have to mind their own business.

"What did she say to you?" Ryan asked.

Sadie sighed. "That I'm not allowed to just turn up on his doorstep."

"I have to say I would echo that sentiment."

"I'm sure you would," Sadie said, rolling her eyes.

"You know I'm doing this to stop you aimlessly driving around places you think various members of his family lived ten years ago."

"I was not going to do that," Sadie protested, pushing the scribbled list of place names further away from her across the table and wondering about this rounding up to ten years thing that everyone was doing.

Ryan had reluctantly agreed to use his contacts to try to find out where Jim was after Sadie had drawn a final frustrating blank, reasoning that someone somewhere must know what had happened to him after he walked away from the band. They still hadn't properly talked about whether *Ryan* was going to do the show yet, and Sadie didn't know how to bring it up, almost afraid to in case the answer was a hard no.

"Where are *you*?" Sadie asked. "It looks like you're in a dressing room."

"In Hollywood, baby! We're filming a cameo on a TV show. It is *cool*."

"Oh, that's awesome," Sadie said flatly, feeling the pang in her stomach that she got whenever she couldn't bring herself to be anything but jealous of Ryan's super cool showbiz life.

She didn't know how he'd managed to be so much smarter than her when they were teenagers, but while she'd walked away from the ashes of their bubblegum pop band with a feeling of unease and disappointment that would stay with her for the next nine years, Ryan had come out of it with enviable guitar skills and a fistful of industry contacts, leaping straight into his next adventure before she'd even had a chance to take a breath.

"It is awesome, but do you know what's more awesome?" Ryan asked.

"What?"

"Coming back to hang out with you for ten days. *That's* awesome."

Sadie peered at the screen. "You want to do the show?" she asked.

"Why wouldn't I!" Ryan said, his stupid lovely face beaming at her through the screen.

"For real?"

"Yes! I wouldn't be here now if it wasn't for Funk Shui. I'm not ashamed of that shit. If we've got some Funk Shui business to take care of, *I am there*."

"Are you sure?" Sadie asked, taken aback. "What about your band?"

"I've cleared it with the guy with the diary, it's all good," Ryan said. "This band can live without me for a couple of weeks. They could get someone else in to play my guitar and no one would even notice. They probably will, actually. Name me one band where you even know what the rhythm guitarist looks like."

Sadie felt like the sides of her face were going to split open from smiling so widely.

"But Funk Shui, that's a different matter – who is going to wear the bright blue satin trousers if I'm not there? You can't replace this face." Ryan grinned at her and, fleetingly, it was as if no time had passed at all and there wasn't an ocean between them.

"I could hug you," she said.

"Well, let's calm down a bit, because, all jokes aside, I am a superstar now, so my entourage will be making sure you don't come within two metres of me."

Sadie laughed.

"It's probably best if we continue to communicate via video call for the duration of my brief visit to England," Ryan said. "And it better not be raining, because I am exclusively sun-kissed these days."

"I'll see what I can do about the weather."

Ryan turned to look behind him, shouting something Sadie didn't catch and making a gesture with his index finger.

"I'm being dragged away," he said.

She nodded. She remembered how it was, being pulled from one thing to the next without any control over your own time. The others had always moaned about it – they were so *tired*; they just wanted a *second* to themselves – but she had never seen it like that. Maybe she'd been different to them from the start.

"Did you get it?" she asked.

Ryan paused.

"Ryan, did you find out where Jim is?"

"You're going to have to pretend you found this out yourself, okay?" he said. "I was never here."

Sadie nodded, stomach churning in anticipation.

"He's in Devon." He looked down at something. "I'm sending you the address now."

"Thank you," Sadie said, the notification momentarily obscuring Ryan's face on the screen.

"Are you going today?"

"I'm going right now."

Ryan nodded slowly. "Honestly, I don't think he's going to want to do it. I can't see why he would. He never looked back, you know? I don't want you to get your hopes up."

"Okay. I won't," Sadie said, hopes already sky high and only gaining momentum.

"You don't even *have* to go there, you know? We could easily do this as a four-piece. It's not like we haven't done it before."

"For like two weeks before everyone realised they didn't like us as a four," Sadie reminded him.

"Well, yeah, but those were different times."

Agree to disagree, Sadie thought.

"How did you find out where he is?" she asked.

"How did *you* find out where he is?" Ryan asked pointedly.

"I'll think of something," she said.

Ryan broke eye contact as a figure appeared at the edge of the screen. "I've got to go," he said, shoving whoever it was back out of shot. "Let me know how it goes?"

Sadie nodded. "I guess I'll see you soon?"

"I guess you will." Ryan winked at her. "Bye, Paws."

The call dropped then and Sadie was left staring at a lingering image of Ryan, momentarily frozen in time.

"Devon," she said to herself, taking out her earphones. "Cool. No big deal. I can drive to Devon on my own."

She walked quickly back to her car, full of nervous excitement. This was a good idea. It *was*. This opportunity wasn't just going to wait around for them to meander back together: someone needed to scoop them all up and throw them into a bag and deliver them to wherever it was they were filming this show. Figuratively speaking.

As she put Jim's address into her satnav she was surprised to see that he was barely more than a couple of hours away, which almost seemed a little easy. She'd pictured crawling into a dark service station in the early hours of tomorrow morning, physically unable to drive any more. Bristol to Devon was a day trip, apparently. Not very dramatic at all.

"Okay, here we go," she muttered, starting the car and exiting the car park.

She had to do this: she had to try. The alternative was just too unbearable. She'd read a career book once that had asked her to list all her major achievements from the last five years, and she'd scrolled back so far in her head that the memories had stopped loading and she couldn't pick out *one single thing* that she was proud of, or that even vaguely counted as an achievement. Jobs that hadn't challenged her. Nights out that were so generic she might as well have just been out the once and had done with it. Holidays that she failed to come back from renewed and suddenly understanding the secret to life. Nothing that sounded anything like the girl with the pink hair who'd cartwheeled around the Eiffel Tower while tourists looked on, wondering why everyone was making such a fuss about five giggling teenagers. If she closed her eyes she could still picture the tiniest details about that day and all those others surrounding it, but everything that had happened since was just a smear of grey across what had promised to be a much more colourful life.

She'd *tried* to be satisfied with reality television and a takeaway on a Saturday night like everyone else, she really had. Tried to ignore the gnawing dissatisfaction; pretended not to hear the voice that said she was wasting her life. She imagined it must feel so calm for them. So *quiet*. But it just wasn't her. Tea and toast and soap operas had never been enough. Mia and Cameron being her entire social circle wasn't enough. Nothing she had done in the last *nine years* had been enough. And she knew now with absolute certainty that nothing would *ever* be enough until she put right whatever it was that had

really gone wrong nine years ago.
    And *five* was the magic number.

6

In hindsight, looking in the box had been a mistake. For so many reasons, including the broken nail and the bloody stupid tears.

She should have left it alone. She knew that, as her legs took her up the stairs to the room at the very top of the house that she didn't really know what to do with. She should have left it alone when her nail bent and tore against the parcel tape, still holding surprisingly strong years after the determined strides to the corner shop and the shaking hands that had wound it around the cardboard. She should have left it alone years earlier when she'd looked around at the pile of things her life had become and decided that that was the thing to carry through the rain to the bus station. That box. The only thing she should have left behind was the only thing she had brought with her.

This stupid TV show. This stupid stupid TV show.

Because she hadn't needed to see any of it again. The grinning faces on the cover of a well-thumbed magazine that had been passed from hand to hand backstage at a summer festival, accompanied by mockery and poorly-concealed delight, the paper crinkled where Fabs had knocked a beer over in excitement and Freddie had leapt across the room with a towel as if it were the only copy in the world. The stupid picture Freddie had drawn her after listening to too much Snow Patrol. Her 18th birthday card from all of them, and the photo from one of the clubs they'd been to that night: glassy eyes and delirious grins and Freddie's hand on her waist. A tatty ticket stub from the first Prairie Dogs gig she'd ever been to – the first *gig* she'd ever been to – and Adam's accompanying plea that she should skip the gig and save the memories for a band worthy of the accolade.

For the whole of the rest of your life, we will be the first band you ever saw play live.

Mabel exhaled, straightening up and pushing open the door into the kitchen.

"Okay?" she asked, too brusquely.

"Yes?" Abbie hazarded, briefly looking up from the carrots she was chopping.

"Good." She paused, tapping a hand against the steel countertop. "You know there's a lunch for five in Kingfisher today?"

"Yes."

Mabel nodded. "Good."

The back door banged open and Liz came back in from her break, glancing at Mabel coolly before turning the tap on to rinse the breakfast pans. Abbie carried on chopping and the radio chattered in the background and Mabel stared at the empty space where a knife should have been hanging before walking out into the canteen without another word, missing the cold air outside that felt as if it had been pressing firmly against her bare arms, holding her together where nothing else was.

Time was creeping on, and although she'd tried everything to rid her body of this unease it swelled in her stomach over and over like a relentless wave. She could forget it for maybe a second and then it came surging back. Hot, like a slow burning. Dizzying, like seasickness. It was totally irrelevant, and she just needed to stop thinking about it, because she'd found the list of bands online and Prairie Dogs weren't on it, so that was that. And it was just as well, because maybe seeing Freddie and Jay again would be like ripping off a plaster, but Adam… Well, that was a much deeper wound and that plaster was saying firmly on.

What an absolute train wreck Granola Fantasy and Prairie Dogs being on the same line-up would be, anyway.

She stormed through the foyer and out into the daylight again.

Fighting it fighting it fighting it. His face and his words and everything else.

Loose dust kicked around her feet as she walked.

Goddammit.

"Christ, you look formidable."

Mabel snapped back to reality to see Jake leaning against a post on the edge of the cycle centre. He took another drag on his cigarette, eyeing her with amusement.

"Have the golf buggies been serviced?" she asked curtly, collecting herself in an instant.

"Yeah, you know, I guess my day is okay." Jake nodded, stubbing his cigarette out and making to flick the remains away.

Mabel bristled – visibly, obviously – and he grinned in satisfaction.

"I wouldn't *dare*," he said, exaggeratedly placing the cigarette butt on top of the post.

She watched as he nudged it neatly into the middle, gaze fixed on it even after his fingers had moved away.

"Yes, is the answer to your question. And it is, as always, a delight to see you too."

"All of them?"

"Every single one. As per your written, emailed, printed, duplicate instructions." His smile looked like a challenge. "So have you seen them yet?"

"Yes, I was here when they arrived," Mabel said, inhaling through the wave.

An exercise in composure. Although torture, in some ways it was a blessing that the bands weren't arriving for another week. She couldn't do *this* next week. There was too much to remember for her to be this irritable and distracted. She *had* to get a grip.

"No, not the TV wankers," Jake said, watching her expression closely.

Mabel wished he'd stop looking at her. Why did people have to *be* like this?

"The girls," he said simply.

She didn't want to ask. Because whoever "the girls" were she knew she should know about it already. By this point it felt like her grasp on the day was nothing more than a wooden bead on the metal spiral of a child's toy.

"By the gate."

She didn't know, and he knew she didn't know.

"Oh. Those girls. I'm going there next," she said dismissively.

"Sure you are," Jake said, nodding.

"Make sure the keys are labelled," she said, taking a step back from the fence.

"They are. *Duplicate* instructions."

She rocked on her heels for a beat.

"You better go and see the girls," he said.

Still smiling. Still challenging.

Mabel turned around without another word, heading towards the rear of the site. Hoping he'd meant the north gate and not one of the others. Not that she minded the walk. All she wanted to *do* was walk. Right back to the days where that was all she *had* done. Movement. Relentless movement. The only thing that had kept it all just about at bay.

She knew something was wrong when Tony was out of his cabin without a sandwich in his hand.

"There you are!" he said, turning as she approached. "Been trying to radio you."

Mabel's hand flew to her belt. No radio. And she hadn't even noticed. At what point today had she completely forgotten to pick up a radio? What else had she missed? How could she not have a radio on her?

Her fingers twitched at her side.

"Maybe you could have a chat with these ladies," Tony said, and Mabel looked past him to see four teenage girls crowded around the edge of the barrier.

Standing like meerkats – too straight, too eager – in the shade of the tall pine trees.

"They're after my sandwiches."

Mabel frowned, nodding and continuing in their direction.

"Hello." One of the girls beamed at her.

Very long hair. Bare arms. Lipstick that was too bright for her complexion; too bright for her *age*. Why were there four of them? Why were they just standing there?

"Can I help you with something?" Mabel asked, trying to work out what was going on.

"No. We're fine."

"Is it okay if we wait here?" the youngest-looking one asked, attracting scowls from the other three.

"For what?

Silence.

"Are you staying here?" Mabel asked.

"Yes," the ringleader said quickly.

Mabel frowned. They should be in school, surely. It wasn't the holidays. It was deeply off-peak.

"You're on the wrong side of the fence if you are staying here," she said, buying herself some time to work it out. "You'd probably have a better holiday actually inside the site."

The girls shuffled awkwardly.

Is this a grown-up? Mabel imagined them thinking. *Do we* have *to listen to her?*
A standoff of sorts, as the five of them regarded each other.

"What cabin are you staying in?"

"Er... five?"

"Really."

Teenage girls. Not dressed for the season. Too much make-up. Staying in a cabin that didn't exist.

The wave crashed over her again.

Oh shut *up*.

She sighed. "I've got things to do. Are you going to tell me why you're here or am I going to have to phone the police and get them to ask you?"

It did the trick. Maybe they were hoping for a soft touch.

"We just wanted to wait until the bands arrived. Then we'll go. We promise."

Oh. Right. Boybands. Of course.

Mabel wanted to smile. To tell them that they weren't nearly clever enough. That they weren't nearly *brazen* enough to get what they wanted. That, actually, it did happen, the things they giggled and daydreamed about. But not to girls like them. And that it was less about lipstick and patience and romance and more about... Well, it wasn't about who you were.

"You shouldn't know about this," she said instead.

"Everyone knows it's being filmed here," one of the girls said.

"We can find out anything," another piped up, as if they had some kind of weird pride in making life harder for other people.

"You can't wait here," Mabel said, mentally doubling the amount of security guards.

"We'll be so quiet. You won't know we're here."

"Go home."

"We just want to see Indigo Lion. We won't even- We just want to see them."

"We can't go home," one of them barely whispered.

Mabel stared at them. Just children. Relying on fictional characters for happiness.

"The bands aren't using this entrance," she said impassively.

She was about to follow it up with a threat when there was a shout from behind her.

"Mabel!"

She turned in the direction of the exclamation, hand touching the empty space on her belt again.

Josie, one of the duty managers, standing a few metres back on the path she'd walked down minutes before.

"We need you!"

She nodded; raised her hand in acknowledgement.

"If you don't leave you'll be removed," she said to the girls. "Don't be here the next time I come past."

She turned around, poking her head into Tony's cabin.

"Get them home, Tony."

He nodded.

"No sandwiches."

His expression was solemn but she knew exactly what was going to happen as soon as she was out of sight.

"Don't feed the seagulls," she muttered, walking briskly to join Josie.

"Groupies. Can you believe it," Josie said with a smile, the excitement of celebrity glistening in her eyes.

It was like a sickness.

"No one's to talk to them," Mabel said as they began to walk. "Where are we going?"

"Oh. Yeah. We've found something. We didn't know what to do about it."

"Okay," Mabel said, letting Josie lead her through the forest, pushing the pace forward as she marched away the memories that she wished meant nothing.

As they came to a clearing in the trees, she could see two of the cleaners standing outside one of the family cabins, rubbish bags piled up at their feet.

"Here," Josie said. "Behind the recycling bins."

"It's so sad," Pam said, pressing a hand to her chest.

Mabel looked at the small wooden bin store and saw nothing.

"In the corner," Josie prompted.

She peered in further and felt her whole body soften when she saw the two tiny kittens: almost circular faces, tiny triangles for ears, bodies draped and curled around each other.

"Oh," she said, taken by surprise.

"Tony said there was a dead cat on the main road early this morning," Josie said. "He thought it was one of the regulars. Same colour." She shrugged. "Like I said, wasn't sure what to do next."

"We should keep them," Pam said.

Becca nodded enthusiastically. "Site pets!"

"They could live in the office."

Soft, dazed expressions. Fuzzy all over. Cream and ginger. The most beautiful thing.

"They can't live in the office," Mabel said, straightening up.

"They could live at the cycle centre? Jake could make them a kennel, or something."

"Jake already has plenty to be getting on with as it is."

"They could be part of the petting farm! Kids love cats!"

"We already have enough pests on site. If we start feeding these two, we'll end up feeding every stray cat that wanders past. And there's no budget for any more animals."

Becca frowned. "It's not like they cost a lot."

Vet bills and vaccinations and flea drops and worming tablets and they were so tiny and so helpless.

"They're feral. You can't have children touching them. It would never pass a risk assessment."

"They're *babies*," Becca said, looking disappointed.

"It might get us a bit of local press?" Josie suggested.

"Meagre, if anything," Mabel said, gaze drawn back to the dim corner and the big eyes blinking out at her. "Not worth it."

"Why don't we send an email round asking if anyone wants them?"

"*You* could have them?" Pam suggested. "I mean, you don't have other pets, or kids, or anything, do you?"

Mabel paused.

The quiet village lane. The fields down the road. The garden she never went in. The open fire she never lit. The empty spaces in the corners of every room that kept her away. Those little furry faces. A saviour. Unconditional love.

"No," she said quietly.

"Are you sure?" Josie was looking at her with something bordering on overfamiliarity, and there was a tiny paw curling hesitantly around her heart, and all she would have to do was scoop one up in each hand to save them.

"Call the RSPCA. Get them to take them away."

Head over heart. It was the *only* way to survive. And what would kittens fix, anyway?

"But they'll have them put down!" Becca protested. "No one wants kittens any more."

"That's not my problem," Mabel said, gritting her teeth and walking away.

7

"Have you ever thought about making a Jenga tower with these flapjacks?"

Adam looked up from the caramel shortbread he was arranging on a plate. "Surprisingly often."

"I wonder if you could make edible versions of classic board games," Esme said, putting the plate of flapjacks back into the cabinet. "Maybe that could be my thing."

"Connect Four with gold coins," Adam offered.

"Pop Up Pirate with chocolate fingers."

He nodded. "Mousetrap with real cheese?"

"Is there fake cheese in Mousetrap?" Esme mused. "Bagsy not clearing those tables," she said as several customers got up at once.

Adam rolled his eyes and picked up a cloth. He knew he let her get away with that too often, but in truth he didn't mind clearing the tables, or tidying up the book display by the stairs that people were forever nudging as they walked past, or any of the other tasks he always seemed to get landed with. What was there to dislike? It was just a job. You did stuff and then you went home. No point wasting energy on actively hating it. It wasn't like you didn't get paid for doing it.

"Is that new?" Esme asked, gesturing to Adam's arm as he carried a tower of cups and saucers back over to the counter.

"This?" he asked, looking at the word scrawled along his skin, the ink slightly more faded every year. "I'd go so far as to say it was *old*. How long have we been working together?"

"Well maybe I don't spend an awful lot of time gazing at your arms."

"Well maybe you should."

He barely noticed it any more, it had been a part of him for so long.

"Very hard to see your arms under all those awful charity shop jumpers,"

Esme said, getting some sandwiches out of the fridge and putting them in the display unit.

"Hey, I have excellent taste in jumpers," Adam said, smiling.

Esme grinned. "What does it mean, anyway? Your tattoo."

"Oh. It's pretty lame," Adam said, deciding that he wasn't going to wear t-shirts any more.

Maybe getting it removed would be as symbolic as putting it on there had seemed at the time. A token gesture towards moving on.

"I'm only going to Google it if you don't tell me."

"I believe you."

"So?" Esme prompted.

"If you must know, it says *always* in Latin."

"Oh."

"Yeah. *Oh* is right. I wasn't entirely in my right mind at the time."

That was an understatement. The pain had been a release at the time, but it hadn't changed anything in the long run.

"A girl?"

"Partly," he nodded, brushing some crumbs off the counter.

Mostly. Entirely.

"What happened?"

Adam paused. "She ran away."

"For real?"

"Yeah."

"Wow."

Silence between them, while Adam focussed studiously on the counter and thought hard about absolutely nothing at all.

"Well that escalated," Esme said.

He smiled, despite himself.

"Was it a long time ago?"

He nodded.

"So where is she now?"

"I don't know," he said.

Oh the desperate things he'd done in pursuit of a ghost.

"Did you... try to find her?"

Adam hesitated, just long enough for Esme to pick up on his reluctance to talk about it.

Because, really, he was starting to irritate *himself*. What was the point of even still thinking about it?

"Sorry, I'm just being nosey. Sucker for a love story." She shrugged.

"It's definitely not a love story," Adam muttered.

"What was her name?"

"Mabel," he said, the word rolling off his tongue like time had never passed, still as electrifying as it ever had been.

Esme nodded, as if this was a satisfactory end to the tale.

"Cute," she said.

And that was that.

Adam shook his head, straightening up as a customer approached. He knocked the spent coffee grounds out of the machine while Esme cut a teacake in half and put it on to toast. He swirled the milk into a wobbly heart shape and put it down on a tray, glancing at the clock behind the counter as the woman gave Esme a handful of change.

And that was that done for another day.

"Are you off?" Esme asked as Adam undid his apron and hung it on the peg in the corner.

"I am," he said, scooping up the pile of books he'd put aside earlier.

"You really should stop shoplifting, you know," Esme said, picking up the hardback on top of the pile. "Or at least steal something good."

Adam smiled. "If I don't read them, who will?"

"What even is this?" Esme asked, flicking through the pages.

"It got made into a film this year," Adam said, watching the photograph he'd been using as a bookmark flutter to the floor.

Esme bent down and picked it up, and he wished he wasn't letting her.

"Is that *you?*" she asked, pointing towards a sandy-haired teenager standing on the edge of the group.

Adam nodded, looking at the smiling faces. That moment of happiness frozen in time. None of them with even the slightest suspicion that all these years later they'd be so far away from the life they'd caught just a glimpse of.

From rock star to barista in the blink of an eye.

Well. Maybe both of those were an exaggeration.

"Yep. Standing on the verge of being almost famous."

He wasn't even looking at the camera. Smiling at nothing, it seemed.

"You were in a *band?*" Esme asked, leaning in to look at the photo more closely. "How have I not seen photos of this before?"

"I think this is the only one I have, actually. We're not even all in it."

"Who's missing?"

"Jonny. He's taking the photo. I think." Adam screwed up his face, inviting that night back into his head again, just briefly. "I think. Yeah."

"What was your band called?"

"Prairie Dogs."

Esme nodded. "I love that."

"Ah yes, our lasting legacy," Adam agreed. "Great name. Shame about the songs."

"Those guys look familiar," Esme said, pointing to the two lanky boys in the middle of the photograph.

Freddie and Jay, arms looped jovially around each other. Not an awful lot of photos like that towards the end.

"Yeah. They were in a much better band."

"Which band?"

"Granola Fantasy."

"No way! I totally remember them!" Esme said. "Were you mates with them?"

Adam nodded. "For a while."

And that had probably been the single biggest mistake they'd ever made as a band. The only *what if* that Adam ever entertained was the one where Jay had gone to a different club and seen a different band and made a different set of decisions with someone else's-

With *someone* else.

"This is too cool!" Esme said. "I'm not even going to pretend not to be impressed! So how many in your band?"

"Four. Me, Harry, Nat," he said, pointing to the photo, "and Jonny."

There was another version of the photo, floating around on the internet somewhere. It had been Betsy, actually, who had emailed it to him.

Oh look who it is! How funny!

And it was so far from funny.

It must have been taken just after the photo they'd posed for. Nat had disappeared altogether in the other version and Jay was creased over with laughter, identifiable only by the dirty blond hair poking out from under a straw hat. Freddie was leaning towards Fabs as if he was about to say something to him, and Harry was pointing in Jay's general direction, smiling widely. Adam couldn't remember what they'd been laughing at, but the way he was staring at the blonde girl, beaming and radiant in the midst of it all, had told him more than he'd even realised at the time about how he'd felt about her.

It had been almost physically painful to look at and not even in his deepest moments of wallowing had he sought it out again. He much preferred the one of the boy smiling at nothing.

"Is that her?" Esme asked, pointing at Mabel.

Adam just nodded.

Maybe that was why he'd kept the photo, so his memories were of how they'd all laughed together instead of how she'd pushed him away. How *he'd let her* push him away.

Enough, he told himself.

He took the photo from Esme, gaze resting on the bin under the counter. What if he just let it go?

What if.

"You need to go home before I ask for your autograph," Esme said, pulling Adam back from his mutiny. "On my chest."

Adam smiled. "First time for everything."

"Did you ever- When you were in the band- No. Just leave," Esme said, shaking her head.

"Leaving. Right now," Adam said, sliding the photo back inside the book. "See you tomorrow."

He clattered down the stairs, phone vibrating in his pocket several times.

Popular today, he thought, checking the screen as he stepped out into the daylight.

A message from Betsy reminding him of his impending homelessness and offering him a spot on her sofa for an indeterminate amount of time – probably inevitable but he'd think about that closer to the last minute – and one from Nat.

Pack your bags – we're in!

Adam stopped.

Well.

That was... What was half way between horror and delight?

A slight smile crept onto his lips as the tide of shoppers ebbed and flowed around him.

He was going to need a bigger bag.

8

The knock on the door wasn't a surprise to Kitty. The girl had been sitting in a car outside the house when she'd popped home at lunchtime, and she was still there when she'd got back half an hour ago. Kitty hadn't recognised her straight away – she had only glanced at the car window to check her reflection as she walked past – but when it had clicked mid-afternoon it had been all she could do not to feign a sudden life-threatening illness and sprint home. She'd eventually made it back five minutes before James and had been trying not to twitch the curtains ever since.

She paused behind the door, considering the curve of the handle as she tried to make up her mind how to play things. It was all going to come out in one big heady rush and she could hardly contain the butterflies in her stomach.

The knock came again and she painted on an enquiring smile, finally pulling the door towards her.

Goodbye, adulthood, she thought, with a fizz of excitement.

"Oh, hi," Sadie said, eyes flitting from Kitty to the hallway behind her. "I'm looking for Jim Redwood. I think he lives here?"

Kitty almost laughed.

Jim.

He was going to hate that.

"Do you- I mean, yeah. He's- I'll get him for you. Hang on," she stuttered.

She'd almost invited Sadie straight in, which wasn't what you did with someone who you were pretending was a complete stranger to you.

Leaving the door slightly ajar, aware that Sadie would be watching her every move, she sauntered as coolly as she could manage down the hall towards the kitchen where James was cooking tea.

"There's someone at the door for you," she said casually, watching as the knife in his hand paused mid-way through an onion.

"Someone?" he asked, putting the knife down and rinsing his hands under the tap.

Kitty shrugged. "A girl. She asked for you."

"I wasn't expecting anyone," he said. "Can you put the pasta on?"

No I cannot put the bloody pasta on! Kitty thought crossly.

It was like going to the loo during the pivotal part of a film. *The Big Reveal.* Absolutely no way was she missing that moment in her *own* film.

She stepped out into the hall just behind James, watching him standing motionless mid-way to the front door.

Oh how she wished she could freeze time and nip round to a better vantage point where she could see both their faces. She could guess at James' expression at that moment: horror, almost certainly, in a similar vein to your mistress turning up at the house you shared with your wife. Honestly, she could not have *written* this!

"Sadie?" James was moving towards the door again.

Sadie hazarded a smile. "Surprise…" she said weakly.

"Of all the people who I expected to turn up on my doorstep…" James shook his head before opening his arms and enveloping Sadie in a hug.

Wait, what?

Sadie's expression went straight from petrified to perplexed, a deep frown resting momentarily over her eyes as James held her tightly against him.

Kitty wasn't sure she'd ever been on the receiving end of such a tight hug from James. What was happening? He certainly didn't seem very horrified.

"What are you doing here?" James asked, stepping back. "No wait, sorry, come in, come in first."

He turned slightly and Kitty froze, caught in the headlights, very obviously not putting the pasta on. But James didn't flinch.

"This is Kitty, my girlfriend," he said, gesturing in her direction.

Sadie nodded, offering her a bemused smile as James closed the door behind her.

You and me both, Kitty thought.

"This is Sadie," he said to Kitty. "She's a *very* old friend. Come through! Cup of tea?"

"Er, yes, okay," Sadie said, following them into the kitchen.

"How do you take it? I wish I could say I remember."

"I don't think I drank tea back then," Sadie said, thawing slightly. "Coffee was cooler. Two sugars, anyway."

James nodded. "Sorry, this has completely thrown me." He laughed. "Have a seat. I will get you a cup of tea."

Sadie perched awkwardly on the edge of a stool and Kitty hovered by the sink, watching her take in the room around her. Had she been expecting a similar reaction to the one Kitty had spent the afternoon imagining? If Kitty felt disorientated by the lack of drama, Sadie must be feeling it ten times over.

"Here you go," James said, passing Sadie a mug over the breakfast bar.

And then he just stood, staring at her, a stupid smile on his face. Kitty noted the lack of tea for her.

"So…" James shrugged. "You look exactly the same."

At least two dress sizes bigger, Kitty thought unkindly.

Sadie took a sip of her tea, putting the mug carefully back down. "Well you don't."

Kitty watched Sadie notice the tattoos that crept down his arm; the black studs in both his ears.

James smiled. "No, I guess I don't."

Another silence, and Kitty tried to work out at what point a lack of explanation would start to get weird, if she didn't already know what was going on. Was it now? Should she start asking the questions?

"So, how do you know each other?" she asked, trying to get into character. "You called him Jim?"

That was the kind of thing she would ask, right? If she didn't know?

Sadie looked confused. "That's not your name any more?"

"Oh, well, Jim wasn't ever really my name. I'd forgotten about that, actually. Jim was more…" He rubbed a hand over his stubble. "What did they say? Accessible, or something like that? James wasn't fun enough?"

"*James* is your real name?"

He nodded. "You didn't know that?"

"I don't know…" Sadie frowned. "Were you ever Jim?"

"Outside of the band? No. That was something they made up. I was James my whole life up to that point."

"They *made* you change your name?"

James shrugged. "Well, they made me do a lot of things."

"Band?" Kitty piped up, almost too late, she realised, getting far too sucked into watching these two people interact.

"Ah, yes," James said simply.

Kitty scanned his face for tension or hesitation or anxiety.

Nothing.

Her stomach was doing cartwheels and his face was doing *nothing*.

What *was* this?

"Sadie and I used to be in a band together. A long time ago now."

Okay, *stop*.

Kitty knew for sure then that this was real life and not a film, because if it had been a film, somewhere at the edge of the set the director would be throwing his hands up in despair and screaming "Cut!". Because that was *not* how you were supposed to reveal Your Biggest Secret. He might as well be telling her about the time that he worked with Sadie in a *bank*. And what was she supposed to say to that, presented in such an underwhelming way? This was going to be a bloody painful conversation to have.

That'd teach her for knowing too much.

"A band?"

She could fly off the handle to make things more interesting, but really that would just be awkward in front of Sadie.

James nodded. "I think I'll skip the tea," he said, reaching for the bottle of whiskey on the kitchen side.

"What kind of band? Like, weddings and old people's birthday parties?"

"I don't know why you'd assume I was in a naff covers band," he said, pouring a hefty measure into a glass.

"You don't know about Funk Shui?" Sadie asked, surprised.

"I didn't think he even liked music," Kitty said casually, watching something cold flicker across Sadie's eyes. "Funk Shui, though. That's quite a name. So come on, tell me everything! This wasn't when you were kids?"

"It was…" James paused. "Ten years ago? Something like that?"

"Twelve," Sadie said. "From the start."

"Oh, okay, so I'd have been…" Kitty pretended to think. "15?"

And she and James had stood in the same room, just metres from each other, on her 16th birthday, and he had absolutely no idea.

"But you wouldn't have been much older… So what, this was a college band?"

"It's hard to know where to start," James said, swilling the gingery liquid round the glass.

Oh either tell me or don't, Kitty thought crossly, bored of the façade already.

"It was a pop band, actually. There were five us – pulled together from various places. Manufactured, by a record company. We *were* really only kids…" James paused. "It didn't feel like that at the time."

"A record company?" Kitty asked, nudging the conversation on. "We're not talking *famous*?"

There were still some things she didn't know, of course, but whether they'd actually make it to the point where the subject got interesting was looking unlikely at this pace.

James smiled ever-so slightly. "We did some stuff," he said, nodding.

"What!" Kitty exclaimed, forcing an expression of curious delight onto her face. "I have so many questions…" she said, leaning back against the counter, feigning wonder. "I can't believe I didn't know this about you!"

James shrugged. "It never really came up."

He was right in a way, she supposed. All the leading questions she'd prodded him with at the start and he never once told her a lie, simply evaded the truth. She'd never asked the *right* question because she'd already known the answer, and there came a point where it stopped being fun, knowing something about someone that they were refusing to acknowledge, so she'd just left it alone.

"You don't even like pop music," Kitty said.

"No," he agreed.

"Should I have heard of your band?" she asked.

And maybe that was the point she took her own lie too far. Maybe the band name should have rung a bell; maybe then when she was inevitably shown a picture and then a video her memory could have become clearer. But it was his fault, not hers. How could she ever have said to him that she knew all along?

"If you liked pop music at the time," Sadie said. "We were in the charts a lot."

Well that corroborated her fake story, at least. James certainly didn't know that she liked pop music at the time. He also didn't know that she still did.

"So you were *super* famous? This is crazy! So where's all the memorabilia? Have you got gold discs and stuff?"

"Oh, I don't know. It's the kind of thing you offload to your parents and they proudly put in a big box."

"You *do* have gold discs?"

"For the album, I think?" James said, looking to Sadie.

"Platinum, actually," she said.

"That's amazing!" Kitty said. "But… Even your mum has never mentioned the band…" She trailed off, suddenly in unchartered territory.

Because that was a good point, actually. It's not like she'd never hung out with his family. But no one had ever mentioned the band. Why hadn't she realised how weird that was?

James shrugged. "My mum's got more interesting things to talk about these days. Like what the neighbours are secretly and or illegally doing with their garage."

"Apparently no one talks about the band," Sadie said flatly. "It's the kind of thing that slips your mind."

"Honestly, I think I'd still be wearing my own band t-shirts," Kitty said.

"Maybe you should have been in the band."

If only.

"Do you have a picture?" Kitty asked. "I'm still not convinced this isn't a massive wind-up."

"I don't. Not here," James said. "I'm sure there's plenty online. Unfortunately."

"Haven't you ever Googled yourself?" Kitty asked. "I mean, *I've* Googled myself and *I* wasn't some teenage superstar."

"There's loads of photos," Sadie said. "And videos. But not much else. I was looking for our old magazine interviews online, but then I was thinking maybe the internet wasn't such a thing when we were teenagers? Does Smash Hits even exist as a magazine any more? What do teenage girls read?"

"The demise of proper pop music is literally the biggest tragedy ever," Kitty said. "Like, I still miss *SM:TV*. What grown-up *really* wants to watch a politics or cooking show in their PJs on a Saturday morning? And kids who think Justin Bieber is pop music are seriously missing out."

"I think the point is that most adults aren't actually watching TV in their pyjamas on a Saturday morning," James said.

"Well maybe you're not," Kitty said.

"I miss *SM:TV* too," Sadie said wistfully. "Those were the best times."

"Were you guys actually *on SM:TV*?" Kitty asked, knowing full well that they had been, because half the time she'd been watching it from the studio audience.

"So many times. It was the most fun. We still are on telly, sometimes."

"Really?" Kitty asked.

"Hardly ever. But sometimes I'll be minding my own business, eating my breakfast, and some music channel will be looking back at old pop bands and suddenly there I am, serenading myself."

Kitty looked at James. "You never let me watch the music channels."

"Precisely because I don't want to be serenaded by my teenage self whilst eating my breakfast. Although I didn't actually think they'd still be playing that stuff these days."

"Nostalgia's a big deal," Kitty said.

Probably because adult life, in comparison to being a teenager at the height of a pop music trend that went hand in hand with terrible miming, dance moves and coordinated outfits, was really really dull.

"Here you go. This was us," Sadie said, holding out her phone to Kitty.

Kitty peered at the image: five teenagers in brightly-coloured clothes, grinning eagerly at the camera like all their dreams had come true. There was Sadie, with her crop-top and lurid lipstick. Mia, who was always dressed in oriental-style clothing for some reason. Ryan, with his blond hair and that grin. Cameron trying to look sophisticated whilst wearing polyester trousers. And James – or Jim – all hair gel and skinny arms. She'd almost forgotten how different he used to look. These days you'd be forgiven for thinking he'd stumbled straight out of a rock band and into their semi-detached life. Who'd have ever thought she'd have ended up with him, out of all of them?

"Oh my God, look at you!" she squealed. "You look so different! I can't believe that's actually you!"

"Me neither," James muttered, looking less and less enthusiastic about reminiscing.

Don't you know, Kitty wanted to shout at him, *how interesting this makes you? How much mileage there is in this? How much I'd rather talk to you about this than house prices and business shows?*

"You look so sweet!" she said.

How this could keep us together.

"How about *you*, anyway," James said to Sadie. "What are you doing these days?"

Sadie hesitated, as if she wasn't expecting to be done with the subject of pop music quite so swiftly.

"Oh, er… Nothing, really. Nothing very interesting. This is the point where I always wish I could say I had some impressive intellectual job rather than just working in a shop."

Well that was boring, wasn't it? Quite the fall from grace. How exactly did you go from pop star to working on the high street? It seemed like almost everyone else who had been in a band during that time was still just about clinging onto some tiny chunk of "the industry" – even if all that amounted to in a lot of cases was "writing for other people" in their home studio. Still, they had a home studio. Sadie wasn't even doing *panto*.

"I didn't figure you for retail!" James said, looking surprised. "I guess I kind of assumed you'd still be doing something to do with music. Or – what do pop music veterans do these days? Radio? TV presenting? I always thought you'd pop up one day where I least expected it. Not so much expecting it to be on my doorstep, but… You're not doing any of that kind of thing on the side?"

Sadie frowned and Kitty's interest perked up again. James was way off track here. Where was he going with this?

"I have to confess I opted out of the whole popular culture scene for bit. I know I should have checked in with you before now, seen how things were going. But, well… Things were a bit messy for a while. And then time passed. You'll have to fill me in."

Kitty felt like she was several steps ahead of both of them. Was Sadie following this?

"On what?" Sadie asked.

"The band! Where you guys went with it. The things you did. You know."

"What things?"

Oh wait- Should she be picking up on the fact that James left the band? Dammit, this was so confusing.

"Oh, were you not in this band the whole time?" Kitty asked innocently.

"Well, practically," Sadie muttered.

"Just for a little bit at the start," James said over her.

Tell me everything, teenage Kitty urged. *Tell me exactly what you were thinking when you were sitting at the back of the group on a TV show looking sad and not saying anything. Tell me the real answers to the questions you avoided in interviews. Tell me about all the drugs you were (probably) taking and which band members you (probably) hated the most. Tell me how long you tried to hang on for and how it felt when you walked away.*

"Oh. Was that a big deal? Leaving the band?" she asked instead.

She hadn't really thought this through: the power she had in this conversation. She could steer these two clueless puppets in any direction she wanted with the right comment or question. But she wasn't big on this level of responsibility and in the midst of it all she couldn't even really remember her motive.

James paused, not looking at either of them. "Probably," he said, almost sheepishly. "But, er… I wasn't in quite the same… *place* as everyone else."

Another pause.

"Long time ago now, though. I'm sure they managed okay without me."

"We didn't," Sadie said.

"What?"

Honestly this was like pulling teeth. Kitty wondered if she'd miss an awful lot if she went and had a bit of a nap for an hour or so.

"We didn't manage without you. It all fell apart."

James frowned. "But you carried on without me? I saw the headlines, at least. You carried on as a four."

"We tried," Sadie said. "Or, I thought we were trying… It sucked after you left, but after the press conference we started doing TV and summer shows again, the normal stuff, and we thought we would just carry on with the album campaign, gearing up to release 'Rise' as planned."

Kitty sighed inwardly. What she wouldn't have given as a teenager to have seen them perform that song live. If it wasn't the best pop ballad ever written then she didn't know what was.

"We performed it once, just after you left, and the fans everywhere went nuts for it. It was perfect. It felt like it was going to be the song that changed everything," Sadie said. "But the record company wouldn't let us perform it again. They kept fobbing us off over the announcement of the next single. Made us perform the same album track at every appearance. The fans started to lose interest. Of course. But that wasn't our fault. And then they dropped us."

James looked mortified. "Sadie, I'm so sorry. I honestly didn't think… I mean, I didn't really *do* much in the band…"

Sadie shrugged. "I don't know whether it was the fans that didn't want it, or the record company that didn't want it. We thought to start with that we'd get another deal but it just didn't happen."

And now Kitty realised how stuck she was. Because this was the stuff she wanted to know. That murky petering out of a band she'd invested so much time in. The unresolved angst and conspiracy theories that the fans were left with. Answers to the questions that still mattered to her, somewhere under all the enforced adulting; that she still wondered about as she trudged through her painfully uninspiring life. And she wanted to exclaim "I knew it!" and

"Those were the worst times for the fans!" and "We hated hearing that album track every time you performed!", and dissect each moment in minute detail with Sadie. She wanted to know how it had felt to be Sadie back then, as well as what James had gone through. She wanted Sadie to know that it had never been that the fans didn't want it.

James had only ever been anyone's second favourite, at best.

"Oh and *then* they kicked us out of the band house and we all had to move back in with our parents. So that was a really special time," Sadie said.

"And then what did you do?" Kitty asked.

"Basically nothing. For a really long time," Sadie said, looking straight at James.

"I'm so sorry," he said. "I thought you'd be okay. But I was…" He sighed. "Young. Naïve, I guess."

"You just disappeared," Sadie said. "You didn't even say goodbye. You didn't say anything."

James shook his head. "I couldn't. That day… I really messed up. I was messing up in general. I always thought I'd see you at some point…"

"But you didn't."

"It took a little longer than I thought to… sort myself out."

Oh this was more like it. The skin on Kitty's arms prickled and she tried to keep her face impassive and blend into the background, barely breathing. It was like eavesdropping in plain sight. There were famous people sitting in her kitchen talking about *secrets* and it was *delicious*. Nothing pressed her buttons more than a brooding messed-up boyband member and faded popstar glamour.

"Why did you have to go?" Sadie asked.

James shrugged, as if he was trying to lift the atmosphere that had descended on them. "It was a lot of things. A lot of things a long time ago."

No! Kitty felt like shouting. *What kind of bullshit PR answer is that?!*

She could see by Sadie's expression and the tense silence that followed that she felt exactly the same.

"I never meant to leave it so long. Not *this* long. I don't know what to say really." James sighed. "Do you ever see the others?"

"Well I live with Mia, so… And Cameron is just down the road. Living the dream with our nine-to-five jobs and shit apartments. Best friends forever."

And probably having more fun than we are, Kitty thought ruefully.

"Obviously we never see Ryan because he's so busy with the band. And too cool for his own good."

"What band?" asked Kitty, completely out of line she realised too late. "I, er, I thought you all worked in shops."

Sadie gave her a look.

Oops.

"They're called Sad Admiral. You've probably heard of them."

No way. No he wasn't.

There was no way Ryan could be in such a big band without her knowing about it. Did *anyone* know about this? She tried to picture the band but all she could conjure up were five blurred outlines. She must have seen them on TV a million times playing festivals and awards ceremonies. How had she not noticed? He couldn't possibly have changed that much.

"I *have* heard of them!" James said. "That's amazing; I had no idea."

"He's only rhythm guitarist. It's not like he's the front man. I guess you wouldn't necessarily notice."

"But they're huge, aren't they?"

Sadie shrugged. "They're no Coldplay. I don't know, maybe he's glad the band ended. All he ever wanted to do was play his guitar. He gets to do that now."

A flicker of something across James' face that Kitty almost didn't notice, preoccupied as she was with trying to think of the most subtle way to get out her phone to look up Ryan and Sad Admiral.

How could she have missed this?

"This wasn't actually a social call," Sadie blurted out.

"Oh?" James lifted his glass. "Am I going to need another one of these?"

A tiny smile. "Maybe."

"How about you?"

Sadie nodded. "Maybe."

James reached into the cupboard behind him and got another glass out, pouring Sadie a drink and pushing it across the counter towards her.

"You're not an easy person to track down, you know," she said, taking the glass.

"Am I not?"

"I suppose it didn't help that I didn't actually know your real name…"

"I wasn't hiding, Sadie," James said.

"I thought you were."

"Why would you think that?"

Sadie paused. "I don't know. I guess I assumed there was a bigger reason for you not getting in touch. Thought you'd moved on."

"Well I did, but that doesn't mean I'm not pleased to see you. We should have done this much much sooner. I'm sorry that we didn't. And I'm sorry that I made such a colossal mess of things for you."

Kitty got the feeling that that wasn't quite the grand apology Sadie had been hoping for. And perhaps not the dramatic reunion either. Well join the club.

"So why now?" James prompted.

"Because I need you for something."

Oh good, they were getting there. Kitty was fairly sure she knew exactly why Sadie had chosen this moment in time to track James down, but she didn't like to count her chickens until she'd actually said it...

"Sounds ominous."

"It's not," Sadie said. "It's a nice thing."

"Which is...?"

"We've been asked to go on a TV show. The band. The whole band."

Kitty watched James' expression.

"Oh! Well I didn't see that coming. What kind of TV show?"

"Did you watch *Village of the 90s?*"

"No."

"Yes," Kitty said.

James looked at her for possibly the first time in this entire conversation.

"When did you watch that?"

Kitty shrugged. "On catch up. When you were out. It didn't seem like your kind of thing."

"Well, no, it isn't."

"So good," Kitty whispered to Sadie.

"I know," she whispered back.

Could they have been friends, Kitty wondered. She'd always written Sadie off for being too... *much*. But maybe they cared about the same things these days.

"That's the show we've been asked to go on?"

"No. It's kind of the same thing, but it's about pop bands. Reuniting pop bands."

"Oh."

"It's not like those other reunion shows where everyone shouts at each other and talks about the past. It's about now. Well, not about *now*. It *is* about then, but more about *recreating* the past than *digging up* the past."

Kitty grimaced inwardly. This was not the hard sell that was needed right now.

James looked at her. "Have you heard about this?"

Momentary shock gripped her, until she realised he was asking if she'd heard about the show, not about Funk Shui being on it.

She nodded. "Little bits. It does seem more light-hearted than the other reunion shows."

"Which I guess you've watched all of. On catch up. While I was out."

Kitty frowned. Well that was a bit unnecessarily snarky considering that putting the music channels on the second he left the house was ever-so slightly less of a big deal than omitting to tell your girlfriend that you'd been in one of the key bands in the country's pop history. And she had humoured his distaste for any kind of popular culture like a bloody saint over the past few years.

"I can't remember how to be a pop star, Sadie," James said, leaning back against the counter.

"No, but that's the point of these shows. They like you better if you're a normal person."

"Yes, exactly. *These shows*. All reality TV is the same."

Kitty had to admit that he was probably right there. No matter what the overall show was about, at some point they were going to have to sit down in a room together and talk about the band. Which really meant talking about why James had left and how sorry he was about the shitstorm that had ensued.

"What do the others think? Can't you do it as a four?" he asked.

"I think we've covered the fact that no one ever wanted Funk Shui as a four-piece," Sadie said. "You don't have to enjoy it. You just have to be there. So I can be there."

"Sadie, don't get me wrong, I want to be able to say yes. For you. I don't want to be the reason you can't do this. But..." He sighed. "There are some things I really don't want to go back to."

And there it was. That look on his face that matched the one he'd worn for much of the six months leading up to him leaving the band. Christ, the fans had called it months before, so how had it come as such a shock to the rest of the band when he'd eventually left? These were the kind of things Kitty needed to hear from the horses' mouths. All she'd got today were bits and pieces, and evaded truths. She needed more.

"Please," Sadie said. "I need to do this. I haven't got anything else."

"Can I think about it?"

She looked at her watch. "Not really. You could have thought about it if I hadn't had to spend two days tracking you down. You know what these things are like: they always need to know the second they ask the question. Apparently they'd been trying to get hold of us for a while but none of us got any messages or anything – I thought they might have already contacted you?"

"This is the first I've heard of it." James took a hefty swig of whiskey and immediately poured himself another one. "What do you think?"

He looked squarely at Kitty, and she was suddenly hit by the realisation that if he didn't agree to do the show then this part of her life might be over.

This house. Her job. The seaside. Him.

"I don't see the harm," she said, trying to sound as nonchalant as possible. "Would it be good closure?"

"I'm not sure closure is what I need," James muttered.

I think it is, Kitty thought. *You're not exactly owning the truth.*

"Maybe it could be about what *we* need this time?" Sadie said hesitantly.

And all credit to her, because that was a ballsy move.

James tapped his fingers against the side of the glass.

Had she done enough?

"Will this do instead of a motorhome?" he asked Kitty.

She nodded, but the feeling in her stomach was unexpectedly sad and small.

"Well I don't know, it seems like a pretty easy way to make amends if you ask me," James said, his tone suddenly light.

"I think we even get paid," Sadie said.

"What's not to like! I was only thinking the other day, wouldn't it be great to get the band back together, for old time's sake."

"You weren't thinking that," Sadie said.

"Well no, I wasn't."

"But you'll do it?"

James exhaled. "Yes, for you, I'll do it. But it probably isn't going to be something I'll look back on and be proud of."

"I might be proud of you," Kitty said.

James looked at her. "Oh might you?"

She smiled. "I might."

"Is this the only bombshell you're dropping today?" he asked Sadie.

"Yes."

"In that case I think I'm going to get on with this Bolognese. Are you staying for tea?"

9

Dinner was awkward. There were several things that Sadie wanted to do after the events of the afternoon and making small talk over a spag bol was not one of them. But what choice did she have? After the lengths she'd gone to to get James – Jim? James? Bloody hell – to agree to doing the show, she could hardly have just sprinted out of there with a jovial "See you in a week!" and hoped for the best.

They'd moved through to the living room after dinner where presumably she was going to have to make even more small talk, skirting around all the topics James didn't want to talk about, of course. She was itching to phone Mia to let her know they could do the show, and she knew she was in trouble for "disappearing" because she could hear her phone buzzing insistently in her bag every 20 minutes, but so far there hadn't been a good moment to take the call. She felt a bit like she was visiting a grandparent she didn't know very well: she wasn't quite sure of the etiquette and was erring on the side of formality just to be safe.

"Here you go," James said, coming into the room and handing Sadie a mug of tea.

"Oh. Thanks."

He sat opposite, avoiding eye contact.

"I like your pictures," she said, for want of something better to say.

He followed her gaze to the big canvas painting of boats in a harbour that was hanging over the fireplace.

"That one's my favourite," he said "They're all by local artists."

Of course they are, Sadie thought. *Because that's the kind of person you are now.*

She was having trouble reconciling this grown-up with the person she'd once travelled around the UK in a glorified minibus with. He was less than three years older than her and yet when she looked at him she saw nothing of herself looking back. Was this where she was *supposed* to be? In a house with period features and local art on the walls and a corner sofa? Had the last nine years passed twice as fast for him as they had for her, or had this always been who he was? Because, Jesus, if she didn't even know his real name, what *did* she know about him?

Which version of you is real? She asked silently, clutching her mug tightly.

She'd like to bet that Kitty didn't know the answer to that question any more than she did. Quite how you could be in a relationship with someone and omit to tell them anything about a really significant portion of your life, she didn't know. First it transpired that Ryan's pop heritage was not common knowledge, then she'd found out Mia and Cameron's friends and colleagues were none the wiser about what they used to do for a living, and now this! Was *anyone anywhere* talking about the band? And, honestly, it looked as if divulging that little nugget of information earlier would really have worked in James' favour because clearly Kitty was *very* into the fact that her boyfriend used to be famous.

"So tell me about Ryan and Sad Admiral," James said. "I can't believe I didn't realise."

"Me neither. He hasn't changed that much. Unlike some people," Sadie said.

James smiled.

"Since when did you wear glasses?"

He shrugged. "Getting old."

Aren't you just, Sadie thought, irritated that, like Ryan, James seemed to be growing *into* his looks, rather than *outgrowing* them like she was. So far it was looking rather like her role in this reunion was to be the one who had let herself go.

"So you said he plays rhythm guitar in the band?"

"Yep."

James nodded. "Figures."

"He got so lucky. The original guitarist left the band, someone mentioned Ryan's name, and the next minute he was gone," Sadie said, knowing full well that luck had nothing to do with it.

"Good for him," James said.

"Oh look, two pop stars in my living room," Kitty said, appearing with a half-empty glass of wine leftover from dinner.

She joined James on the sofa, leaning forward to pick up the TV remote from the coffee table.

"What's the best channel for old pop music?" she asked Sadie.

"Oh, er, I don't know. It's not, like, a regular thing," Sadie said, regarding Kitty suspiciously.

The jury was out on this one but something was definitely off here. Was Kitty a lot younger than James? Sadie would have liked to entertain the idea that Kitty was genuinely star-struck and just trying too hard, but seeing as she hadn't ever heard of Funk Shui it seemed unlikely.

"What are you doing?" James asked.

"Research," Kitty said, flicking through the channels. "Can't be hanging out with a load of pop stars and not know who anyone is."

"I'm sure they'll give you a leaflet," James said dryly. "And over here we have ex-singing sensation Noah Scott, now languishing in the West End with a moderate alcohol addiction and a small dog. To your left you'll see 911, who are getting on a bit now and the backflips aren't quite what they were. In fact, we've got a paramedic on standby just in case."

"I thought you didn't know anything about pop music," Kitty said.

"He doesn't," Sadie said. "911 are a completely different era."

"Do we really have to have this on?" he asked, as Kitty settled on a channel.

"You need to reconnect with your inner teenager," she said.

"My inner teenager is just fine, thanks," James muttered.

The channel ident played and Sadie suddenly realised that she was the only person in the room wearing shoes. Well that was embarrassing. What if the whole time she'd been there James and Kitty had been inwardly sighing at her stomping all over their polished wooden floors?

"Oh!" Kitty exclaimed. "Is this the show?"

Sadie looked at the TV, watching as a *Village of Pop* logo appeared and shots of what looked like a holiday park floated across the screen. Her heart didn't skip a beat so much as do the long jump, and she leaned forward as Kitty turned up the volume.

"Filming is due to start soon for the brand new 'Village of...' series, as a host of defunct pop bands prepare to be thrown back together for the reunion to end all reunions," the presenter said, over a montage of old music videos.

Kitty let out a squeal of excitement and Sadie took in the grinning faces and garish outfits of the people she used to know, everything that had happened in the last few hours fading out.

"In a twist to the usual format, they'll also be joined by the UK's biggest chart-toppers, Indigo Lion, who are taking a break from their UK tour to do the show. Here's everyone's favourite heartthrob, Theo Monroe, with a few words about their involvement in the show."

Never mind James' multiple personalities and his flaky girlfriend: *this* was all that mattered. And she'd done what she came here to do.

"Who are Indigo Lion?" Kitty asked.

"A big deal," Sadie said, feeling the goosebumps spread down her arm as she shifted in her seat. "Actually, I think I'd better give Mia a call: she's probably wondering where I am."

She stood up, dipping into her bag and retrieving her phone.

Eight missed calls.

"Back in a sec," she said, heading out into the hall.

She selected Mia's number and perched at the bottom of the stairs as the phone began to ring.

"You better be dead or abducted because Mia is about to launch a nationwide manhunt here."

Cameron's voice on the other end was not what she wanted to hear. He was such a control freak. Why did he have Mia's phone?

"Is that Sadie? Is she okay?" came Mia's voice in the background.

"Can I talk to Mia?" Sadie asked.

"Where are you?"

"Can I just talk to Mia for a minute?"

"What are you up to?" Cameron pressed.

"Cameron, please, will you just put Mia on?"

"Where are you though?"

"I'm at Jim's house," Sadie said tersely. "Okay? Will you put Mia on? I need to talk to her."

Silence.

"What have you done," Cameron muttered finally.

"Sadie?" Mia was high-pitched and agitated.

"Sorry," Sadie said, suddenly feeling sheepish and silly at not having told anyone where she was going.

"You didn't come home from work! I didn't know where you were!"

"I know."

"What's happened? Where are you?"

"I found Jim," Sadie said, tracing the stripes of the stair carpet with a finger. "I'm at his house."

"Oh!" Mia paused. "So you're okay? Why didn't you tell me?"

"Because you wouldn't have let me come."

"Sadie, you're an adult, I can't tell you what to do."

"You would have made Cameron come with me."

Mia laughed. "Well maybe. So, gosh, you're at his house now? Have you talked to him?"

"He made me dinner."

"Was it okay?"

"The food?"

"No!"

Sadie smiled. "I know, I know. It was…" She looked back towards the living room, lowering her voice. "It's been a bit of a weird afternoon."

"I don't think I'm very surprised by that."

"He was so pleased to see me, Mia. Nothing like what Cameron said. It was like… Like I was a really old friend that he'd lost touch with. Like it was a good surprise, not something from his past he'd rather forget."

"That's good! *Is* that good?"

"It was, but then…" Sadie looked over her shoulder again. "He's got this girlfriend who didn't even know he was in the band. I think they live together. And she didn't even know. And *he* didn't know that the band split up after he left. Like, how could he not have known that? It's like he erased the whole thing from his mind. From his life! But then why was he so pleased to see me to start with?" She shook her head. "I don't think anything we know is true."

"What do you mean?"

"I don't know, there's just something weird about it. He kind of made out that leaving the band wasn't a big deal. Like, he said sorry, but…" Sadie paused. "He's so different. To how I remember him."

"How so?"

"He's… He's such a grown-up."

"Oh!" Mia said. "I guess that's just something that happens to people. It has been a long time."

"You're not a grown-up."

"Am I not? I feel like a grown-up."

Sadie frowned. "I don't."

"Well… People are different, I suppose," Mia said. "So did you ask him about doing the TV show?"

"Yes. He didn't really seem that keen but I talked him into it. He said he'll do it. And Ryan: I spoke to him too. Okay? Are you and Cameron still in? Shall I email the show people back?"

"Yes, I suppose you should. Cameron's in a mood but I'll work on him," Mia said. "When are you coming home? Are you supposed to be working tomorrow?"

And today, Sadie thought.

Not all the missed calls had been from Mia.

But things like work seemed so irrelevant now! How could she possibly spend the next five days in the shop when she was about to be catapulted into something so huge? Shouldn't she be working on her public image and fabricating her backstory, or whatever it was that they were doing when they were "advised" to delete their old email accounts and any other online evidence that suggested they'd been individual autonomous teenagers before the band. What if it got out that she was working there and people could just pop in and buy chocolate from her? That didn't seem very showbiz. Who was going to help them do all this PR stuff this time around?

"I'm not sure," Sadie said, answering both of Mia's questions at once. "What if Jim changes his mind?"

"I thought he said he'd do the show?"

"He did! But what if he changes his mind?"

"Sadie, you can't stand over him for the next five days to make sure he doesn't. You just have to trust him."

"But…"

"Come home now," Mia said. "You've had a busy day."

Sadie looked round at James' classy hallway and had a sudden longing for her messy flat with the pompom fairy lights strung across the wall, llama cushions on the second-hand sofa and charity shop chick lit on the bookshelves.

Okay, she thought, almost relieved. *Enough now. Mission complete.*

It was time to get back to where she belonged.

10

The kitten issue had got out of hand.

Mabel looked across the room at the two balls of fur currently climbing up and flopping back off the arm of the sofa.

Actually, out of hand seemed like an understatement.

It had felt like a conspiracy. The local cat shelter was at full capacity so they had been asked to foster the kittens themselves until a permanent home was found. Suddenly every single member of staff had their hands full with children, dogs, house rabbits and elderly relatives with allergies, and all eyes had turned to Mabel. So here they were, in her previously fur-free personal space. Never mind the fact that she'd be working non-stop for the next two weeks. Never mind the fact that she didn't have the slightest desire for feline company – or *any* kind of company, for that matter.

They weren't in the cottage, at least. The three of them were set up in one of the older cabins in Zone D, removed somewhat from all the chaos, but close enough to throw on some clothes in the middle of the night if needed. As much as she wanted to be as far away as possible from the impending madness, she'd rather staff knew she was around and likely to appear at any moment. Experience had shown that things ticked along more smoothly that way, with one eye on the pot at all times.

This cabin was her favourite, anyway. But she liked it a lot better without kittens in it.

Reaching down behind the wooden cabinet, Mabel unplugged the small TV and carried it carefully through to the bedroom, resting it gently on top of the slim chest of drawers. She turned it slightly to the side so the plug would reach the socket and went back for the remote. The kittens looked at her curiously, as if they'd been so busy throwing themselves off furniture that they'd only just noticed she was there.

"This was not my idea," Mabel said to them, picking up the remote and the pile of DVDs she'd brought from home.

Taking that as an invitation, both kittens enthusiastically fell off the sofa and trotted after her into the bedroom, immediately disappearing under the bed. Mabel tried to ignore them, stacking the DVDs next to the TV in two piles, making sure the spines of the cases were perfectly aligned. One pile for watching and one for falling asleep to.

The films for watching were mostly ones she'd picked up from the charity shop yesterday, with a few old favourites that she could rely on for comfort on the most difficult day. In comparison, the films for falling asleep to were a carefully curated collection, honed over the course of the last nine years. It was rare that a film from the watching pile made it to the falling asleep to pile. All those years ago, after walking and vodka both became impractical as coping mechanisms, watching endless fictional representations of other people's lives had proved a much healthier distraction. Old films, new films, foreign films, anything served to fill the silence; to take her away from both where she was and where she wasn't. There wasn't a cinema nearby that you could get to without a car, and Netflix wasn't tangible enough, so her DVD collection had become the only real thing she owned.

She'd started reading film magazines when she'd begun working at the holiday village and found there were too many gaps and silences during evening shifts. *Little White Lies*, *Sight and Sound*... The magazines that didn't talk about anything *real*, only fiction. And it had to be magazines: books were too personal; too invasive. She much preferred the physical distance of watching a film contained on a small screen at the edge of a room. Reading a magazine served the same purpose.

There was a strange noise from across the room and Mabel looked round to see both of the kittens trying to scale the curtains. She hurriedly plucked them from the fabric, one in each hand, and set them back down on the floor, sweeping the curtains up onto the windowsill.

"I don't think you should be in here," she muttered, trying to herd the kittens back towards the living area.

They skittered around her feet as she walked.

This is ridiculous, Mabel thought. *What am I supposed to do with them?*

Josie had taken them to the shelter to be checked over and apparently they were old enough to be without their mother as long as they were kept inside for the time being, but what happened when they were left alone?

Wasn't the mother cat supposed to keep them in line; teach them basic cat etiquette? What else were they going to climb left to their own devices?

This was her *favourite cabin*.

One of the kittens started to sniff the floor, padding around in a circle.

"Oh no no no…" Mabel scooped him up and practically flung him at the litter tray that Josie had set up by the door.

She watched him do his business, horrified at the thought of it almost happening on the carpet instead. When she'd protested to her manager, Diane, about potential damage to the carpets, she'd said it didn't really matter; that the carpets could be cleaned, or even replaced if necessary. It was their oldest cabin and they rarely rented it out, even in peak season. It was probably due a refurb. But Mabel liked the outdated orange and beige colour scheme and the furniture that didn't make the best use of the small space. She liked that it went unnoticed almost: cast aside for bigger, shinier things. She'd holed up in this cabin so often it felt more like home than anywhere else.

"I don't want this."

She sighed, sitting down on the sofa, dismayed at the situation.

As if the next two weeks weren't going to be awful enough without having to clear up after two feral animals. The bedroom door was staying closed, that was for sure.

Two furry faces appeared by her elbow, accompanied by the sound of tiny claws on fabric. She watched as they stepped unsteadily onto her lap and then proceeded to scale her jumper until they were both – somehow – curled on her right shoulder, tucked into her neck. And there they stayed, vibrating against her skin.

"This isn't going to work," she said quietly. "I have things to do."

The kittens continued to vibrate, pushing their faces into her hair and against each other. It was the strangest sensation and Mabel sat still for just a second, thoughts drifting unchecked to a past life, the faded images of a gaggle of boys and a teenage girl in dirty vans and dingy music clubs so far removed from this reality.

Small stupid memories, like the first time she went backstage with Prairie Dogs and it turned out that backstage was just a room.

"I wish I could reassure you that it'll get more exciting later, but you should probably try to come to terms with the fact that standing in a grimy back room holding a drum that you don't know what to do with is about as good as it gets."

Mabel sighed heavily and one of the kittens squeaked in protest.

Those small stupid memories had been the ones that had stuck. Sharp fragments that had pierced her skin like tiny needles, no matter how fiercely she fought to be rid of them. It took an awful lot of effort to train yourself not to think about something; an awful lot of effort to pretend you were succeeding. She'd come all this way to start again, just so she could lie to herself every day that it didn't still hurt; that her stomach didn't still twist with regret and revulsion.

What started as a slow trickle quickly became a waterfall of memories she didn't want, their faces and voices back in her head against her will. A private showreel of mistakes, playing on repeat. Adam waving at her across the crowded train station the first time they met. The Counting Crows song that had been playing on the radio as they drove across town. Joking with him in an alleyway as she helped them load their kit into a venue. The smile he'd given her from the stage that had made her feel like she was part of something. Chinese food in the middle of the night. The frisson of excitement that her nondescript summer had just got vastly more interesting…

Those small stupid memories that weren't even still valid. At best, they were a false representation of what didn't happen next; at worst, a cruel reminder of what could have been the start rather than the end. Picnics in the sunshine that were more beer than baguettes. Running up to the railings in amazement the first time she saw the pelicans in the park. Smoothies and street food by the canal. The way Freddie's face lit up when hers did; his hands on her waist as he found her in the darkness of someone else's gig. And then, the way she quickly learned to manipulate his emotions to suit her. The friends she stopped calling back because they were too boring. The gaze that curiously lingered just a little too long whenever she caught Jay's eye…

She should have gone home. She should have had a few days in the city catching up with her step-brother and then gone home to pack for university. Adam wasn't supposed to pick her up from the station – Nat was. She wasn't supposed to meet the rest of the band at the shabby studio they practiced in. They weren't supposed to have a gig that weekend. She wasn't supposed to be a part of any of it. She should have been long gone by the time Jay happened across the band in one of their regular haunts two weeks later. Long gone when they went home all starry-eyed and sat around the kitchen table drinking beer and excitedly talking about superstardom until morning. She should never have even met Freddie.

How it was supposed to happen: big band sign very small band to their new record label, help them make a great album and take them along on their world tour. Fame. Fortune.

How it actually happened: none of those things, and then some.

Who would have thought that one girl could do so much damage?

Not Freddie, when he caught her eye from across the professional recording studio they found themselves in. When he kept finding excuses to go on the coffee run with her. And when he finally kissed her on a dim staircase backstage before a gig.

Not Jay, when his hand brushed hers a little too often to be coincidence. When he suggested going to the kind of club where no one would say "Hey isn't that Freddie Armstrong's girlfriend?" or "What is she doing out with Jay Harper?". When they were dancing too close in the darkness, the air between them crackling with electricity.

Not even Mabel, when a look passed between her and Jay and she knew she was about to do something terrible. When the tantalising thrill of crossing that line was so strong it was almost inevitable. When Jay pulled her closer and whispered in her ear, crass ugly words, and she followed him to the toilets, her heart pounding so hard she felt like she was floating.

Did Nat know what she was capable of, right at the very start, way before the pelicans and the lingering gazes, when he reminded her about her return train ticket?

Did Fabs know, when he said more with a hard stare than he ever could have with words?

Did Adam, outside Jay's flat, with "He isn't good for you", "Just come to mine for a bit" and "This isn't you"? When she pushed him, when she was vulgar, when she accused him of being jealous? When he wouldn't leave; when she slammed the door in his face and pretended she hadn't seen the tears in his eyes?

Those small stupid memories became sharper towards the end. The back of the toilet door and the little packet Jay slid out of his shirt pocket afterwards. Arguing with her dad down the phone about deferring her university place and hanging up on him when he just wouldn't listen. The hand that snaked up her thigh in the back of the van on the way to a gig. The lies she told Freddie when she slunk into bed beside him in the middle of the night; the times she didn't make it back to him at all. The stark white room she ended up in, alone and empty. Freddie shouting at her in a dark car park, his face streaked with tears as she turned away from him, feeling nothing.

The bottle of wine in her cold hand as she climbed the steps to Adam's flat, needing something – anything – to numb the pain. The way he wouldn't sit on the same sofa as her, watching her warily as if he knew why she was really there; as if, finally, he saw right through the paper-thin fabric of her facade. When she tried anyway, in nauseous desperation, to lose herself in him: his hand on her cheek and a strange expression on his face.

"Not like this."

When being there with him was the most horribly comforting thing she could ever imagine; when not wanting to leave meant she knew she had to. When she took the money from the tin in the wardrobe – one final terrible act to make sure he could never care about her – and walked away from everything.

Mabel brushed the tears from her face, untangling the kittens from her hair and setting them down on the sofa, before walking out of the cabin towards all the things she was supposed to be doing.

People didn't change. She felt that inherently. You could fight it, put enough obstacles in the way of your true nature to delay treading the same path over and over, but you couldn't change who you were. It was *in her*, this gift for indiscriminate destruction that she never asked for and didn't want. She could feel it constantly, straining just under the surface, barely suppressed by the weight of her disgust and self-loathing; at all times just one careless mistake away from being the version of herself that she'd tried to leave behind.

She wished so badly that she could have been the person Adam thought she was at the very beginning. Who *she* thought she was, if she'd ever given it much thought at all. But the way that she could hurt people so easily, so carelessly, so *naturally*, caught up in the thrill of lust and desire, only to realise in horrified hindsight… The thought that she could inadvertently treat someone like that again…

It would only take a moment to fall into something here with someone like Greg, she knew that. And then who? Jake? Someone nicer than Adam? Someone more destructive than Jay? A few exhilarating highs, and a fresh set of reprehensible lows to add to her collection. And after she'd finished trampling all over them, as she so inevitably would, the only thing left would be even more regret, and this hot burning shame.

11

There were children everywhere. And women. Just a lot of people in general, really, Nat having neglected to mention that he'd also invited the Granola Fantasy boys and their families to this pre-show Prairie Dogs reunion.

Adam had imagined catching up with Nat, Harry and Jonny over a couple of beers, finding out what they'd been up to recently, having a laugh like old times; speculating what they were getting themselves into with this TV show with a bit of false bravado thrown in for good measure… In comparison, this elaborate barbeque gathering at Harry's swanky house in the Cotswolds with everyone's wives and children in tow seemed a bit much. Jonny wasn't even bloody there, having pointed out that it didn't make any sense for him to travel three hours across the country and then the same distance back when he only lived just over an hour away from where they were filming the show in two days' time. It didn't really make sense for *Adam* to come over from Cardiff and go back again, only to drive pretty much straight past on Monday morning, but that was irrelevant anyway seeing as he didn't actually have a home any more and all his belongings were in the back of his van.

He was feeling Jonny's absence even more keenly amongst all these adults drinking hipster beer, and talking about mortgages and renovations and childcare. It wasn't like he hadn't seen them at all since the band petered out, but clearly their lives had accelerated in a completely different direction to his during that time. He wasn't entirely sure how many of the small children charging around the garden belonged to Nat and Harry, but he was pretty sure that none of them had been present the last time they'd met up. It didn't feel *that* long ago since Nat's wedding, which was definitely the last time they'd *all* been together, and the only time he'd seen Freddie, Jay and Fabs at all since the band days. Maybe most of these children were actually theirs?

He wandered across the decking and perched himself on a picnic bench, watching Nat's wife, Annabel, and Freddie's partner, Jen, herd a blond toddler away from the stream at the end of the garden.

"Hello mate," Nat said, sitting down next to him. "This is all right, isn't it?"

Adam nodded slowly. "Busy," he said.

"Hmm."

"Bit like a crèche?"

Nat laughed. "Yeah, I know, not your thing."

"It's not that, I just feel like I missed the memo about bringing along a wife and child."

"Ah it's not just you! Jay's over there, he's not brought anyone. I don't think he's... You know."

Adam followed Nat's gaze to where Jay was leaning against a wall near the barbeque, smoking and talking to Fabs.

"Are you sure all these children belong to the people here? Are we old enough to have this many children?"

Nat laughed again. "They're all Fabs' and Freddie's – they've got a few years on us yet."

"Well I'm sorry to have to say this but your wife has really let herself go. I mean, look at that belly – it's enormous."

Nat grinned. "Only a few months to go now."

"That is terrifying."

"I know, I know." Nat smiled, gaze lingering on Annabel and her considerable bump. "So this is quite a place, right? Who knew there was more than one way to end up with a pool in your basement?"

Adam nodded. "It's impressive."

"He built it himself, you know? And I'm sitting in my "doer-upper" Googling the difference between an orbital sander and a belt sander, wondering how I'm going to make the place habitable before Annabel divorces me." Nat shook his head. "You should come and see my place. Annabel hates it. I mean, I'm starting to. It's a wreck."

"Ah, well, I'll see your doer-upper and I'll raise you no fixed abode."

"No way! What happened?"

"Oh, I was renting a room from a mate; he needed the room back. I figured I'd do this show and work the rest out afterwards."

"Come live with me, man! You can help me do up the house! Plus, free childcare."

Adam laughed. "I hadn't previously considered au pair as a career option, but…"

"I'm serious, I'm serious. You can't do the show knowing you've got nowhere to go afterwards, that's a shit thing to have hanging over you. Maybe not the free childcare, but come back with me and Annabel afterwards, just for a bit. We can hang out – it's been ages. I don't like you living the other side of the country. I miss you." Nat clapped his arm around Adam's shoulders as if they'd seen each other yesterday; as if they were still the same scruffy teenagers that had grown up messing around in a shit town with nothing better to do than get a few mates together and call themselves a band.

How easy it was to forget where they came from – who they had been – when life had moved on so much.

"How did we even end up so scattered all over the place? Where the fuck even are we right now?" Nat exclaimed, gesturing around with his beer. "This village looks like a film set."

"Yeah well, *women*, for a start," Adam said.

"Why else would we do anything," Nat agreed, nodding. "You know, you could get a shit job anywhere."

"Ah mate, my shit job where I am barely pays my rent, I don't think London is an option at the moment."

"You could get a non-shit job?"

Adam just shrugged. *Could* he? Working afternoon shifts in cafes, being in bands, gigging and drinking too much, daytime TV and cold pizza… Should life be about more than that? Did it *have* to become something more, if you didn't mind that it wasn't? Maybe he *could* scrape together enough skills and achievements to blag his way into some kind of entry-level nine-to-five job, but for what? To work his way up, for more money, to get a house, to be an accomplished adult, to be husband material? Did he want that? Would it make him happier than what he already had?

"You'll come to mine for a bit though?"

"Yeah, sure, that sounds nice. Thanks, man."

"Sorted." Nat sat back against the bench, surveying the scene.

Annabel and Jen were still refereeing various children (one of whom seemed to have split into two identical children) down on the lawn. Harry was at the barbeque and his girlfriend Emma was bringing various plates and bowls of food out from the kitchen. Fabs was kicking a ball to a little girl, with his wife Sara watching nearby. Three older children were attempting to scale a tree in front of the stream. Adam couldn't see Jay any more, but that wasn't any great loss to anyone.

"This is a great idea. Why don't we do this a lot?" Nat asked, looking satisfied.

When they'd seen each other previously there had always been a slightly weird dynamic between the two of them owing to Adam pining over Nat's estranged step-sister and no one talking about it, but that didn't seem to matter so much today.

Adam paused. "Is this going to be okay? Us being on the show? Freddie, Jay… I don't know, I just feel a bit… It's not going to get stupid, is it?"

"It's all good here," Nat said. "I spoke to Freddie about it before I called the number you gave me. I wouldn't have called them if he wasn't cool with it."

"I feel like we're going to get dragged into something."

"Nah, we're just filler, man. We barely got started. No one's even going to notice we're there."

Adam raised his eyebrows sceptically.

"What's the worst that can happen?" Nat continued. "Even if it does go tits up, who's going to care? It's not real life any more for any of us. It's a free holiday! We all get to hang out and dick around with the band again. It's cool, honestly."

"What are we going to say if they ask about the end of the band? Or what the end of Granola Fantasy had to do with us? Isn't that quite a popular topic on these kinds of shows?"

Nat shrugged. "We ended because they ended. What's to tell? It didn't quite take off, we had a bit of a break and then it just didn't feel the same afterwards so off we went to get normal jobs."

"Yeah but you know that isn't really how it happened," Adam said, that uneasy feeling not going away.

"It kind of is."

"You don't think that anyone behind this show knows it's a bit more complicated than that?" Adam asked. "You only have to Google Granola Fantasy…"

"The point of these reunion shows is to straighten out all the rumours and PR lies and give bands a chance to set the record straight about what really happened," Nat said.

Adam frowned. Well that didn't sound at all rehearsed. Why did he get the feeling that this had already got stupid? Nat and Freddie had spent a lot of time together after the two bands imploded: it was a weird kind of symmetry that Freddie had dated Nat's sister, and now Freddie's sister was Nat's wife. Being that the two of them continued to see each other a lot, Adam got the feeling that there was something about this TV show that he wasn't in on.

"But it ended how it ended, Nat. Surely they're going to have to talk about what happened? Not sure why they would want to, but they're going to have to."

"Look," Nat said, starting to look a bit shifty. "There's a different version of how it ended, okay? They're not going to talk about… You know. All that."

Adam narrowed his eyes. "Why *are* Granola Fantasy doing the show?"

"You can't tell anyone," Nat said, lowering his voice.

"I already don't like this."

"There are a lot of bands who've done shows like this who are touring the country now – properly, not just doing Butlins as a novelty act once a year. Freddie wants that. But we've looked at these shows: it's not enough to just go along and tell the truth. The bands that come out of it with the good stuff all have a similar story: one of the band fucks it all up, usually it's drugs, then he pulls himself together, the band forgive him, the feud is healed and all the women go crazy for them," Nat said. "But what actually happened… It's not the right kind of story. Nobody came out of that shit looking good."

"They're going to lie?" Adam asked. "I assume it's Jay they're going to throw under the bus?"

Nat shrugged. "We all know Jay was smacked off his face for the majority of the time the band was together, it's not so hard to believe. You just leave some bits out and amp up some of the stuff that did actually happen."

"Does Jay know about this?"

"Yeah, of course."

"And Fabs?"

"It's not my idea, man: it's theirs."

"This was the plan even before we were doing the show?" Adam asked.

"Yeah, but they can still totally pull this off with us there. It's *better*,

Freddie thinks, with us there."

"You know when you said we weren't going to get dragged into something…"

"What's it to do with us, as far as anyone else knows?" Nat said. "We thought about telling you guys, but Freddie doesn't think Jonny and Harry can pull it off. This way, if they do get asked about what happened they'll just be echoing what the press said at the time, which suggests that the two bands weren't that close and none of us really knew what was going on."

Adam frowned. "So what am I supposed to say? What are *you* going to say?"

"Don't worry about it! It doesn't really matter what you say. It's supposed to be a mess." Nat put his beer down and stood up. "I'm going to grab some food, mate."

"Nat." Adam paused.

He didn't want to ask. But he had to ask.

"Did you ever hear from her?"

Nat sighed. "You need to stop asking me that," he said, a look of pity on his face. "I don't think she's worth ten years, is she?"

Adam just shrugged and Nat continued his descent down the steps onto the patio.

It made sense that they'd lie. They were already experts at skirting around the subject: nobody so much as mentioned her name these days. It was a relief in a way, them all consciously writing Mabel out of their shared history. The last thing Adam wanted to see on TV was a blow-by-blow account of what had actually happened. Nat was right: nobody came out of that looking good. Not Freddie, not Mabel, and certainly not Jay.

Adam had spent approximately 99% of the intervening years blaming himself for what had happened to Mabel. By the time he'd realised what was going on it had already got out of hand, and even then it turned out that he didn't know the half of it. Was he too busy giving her the benefit of the doubt? Clinging to an image of who he thought she was? Would he have spotted it earlier if he wasn't so attached to the nice bits; the in-betweens? Like the nights when he'd come back to his crappy house share and find her sitting on his bed, all big socks and elaborate hot chocolate. Nights when she was inexplicably neither with Freddie nor Jay. Nights when he got a glimpse of the girl he'd spent so much time with at the start; who'd chosen Freddie over him without even realising it was a choice.

She was so volatile towards the end; so different. It was too easy to say the wrong thing, and too hard to come back from it once he had, so instead they'd spend hours playing computer games, watching DVDs and ordering stupid things from the shopping channel, not talking about why she was there with him or why she looked so tired. Perhaps he'd pulled away from her towards the end, even before she'd pushed him, but it just got so hard to be her friend, in more ways than one.

It seemed inconceivable that Freddie hadn't known the full extent of it, and why – surely knowing the things that Jay was into – he was happy for Mabel to spend so much time with him in the first place. Was he somehow to blame too? Could he have stopped it from happening? Was he really so busy carrying the band with his number one singles and catchy album tracks that he hadn't noticed Jay was busy fucking his girlfriend?

Adam looked up as someone put a beer on the table top behind him.

"Thought I'd come say hi," Freddie said, sitting down. "How's it going?"

"Thanks," Adam said, taking the beer. "Yeah it's… It's going."

"It's good to see you, man. It's been a long time."

"Yeah, same. I was just thinking that the last time was probably Nat's wedding."

Freddie nodded.

"I hear all or several of these children belong to you?"

"Er, those two…" He pointed to the very small blond duplicates. "And…" He looked around. "Oh, that one in the tree. Dark hair, devilish grin."

"You've got your hands full."

"Jen's got her hands full. I just do as I'm told."

Freddie paused and it occurred to Adam that they'd never really done this. Nat's wedding had been big and busy, and after a few awkward pleasantries with Freddie and Fabs he'd retreated to the safety of getting hammered with Jonny and Betsy. The demise of Granola Fantasy had come about so swiftly and so explosively that by the time Adam had recovered from the aftershock the opportunity to talk to Freddie properly about any of it had never come up. They all moved away, moved on and assumed that one day they'd forget it had ever happened.

"So Harry was saying he reckons he hasn't picked up a guitar for at least five years," Freddie said.

"How does he feel about drum kits, because I'm not sure I can even remember how to hold the sticks," Adam said, content to have the kind of conversation where they didn't mention any of the things they'd never talked about.

"You don't play any more?"

"Not for a long time. I mean, I still play, but guitar not drums."

"Gigging?"

"Yeah, just locally, you know. Me and a mate. So small-time."

"Gigging is gigging," Freddie said. "You might get some bigger stuff after the show."

Adam shrugged. "I don't know. Small-time is simple."

"Yeah."

"How about you?"

"Ah, I'm the man behind the desk now: I've got a studio at home. It's pretty small-time too, I'll be honest, but it keeps my hand in. You and your mate should come and put some tracks down. I'm not bad."

Adam smiled. "Thanks, man. I might take you up on that if we manage to cobble together more than three songs."

He'd never really had anything against Freddie. He'd always seemed like a good guy and he was an exceptional songwriter: even writing pop songs his lyrics were more intelligent and sophisticated than the genre deserved. It had been inevitable – and fair enough – that he'd get the girl: back then he'd had a rock star swagger that had put him in a different league to Adam, and he was pretty sure Mabel had never seen him as anything more than a friend, anyway. If she'd never met Freddie there probably would have been someone else, sooner or later, but honestly Adam would have been more than content to fall into the BFF role. He didn't know why she'd felt she had to disappear, but he didn't think he'd ever stop wishing that she hadn't. You'd think nine years would be enough time for the memories to fade, but it wasn't, not really. Some people leave a void that you can never patch up.

"You don't write any more?" Adam asked.

Freddie made a face. "Not for a while."

"That's a shame, man. Your lyrics were something else."

Freddie looked surprised, but stayed silent.

"I hear Fabs is writing for some pretty big names these days?" Adam asked.

"Yeah, he's doing better than the rest of us. It took a bit to get him to agree to all this."

"Oh really?"

"Oh he doesn't need this. He's more doing it for the kids, so they can see him play the old stuff. He said they don't think he's cool." Freddie smiled. "He's got a point to prove."

"Nat said you guys might go back on the road afterwards, though?" Adam paused. "I realise I'm not supposed to know that."

"Oh no, you're all right, it's not a secret. We're all friends here."

More or less, thought Adam.

"I think he'll do it for a bit, but we'll see. We might have a vacancy for a new drummer." Freddie grinned.

"We'd be entering dangerous supergroup territory there," Adam said, although obviously there was no way in a million years that he'd volunteer to be in a band with Jay.

"Everyone loves a supergroup."

Adam hesitated, not quite able to leave it alone. "So this alternative ending…"

Freddie sighed. "You know, it's not *just* about pitching it right to get the band back together. I didn't think it was a good idea to dredge all that shit up again. How it ended was really…" He shrugged. "I've got kids now: Ava's seven. Maybe she hears about it from someone at school, or maybe she looks it up on YouTube in a couple of years, but I don't want her to know about all that."

"Makes sense."

"And Jay won't talk about it, anyway, so it's less aggro this way."

"Oh?"

"I don't know, he's still really touchy about it all. I mean, *I'm*…" Freddie shrugged. "You know, time moves on, doesn't it? But with Jay, it's just one of those things you don't bring up."

It was almost sickening how much of a good guy Freddie was, Adam thought. Sure, they all lost their careers over this, but Freddie was the one who was really wronged by the whole thing, and to allow *Jay* to be the one who was having a hard time getting over it was taking friendship to a whole other level.

"And maybe it's not fair on her either to drag all that up again. Wherever she is now," Freddie said. "She did a lot of stupid shit but that doesn't mean we have to keep going on about it."

"But you guys are okay?" he asked.

"Me and Jay?"

"Yeah."

"Seems like a long time to hold a grudge against a mate," Freddie said. "We're all okay, aren't we?"

"Yeah. Sure." Adam nodded, not entirely convinced.

"Jay is Jay, man. You take him or leave him."

"Did I hear my name?"

Adam exhaled slowly as Jay appeared beside the picnic table.

"Just trash talking you to Adam," Freddie said.

"What's new?" Jay said, taking a drag on his cigarette. "You okay?"

Adam nodded stiffly. "How's it going?"

There'd always been a low-level arrogance to Jay that he couldn't get on board with and it emanated from him still, even without the celebrity status.

"Can't complain," Jay said. "Although I haven't built my own house recently so I guess it's all relative."

"Harry built this place himself?" Freddie asked.

"If the rumours are true," Adam said. "His old man's got a building company so Harry went to work with him after the band. I guess he found his niche."

"All right for some, isn't it," Jay said. "Shame we don't all have a family business to fall back on. What are you up to these days?"

"Not building my own house," Adam said. "Gigging a bit, working in a café the rest of the time. Nothing much."

"Not with Prairie Dogs?"

"Oh, no, just an acoustic duo with a mate."

"I see you also forgot to bring your wife and child," Jay said. "Same."

"Ah, shut up. You said you didn't want any of what I had," Freddie said.

"I don't! Seems like a whole load of hassle."

"You're a dickhead." Freddie smiled. "We're not married, anyway."

"I thought you were going to elope, or some shit like that?" Jay asked.

"We were, but then the twins happened and now we're too tired to do anything romantic. Or anything, really."

"Is Jen coming next week?"

"No, Ava's got school, plus trying to go anywhere with two toddlers requires a whole lorryload of stuff. Jen's mum's coming to stay while I'm away instead."

"Now *that* sounds like a band reunion," Jay said. "I hope they give us free booze."

"Man, I can't wait to play with you and Fabs again," Freddie said.

"Is he flying solo?"

"I guess so – his kids will have school too."

"More time for beer," Jay said.

Adam thought about Betsy and how she'd read the paperwork over his shoulder and begged to be his plus-one for the show. He'd refused point blank on the basis that she was far too nice and the last thing he wanted to do was throw her to a bunch of ex-celebrity vultures to be taken advantage of. Her eyes had lit up at that point and she'd assured him that she'd rather like to be taken advantage of by a load of aging pop stars. But the thought of someone like Jay getting his claws into her…

"You know part of the agreement for being on the show is that you can't get together beforehand and practise?" Freddie said. "I love that. We're going to be awful. They even said not to look up old song lyrics."

"But this is okay, right?" Adam said, gesturing around him.

"I guess they'd rather we weren't all catching up two days before we start filming…" Freddie shrugged. "It didn't seem like a great idea to go in cold, you know."

"Can't have you gate-crashing the show at the last minute without even saying hi," Jay said.

There was a smile on his face but not in his words, and there was that uneasy feeling again. But what could Adam really do at this point? The train was on the tracks; everyone else was on board and having a lovely time. He was the only person with one foot still on the platform.

"You've got to play reality TV at its own game," Jay continued. "They'll get what they want, but on our terms, not theirs. Nothing to it."

"I'll drink to that," Freddie said, raising his beer bottle into the air. "To getting the band back together. And having some fun!"

12

"Are you leaving me?"

Kitty looked up from the open suitcase and smiled.

"No! Packing!"

"I see," James said, coming further into the room and sitting down on the edge of the bed.

"When are *you* packing?"

James shrugged. "Tomorrow. I'm still trying to finish up this work stuff."

Kitty pulled a dress off its hanger and folded it into a messy square.

"You are still going?" she asked, the constant butterflies in her stomach suspended in mid-air for a moment.

"Of course."

"Because you promised Sadie," Kitty said, turning back to the wardrobe.

"I did."

"She thinks you're not going to do it."

"I know she does. I know Sadie very well," James said.

Kitty put another dress into the suitcase.

"Still?" she asked, looking at him again.

James nodded slowly. "I think so."

Kitty moved over to her dressing table, opening the marble box and pairing up the earrings inside, her back to James so he couldn't look her in the eye.

"Were you lying to her about why you left the band?" she asked carefully, catching a glimpse of his expression in the mirror.

He looked up, a faint frown on his forehead. "No," he said.

Are you lying to me? Kitty thought.

"It just wasn't me, I guess." He sighed. "I don't know. Another lifetime."

The butterflies surged upwards. So curious. So many layers she knew nothing about. This man she'd spent years with, thinking that she knew his only secret. But where would be the fun in him answering all her questions straight away, anyway?

"What's this?" he asked, picking a book up off the bed and turning it over.

"A book I'm taking," Kitty said breezily, waiting for the inevitable.

James flicked through the pages.

"But what *is* it?"

"A book."

"Is this young adult fiction?"

Kitty shrugged.

"You don't read books like this," James said, looking confused.

I don't read books like this around you, Kitty thought.

Maybe she didn't have to answer all his questions, either.

Because, honestly, she was fed up of the eggshells he put out for her to trip over. She hadn't realised how much of herself she'd given up to tiptoe around the thing he wasn't talking about. He'd renounced a part of himself so vehemently that he'd inadvertently expected her to do the same. Music channels, reality TV, mainstream radio, celebrity magazines, musicals, pop star memoirs, social media, Simon Cowell, *teenagers*: all frowned upon in James' pursuit to erase his former fame from his life. And she was *bored*. Wasn't he bored? When they'd first got together Kitty had thought she could let go of "childish" pursuits like pop music and young adult fiction, and embrace adulthood – *for him*. And maybe it was about time she "grew up" anyway, right? But it turned out that without those things she didn't truly feel like herself, and she just wasn't sure it was worth it any more.

But. Now wasn't the time for a confrontation about any of that. Not when she was about 36 hours away from being teleported back to her teenage years.

"Tell me a story," she said instead, taking the book off him and putting it in her suitcase. "Packing is so boring."

He frowned. "A story?"

"About when you were in the band."

He shifted on the bed.

"You don't want to know about all that, do you?"

So much. So so much. More than you could ever possibly imagine.

"Why wouldn't I?" she asked, returning to her dressing table. "I want to know everything."

"I think it's a lot more boring than you're imagining."

"I bet it isn't."

She watched him some more in the mirror as she started to line up the make-up she was taking.

This was a full-scale operation. James was about to be a celebrity again, which meant she was about to be the *girlfriend-of*. And girlfriend-of was a big deal: Instagram was full of the wives of reunited boyband members and their book deals, YouTube channels, podcasts, magazine shoots, chat show appearances and mum blogger award ceremonies. Being girlfriend-of automatically made you someone. It was the ideal platform from which to launch a fabulous yet reasonably low-key career: just enough notoriety so you didn't have to do your ordinary office job any more but not so much that you couldn't still get the tube to your book launch.

She'd done her research. There seemed to be a couple of ways into this: you could be charmingly down-to-earth in both personality and looks with no obvious talents but a level of intelligence (book deal, most likely about something parenting-related, and an adoring social media following), strikingly pretty and a super nice person to boot (endless freebies in the post for you to use/wear/eat/drink and rave about on Instagram; maybe modelling) or exuberant, klutzy and instantly lovable (Z-list TV presenting, small town Christmas light switch-ons). If you had a triumph over adversity story to tell (mental health, infertility, weight loss) that would immediately become your distinctive trope and was a fast-track to all of the above.

From there it was an organic process. Your boyfriend's popularity would begin to grow again, somewhat taking him by surprise, so you'd find yourself inadvertently being photographed while the two of you were doing normal things, like shopping or out for dinner. He'd also start being invited to more red-carpet events, so you'd increasingly be photographed sweeping past the cameras and the fans on his arm. These photos would end up on gossip websites and in magazines, and fans of your boyfriend's band – who were now adults and capable of some serious internet stalking – would look you up online, because the girlfriend-of is the *in*: much less famous, somewhat oblivious and therefore much more likely to share intimate details of *his* life on social media and respond to your try-hard comments on their photos.

You didn't have to be extraordinary, you just had to be *noticed*, and one way or another Kitty was going to be noticed this week.

"Oh wait, do I need to bring all my make-up? Will someone be doing our make-up?"

"I don't think you're going to be on camera, Kit," James said.

"I might be," Kitty said lightly.

"They tend to keep girlfriends away from all this kind of thing."

Maybe in the world of pop music that you're from, Kitty thought. *Welcome to the new age.*

"Is my phone on the bedside table?" she asked.

James looked behind him. "Yes it is."

"Can I have it?" She held out her hand as he leaned across the bed to pass it to her.

"What are you doing?" he asked, watching as she got up on the stool to take a top-down photo of her assembled make-up collection.

"Nothing," Kitty said, quickly uploading the photo to Instagram.

#packing #excited #villageofpop

That should do it.

"What did you tell work?" James asked, pushing Kitty's suitcase over slightly and settling back against the headboard of the bed.

"Just that you'd booked a last-minute holiday," she said, zipping her make-up bags up.

"Your boss didn't mind the short notice?"

Kitty shrugged. "I've got to take those days left over from last year by the end of the month, anyway."

"Wouldn't it have been better to explain the situation? It's a better reason for needing almost two weeks off than just wanting a holiday."

"I could hardly tell them that it turns out my boyfriend used to be famous, could I?" Kitty said, looking James square in the eye.

He looked momentarily wrong-footed by the directness of the comment.

"No one talks to me at work, anyway," she said, brushing it off. "They don't care either way. It's not an issue."

They hadn't talked at all in the last three days about the elephant in the room: *why didn't you tell me.* Things they had talked about: who was going to feed the cats, would there be Wi-Fi there so James could do a bit of work, did they need swimming costumes, when should they leave on Monday morning to miss the work traffic, should they cancel the Sainsbury's delivery this week, what time should they set the lamps to come on in the evenings while they were away, which service station were they going to stop at, did they need to take two phone chargers or could they share one, and how many car snacks were required for a five-hour journey.

"Come here," James said, patting the bed next to him.

"I'm packing," Kitty said, feeling unreasonably irritated by his presence.

"Come here."

She relented, sliding her suitcase down to the end of the bed and crawling into the leftover space next to him.

She pressed her finger to the tiny hole in his chin. "You never use this any more."

"The piercing?"

Kitty nodded.

"I thought I might let it heal up, actually."

"Why?"

Kitty's heart sank the way it did every time James put a part of himself away in a box and took another step away from his youth. Yes, people evolved over time, and she knew she should love him regardless, but she was afraid that one day she'd wake up and realise he was wearing chinos and a fleece and shoes from Clarks, and she didn't know how that would make her feel.

"I think I'm too old."

"You're 31, not 81."

James smiled.

"Put it back in for the show."

"Really?"

"Trust me."

If James couldn't see that him turning up looking like a rock star compared to Sadie – soft around the edges and wearing supermarket clothes – was going to delight the producers of the show then it was going to have to be up to Kitty to ensure that he gave the performance they needed to catapult Funk Shui back into the spotlight.

"I like this…" She said, tracing a finger down his shirt.

Deep blue, covered with brightly coloured birds, rolled up to his elbows and tight across his chest. He wore things like that without a hint of self-consciousness, pulling it off effortlessly in a way that many couldn't. You noticed when James walked into a room. Kitty wondered if he knew that.

"Me too," James said.

"Did you ever look them up on Facebook?" Kitty asked.

"Who?"

"Your bandmates."

James paused. "No... I never thought about it."

"Do you want to now?"

"I'm not on Facebook any more."

"I am."

"Do we have to?" James asked reluctantly.

"Aren't you curious?"

"Well I'm going to see them all in two days..."

Please don't be boring, Kitty silently implored. *Please don't keep being so boring.*

Oh the constant disappointment of curtailed spontaneity. Where would they be, she sometimes wondered, if James was a yes person; if he wasn't so cautious, so thoughtful. If, when she said "Let's have a party!" he grabbed a bottle of gin and some glasses instead of spending the next week researching gas barbeques and muttering about having some people round sometime in the summer.

"Tell me about them," Kitty pressed. "Who they used to be."

James was silent for a moment. "I don't know if my memories are anything more than caricatures by this point."

"Draw me a caricature, then."

Another pause, while Kitty held her breath.

"Okay, okay. So there was me, Sadie, Mia, Ryan and Cameron. Sadie was... Well you've met her now, but back then she was always the most excited about things. So enthusiastic about everything. Impulsive, and she didn't always think, so she got herself into trouble sometimes. She was impossible to win an argument against. She'd keep you up when you should have been asleep: she never seemed to switch off. It seemed like she was happy all the time. I don't know if that was the case, but..."

Kitty nodded. So far so predictable.

"Mia was the yin to Sadie's yang," James continued. "I'm not really surprised that they're still so close now – it was almost like Mia was everything that Sadie lacked. She needed Mia to function as a rounded human being: without her she'd be all go go go all the time. She was always so calm, so diplomatic. She was the person you went to when you were wound up about something and she made you feel better."

"She sounds nice," Kitty said.

"She was nice. I don't think I ever heard her say a bad word about anyone."

Mia had never really interested Kitty. *Nice* isn't really what you're looking for when you're a teenage girl. Nice is one-dimensional. Nice isn't sexy. Nice won't break your heart in a hotel room.

And that's what you yearn for. Not just attention. Not a discreet happily ever after. You want the sweeping public displays of affection. The heart-wrenching love triangle or the angst-ridden breakup that lends itself to long cold walks by the river, feeling stoic and brave. And you want all of that right up to the point where you find out the hard way that those moments aren't dramatic and romantic, but small and quiet and sad, and they leave you feeling empty, not brave.

James paused, but Kitty could fill the rest in for him.

Cameron was an acquired taste. You had to really look hard to find what his fans saw in him. He was inoffensive, but therein lay the problem: he had nothing to say for himself. Average-looking with an average personality. Nice, like Mia, but where Mia had something of an air of being wise beyond her years, Cameron had nothing. The girls who liked Cameron were the ones writing slow, gentle fan fiction, where falling in love took a long time and nothing dramatic really happened. The girls longing for the love triangle overlooked him entirely.

But Ryan…

Kitty thought about the photos of Sad Admiral she'd spent the best part of an evening trawling the internet for while James had been holed up in his study. Sure enough, there he was: Ryan Malone, as gorgeous as he'd always been, only this time he was hidden at the back of the band instead of being the shining spotlight at the front. A different hairstyle in pretty much every photo she'd found – he hadn't lost his vanity, clearly – but the exact same glint in his eye that she might have walked off a cliff in pursuit of when she was 15. Ryan Malone: charming, funny and every bit as much of a heartbreaker as he looked.

"Who were you in the band?" Kitty asked.

James looked at her like it was a trick question.

"Very naïve," he said, as if that was a proper answer.

"What do you mean?"

"Oh, I suppose being in the band didn't turn out to be quite what I was expecting."

"You said to Sadie you weren't happy in the band?" Kitty asked, tiptoeing through the conversation, expecting the walls to come back up at any minute.

"Not towards the end," James said.

And what happened? Kitty implored silently. *Where did that cheeky energy go? The guy with the infectious laugh: Ryan's comedy partner in crime. Where did he go, and why didn't he ever come back?*

And why isn't he here now to be my *comedy partner in crime?*

There was more than one reason why being James' girlfriend had turned out to be a disappointment.

"Did you get on with the other guys in the band? Cameron and Ryan?" she asked, knowing it was pointless to ask the questions she really wanted to.

"Mostly. Cameron could be… *difficult*, sometimes."

"Oh?" Kitty asked, having never made a greater effort in her entire life to sound nonchalant.

This information she *hadn't* known. In her long and illustrious career as a fangirl she had never once heard anyone suggest that Cameron and James weren't good friends, so they'd hidden that astoundingly well.

"I'm sure he's a decent enough bloke these days. We just didn't quite see eye to eye on things," James said.

"What kind of things?" Kitty squeaked out, but of course James didn't feel like talking about it.

He shrugged. "I don't really remember the specifics. Male ego, maybe."

"And Ryan?" Kitty hardly dared ask.

James smiled, but it was heavy with something akin to sadness or regret.

"Ryan was probably the best friend I ever had," he said.

So why isn't he still?

"Do you miss him?" Kitty asked, but it was one question too far and James' smile disappeared.

"No. No, it was a long time ago. I'm sure we're all different people now." He got up off the bed. "Anyway, I better get back to work."

And with that he was gone.

Kitty sighed to the empty room. There was a part of her that knew she shouldn't still care about any of this in her late twenties; that this *was* one of the things she should definitely have let go of by now. And yet, she did still care, and she was beginning to suspect that, actually, you don't ever get over loving a pop band that much. Perhaps something so significantly chemical happens in your teenage brain that you are irrevocably changed, in a way that people who bypass the fangirl phase entirely never are. And it really did seem like there were only two types of adults in this world: those that once loved a pop band, and those who have no idea what you're talking about.

Was it worse when the band you loved fizzled out under murky circumstances? With no closure and no goodbye are you forever held in limbo, no matter how hard you try to forget?

And when you give your heart to a boy in a band do you ever really get it back?

TEN DAYS TO
THE LIVE SHOW

13

"Is this it? Oh my God." Sadie wound down the car window as Cameron pulled off the main road onto a narrow lane lined with unkempt hedges.

"What are you doing? Put the window back up," Cameron said.

"Is this place going to be really small? I thought it would be like Center Parcs. Why did we just drive through a village? Are we nearly there?"

"If you don't calm down you're going to have to sit in the back with Mia. Or in the boot," Cameron added under his breath.

"I'm so excited," Sadie said, bouncing her legs.

"We noticed."

"Can't wait," she whispered to herself, scanning for something that looked like a holiday park through the gaps in the hedge.

Any minute now, surely.

The journey had felt agonisingly long, not helped by the fact that they hit every bit of morning rush hour traffic going. She'd eaten all her car sweets in the first 30 minutes and had needed to stop for a wee three times during the four-hour journey. She felt sick, she felt tense; she was so excited that it felt like she might turn inside out at any minute.

"Are you sure this is the way?"

"Yes," Cameron said. "You can see on the satnav that this is the way. I have followed the satnav the whole way here so far and, funnily enough, it has taken us to the exact place we asked it to take us."

"I can only see fields," Sadie said. "Shouldn't there be a forest?"

"I had nothing to do with the design of the place, so unfortunately I can't answer that question."

"Aren't you excited?"

"I'm excited to not be driving any more," Cameron said.

"I'm excited to see Ryan," Mia said, smiling from the back seat. "Did you say he was getting there after us?"

Sadie scrolled back through the messages on her phone.

"He said they told him to get there at midday. Are you sure they said half 11 to you?"

"Yes, definitely half past 11 for us."

"Why would they tell us different times?"

Cameron slowed down as the lane curved round to the left and the entrance to Meadow View Holiday Village swam into view. Sadie squealed with excitement.

"I think this might be why…" Cameron said as they pulled into the car park.

"Oh my God… Is that for us?" Sadie asked, her stomach doing somersaults at the sight of the camera crew standing next to a woman with a clipboard.

She watched, every hair on her arms standing on end, as the women pressed a small black button clipped to her top and said something into it. Camera held aloft. All eyes on them.

"Oh my God, I'm not ready for this…" Sadie said, not feeling quite so steady or excited all of a sudden. "I didn't know there'd be… My hair isn't… I can't remember how to… I'm not ready…"

She felt like she'd just drank a million cups of coffee. Her hands were shaking. She needed another wee.

"Hey," Mia said, reaching over the seat and putting a hand on her shoulder. "This is what we're here for. You *are* ready. Okay?"

Sadie nodded.

You are a pop star, Sadie Dawes.

"Okay."

She took a deep breath, unclipped her seatbelt and got out of the car, making sure Mia and Cameron were with her before walking towards the woman, so aware she was being filmed. It was like her body couldn't remember how to behave normally. Did she usually walk like this? Was this always what happened with her hands? She tried not to look at the camera.

"Welcome to Village of Pop!" the woman said, smiling widely at them. "My name's Helen. I'm part of the production team working on the show. It's so good to meet you all!"

Sadie half expected her to ask to see some ID, or at least to ask their names, but she paused only to shake their hands.

She knows who we are, Sadie thought, an unexpected lump coming to her throat.

It had been such a long long time since someone had known who she was...

"How was your journey?"

"Not too bad," Cameron said, everyone nodding in agreement.

"Great." Helen smiled some more. "So, I'm going to jump straight in and get you all set up today. I'm sure I don't need to mention that you are being filmed. We know this might take a bit of getting used to, so please don't worry about it too much at the moment," she said. "We're going to capture a lot of footage to make sure we have everything we need for the show, but the likelihood is that we won't use even half of it, so just try and be yourselves. I do need to make you aware that you will be being filmed at all times, apart from when you are in your accommodation and during specifically designated free time. Now if I could get you to sign your lives away here..." She held out the clipboard. "It's just to say that you consent to being filmed whenever necessary and without prior warning, and that you're happy for us to use any footage we capture in whatever way we deem appropriate without seeking additional approval from you."

"No big deal then," Cameron muttered, but he took the clipboard and signed anyway, passing it on to Sadie.

"Okay then!" Helen said. "Let's get started. We've got some really exciting things lined up for you all over the next ten days: I hope you're ready for some long days! I need to stay off camera as much as possible, so I'll just talk you through what's going to happen today and then I'm going to leave you to it."

She pulled a piece of paper from the clipboard and handed it to Sadie.

"So this is the map, and we are... *here*. The first thing you're going to need to do is find your way to your cabin, which is this one here." She pointed to a little grey square towards the middle of the map. "It's not too hard to find: you just head up towards the lake and then you take this track and it's about mid-way down the row. Number 45. Okay?"

Sadie nodded. This was really happening, wasn't it? She still had goosebumps all over.

"Once you get to your cabin, you'll have about an hour to get settled. You guys are quite lucky because the people with a later arrival time are pretty much going to be whisked straight off. If you want to get changed or anything, that's fine, but we do ask that you only dress up to the extent that you would if you were meeting friends for lunch, or something like that. Keep it fairly casual. We want this to be really natural for the viewers: give them an insight into the real people behind their teen idols."

Teen idols.

Sadie realised she hadn't really thought about the fans in all of this. Would they really still care? Wouldn't they all be proper adults by now with more important things going on? What even happened to fans after their favourite band broke up? Did they just wander off like a herd of zombies and find a new band to shower with adoration? Or did they power down like robots, poised to reactivate ten years later once the pop bands of their youth got a bit strapped for cash and bored of normal life and decided to have another crack at fame? She'd been 16 when the band had formed; she'd never been as intense about a band as their fans had been about them.

"We'll be doing all the on-camera reunions from one o'clock. Someone will come and get you when it's time; if you could stay in your cabin until then that would be great. There's a full schedule in the welcome pack so you can see where you need to be and when across the next ten days. I will say that the schedule is quite full-on, but it's all been planned out with making this experience into a really fantastic TV show, so if you can try to be where you're supposed to be as much as possible we would appreciate it."

Sadie continued to nod. It was a bit like when you bought car insurance and they read out all the terms and conditions that you couldn't possibly be expected to take in there and then.

"And I think that's about it! If you need anything at all there are phone numbers in the pack: please feel free to call us any time. We're really excited to have you all here." Helen beamed at them again. "Someone will bring your bags along behind you, if you wouldn't mind leaving your car keys? We'll bring them back with the luggage."

"I think it's all in the boot…" Cameron said, pulling his keys out of his pocket.

"Great, we'll sort that out for you. Any questions?"

So many, Sadie thought, shaking her head.

"Okay! You are free to go," Helen said, sweeping a hand towards the forest as if she was ushering them into a magical world.

Sadie gripped the map as the camera crew moved into position in front of them, feeling Mia and Cameron bunch in more tightly beside her.

"What do we do now?" she muttered, eyes fixed on the piece of paper.

"We find the cabin as quickly as possible. Preferably stay inside until all this is over," Cameron said, pointing at a completely random point on the map.

"What are you doing?" Sadie asked.

"I'm pretending to point to things on the map."

"Why?"

"Because that camera crew over there are expecting us to do something other than just stand here," he hissed.

"Why don't I be in charge of the map?" Mia suggested, taking it from Sadie, a smile pasted onto her face that didn't match the words she was saying. "I can see where we need to go. Come on."

She started walking and Sadie hesitantly followed suit, the camera crew moving backwards in time with their progression.

"Are we supposed to just talk amongst ourselves?" Sadie whispered.

"I'm not saying anything," Cameron said, walking behind them.

Mia turned around, still smiling. "Cameron, you are being filmed. If you look grumpy, they are going to use it. If you look grumpy *enough* then that's *all* they're going to show of you."

"He *is* grumpy all the time," Sadie said.

"Well it'll be accurate then, at least," Mia said, nudging her.

And this time the smile was real.

"Let's just try not to fall out on camera before we've even got started, yes?"

Funny, Sadie didn't remember Mia being this sharp first time around.

"I think this is so beautiful, anyway," she continued. "I can't remember the last time I was around so many trees."

Sadie looked around her, careful not to so much as glance at the camera crew.

"I don't think I can believe we're actually here," she said. "It just seems like we're on holiday. Apart from the camera crew."

"It sort of is a holiday."

"It sounds like a lot of hard work to me," Cameron said.

"You know, this is my favourite part of any holiday," Sadie said. "The bit when you arrive and you don't know what it's all going to look like. Seeing your accommodation for the first time. You know when you go into a caravan and all the doors are closed and it seems like there can't possibly be actual bedrooms in such a tiny space. It's so exciting. Maybe I'll just think about that."

"We'll get the hang of this," Mia said. "It's a big day."

Sadie nodded. "Do you think Ryan's going to get the exact same spiel from that woman when he arrives?"

"I think we're on a conveyor belt of the once famous," Cameron said. "Is this the path we're supposed to be taking?"

Mia laughed. "I thought you meant metaphorically, for a minute." She looked at the map. "I don't think so. We're not anywhere near the lake yet."

"That sign says Cabins 122 to 145," Sadie pointed out.

"Has anyone considered that we don't actually need this map seeing as there is a camera crew in front of us who definitely know where they are going?" Cameron said.

"I think they'd still follow us if we went the wrong way."

"Why don't we find out?"

Sadie looked at Cameron suspiciously. "What are you about to do?"

He grinned. "Well I think it's this way!" he declared loudly, striding off the main path, Sadie and Mia following in his wake.

"What are you doing?" Sadie giggled. "The camera crew are going to be cross!"

She could hear the crunch of footsteps behind them but she daren't look round.

"Hey, we're autonomous human beings."

"But we're supposed to be going to the cabin!"

"I am going to the cabin. Just keeping them on their toes."

Suddenly the camera crew ran past, righting themselves on the path in front of them, and Mia, Cameron and Sadie were all smiling then, the excitement starting to bubble up through the nerves.

"Ooh look, these are so cute," Sadie said, as they emerged onto a road lined with low wooden buildings. "Do you think ours is going to be like this?"

"I don't think this is a very good short cut," Mia said, looking at the map again.

"We're only 100 cabins away. Can't we just count down until we get there?"

"I don't think it quite works like that. I think we're going to end up on the wrong side of the lake if we keep walking."

"Do you think anyone else is actually here yet? It seems so quiet," Sadie said, taking a deep breath of the cool air.

It smelled like adventure.

"What's down there?" Cameron asked, pointing at another path cutting away from the line of cabins.

"It doesn't look like there's *anything* down there…" Mia said.

"Let's find out, shall we?" Cameron said, changing course again.

This time Sadie did look at the camera crew, shooting them an apologetic look, but they just smiled and shrugged.

"Okay, give me that," she said, taking the map off Mia and cutting in front of Cameron. "I don't know who made you the boss of this hike."

After a few minutes the camera crew overtook them again, staying in front of them until they came out onto another row of cabins, at which point they moved to the side.

"I guess we're here," Cameron murmured as Sadie scanned the numbers on the front doors.

"There!" she pointed, taking off across the tarmac towards cabin 45, trying the handle as Mia and Cameron caught up with her.

"Why would you run when we're being filmed?" Cameron said, following her through the front door and closing it firmly behind them. "*Will* we get used to that? I feel like I'm Ed Sheeran."

"You wish you were Ed Sheeran," Sadie said, looking around her. "This is so cool! Where are the bedrooms? Bagsy the best one!"

She flung open the first door to the right of the living area, stepping into a room with twin beds. Another twin bedroom next door to that, and then a double. The fourth door led into a small bathroom, but the only other door in the cabin opened onto a broom cupboard.

Sadie frowned. "Why have we only got three bedrooms? Are we sharing rooms?"

Cameron was already rifling through a hamper of food on the dining table. "Why would we need to share rooms?"

"Well where's Ryan going to sleep?"

"I'm not sure you quite get the concept of a reunion."

"He's probably got his own cabin," Mia said, filling up the kettle. "I expect it's like that for most of the bands. We're lucky that we see each other all the time so we get to bunk up together."

"Oh," Sadie said, feeling a bit deflated, images of her and Ryan curled up on the sofa with a bottle of wine in the evenings going up in smoke.

Not quite the reunion she was imagining, then.

"Tea?" Mia offered, handing her a mug.

"It's like a Boots meal deal in here," Cameron said, a boxed sandwich in each hand. "We'd better eat if they're coming for us in an hour. Egg mayo?"

Sadie nodded, joining him at the dining table.

"Did you know that M&S invented the pre-packed sandwich?" Cameron asked.

"That doesn't sound true," Mia said, putting a mug of coffee down in front of him.

"It is true!"

Cameron threw a packet of crisps in her direction as Sadie picked up a cardboard file from the table.

"That the welcome pack?" Cameron asked, mouth full of ham and pickle.

"I think so," Sadie said, flicking through the sheaf of papers. "Oh, this must be the schedule. Wow, she wasn't joking about being busy."

Mia peered over her shoulder. "What's a treetop adventure course?"

"Ooh we're having a photoshoot tomorrow!" Sadie said, feeling her spirits lift a little.

The schedule read like a kids' holiday camp brochure: bowling, crazy golf, pottery painting, forest campfire evening, Segway experience, *roller disco*... And lots and lots of rehearsals.

"Let me see," Cameron said, leaning over to look. "Christ, is all this compulsory?"

"Are these activities all happening on site?" Mia asked, pulling another copy of the site map out of the pack. "Oh, look, there's the petting zoo. Maybe they are."

"90s theme evening!" Sadie exclaimed.

"Yoga?" Cameron wrinkled his nose.

"This is amazing," Sadie said, leaning back in her chair. "I didn't know it was going to be like this! I thought we'd just have a go at being a band again and then hang out in the swimming pool the rest of the time."

"I'm not sure I've brought the right shoes for all these activities..." Mia said.

"Do you think we all get to do all of this, or will they split us into groups?" Sadie asked. "How many other bands are here?"

"Maybe there's a list..." Mia said, flicking through the rest of the sheets in the pack.

Sadie's phone buzzed on the table: a three letter exclamation from Ryan. *WTF!!*

She smiled. "Ryan's here."

She fired back a reply – *What cabin are you in??* – but her message just hung there, unread.

There was a loud knock on the door and all three of them jumped.

"Jesus," Cameron said, getting up to answer it. "We need to calm down or we're not going to make it through the next ten days."

He reappeared a moment later with his car keys and their bags.

"Just the luggage robot."

"Was it really a robot?" Sadie asked.

"What do you think?"

"I think... No?"

"I think it's going to be a very unusual day," Mia said, tidying the pieces of paper back into the folder. "To say the least."

14

Kitty watched James sign his name on a piece of paper and wondered how it was possible for a moment, which surely had happened at normal speed, to have passed by in such a flash that her brain had no recollection of it happening at all. They'd pulled into the car park – the cameras were rolling already! – and then she'd blinked and suddenly she was standing in front of a woman talking about maps and schedules. She could imagine that she had indeed got out of the car and walked towards where she was currently standing, but it wasn't much more than an educated guess seeing as that section of her memory was completely blank.

And that moment – her arrival, *on camera* – would really have been something to hold onto if James continued to be as weird as he had been for the last five hours. Five hours, in almost complete silence. It had felt twice as long as that, and okay, sure, James kind of suited the brooding look, and she couldn't deny that she found it just a teeny bit sexy, especially when she imagined that his inner turmoil was something to do with the imminent reunion with his former bandmates, which, yes, made her feel like she was in some kind of real-life fan fiction, and he did look exceptionally gorgeous today. But still. *Five hours. In silence.*

"Okay, so I'm afraid I'm going to have to split you two up now, just temporarily, so we can get some footage of Jim – sorry, *James* – walking to the cabin," the woman said, and Kitty's heart sank.

Were those few seconds that she couldn't even bloody remember going to be the only time she'd be on camera over the next ten days?

"I'm sure you don't want your face broadcast to millions to people, do you?" she said, smiling at Kitty. "I know I don't!"

Kitty managed a wan smile in return, glancing at James.

"You can come with me, Kitty, and we'll bring the bags."

Oh, wait, it just got better.

"James, if you head off in that direction, the camera crew will follow you to your cabin. I'll get Kitty back to you, don't worry," Helen said, like she was some kind of pet or accessory.

She had to admit, being *girlfriend-of* didn't seem to be counting for much so far.

"You'll need the car keys," James said, pulling them out of his pocket and putting them in Kitty's hand. "Okay?" he asked quietly.

She nodded firmly, embarrassed that he clearly knew this wasn't living up to her expectations.

"See you there," she said, feigning nonchalance.

He held eye contact for just a little too long before nodding and moving towards the camera crew.

"Right then. Let's get your bags," Helen said, steering Kitty towards the car. "Have you two been together long?"

"Four years," Kitty said, opening the boot and hauling out her enormous suitcase, wishing she'd packed a bit more conservatively.

Four years, but who was counting any more? Except maybe her mum and James' smug married friends. It had seemed like a dream come true when they'd first met at the art gallery she was doing admin for, her breath catching in her throat when the guy from the graphic design company that was helping them rebrand turned out to be Jim from Funk Shui. She'd been 23 and bored, and he'd been up from Devon for the weekend to get to know the business better. And maybe she hadn't entered into things entirely honourably right at the start, but he'd been funny and cool and romantic, and he'd side-lined her ulterior motive with grown up dates at fancy restaurants, impromptu weekends away in picturesque yurts and phone calls that ran into the early hours.

She'd been the talk of the office – *"Did you hear Kitty's dating the hot website guy?"* – and one weekend at his place he'd asked her not to go home, ever. What a gutsy move – what an adventure – to leave behind everything you knew and move to the seaside for a *boy*.

"Lucky girl," Helen said, but maybe she wasn't.

Maybe neither of them were.

"Well I expect you're very aware of how these things work, but we're saying it to all the plus-ones: of course it's been a while since a lot of the guests were in the public eye, but I'm sure you appreciate there is still an element of fantasy involved between the stars and the viewers."

Kitty put James' much smaller case next to hers, not feeling massively enthusiastic about where this was going.

"You're more than welcome to be here, of course, but when it comes to "where are they now" it's not really the wife and kids domestic element we're focusing on. Or that the fans necessarily want to see."

Kitty looked at Helen. In her forties, probably. Wedding ring. Clothes from Joules. Aging girl-next-door hairstyle. Who would be the better card in a game of Top Trumps?

Helen: works for a TV company.

Kitty: girlfriend of someone who was famous ten years ago.

"Think of the site in two parts," Helen said, handing Kitty a slim folder. "These plans show where we're filming each day: if you could stick to the green areas, that would be really good for us. Obviously when we're not filming you and James are free to use any of the facilities you like. Your cabin is towards the outskirts so you shouldn't get caught up in anything. There's perhaps only a couple of times where you'll have to stay put for a while."

Oh goody, Kitty thought.

"Ah, here's your shortcut," Helen said, looking up as a golf buggy pulling a trailer appeared from the trees. "You'll be unpacked and making a cup of tea before James gets to the cabin."

And there I shall stay, Kitty thought, flicking to the first sheet in the folder and taking in the huge swathe of red across the map.

"This is Ray," Helen continued, gesturing to the silver-haired man behind the wheel of the golf buggy. "He'll take you where you need to go. Hop in and we'll get your bags."

Kitty climbed into the passenger seat as Ray loaded the cases into the trailer. She pulled her phone out of her handbag and took a quick photo across the steering wheel looking towards the forest. Phone signal was weak but just enough to upload the photo.

#plusonelife #sopeaceful #villageofpop

She'd had a nice slew of new followers since her last post and a few curious comments about where she was going, which she'd left unanswered. It didn't quite make up for James' lack of enthusiasm draining the life out of her, or the fact that "plus-ones" – *how rude* – didn't actually seem to be welcome at all, but it was something, she supposed.

"Is everyone here already?" she asked Ray, peering through the trees as they bumped slowly along a track.

There was no sign of life anywhere: so much for the place swarming with the relics of her youth.

"I don't know about everyone, but you're my last fare of the day."

"It just seems so quiet."

"Not much happening on the outskirts. There are quite a few people where you're staying, though. I've been back and forth all morning."

Yeah, on Exile Street, Kitty thought.

She was assuming all the wives and girlfriends were being dumped in the same place. Was it really necessary, though? Would the grown-up fangirls be tuning in and buying tickets for the tour – she assumed there'd be a tour – still harbouring the misconception that they might stand a chance with their teenage crush? Sure, that's how it *used* to work: you didn't want to catch a glimpse of a tetchy-looking girlfriend being herded to a car while the band posed for photos with fans at the back gate, you wanted to *be* the girlfriend. No one was interested in the rare boyband member who insisted on being honest about his long-term relationship; if you were, it was only because you hoped you'd one day get the opportunity to break them up. Otherwise, what was the point? Did anyone *really* become a fan of a band and *not* ultimately want to end up marrying the best-looking one?

Fancy thinking that all you needed to be happy was a boyfriend in a band.

They emerged from the trees onto a proper tarmac road lined with wooden cabins and Kitty sat up a little straighter. Was Ryan in one of these cabins with his plus-one? She could hear a baby crying in amongst the birdsong. There'd been no mention of any of that on the internet and she couldn't exactly picture it, but stranger things had happened. They were that kind of age and he was part of the L.A. set now: maybe he had a low-key Hollywood wife and a couple of golden-haired kids.

And so what if he did, right? So what if he did.

"Here we are," Ray said, pulling to a stop. "You're in this one."

Kitty could see lights on in a few of the cabins opposite as she picked up the smaller suitcase and carried it up the short path behind Ray.

"I'll leave you to it," he said, and she nodded, opening the front door and stepping inside.

No sign of James, like Helen had said. So what was she supposed to do now? She wished they'd got there earlier so she could have watched everyone else arriving, but she supposed she might see a stream of pop stars walking past as they were frogmarched to their official reunions. But these maps, and the whole staying put thing... She was *right here*: was she really going to have to watch all of this on TV like everyone else? The cabin was nice enough but she wasn't in it for the peace and quiet.

She pulled their suitcases into the bedroom and flicked through the paperwork on the table, taking a picture of the schedule, just in case. They'd been somewhere like this on holiday a couple of years ago, packing a lot of pear cider and not much else, and they'd bought a waterproof disposable camera and taken it to the swimming pool, delighted with themselves and their blurry shots of the water slides. Who knew where those pictures were now. Probably at the bottom of a drawer. Somehow she couldn't imagine them doing something like that these days.

The front door opened as she clicked the kettle on.

"Oh hello," she said, looking in the cupboards for a couple of mugs.

"How did you get here before me?" James asked, unlacing his shoes and leaving them by the door.

"Teleportation," Kitty said, willing him to smile, just once. "How was your walk?"

"Very weird."

"Did it take you right back to the good old days?"

"Not exactly," James said, poking at the hamper of food on the dining table. "Have you eaten?"

"No, I was waiting for you."

She debated telling him what Helen had said to her about the plus-ones and showing him the maps, but what would it really achieve? He'd do his "sorry life isn't working out quite how you were expecting but I'm not sure what I can really do about it right now" face and she'd do her "you win some you lose some" face and that would be that.

"So what were they filming?" she asked instead, handing him a coffee. "Just you walking?"

"Yeah. I can't imagine it'll make for riveting TV," James said, opening a sandwich. "I mean, I get what they're doing, but it seemed a bit unnecessary. We could have faked it in half the time. Have we got plates?"

Kitty nodded, going back over to the cupboard and getting one out.

"Thanks. Are you not eating?"

"I'll have something later. When do you have to go back out?"

James looked at his watch. "I don't know. It's after one now."

Kitty didn't say anything more, just watched him eat his sandwich, more and more convinced with every interaction they had that she was witnessing a person shutting down before her eyes. He hadn't been the same since Sadie turned up on the doorstep, and she knew something was wrong because she hadn't had to go to elaborate lengths recently to avoid talking about the things she didn't want to talk about. Things like buying a house together; things that made her feel suffocated, like her life was closing in around her. James had simply stopped bringing those things up – abandoned all his heavy hints – and with it he had visibly withdrawn to somewhere that Kitty found she couldn't get to.

"Are the bags here?" James asked, getting up suddenly.

Kitty nodded. "In the bedroom," she said, pointing to the doorway.

James disappeared for a moment and came back out clutching a half-empty bottle of whiskey. Kitty frowned. Of all the things she expected him to pack...

He'd only taken a sip when there was a knock on the door. Kitty couldn't meet his eye.

"Can you?" he asked.

She nodded, leaving the dining room and opening the door to a different camera duo, laden down with kit.

"Jim from Funk Shui?" one of them asked, grinning at her.

Kitty cast a glance back to where James was standing, but both the whiskey bottle and the glass were gone.

"Come in," she said, forcing a smile.

She'd never seen James drinking in the day before, and something about it disquieted her on a level she couldn't articulate.

"All right, mate? Ready for your close-up?"

The three men shook hands while Kitty hung back.

"So we're going to film a quick Q&A segment first, and then we'll take you over for the reunion. We'll go outside, if you don't mind: the light's better."

They swept back out through the patio doors and Kitty watched them through the glass: lips moving soundlessly, James looking awkward and uncomfortable perched on a chair with his back to the woodland. She was in the shadows even now, still skirting round the edges of everything she wanted, and the sinking feeling in her stomach suggested that maybe being here didn't make things any more right between them after all.

15

"So what do you want me to do? Just walk, or should I be saying something?"

"Just walk, mate. Pretend we're not here. You know where you're going?"

Adam nodded, thrusting his hands into the pockets of his hoodie and starting out down the path that led away from his cabin.

This was all so much weirder than expected. It felt a little bit like he'd accidentally signed himself up to a cult and now it was too late to change his mind, from the reading of his rights on arrival to the way he'd only just put his bag down when there had been another knock on the door and he was being briefed about the next bit. Everyone else had already arrived, by all accounts, but who knew where they were. He had to say he wouldn't be entirely surprised if he was ushered into a dim room, tied up and shot.

Oh and he could not *wait* to watch the car crash of an interview he'd just done along with an audience of however many thousands of people when it aired on TV. He hadn't been prepared for it at all, stumbling over pretty much every question as he tried to remember what Nat had said to him about *The Official Line* at the barbeque.

How long since you've seen everyone? Are you still friends? How do you feel about seeing them again?

They were already asking him questions about Granola Fantasy and he was sure he was getting it all completely wrong. Had Nat and Freddie expected this level of interrogation? Exhausting. So much for just playing some music and having a few beers with old friends.

"Right, Adam, we're just going to hold you here for a moment, check they're ready for you." The guy not holding the camera pressed the microphone clipped to his polo shirt. "I've got Adam Anderson in location 2A." He listened to the response in his ear and nodded. "Okay, moving to 2B. You see that low building over there?" he asked, talking to Adam again.

"You're headed for that glass door. Once you're in there's another door immediately on your left and that'll take you into the room where your reunion is. Go in when you're ready. We'll leave you at the first door, but there'll be cameras in the room filming as you go in, and they'll be filming the entire time. Try not to look at the cameras and just be yourself."

No big deal, Adam told himself as he walked towards the building. *It's just Harry and Jonny and Nat. We're in it for the money and the free food. We don't have to buy into the rest of it.*

He reached the building, pushing open the door and stepping into a lobby area.

"Big moment," a woman said, smiling at him.

He nodded, idly wondering whether he should have made more of an effort than a hoodie and jeans.

"Ready to go in?"

"Think so."

The woman smiled again. "Enjoy it," she said, gesturing at the door.

Adam pushed it open and stepped into a large room: wooden floors, white walls, lots of windows, lots of cameras. He saw Nat first, coming towards him, arms outstretched and a weird look on his face.

"Keep smiling," he muttered, pulling him into a hug. "Mate! It's so good to see you!" he exclaimed, stepping aside so Adam could see the rest of the people in the room.

He was the last one to arrive, evidently. Harry was there, and Jonny, clapping him on the back, and then Adam could see the reason for Nat's comment, because hanging back slightly at the side of the room were Freddie, Fabs and Jay. None of whom he had previously noticed being members of Prairie Dogs…

"What are you guys doing here?" Adam asked Freddie under his breath as they shook hands for the cameras.

"No idea," Freddie muttered, with a wide smile that didn't quite reach his eyes.

A few more platitudes and that was the grand reunion done, it seemed. They stood, awkwardly, Nat bridging the gap between the two groups.

"What now?" Jonny asked.

"Who knows. A swarm of mosquitoes? Perhaps a stampede?"

Jonny laughed. "Ah man, that would be next level! Imagine that! If this wasn't what they said it was at all and we were stuck in some *Jumanji* shit!"

"Still waiting on the evidence that we're not," Adam muttered, looking up as a door on the far wall opened and the woman he'd met in the car park strode out.

"Hello everyone!" she said, looking particularly pleased with herself. "I'm sure you're all wondering what you're doing here at the same time. I wouldn't say we've brought you here under *false pretences*, but we've got a slightly different challenge for you guys, which we hope you'll enjoy." She paused momentarily to look around the room, like a cat when it knew it had its prey beat.

A very big cat with very big claws.

"What we realised when Prairie Dogs came on board was that the trajectory of these two bands were so closely linked that you almost can't have one without the other. So, for the purposes of this show, all seven of you are going to be performing together as one band. A supergroup, if you will."

And that's when Adam realised that it wasn't *their* reunion at all; it wasn't anything to do with them, in fact. This was Granola Fantasy's reunion, and they were just a playing piece in the story. But how all this fitted into Freddie's plan to relaunch themselves as a proper band he wasn't sure. Probably not well.

"Fuck," someone muttered, although Adam couldn't tell who.

Jay looked *furious*, though.

"Banging," Nat was nodding. "I like it. What are we called?"

"Granola Dogs," Jonny said. "Prairie Fantasy?"

"That part's up to you. Each band is performing four songs at the concert at the end of the show, so you'll be doing two together – one Granola Fantasy track and one Prairie Dogs – and then you'll each do one song with your original line-ups. So a bit of both. You can talk specifics in rehearsals tomorrow, but for now we're going to do a big group interview with you all, then individual ones, and then it's on to the first activity. I'll leave you in the very capable hands of Lewis. Enjoy the rest of your day," Helen said, exiting stage left.

Adam exhaled slowly, watching everyone process the news.

"Cereal Hounds," Jonny said. "Meadow Dream."

"A supergroup after all," Freddie said, raising an eyebrow at Adam.

"Who'd have thought."

"Wait, we all play the same instruments, how's that going to work?" Jonny asked.

"I've been saying for a long time that the drummer is the most important part of the band." Fabs said. "Having two can only be a good thing,"

"Maybe I'll just do the bass drum," Adam said. "I'll be the foot."

"Hey, he's a session drummer! You don't even drum any more!" Jonny exclaimed with glee.

"Yeah," Adam said. "Thanks. I realise the vast chasm between my skill level and his."

"I'll take it down a notch for you," Fabs said, grinning.

"Fucking hell," Adam muttered, shaking his head.

"So, two drummers…" Jonny looked around the room. "Two bass players, three guitarists. A fist fight over the vocals."

"I'm game," Harry said. "Sounds cool."

Yeah, Adam thought. *Just a bit of fun. A bit of completely innocent, not-at-all-calculated, entirely-free-of-consequences fun.*

"What do you think, man?" Freddie asked, nudging Jay just slightly too hard.

"Cannot wait," Jay said, expression stony.

"Okay, guys, so if we could have you over here for the group interview?" another member of the production team called to them, gesturing to a curved sofa and a line of stools at the far end of the room.

Jay muttered something about S Club 7 but followed them down regardless.

"Okay, great, so if we have Adam, Jonny and Fabian at the back, and then Nat and Freddie, you sit on the sofa in the middle, and Harry and Jay either side. That's perfect."

"We're just the backing singers," Jonny whispered, looking like he was enjoying himself a lot more than Adam had expected. "We're The Supremes."

Or maybe he was just high. It was hard to tell which was the most likely.

"Aaaand, we're rolling…"

A guy with too-cool glasses – Lewis? – sitting just to the left of the main camera picked up a clipboard.

"You've just been given the news that you're being merged into a supergroup. How are you guys feeling about that?"

Bobbing heads and a broad murmur of assent rippled across the group.

"We're very open to the challenge," Freddie said. "I think I speak for all of us when I say that we've come into this with no expectations, and we spent quite a lot of time together back in the day so we're all familiar with each other's songs."

And there was that sweet media training, Adam thought.

"I mean, I'm not saying there's not going to be a fist fight for the lead vocals..." Nat chipped in.

Freddie laughed. "We can take that outside after we're done here."

Adam wished someone was holding up a cue sign so he knew when he should be laughing, and applauding, and keeping his mouth shut. And he really *really* wished that he didn't know about Nat and Freddie's secret agenda.

"Can you tell us a bit about how your paths first crossed as bands?" Lewis asked.

"Yeah, so the four of us – me, Harry, and Adam and Jonny back there – were playing a lot of local gigs, and Jay saw us playing one night and came to talk to us after the show," Nat started.

"And you were a big deal at that point?" Lewis said, aiming his question squarely at Freddie.

"Yeah, we were doing pretty well: we'd put a couple of good albums out, had a feel for the way things worked in the industry. I think our success was quite unexpected to us – we still felt like a local band at heart – and we had this idea that we'd start our own label and give some other unsigned bands a bit of a leg-up."

"To mould them in your image."

Freddie hesitated. "I wouldn't say *mould them in our image...*"

"It's hard to get a break, you know," Jay said. "You don't just need hard graft."

"Yeah, we felt we were in a position where we could help some other bands get their break," Freddie said.

"So you found Prairie Dogs..."

"Yeah, Jay found them."

"Do you wish you hadn't?" Lewis asked Jay.

Jesus, Adam thought, very glad he'd been shoved in the back row.

"That's, er..." Freddie faltered as Jay remained silent.

Adam really hoped, for all their sakes, that Jay had his game face on right now.

"Because it didn't really go very well from there, did it?" Lewis asked.

"In hindsight, it probably wasn't a very good time for us to be trying to pull off that project," Freddie said, recovering. "There was a lot going on in the band at the time. I think we all actually do regret bringing these guys into something we couldn't follow through on."

"It seemed like Prairie Dogs got a bit of a taste for the limelight: we saw a lot of pictures of you all at festivals, and in clubs, but not a lot of actual music going on…"

"No, and that was the fault of our youth, I think," Freddie said. "Very easy to get caught up in the good times. We put down a lot of tracks with these guys in the studio, it was just unfortunate that we didn't get the opportunity to do anything with the songs before things went a bit south. We got some good stuff out of them; they deserved more."

"So do you feel like Granola Fantasy owe you an apology?" Lewis gestured at Nat and Harry.

"No, man, not at all," Nat said. "Obviously we were gutted that it didn't go any further, but we had a great ride. It was just circumstances at the time."

"You wouldn't say that you contributed to the fallout at all?"

"I think taking on these guys was a bigger deal than we initially thought," Freddie jumped in. "It probably added to the stress of what was going on at the time, but these guys certainly aren't to blame."

Was this smug git buying their story? Adam couldn't tell. Was he fishing, or digging? Who had the upper hand here?

"It has been said that things changed quite quickly for you once Prairie Dogs came on the scene. There was talk of a very different dynamic within the band…"

"Well I'm not sure who would know that much about what was going on other than the three of us," Freddie said.

"And your four new friends."

"We didn't spend every second together. You know as well as I do that press photos can paint whatever kind of picture you want. It's rarely a reliable measure of the truth."

"There is a certain series of photos that it's surely hard to interpret in any other way…" Lewis said.

Adam could see how the photos of Freddie pinning Jay against the wall and hitting him square in the face could have been a bit of an indication that all was not well towards the end. Unfortunate that that had happened in full view of a delighted paparazzo but there was no accounting for the timing of revenge.

"Do you want to talk about that?" Lewis probed.

Freddie laughed nervously. "No? Is that an option?"

"How about you, Jay?"

"It was a long time ago, mate," Freddie said firmly. "Water under the bridge."

Adam would have thought they *would* have wanted to talk about it actually, given that it was a pretty convenient way to shoehorn their reworked version of the truth into the picture, but what did he know?

"How does it feel to all be back in the same room?"

"Feels like it's about time," Freddie said, looping an arm around both Nat and Jay's shoulders.

Lewis nodded, looking satisfied. "All right, that's a wrap! Thanks guys. Jonny and Adam, if you could hang on here for a minute, and if everyone else could follow me please…"

"First to be executed," Jonny said, winking at Adam.

"Right guys," said another very trendy female crew member, nameless and appearing out of nowhere, as seemed to be the thing here. "We're going to kick off the individual interviews with you two. Adam, you're going to do yours in here, so make yourself comfy on the sofa and I'll be back in a minute. Jonny, follow me."

She swished through a door with Jonny trailing behind her. Adam did as he was told but it felt like a trap. This really wasn't a holiday, was it? It was all very *Big Brother*, just with more walking.

"Hi!" The woman reappeared and sat down in the chair Lewis had occupied before. "So we're just going to have a super casual chat, if that's okay with you?"

Adam nodded.

"It won't take very long and then you can go back to the rest of the group. Just a few questions." She picked up the clipboard and folded the top page over. "Okay! So you guys were effectively plucked out of nowhere by Jay. What was the plan? What was supposed to happen next?"

"Ummm…" Adam tried to think back.

What *had* been the plan? What had Jay said to them right at the start that had got them hooked in?

"Well, we'd been together as a band for quite a long time, so we already had loads of original material that we'd written. We started recording it in a studio with Freddie producing and I guess the plan was to release something eventually?"

The girl looked unimpressed at his patchy recollection.

"The thing was, back then we weren't really very focussed on the long term. We were 18 and we suddenly found ourselves in a proper recording studio with a bunch of famous people and a lot of free alcohol, and we were basically having the best time of any 18-year-old ever. We weren't that bothered about where it was going. Well, I know I wasn't."

"Was it just free alcohol?"

Adam shrugged. "I can only speak for myself."

"And you were going to go on tour with Granola Fantasy? That was where it was going, wasn't it?"

"Sounds like you know all this already."

"Pretend I don't," the girl said, with a smile that was the opposite of reassuring.

"Okay. Well, yes, eventually we were supposed to be going on tour with them."

"And that didn't happen."

"That didn't happen," Adam agreed.

"Can you tell me why?"

"Granola Fantasy split up, so that pretty much put an end to the tour, I'd say."

"What do you know about why they split up?"

"I think it's common knowledge that things between Fred and Jay were a bit volatile towards the end."

"Do you know why that was?"

Adam shook his head, not really wanting to give her anything at all but at the same time feeling the need to lead the trail away from Prairie Dogs a little.

"There was a point, towards the end, where we started to wonder whether it was the kind of thing we wanted to be involved with. Things were tense between them and I think we could kind of sense that it was a sinking ship. I wouldn't say we distanced ourselves from them but we didn't see them as much. So I'm not really sure what was happening between them at that point."

That was a good lie, right?

"Do you know why things were tense?"

Adam shook his head again. "There were whole weeks where I didn't see Jay at all. I don't really know what was going on then."

The girl visibly perked up at this and Adam knew immediately that that had been exactly the wrong thing to say.

"When would you say things became tense between Freddie and Jay?"

"Oh man, I don't know. You'd be better off asking Fabs: he was actually there," Adam said, wishing this would all go away.

Was this really what he'd signed up for? Was it too much to hope for some questions about his actual band?

"How well did you get to know Freddie and Jay?"

"Not that well."

"You seem to be in all of the pictures."

"I think that's fairly inaccurate."

"A lot of the pictures."

"Well, yeah, I was, but being in the same place as someone isn't the same as getting to know them. We honestly weren't that close."

"They weren't your kind of people."

"You know, it's hard to find common ground with three guys selling out arenas when a minute ago you were playing for a pint in your local."

"So you didn't get on?"

"We got on fine," Adam said, trying to get the defensiveness out of his voice.

He didn't even know what he was being defensive about, for God's sake. He just got the feeling he was being goaded and it put his back right up.

The girl paused and Adam thought it might actually be over, but no such luck.

"Wouldn't you say it seems strange that Granola Fantasy were pretty much poised to take over the world, and then within six months of them teaming up with you guys it was all over?"

"Look, I can't comment on what it looked like from the outside, or how much of a coincidence it all seemed, or talk you though it from Fred or Jay's point of view. I can only tell you what it was like for me."

The girl paused. "So tell me what it was like for you."

Never, Adam thought. *Not a chance in hell.*

"I'll walk you through the edited highlights," he said.

16

"Who do you think will come in first?" Sadie asked. "I can't believe we're going to be a band again! Oh my God, I can't wait."

"I'm excited to see both of them," Mia said, smiling.

Cameron said nothing, but what was new there.

They'd been waiting in this room with the cameras for what seemed like ages, and Sadie felt like she was going to spontaneously combust with anticipation. What would it be like seeing Ryan again? Would it be weird? Would he be different? Would he really have an entourage with him? Would he just shake her hand and say it was nice to see her? How long had it even been since they'd been together in the same room? Years, certainly. It felt like forever.

A crackle on the radio and the mobile camera crew moved towards the door. Sadie's heart was hammering in her chest; she felt Mia's fingers lace around her own. The door handle turned and Sadie let out an involuntary squeak. Everything was in slow motion.

And then there he was. His hair was different but his face was the same and before she could stop herself Sadie was hurtling across the room towards him. He caught her in a hug, laughing, as she buried her face against his shoulder.

"Hey, Paws," he murmured as tears came to her eyes. "Are you crying on me?" he asked as they separated.

Sadie shook her head, grinning and wiping her eyes.

"Your hair looks so stupid," she said, his grin matching hers.

"I came dressed for the 90s, I don't know what your excuse is," he said, punching her softly on the arm.

There were lines on his face that she hadn't seen on Skype and a physique showing through his t-shirt that she wouldn't have expected. He had a tan and his eyes were sparkling and he smelt *really* good.

"There she is," Ryan said, aiming his next hug at Mia. "Lovely as ever."

Mia's cheeks were bright pink as Ryan turned to Cameron with a manly handshake that inevitably merged into a full-on hug.

"Hello, mate, how's it going?"

"Welcome back to England," Cameron said, a bigger smile on his face than Sadie had seen for a while.

"I vaguely remember it," Ryan said, nodding. "Haggis, right? Kilts?"

Sadie laughed. "It hasn't been that long."

"Ah, man, I feel like we've been touring forever."

"The hardship," Cameron said.

"Yeah, it's rough." Ryan grinned, looping an arm around Sadie's shoulder and giving her a squeeze. "Guys! This is cool. Who'd have thought."

"Where are you staying?" Sadie asked.

"Oh, just this little place with a hot tub and an indoor pool. It's like a treehouse pod. Entirely automated housekeeping. Very low-key."

"You are not."

Ryan shook his head. "I am not. I'm slumming it like the rest of you mere mortals. Although I kind of thought we'd all be bunking up together. Are you guys sharing?"

"Yep."

"Jealous. I'm rattling round a two-bed cabin on my own."

"I'll swap you," Cameron said, still smiling.

"So who else is here? Who've we seen?" Ryan asked.

"No one!" Sadie said. "We don't know who else is here."

"Ahh, what was that girl group I was especially fond of back in the day?" Ryan winked at Cameron. "Hope they're here."

"You're awful," Sadie said, elbowing him.

"The one and only." Ryan grinned. "What have you been doing this morning? I ate four of those welcome basket sandwiches in a row. Not that everything's about achievement, but just saying."

"Pacing," Cameron said, looking pointedly at Sadie.

"Did you come straight from the airport?" Mia asked.

"Yeah, man! We had a show last night! Honestly, I'm not sure if I'm asleep or awake right now," Ryan said, blinking exaggeratedly. "In all seriousness, when can I lie down? Are we done here? It's been good to see you."

"You have to stay with us now," Sadie said.

Ryan nodded. "All right, you've twisted my arm. So what's next?"

"We need one more," Mia said, and Sadie felt the mood drop almost instantly.

"Of course," Ryan said. "So where is he?"

"Here somewhere, I guess," Sadie said.

I hope.

Every time she'd seen a crew member today she'd half expected to be taken aside and told that James hadn't turned up and they were being kicked off the show. The very tiny rational part of her brain said that if he hadn't turned up they wouldn't have even made it as far as this room, but until she actually saw him standing in front of her she wasn't counting any chickens.

"You saw him?" Ryan asked Sadie.

"Last week."

Ryan raised an eyebrow in question and Sadie shrugged in return. Then the radio crackled again and her stomach lurched. The four of them turned to face the door, Ryan's arm around her, his hand squeezing her shoulder.

"Here we go," he murmured, as the door opened and James stepped into the room.

"Gosh," Mia whispered, because of course she hadn't seen any of this before.

The short hair, the stubble, the piercings, the tattoos curling out from underneath the rolled-up shirt sleeves. He looked like a completely different person; different even to the person Sadie had eaten an awkward spaghetti Bolognese with six days ago. If she were being truly objective she might have said that he was giving Ryan quite the run for his money in the heartthrob stakes, but James wasn't smiling and that warmth she'd felt from him so briefly before was nowhere to be seen.

The five of them regarded each other for a few moments before Ryan stepped forward.

"What time do you call this?" he said, holding out a hand.

James met him in the middle to shake hands and everyone in the room let out a collective breath.

"Took a little longer than I thought," James said.

Ryan nodded and Sadie didn't know whether they were talking about right now, or something bigger.

"You look well," Ryan said.

"So do you," James said. "The blond is holding up remarkably well."

Ryan smiled, seeming surprised by the dig. "I'm so very L.A. now."

"So I hear."

"Have you met the kids?" Ryan asked, sweeping an arm towards Sadie, Mia and Cameron, still clustered together.

"I don't think I can believe what I'm seeing," Mia said, approaching James with her arms wide and pulling him into a hug. "It's been such a long time."

"I'm sorry for my part in that," James said.

Mia smiled. "You're back now."

"You made it," Sadie said, also giving him a hug. "Thank you."

James just nodded. He turned to Cameron and there was a moment – just a fraction of a moment – where Sadie thought that perhaps this wasn't going to go as she'd imagined. But then James held out his hand and Cameron reciprocated, and that was all five of them, reunited.

"This is all new to me!" Mia said, waving a hand over James' general appearance, turning the attention away from the fact that James and Cameron were yet to say a word to each other. "I don't think I'd have recognised you in the street."

James ran a hand over his hair and smiled self-consciously.

"Well, we've all got new hair," Ryan said.

"This suits you," Mia said to James. "Very handsome."

"Oh all right, Jim Fan Club."

"It's James, actually, these days," James said.

"Huh," Ryan said. "Well, 10 points for a name change."

Sadie was watching them watching each other. This was going to be all right, wasn't it? Everyone seemed okay. Ryan's energy was irrepressible, even in the most awkward of situations, and she could see the tiniest hint of a spark between him and James, like the old old days; a muscle memory of how things had been at the start. Sure, James looked thoroughly daunted and Cameron was being very Cameron about it all, but they were a band again, one way or another. She felt like she was very cautiously stepping onto cloud nine.

"Right, guys!" A shout from behind them and the reality of the situation – the cameras, the schedule – came rushing back in. "There's a glass of champagne for you all out on the balcony while we do the individual interviews. Sadie, we'll do your interview first. If the rest of you could head out through those double doors, please…"

Sadie watched her bandmates leave without her, feeling a pang of missing out on the first exciting moments of catching up. The lights and cameras were all set up around a high stool in the corner of the room; she settled herself onto it and looked expectantly to a girl with a clipboard sitting beside the camera. Her hands felt a little bit shaky at her sides but it was as much adrenaline as it was nerves. She'd done a pre-reunion interview at the cabin with Mia and Cameron earlier which had been a good warm up, so how hard could a solo interview be?

"Okay!" The girl with the clipboard smiled warmly at her. "Welcome, Sadie! This'll just be a quick one, while the reunion is super fresh. If it's okay with you we'll dive straight in?"

Sadie nodded.

"Great! So the five of you have just been in the same room together for the first time in nine years. How did that feel?"

"Amazing! I don't think I've really processed it. It's like a dream come true."

"So you were keen for this reunion?"

"So keen."

"Do you think everyone else in the band feels the same?"

Sadie paused. She realised that she'd never actually discussed this with anyone outside of the band, and certainly not a stranger. She wanted to be honest in all the interviews, but a nagging feeling at the back of her mind wondered whether there was such a thing as being too honest in a situation like this. Did being diplomatic with her answers still count as telling the truth?

"I don't think they miss the band like I do," she said. "Obviously Ryan is still doing music, so I guess this is more of a novelty for him?"

"So would you say the others are slightly less enthusiastic about it all than you?"

Sadie shrugged. "Maybe a little bit. But they're all on board with doing the show. We wouldn't be here otherwise."

"And how do you think the reunion went?"

"Really well."

"There wasn't any tension between anyone?"

"Not that I noticed."

"Not even with James? Isn't it right that you hadn't seen him since he left the band?"

"I think we're all seeing this as an opportunity to make amends for the things that happened in the past," Sadie said carefully.

"Like James walking out on the band."

"I guess."

"How do you leave one of the biggest pop bands in the country without telling anyone?"

She hesitated. "I don't know. One day he just wasn't in the band any more."

"So you guys carried on as a four-piece for a little while, but ultimately split up."

"Well, the record company dropped us," Sadie said.

"And how did that make you feel?"

She paused again. Could she be honest *here*? When it was just her feelings at stake?

"Lost," she said. "Really lost. I've never found anything to fill the gap that the band left."

"Why did James leave the band?"

"I don't know."

"He never told you?"

Sadie shook her head.

"Why didn't you get in touch with him before now?"

"We were angry," she said. "To start with. And then time passed, and things got even worse for us, and I blamed him for everything that my life wasn't. I suppose I didn't feel like reaching out at that point."

"Is it a question you want to know the answer to?"

"I don't know," she said. "Maybe."

She'd thought that it was something she'd *needed* to know. That evening she'd spent at his house, the lack of answers had been infuriating. But now, seeing everyone together again... He'd come back. He was doing the show. Maybe the *why* didn't matter as much as she thought it had? Maybe him just being there with them was enough closure for her to be able to move on.

"Okay, that's great. I think we'll finish there for now," the girl said. "Can you send James in?"

"Sure." Sadie hopped off the stool and made her way to the doors that her bandmates had disappeared through earlier.

She could see them through the glass: talking, drinking... Everything still looked fine.

"Hi band," she said, stepping out onto the decking. "They want you next, James."

He nodded, putting an empty glass down on the table before heading back inside.

"Are you seriously calling him *James*?" Cameron asked.

"That's his name!" Sadie protested, taking a glass of champagne from Mia.

"How was your interview?" she asked.

Sadie shrugged. "It was okay. I don't know if I talked enough; I feel like I should have given longer answers to the questions. I wish I could remember our media training properly. All I can remember is that I need to know my message points, but I can't remember what message points are."

"Well don't look at me, I can count the number of interviews I've done recently on this fist," Ryan said, holding up a fist to demonstrate. "As in: no one cares what the rhythm guitarist has to say."

"At last you'll get your time in the spotlight," Cameron said.

"It's my time to shine!"

"Is there anything better than champagne in the middle of the day?" Sadie said, peering over the edge of the balcony into the lake. "Are there cameras out here?"

Ryan shook his head.

"Oh. I thought they'd be everywhere. So what happened after you came out here?"

"We made a secret pact without you. Just the four of us. You're not involved. It's very secret."

Sadie laughed. "You did not! What do you think about James? He's hot, right?"

"Gross. You can't say that, it's like incest," Ryan said.

"He's definitely very good looking these days," Mia said. "Very handsome."

"He thinks he's better than us," Cameron said.

"Oh I don't think that's true," Mia said. "He's just different."

"I don't think it's even him."

"Oh Cameron."

"He was never really one of us."

"That's not how I remember it," Sadie said, the conversation souring before her eyes.

"Well we all know the track record of your memory," Cameron scoffed.

"What do you think?" she asked Ryan.

He just shrugged.

"What's that supposed to mean?"

"I don't know."

Sadie frowned.

"What do you want from me, Paws? I don't know the guy. I'll make the effort for this but we're not going to be BFFs."

"What's Paws?" Mia asked.

"Ah, you remember: Sadie went through that phase of wearing those tatty fingerless gloves everywhere," Ryan said.

"Oh no, those purple and black things!" Cameron exclaimed. "Was that when you had the purple hair?"

"No, the purple hair was later," Ryan said. "Remember you wanted to dye it black and David *expressly forbade* you?"

"Remember when you had stupid bleach blond hair? Oh no wait, that's right now," Sadie said.

Ryan smiled, meeting her eye. "I missed you," he said. "I didn't know how much."

Sadie's heart filled all the way up to the top as she looked away, overcome.

"Classic Malone charm," Cameron said.

"Hey! I missed all of you!"

"Oh sure. L.A. life is so hard."

"Home is home," Ryan said. "I mean, trust me, I hate the thought that you guys are home as much as the next guy, but there it is. I'm glad you talked me into this, Paws."

"I didn't…"

"Shhh." Ryan put a finger to his lips. "I told my cool friends that you dragged me kicking and screaming all the way back to England."

Sadie grinned. "Well I didn't miss you one bit."

"Now we both know that's nonsense."

"Oh whatever."

Sadie leaned back in her chair as the conversation continued around her. This was nice. Wasn't this everything she'd wanted? And so much more than she'd had just a few days ago. Maybe she didn't need to worry about whether she could ever get her friendship with Ryan back on track, or why James had done the things he did all those years ago. Perhaps she'd get a proper apology or an explanation from James at some point, but perhaps he just simply wasn't the person she had thought he was. Regardless, she could relax now, couldn't she? Enjoy whatever this was going to be. It was happening; they'd made it. It was all good from here.

17

Kitty looked at the clothes strewn over the bed and then back at her reflection. Was she pitching this right with a loose grey t-shirt tucked into a short black button up skirt? She pulled her hair back into a ponytail, studying herself critically in the mirror. She had to look like she belonged in this strange twilight world of half-celebrity: glamourous enough to spark interest but incredibly casual at the same time, as if any attention she might get was entirely unexpected.

She slipped her feet into her favourite pair of Vans and perched a pair of sunglasses on her head.

Good enough.

She folded up the sheet of paper she'd taken out of the folder and tucked it into her back pocket along with her phone. Nice of them to let her know exactly where the celebrities would be each day. There was a small child riding a bike with stabilisers down the middle of the road and Kitty smiled at the mum hovering nearby as she walked past. She'd done a bit of digging into the bands and their potential plus-ones before they'd left, but the face didn't ring any bells. It had been hard to find details on everyone, though: there were a whole bunch of ex-pops stars here not doing anything of note any more.

She'd considered several times on the drive up that, short of being their saving grace, this might actually be the end for her and James. She wasn't sure there was actually a whole lot to lose at this point. Would it always be a disappointment, falling in love with who you thought someone was? She'd made a big decision based on a previous version of James, and even that was mostly information gleaned from afar. As it stood, the packaging had said one thing but what had turned out to be inside was markedly different: he was a cheap eBay knockoff of the genuine article. Was it possible to reframe how you saw someone; to appreciate what they actually were, rather than what you so badly wanted them to be? Did she even want who he really was? Did she even *know* who he really was?

If this really was it for them, though, she absolutely couldn't walk away without *some* answers. He could insist all he liked but she would never buy the line that he'd left the band because fame just wasn't for him. There's fame not being for you, and there's looking deeply *deeply* sad during every TV appearance past a certain date, no longer interacting in any way with your bandmates on stage and not saying a word in interviews. He went straight to the car after shows while the other four posed for photos and signed body parts at the back gates. A friend of a friend – and you were all friends if you were fans of the same band back then – had won a competition to have lunch with the band in a swanky London restaurant, and apparently James hadn't said a word throughout, eventually leaving early. Dodgy tummy, their PA had said at the time, but the larger issue wasn't addressed once. It had been like watching a ghost towards the end: every single fan felt his unease. Instead of gushing about how much they loved them, more and more fans would simply ask "Is Jim okay?" whenever they got a chance to talk to the band. Collectively no one could bear seeing him looking that sad.

Kitty hadn't known one single fan that had blamed James for leaving the band. It had felt impossible that there would be any other outcome. If they felt anything it was relief – *for him* – the way you might feel glad that a beloved family pet was no longer suffering. You could say what you wanted about teenage fangirls, but the community she used to be part of only ever wanted the best for James, even if it meant losing the thing they loved the most. They hoped he would be happy. They still asked "Is Jim okay?" every chance they got.

Even if she was the only person in the world still wondering, she couldn't leave without knowing *why*. The fact that she still cared after all this time suggested that she probably always would. Carve it on her gravestone: *is Jim okay?* She'd ask him outright if she had to, if it was the end. She'd make up something about watching some old clips of the band on YouTube and ask him all the questions she'd spent the last week trying to nudge into his field of vision. But not yet. She had some other things to do first.

Hearing footsteps nearby, Kitty slowed down the rate that she'd been stomping through the forest.

"Are you lost?"

The woman on the path in front of her looked stressed. She was slight, with blonde shoulder-length hair. Plain black top. Straight-legged black trousers. Not enough make-up to be TV people.

"No," Kitty said, flashing her most exuberant smile. "I'm press."

The woman frowned slightly.

"Well," Kitty said, trying to channel whatever it had been that had got her into so many places she shouldn't have been as a teenager. "Blogger. I do unofficial backstage pieces on this kind of thing. Helen feeds me stuff and I create the hype. You know Helen?"

The woman nodded, not looking convinced.

"Shouldn't you be in the media centre?"

"Oh I'm just having a break, actually. Thought I'd have a bit of a walk, get to know the place. It's amazing here, isn't it?"

"It has its moments." She paused. "It's really pretty out towards the perimeter. If you go down that path there until you hit the fence, you can follow the stream back to the centre."

"Oh, thanks! I'll do that," Kitty said, nodding enthusiastically.

"Enjoy," the woman said, smiling tightly before turning and heading away from Kitty.

Kitty eyed the path she'd pointed to. She supposed a little detour wouldn't do any harm. The whole point of this excursion was to get the hang of the layout of the place, anyway.

It took her about five minutes to get to the fence. She caught a glimpse of the stream through the trees to her left, and then she saw something much more interesting. Stepping off the path, she picked her way through the undergrowth towards the group of girls clustered behind a wooden barrier, mostly on their phones, looking cold in the shade of the forest. They all looked up as she approached.

"We're not doing anything wrong," one of the girls said.

Kitty shook her head. "I didn't say you were."

"Aren't you here to tell us off?"

"No."

"Oh."

"Are you a famous person?" a different girl asked eagerly.

Kitty smiled. "Who are you waiting for? I thought all the bands were here already."

"Are they?" a younger girl asked, looking worried.

"No, they're definitely not here yet. Amber said the cars didn't leave until lunch time," the first girl said.

"Big fans?" Kitty asked.

"The biggest."

"We're kind of like… Not even really fans. We're pretty good friends with the band."

Are you really, Kitty thought, not believing it for a second.

"They totally know our names."

"Connor replied to one of my tweets."

"Oh, Indigo Lion," Kitty said, nodding.

"Do you know them?" one of them asked, too quickly.

"No. But I used to do this kind of thing when I was your age," Kitty said.

"Which band?"

"Funk Shui."

The girls looked blank.

"They're one of the bands on this show?"

"Oh. We don't really know anything about those bands." The girl looked sheepish.

"Were you a groupie?"

Kitty smiled, amused. "No. I thought I was. But that's not what we were."

Groupie seemed too rock and roll a term for a handful of girls loitering at the back gates of an arena when they should have been at school, armed with crisps and bin bags – the trusty all-weather accessory – and prepared to go 10+ hours without having a wee, all in the pursuit of catching a glimpse of their heroes as they drove through the gates.

"Did you meet the band?" the girl at the back asked, interest piqued.

"Oh yeah. Loads of times."

An actual gasp from the crowd.

"What happened?"

Well, where to start? Kitty thought.

Admittedly she hadn't been one of those girls with the bin bags for very long. She couldn't remember exactly what she'd said to Ryan the first time she'd managed to get close enough to him, but she could remember the look he gave her after she'd said it, heart hammering, hands shaking so much that the photo she'd taken of the two of them was blurry. The second time she got really lucky: he arrived at a venue much earlier than the rest of the band, and at that time of the day it was just her and her most diehard fan friends hanging around just in case. If there was one thing you could say about Ryan it was that his love of being centre of attention really worked in the fans' favour: he stayed out for much longer than they would have expected that morning, smoking and chatting.

"Don't tell the fans I smoke," he'd said, and they'd all giggled, suddenly in on this huge secret.

The third, fourth and fifth time... Well, it wasn't long before Ryan was slipping her backstage passes as he was rushed past, telling security guards to let her and her gang in, ducking them under ropes. They were the elite, the gold-standard of fans, or that's what they thought at the time.

"Josh waved at me once at a show. I swear he recognised me," one of the girls said, her eyes sparkling.

"Oh my God, did you *die*?" a girl at the back shrieked.

"Did you ever go backstage?" the girl nearest to the barrier asked Kitty.

"Yep."

"You *were* a groupie!" another girl squealed.

Kitty laughed.

"How did you get backstage?"

"Most of the time I was invited."

"By who?"

"One of the band."

"What!"

"Which one?" a girl asked, thrusting her phone at Kitty.

She'd pulled up an old picture of the band, thankfully without the luminous outfits this time.

"Him," Kitty said, pointing to the screen. "Ryan."

"Were you his girlfriend?"

"No," Kitty said. "No, definitely not."

She perhaps hadn't started out intending to embark on such an all-consuming fangirl career, but the success of her endeavours and the attention from Ryan had been intoxicating. Before she knew it she was in with the stalker set of fans who were slightly older and much more organised, and she was getting all the info along the grapevine about where the band would be and when. They were front row in TV audiences, they waved them off at airports, they brought them coffee when they were in the studio and they spent so much time backstage that they came to be on first name terms with the band's families. Those other fans, the ones who just dipped into it every now and then, didn't stand a chance. It was a good day when Kitty got a fond eye roll from David, their PA, having turned up somewhere she shouldn't have known about yet again. There were a lot of good days.

One of their best tricks was to leave whatever arena the band were at well before the end of the show and get to the hotel before them. At the start they tended to all be swept into the bar along with the entourage, but increasingly frequently David would appear ten minutes after the band had gone in and pluck one or two girls from the group. Sometimes he'd say "Just Kitty" – she started to live for those two words. It didn't go down too well with the rest of the fans, but teenage girls back then were fickle like that: give them half a chance with their celebrity crush and they'd drop their friends without a second thought.

"And what happened next?"

The girls at the barrier were rapt, listening wide-eyed as Kitty gave them the edited highlights. It wasn't often she had an audience for this kind of anecdote: not really the kind of thing you could typically bring up at after work drinks on a Friday. And what did happen next definitely wasn't something to boast about.

It had seemed for a while like Ryan picked her out of the crowd every time. Those golden days when they stayed up later than the rest of the band in hotel bars, talking and teasing and laughing. When she felt luminous in his gaze. She was let into whatever backstage area she wanted to get into – she ditched the bin bags and just waltzed straight up to the door under the watchful gaze of the normal fans – and Ryan asked for her number under the pretence of wanting to send her a link to some website he'd been telling her about. She never messaged him first but he'd feed her titbits and tipoffs to make sure she was everywhere he wanted her to be, first in the queue. And, seemingly so close to the inner circle of the band, it felt like she was teetering on the edge of finally being part of something.

Kitty didn't feel like that again until she met James all those years later, and it didn't take her long to imagine a whole world of glamourous possibilities opening up in front of her. New Year parties and summer barbeques with his ex-bandmates; perhaps a group holiday to a Scandinavian country over Christmas where they'd all share a big log cabin. Then, eventually, they'd start to settle down: they'd be VIP guests at each other's weddings, her kids would play with Sadie's kids, and there they'd be, forever linked, and she'd be a part of that shared history.

But James' actual friends were boring and already settled down, and the most exciting it got was sharing a bottle of wine with another couple that she had nothing in common with in Pizza Express on a Saturday night. And so she remained, forever searching for another taste of that feeling.

"I don't think they do this any more, but when I was your age they had these magazine tours where they put a whole load of current pop bands on one line-up and toured them around the country. I don't know how it would even work these days. I can't see Ariana Grande coming over to do the Smash Hits Tour," Kitty said. "Anyway. The Holy Grail for fans was the end of tour party. I never heard of another fan ever getting in."

"Did you get in?"

Kitty nodded. "Ryan told me where it was going to be. I messaged him when I got there and he appeared out of nowhere, pulled me inside and put a glass of something in my hand."

"Was it amazing?"

"It was *amazing*. Imagine every band you listen to at the moment in one room, acting completely natural, all just being mates with each other. And a lot of them with girlfriends and boyfriends you hadn't even known existed while they were doing magazine interviews about being young, free and single."

"So what happened at the party?"

"Well me and Ryan were having such a laugh, but then David came over and was like, "I don't think she should be here". And Ryan really didn't like it when David told him what to do, so he said that we were leaving and he just grabbed my hand and we left. He was really drunk, and I guess I was drunk too, and suddenly he was kissing me, in the middle of the street."

And that poor, naïve, 16-year-old girl thought it was the beginning of everything, when it was actually the end. The rest was pretty clichéd, if she was honest. Ryan took her back to the hotel and it was probably a blessing that Kitty couldn't remember much about what had happened after they'd fallen giddily onto the bed. You could probably go ahead and assume, without being too far off the mark, that two drunk teenagers having sex wasn't going to be much to write home about. Especially when one of those teenagers had absolutely no idea what she was doing. The one thing she could remember, with absolute clarity, was the certainty that she was going to wake up in the morning as Ryan's girlfriend. And, of course, that couldn't have been further from the truth.

She didn't get another message from Ryan after that night and he never responded to any of hers. From then on it was never her that he picked out of a crowd or snuck backstage. She told the few friends she had left that *she'd* dropped *him*, but no one even believed that anything had happened between them in the first place. She found herself back on the outskirts of the fandom, with absolutely nothing to show for it. Perhaps this was something that these fans really did need to know, but Kitty couldn't bring herself to shatter their dreams like that. And what were the chances, anyway, of one of them repeating her experience with Indigo Lion? Funk Shui had been nothing in comparison to their current level of fame. These girls would be lucky to even catch a *glimpse* of them.

"I'm sure you can use your imagination for what happened next," Kitty said.

She should have been bitter; should have taken a step back and realised that Ryan had done exactly the same to every girl that had come before her and would do the same to all the ones that followed. But instead, that 16-year-old girl who hadn't grown into her looks yet but was already funny and kind and bold, took it as quality critique: she wasn't pretty enough, skinny enough, cool enough, *vibrant* enough. And, 11 years later, it was no accident that she'd replaced funny, kind and bold with all of those more important traits.

"Can I give you some advice?" Kitty said to the girls. "You need to stick together. Okay? No matter what. Support each other. It's not easy. But it's important."

They looked puzzled but they nodded anyway. For here was a woman who had had sex with a celebrity and was deserving of their unwavering respect.

"Can I get a photo with you for my Instagram?" the girl at the front asked.

"Oh! Sure!" Kitty said, ducking under the barrier to pose for the photo. "What's your handle? I'll follow you. I'm going to try to get some behind the scenes stuff for mine."

Nothing like a few impressionable teenage girls to blow up your Instagram.

"Can you send us some pictures of Indigo Lion?" one of the girls asked.

"Can you sneak us in?" another asked.

Kitty laughed. "I don't think I can sneak you in, but I can try and get you some bits of your boys. Let me give you my number. Maybe add me to a

WhatsApp group with all of you in, or something?"

"You're so cool," the youngest girl said, grinning at her.

Cute.

"I'd better head back," Kitty said, turning to go. "I'll let you know if I see anything interesting."

"Wait, why are you here?" the ringleader called after her. "Did you marry Ryan?"

Kitty just smiled.

No, she thought. *But I've waited a really long time to show him what he's missing.*

18

It was worse than Mabel had imagined, them being there. Oh the unease that had settled in her stomach at midnight. And by morning, the place that had been her salvation no longer felt like hers. She imagined the layers she'd pasted onto herself over the years starting to peel off; all the things she despised starting to show in patches underneath. She was headed over to the office to get on with some work but she didn't know if she could even be around people when she felt like this. She had to go now, though: she'd stayed in for most of the afternoon when she knew the bands would be moving from their cabins to the main square, and now she had a tiny window of opportunity to get across the site before everyone was released back into the wild.

Was this kind of behaviour sustainable for ten days? She wasn't sure, but it gave her something to focus on, at least. She was just going to keep putting one foot in front of the other for as long as possible and–

Mabel's head jerked up as she heard footsteps on the path in front of her.

She stopped still, frowning, blinking, trying to get the image before her to make sense. It was, perhaps, a similar sensation to a giant wave rearing up before you: for a moment she couldn't believe what she was seeing. It was *so* improbable it was like her brain lagged behind for a beat while it tried to work out how to process the information.

Because there ahead of her, in the last place he should ever be, was Adam.

He hadn't seen her yet: he was still about 10 metres away from her, frowning at the phone in his hand. Every impulse in her body was screaming at her to move but all she could do was watch as he put the phone in his pocket and looked up.

He stopped too and it was as if, just for a moment, they were suspended in time together, held by a forcefield, just staring at each other. She vaguely registered the look of shock on his face; she thought perhaps he said her name. Then the wave reached its breaking point, instinct took over and she turned and ran.

She flew through the forest without looking back, without really knowing *why* she was running, feet crashing through bracken and red campion, stumbling over tree roots. She ran so fast the landscape blurred around her and she lost her bearings, imagining all the while that she could hear Adam just moments behind her. She burst out onto a deserted street, feeling entirely exposed without the cover of the trees, and hurled herself at the front door of the nearest cabin, relief coursing through her as the handle gave way and she virtually fell inside. Her whole body trembling, she slid down the wall opposite the door, squeezing her eyes tightly shut and trying to regain control of her breathing as huge swells of dizziness engulfed her.

Mabel didn't know how long she stayed there, sitting against the wall, but all the fight was gone from her by the time she heard footsteps outside and the swish of the front door.

"Oh. Hello." The girl with the copper-coloured hair that she'd met in the woods earlier that afternoon looked around, as if she was trying to work out whether she was in the wrong cabin. "Are you okay?" she asked, peering at Mabel.

"Are Prairie Dogs doing the TV show?" Mabel stammered, realising for the first time that her face was wet.

She hadn't even noticed she was crying.

"What?" the girl asked, looking confused.

"Are Prairie Dogs supposed to be here?" Mabel urged, needing some kind of verification that she'd really seen what she thought she'd seen, and that she wasn't finally losing it.

"Er… Yes?" the girl said, still frowning.

"But they weren't on the paperwork," Mabel murmured.

"They were definitely mentioned in an article I read at the weekend…" The girl paused, still standing by the front door. "Are you… hurt?"

Mabel shook her head. She thought she might quite like to stand up and go back to her cabin, but her legs had other ideas, wobbling beneath her as she tried to get up from the floor.

"Oh! Okay…" the girl said, catching Mabel as she veered sideways.

She steered her towards the sofa, standing over her as she sat down.

"Can I make you a cup of tea?" she asked awkwardly.

Mabel nodded in defeat and the girl moved off towards the kitchen.

She couldn't think of anything but his face. It was like the image had burned itself onto the back of her eyelids. Even in the darkness, there he was. He looked exactly the same, as if all that time had never passed. She felt sick. *How* could he be here? *How* could she not have known?

"I'm Kitty, by the way," the girl said, handing Mabel a mug and gingerly sitting down on the sofa next to her.

"Mabel," she whispered.

Kitty nodded in acknowledgement. "I didn't know how you liked your tea…"

Mabel didn't say anything, just clutched the mug between both her hands, wishing it was hot enough to burn her: that all too familiar yearning for something to hurt her more on the outside than she was hurting on the inside.

"We met in the woods earlier, didn't we?" Kitty asked.

Mabel nodded, still staring at the tan-coloured liquid.

"Do you work here?"

There was a bang, the sound of voices from outside the cabin, and Mabel flinched, the tea rippling across the mug.

"Are you sure you're okay?" Kitty asked. "I would leave you to it but you're kind of in my cabin… Can I call someone for you?"

Mabel shook her head. "I'm sorry… I don't think I can explain…"

Kitty smiled encouragingly. "It's okay. We can just drink tea. As long as you're not going to pass out, or anything."

"I don't think so."

"Stay until you feel better," Kitty said. "I'm not supposed to leave the cabin, anyway."

"Why not?" Mabel asked.

Her voice didn't sound right, like it wasn't really her talking. But then nothing was right any more. The best she could hope for was that this wasn't actually happening and she was having some kind of psychotic episode.

"Well," Kitty smiled sheepishly. "Obviously I'm not a blogger…"

"These cabins are for people with plus-ones," Mabel said, realising where she was.

But there had been no questions marks, no TBCs on the list she'd been given, and no one had asked for any extra cabins to be made ready. *How* were Prairie Dogs here?

"That's me," Kitty said. "Someone make me a t-shirt quick so I'm not accidentally mistaken for a person of worth."

"Whose plus-one are you?" Mabel asked, praying that this girl was not connected to one of Granola Fantasy.

"James from Funk Shui," Kitty said. "They got asked to do the show pretty late, though. Apparently some bands dropped out? Maybe the same happened with Prairie Dogs?"

Mabel was sure Funk Shui hadn't been on the original list either.

She took a sip of tea, trying to ground herself. What was she going to do?

"So what do you do here?" Kitty asked.

"Me?"

Kitty nodded.

"I'm the Assistant Site Manager," Mabel said.

Maybe Kitty would keep asking questions and she could just focus on that.

"Oh wow. That sounds so cool. Are you in charge?"

"Mostly."

"I'd love to be in charge of something," Kitty said. "Is it fun?"

Mabel thought for a moment. *Was* it fun? She wasn't sure she noticed, day-to-day, whether she was actively enjoying things. She felt more like she was just endlessly navigating the hurdles that cropped up, as if every day was nothing more than an annoying fly she kept swatting away.

Was that a life?

"It's okay," she said, feeling like that wasn't nearly enough.

Hadn't this job given her something to get up for every day? Even if that was only because it would descend into chaos without her. Diane made her feel respected and capable; she wasn't sure that any of the other staff thought very much of her, but they didn't put up too much of a fight either. When she was here, working, she had something. She *was* something. Perhaps it wasn't a purpose exactly, but it was a hell of a lot more than she'd had before.

"It's a good job," she tried again.

"How did you get into it?"

Mabel scanned back through the last few years, isolating the mundane memories that didn't mean anything; blurring out the rest.

"By accident, I suppose. The person who interviewed me told me they couldn't find anyone who wanted this job: you kind of find yourself working all the time, especially in the summer. I didn't have the experience, but I also didn't have any ties or commitments that would get in the way of work, so they gave me a chance."

She was so unused to explaining anything about her life to another person that the words came out stilted, as if conversation were a muscle you had to use regularly or it would seize up.

"Hmm. Maybe I could do something like that," Kitty said. "I think me and my boyfriend are going to break up."

"The boyfriend you're here with?"

Kitty nodded. "I thought coming here would fix things, but I don't think it's going to." She shrugged, not looking overly distraught. "It's kind of complicated. What did you want to be when you were younger?"

Mabel hesitated, thrown by the question. "I don't know," she said, toying with the idea of telling Kitty something real.

There was something disarming about her, like it might be possible just to sit here and chat about nothing and pretend that she did this kind of thing all the time.

"I was supposed to do a psychology degree, but I didn't..." Mabel said, nudging at the boundaries of her discomfort.

"How come?"

"There were other things that seemed more important at the time."

"Did you go to uni at all?" Kitty asked.

"No."

"Me neither. Do you regret not going?"

Mabel nodded slowly.

It wasn't exactly top of the list of things she regretted, but it was up there. The life that could have been, if only she'd got on that train and just gone home.

Kitty gasped suddenly and Mabel flinched again.

"Oh my God, I forgot to ask my friend to feed the cats! Shit!"

She picked up her phone from the coffee table, her long nails clicking against the screen as she tapped out a message.

She grinned at Mabel. "I'm the worst! James would have killed me!" She paused. "I wonder if he'll let me take my cat when we break up... Do you have any pets?"

Mabel thought: this girl is so strange, she's all over the place, I need to leave.

But then she thought: when was the last time I actually talked with someone like this over a cup of tea?

And then she thought: maybe this isn't worse than being alone right now.
"More tea?" Kitty asked, holding up her empty mug.
And, despite herself, Mabel nodded.

19

"Nat!" Adam burst through the door of the sports bar where he'd left his band mingling and drinking with everyone else. "Fuck fuck fuck."

He scanned the room, spotting Nat talking to a couple of people he didn't know over in the corner.

"Nat!" He pushed through the awkward groups of people until he got to him. "I need to talk to you," he said urgently, breathing heavily, one hand on Nat's arm.

Nat frowned, looking from Adam to the two people he was with. "I'll catch up with you later," he said to them, stepping away with Adam. "What's going on?"

"She's here," Adam said. "I saw her… She was there… I lost her…"

Nat looked at him like he was crazy.

Did he look crazy? *Was* he crazy?

"Let's go outside for a sec," Nat said, gesturing to someone across the room and ushering Adam back out of the bar.

Jonny banged through the double doors just after them.

"Hey man, did you get my filters?" he asked, doing a double take as he looked properly at Adam. "What happened to you?"

"Mabel's here," Adam said.

Nat and Jonny exchanged a glance.

"*Mabel* Mabel?" Jonny said.

"What do you mean *she's here*?" Nat asked.

"I saw her. In the woods."

"Why were you in the woods?"

"I dipped out," Adam said, really thinking that this was not the part of the story that needed the explanation. "I went to get my jacket, and Jonny wanted me to grab his filters."

"And a sandwich," Jonny said.

"She was there. Just walking down the path. Fucking hell!" Adam exclaimed at the sky.

"How can that be possible?" Nat asked carefully.

"I don't know! But she was there! And she ran, and I lost her."

"She ran? *Dude*," Jonny said, patting his pockets. "I wish I had my filters."

"How can she be here?" Adam shook his head, pacing hopelessly across the flagstones of the square.

"You're sure it was her?" Nat asked.

"It was her," Adam said. "My whole fucking world just imploded. It was her."

Nat exhaled slowly. "Shit."

"Is she here because we're here?" Jonny asked.

Adam shook his head. "I don't know. She was wearing, like, office clothes and she had a thingy around her neck. Like a…" He gestured, trying to find the word. "A key fob."

"Plus why would she have run," Jonny said.

Yeah. Why *had* she run. In all the millions of seconds Adam had spent daydreaming about what it might be like to unexpectedly bump into Mabel one day, not once had he imagined her running away from him. And he'd thought she'd already broken his heart as much as it could possibly break.

"You think she's with the TV people?" Jonny asked.

Adam shook his head.

That look on her face. Absolute horror. Like *he* was where he wasn't supposed to be, and not the other way around.

"I've got to find my aunt."

"Oh right! Your aunt works here! Yeah that's a good shout, man," Jonny said. "Want me to come with?"

"Or you could just leave it," Nat said, looking Adam straight in the eye, in a way that only a person you'd known since you were kids had the right to.

And here was the unspoken distance between them. A whole canyon full of what Nat thought about how Adam felt about Mabel that they'd never really be able to cross. 20 years of friendship reduced to nothing.

Adam sighed. "You don't think I could really do that?"

"I think she's trouble, and I think Freddie could do without this." Nat paused. "So could you, to be honest."

"What's Freddie got to do with it?" Adam said.

"Oh what's Freddie got to do with it. Come on, man," Nat said. "It's got more to do with Freddie than it has to do with you."

It stung more because he knew Nat was right. The only part of this that was his business was the part he'd constructed in his own head.

But why had she *run*.

"Cover for me, right?" Adam said, walking away from them both.

He didn't have a plan. He was just going to keep walking until he either saw a sign or found someone to ask for directions to the main staff office. How big could the site be?

He couldn't think of anything but her face. She looked exactly the same, as if all that time had never passed. He felt sick, like he'd drunk too many strong coffees too fast. How could he have been so close to her all day and not have known? Would he ever have known if he hadn't taken a detour on the schedule?

Why had she run?

Of course there were no signs to where he needed to go, but at some point he ran into a guy in uniform sweeping blossom off a path who told him that the staff offices were based out of the Visitor Centre and pointed him in the right direction. Adam was out of breath by the time he reached the low building, his heart pounding. Would she be in there? Was this where she'd run to? He stepped into the lobby and went over to the reception desk.

"Is Diane Cooper around here anywhere?" he asked.

The blonde girl looked up and gasped. "Oh my God! You're a famous person! You're from that band!"

Well he hadn't been expecting that. And if it had been any other time...

"I'm Diane's nephew," he said. "Is she here?"

The girl nodded enthusiastically. "I'll call her," she said, picking up the phone. "Diane! You never said you had a famous nephew!"

A moment later the door behind the desk opened and Diane appeared, smiling so warmly that for a moment Adam forgot why he was there.

"I was wondering when I'd see you!" she said. "Come through!"

Adam could feel his hands shaking as he followed her into the small office. It was pretty apparent that it was empty, though. Mabel wasn't there.

"Do you work with someone called Mabel?" he asked.

Pleasantries would have been unbearable at this stage. He just needed to know where she was.

The smile didn't leave Diane's face. "Yes! Do you know her?"

"How long has she worked here?"

Diane thought for a moment. "Oh, gosh. It's been years. I couldn't tell you exactly."

Jesus. All this time. Right under his nose.

"Where is she?" he asked.

Now she frowned. "Are you all right, Adam?"

He shook his head. "I really need to see her, Diane."

"Well I'd love to help but I don't know where she is at the moment. She's here, somewhere, but I couldn't tell you where." Diane paused. "How do you two know each other?"

"She's Nat's sister," Adam said, and he could see Diane trying to work out who Nat was and how this all fitted together. "I knew her when we were in the band."

Perhaps if he sounded slightly less deranged there might be a better chance of him getting the information he needed.

"Sorry," he said, pulling it back a notch. "I don't mean to come in here being all weird. It's just I saw her earlier and it was a bit of a shock, and… I could just really do with talking to her."

Diane looked at him for a minute, before nodding. "She's staying on site for the next ten days," she said. "She might be at the cabin."

She picked up a leaflet from a nearby desk, unfolding it and putting a pencil ring around a tiny numbered square towards the edge of the map.

"I hope this isn't a bad decision on my part, Adam," she said, handing it to him. "She's one of my best people."

"Thank you," he said, hugging her. "I'll come and see you properly soon."

"Do," Diane said. "You can come back here any time, okay?"

He nodded, grasping the map tightly and leaving the office.

How many times had Diane invited him to come up for a free holiday? How many times had it seemed like too much effort to actually go? He couldn't get the time off work, couldn't afford the petrol to get there, couldn't get Betsy and Henry organised enough for them all to be free at the same time… How different would this moment have been if he'd been there for a holiday; if he'd gone to Diane's office to be introduced to the people she worked with and Mabel had just been there?

And then, a horrible sinking feeling as he strode across the site: if Mabel worked here, did she know that he was going to be here for the show? Because Diane knew. Would she have bragged about it in the office, or was it of less consequence to her than that? And if Mabel did know... Did that mean that after all this time she still didn't want to be found?

Adam knew he wasn't really this guy. He wasn't this guy about anything. But with her... Well, he didn't know *who* he was with her. Did she expect him just to leave it? To just shrug it off like he had back then as she'd zigzagged away from him. Did she even know how hard he'd tried to track her down over the years? Hadn't he been patient enough?

He saw the perimeter fence loom up in front of him and a cluster of cabins that didn't look as new as the one he was staying in. There were no lights on in any of them; no sign that anyone was here at all.

Please be here.

Of all the times he thought he'd come close to finding her, this was the one that would break him. The very last stop at the end of the line. And he realised, as he approached her cabin, that he didn't have a Plan B; that every moment of his life for the last nine years had been nothing more than treading water until he found her. He'd kept himself, and his life, a blank canvas, just waiting for her to come back and put her mark on it. And not once had he ever considered that she might not actually want to.

He walked up the wooden steps to the front door of the cabin and knocked.

Nothing.

He knocked again.

"Mabel!" he shouted. "Mabel, please! I just want to talk to you!"

He banged again on the door, so hard that the sound seemed to reverberate through the trees around him. Breathing heavily in frustration he went over to the window, cupping his hands around his eyes to peer through into the dingy room.

Two kittens on the sofa stared curiously back at him.

He stepped back.

She wasn't there.

With his back to the wall he slumped to the floor, head in hands, not knowing what the hell was supposed to happen next.

20

Mabel looked at her watch. "It's getting late. I really need to feed the kittens."

"Do you think he'll still be there?" Kitty asked.

She'd managed to fill in some of the pieces of what was going on over the course of the afternoon; enough to get the general gist. Mabel hadn't had much of a choice there: her reaction when she'd got the phone call from her boss hadn't been the kind of thing you could leave unexplained. Kitty couldn't quite work out at this point whether Adam was a bad guy or whether Mabel's "history with him; with the band" was enough in itself for her to want to avoid seeing him. All she did know was that Mabel didn't seem to have anyone else to support her in this, and you didn't leave another woman in need at the mercy of a past relationship, whatever form that had taken.

Girl power and all that.

"I don't know," Mabel said.

Kitty couldn't tell whether the look on her face was just worry, or fear.

"I wish Diane hadn't told him where I was staying."

"Yeah but who knows what he said to her to get that information. He could have made anything up. At least she told you what she'd done."

Mabel shook her head. "I can't believe she's his aunt…"

"People always say it's a small world, but it totally isn't. How things like that actually happen is completely nuts."

"I don't know what I'm going to do," Mabel said. "I need to get back there."

"I could go. See if he's still there. If he's not I could feed the kittens for you."

"Oh, you don't have to do that…"

Kitty shrugged. "I'm not doing anything. James will be off doing his pop star thing for God knows how long. I was only going to try and stalk them around the site."

"Are you sure?"

"I'll just go and have a look. It's not that far from here, is it?"

Mabel shook her head. "You just follow this road out to the edge."

"Okay then." Kitty stood up and slipped her shoes on.

"Don't let him see you," Mabel said. "He might follow you back here."

Kitty smiled. "Don't worry, spying on people is one of my top skills. Although if I get told off for being out of the cabin I'm blaming you."

Mabel just looked worried.

"That was a joke," Kitty said, smiling encouraging at her. "Don't you go anywhere. I'll be back."

There was another small child on a bike in the street. Was that all you did with small children? That whole world was beyond her. Couldn't see that happening with James – or anyone – any time soon.

She walked alongside the neat rows of cabins until the forest closed in around her. Stepping off the path she picked her way slowly through the undergrowth until she had a clear line of sight to Mabel's front porch.

No mistaking it: Adam was still there, sitting with his back against the front door, arms folded across his knees. This certainly hadn't been the drama she'd been expecting from this trip but she'd take it! See also: helping out a friend. Obviously that was the main thing here. *Obviously.*

Kitty had, of course, been aware of the existence of Prairie Dogs back when they'd been almost famous. It had been a much worse ending for the fans than the whole Funk Shui debacle: rumours of addiction, in-fighting, some kind of feud between Freddie and Jay, and sketchy reports of a girl that had something to do with it that cropped up again and again in fan chatter. The fact that both bands were on the show seemed to suggest that Prairie Dogs had indeed played a key part in the downfall of Granola Fantasy, and Kitty imagined that the fans were waiting to watch the fallout with baited breath.

Mabel had been so vague when she'd been talking about Adam that Kitty didn't know if he was an ex or not, but judging by the state she'd been in when Kitty had found her and the pure anguish on Adam's face right now, their history together was Big. And she wondered: if she broke up with James, would he track her down and sit outside her front door until she talked to him? Would she find herself in uncontrollable tears if she was to bump into him in the street one day after the event? Somehow she thought not. Did that mean that what they had wasn't enough?

When she got back to the cabin Mabel was exactly where she'd left her.

"He's still there," Kitty said, sitting back down on the sofa.

Mabel looked dismayed.

"You don't think… It's not a good idea to talk to him?" Kitty asked.

Mabel shook her head vehemently.

"Never?"

"I can't…" Mabel whispered. "Oh, what I am going to do about the kittens?"

"Well he can't stay there forever, surely," Kitty said. "He's not even supposed to be there now, I bet. If James is filming, surely everyone is filming. We'll just have to wait until he goes."

"I'll have to move everything to another cabin," Mabel said, looking more and more panicked.

"Why don't you stay here?" Kitty asked. "I don't like the thought of you being on your own. I'm going to be here all the time. We could look after the kittens together? I love kittens."

Mabel paused, looking like she was weighing it up in her head.

"I don't think I can. I.…" She hesitated, looking awkward. "I don't sleep well…"

"Are you going to sleep better on your own when you know Adam is here somewhere?"

Mabel didn't answer.

"I can go and get whatever you need from your cabin. You can have your own room here. You don't have to hang out with me all the time. It's just… There was a time when I really needed a friend and I didn't have anybody. I know what it feels like. I just want to help."

Eventually Mabel spoke. "I fall asleep to films," she said, as if it was the most shameful revelation in the world. "I can't sleep if it's quiet."

Kitty nodded. "I think we can handle that."

There was so much she wanted to ask Mabel. What did she do to attract these fascinating people who wouldn't talk about what had happened to them? Patience was a virtue all right.

"I'll go to the cabin later, when it's dark. I'll take James. I'll get him to punch Adam if there's any trouble."

Mabel looked alarmed.

"That was another joke," Kitty said. "I don't think James would ever punch anyone."

As if on cue, James came through the front door, slamming it crossly behind him.

"Or maybe he would..." Kitty murmured. "Hello," she said brightly, jumping up from the sofa and following him into the kitchen.

He leaned back against the workshop and sighed heavily.

"Sorry," he said, rubbing his eyes. "Long day."

"James," Kitty hesitated, realising that perhaps the decisions she'd made that afternoon were not going to be compatible with this mood that had stormed into the cabin. "We have company," she said lowering her voice.

"Who?" James asked, looking over to the sofas.

"Her name's Mabel. She's having some trouble with... someone here. She needs to lie low for a bit. I told her she could stay here."

James looked mildly irritated. "Oh, what? Can't she just tell the people who work here and get them to sort it out?"

"She *does* work here," Kitty said.

James frowned, the way he always did when Kitty did something that he was sceptical about.

"What are you doing," he muttered, moving towards the sofas. "Hi Mabel, I'm James," he said, holding out a hand to her.

Mabel shook it and smiled weakly.

"Sorry if this is a pain..." she started.

"It's not," Kitty said firmly.

James was still looking at Mabel, something about his expression that reminded Kitty of watching him on a TV screen. Those deep brown eyes that held so much and gave you nothing.

"Drink?" he asked finally.

Mabel nodded.

Kitty watched him as he brought the whiskey back into the kitchen and poured out two glasses. He handed one to Mabel and there was a startling similarity in the way they drank: both a desperation and a relief. Perhaps you couldn't see it so much in isolation, but here, stood next to each other, it was plain to see that these were two people in a lot of pain. Something real had happened to them and it wasn't over.

And all Kitty could think was that she wished she knew what that was like.

NINE DAYS TO THE LIVE SHOW

21

Sadie looked at herself in the mirror, marvelling at how the make-up artist had somehow managed to turn her back into a pop star in the space of half an hour. She looked like *herself* again, for the first time in a very long time. Was this really all it took to see a face in the mirror that she recognised? She could have taken a make-up class and saved herself nine years of moping.

"Thanks, it's amazing," she said, getting out of the chair and heading back outside to wait for whatever came next.

It hadn't taken very long at all for the paved area in between the main buildings to become the unofficial place where they all congregated, perching on picnic benches or on the walled edge of the fountain in the middle. The cabins were so spread out and the route back was steep, and once they were down here there almost didn't seem any point leaving. Sadie didn't know about anyone else, but she didn't feel much like a pop star when she was alone in the cabin. Here, they were a force to be reckoned with.

Ryan wolf-whistled her as she approached the bench that most of her band were occupying.

"You look like Baby Spice," Cameron said. "During the bad phase."

"You two bring out the worst in each other," Sadie said, sitting down.

"I didn't even say anything!" Ryan protested.

"I like this," Mia said, pinching the fabric of Sadie's outfit between two fingers. "Do we get to keep the clothes?"

They'd dressed her in a cropped black jumpsuit and pristine white trainers and she felt cooler than she'd ever felt in her entire life. How did someone she'd never met have a better grasp of her fashion sense than she had herself? Why didn't she own a jumpsuit? Honestly, she had spent nine years absolutely failing as a woman.

"Well I'm never taking this off, so they'll have to cut me out of it if they want it back," Sadie said. "You must be next: I think they've done nearly everyone else."

"I'm excited," Mia said.

Sadie smiled absently, unable to help her gaze drifting over to where James was sitting, several benches away, with Jay from Granola Fantasy, Tom and George from Kingpin, and Hayley from Polar Opposite.

"I wish he'd hang out with us," she said.

"Give it time," Mia said. "It must be so weird for him."

"It doesn't look very weird for him to hang out with them," Sadie said. "Or the people he was with earlier. Why does he hate *us*? Isn't it the other way round?"

"I think we're actually the only band sitting together," Mia said, looking at the other clustered groups. "Everyone's just catching up."

"Okay," Sadie said, getting up. "Then I'm going to catch up with George."

She shimmied round the benches and sidled up next to him. James was saying something to the group about kittens, nodding at her in acknowledgement as she poked George in the arm.

"Hi!"

He turned, a huge grin on his face when he clocked her.

"It's you!"

"It's me!" Sadie smiled too. "I didn't see you yesterday at all!"

"I know! I was doing a very lengthy interview about Aimee." George pulled a face. "They asked about you, though."

"Did they!" Sadie exclaimed, failing to be nonchalant in the slightest.

George nodded. "A tiny cameo."

"Oh, well, I'm flattered that anyone even noticed."

"You look amazing," he said, giving her the onceover.

Sadie did a strange curtsey thing that she regretted instantly, beaming nonetheless.

"Thank you! I have been restored to my former glory," she said. "So, tell me everything! How are you? What are you doing with yourself these days?"

"I'm busy! Got loads of projects on the go! It's all good!"

"Like what?" Sadie asked, seeing the same look in George's eyes that she'd seen on just about every other person she'd talked to so far.

Craig, who was a Music History lecturer now. Lauren, who ran an amateur dramatics club for kids. Lee, who advertised his guitar lessons in the local paper. Natasha, who had been in the identity parade in *Never Mind the*

Buzzcocks once. Gemma, who almost got to represent the United Kingdom at Eurovision.

Their lives were all *just so great*. And she didn't believe a word of it.

"Well I've been doing panto," George said. "There are some great theatres near where I live now. I did this touring show, like a 60s retrospective, which was awesome. I've done a couple of musicals…"

"In the West End?" Sadie asked.

"No. Just… With this theatre company. Locally."

Sadie nodded, suspicions confirmed.

"I'm writing one of my own too. That's going really well," he said, brightly.

"You're not doing music any more?" Sadie asked.

"Well, *musicals*."

"Not really the same though, is it?"

"All right, negative," George said with a smirk. "Sure, it's not Glastonbury, but it's something."

Sadie smiled. "Sorry. I just… Everyone keeps telling me about how great their lives are now, but it just sounds like making do to me. No one has come out and said, "God I miss being in a band, isn't life shit these days". Even though it kind of is."

"What are *you* doing these days?"

"Nothing. I work in a shop," Sadie said. "I couldn't be further away from music if I tried."

"Wouldn't you rather be doing *something*?"

Sadie sighed. "I don't know that I even had the chance. By the time I realised you had to go looking for those opportunities and *next big things* it was too late."

It had faded so fast, the lustre that surrounded her at the peak of her fame. The glow that had set her apart from the ordinary people on the street; that saw her singled out in a busy supermarket. The glances, the whispers, the poorly-concealed cameras pointed in her direction. These days she felt like she could walk around the supermarket naked and no one would bat an eyelid. Did the aftermath of fame somehow make you less visible than you were before? Oh that daily disappointment as customer after customer looked her right in the eye and never once realised who she used to be.

"We're all just making the best of it, aren't we?" George shrugged. "Course it's not *enough*. I'd give anything to be releasing music people actually care about. I've put a few bits out myself, and the fans we've got left have supported it to an extent, but it never goes anywhere." He raised an eyebrow. "I'll be honest, it's not great for the ego to admit that I can't write the kind of song that anyone would want these days. We weren't in bands because we were talented, were we? It was a different time. Music's moved on without us. I don't know if there's really a place for us there any more. Not like that, anyway."

He was right, wasn't he? She *hadn't* been in the band because she was *talented*. She could sing well enough, but mainly her looks and personality had fitted the role, and she had really just been in the right place at the right time. Someone else could quite easily have been in the band in her place, whereas Ryan's talent for guitar had been there before the band, lying dormant until it was needed. It *wasn't* just because of his good fortune that he had ended up in another band.

"You've made me think way too deeply about this. Now I'm depressed." George laughed.

Sadie smiled. "Sorry! It's just so hard, isn't it, to go from such heights to never getting another break for the whole rest of your life? I find it hard, anyway. To accept that this is it; that we're not worth more than where we've ended up."

"I think *you're* worth more than working in a shop," George said. "And I don't know, musicals and local theatre shows and panto kind of feel like success if you forget about what we had before."

"I don't know if I can…" Sadie said.

"Might be better than nothing?"

She nodded thoughtfully. "Maybe."

"Well if you ever get the urge to be in a panto, I can hook you up."

She smiled. "Thanks."

Mia appeared next to them then, looking completely perfect in a dark pink pleated skirt and white top, her black hair cascading down it in soft waves.

"Oh no way, you got sparkly Converse!" Sadie said.

"I like the wardrobe people," Mia said, looking quietly delighted.

"You look so lovely."

She smiled. "I think we're going in for the photos now."

"I better find the rest of my band," George said. "See you in a bit."

Sadie locked eyes with James, hesitating for a second before linking her arm with his.

"Come on then," she said, leading him and Mia towards the bottleneck of pop stars at the entrance to the main building.

It felt *horribly* awkward being in his personal space, but she stubbornly stuck with it and didn't break contact until they were at the door. Once inside they quickly found Cameron and Ryan and allowed themselves to be herded into position with all the others in front of a ceiling-height glittery backdrop strung with silver and gold stars. It looked fairly rubbish in real life, but Sadie was confident the TV people knew what they were doing here. The press shots from *Village of the 90s* had looked amazing: you needed to see it through a camera, not your eyes.

Funk Shui were put at the front, with Granola Fantasy next to them. Sadie took this to mean that they were either the best looking groups or the most famous. Probably both. Kingpin, Polar Opposite and Prairie Dogs were perched precariously on a row of low staging units directly behind them. There was no sign of Indigo Lion, but Sadie guessed they were just too much of a big deal to associate with the has-beens. The photographer started shouting directions and tweaking people's poses and Sadie laced her fingers through Ryan's without thinking, trying not to blink or let her smile drop. Everyone jumped at a loud bang from behind them, and then looked up in delight at the confetti floating down over them.

Now that's what you call a photo, Sadie thought, grinning wildly at Mia and squeezing Ryan's hand.

They did their band shots next, complete with wind machine, lining up with their backs to the camera.

"And after three, turn and pose!" the photographer shouted.

Head tilted to the side, hand on hip.

Nailed it.

This is the photo that will come up in Google searches, Sadie thought, adrenaline racing through her. *This is the photo they'll use on websites and in magazines.*

She felt like a hundred million billion dollars.

"That's perfect, thanks guys!"

They were ushered to the side, Polar Opposite taking their place. Sadie couldn't tell if she was breathing too fast, or too slow, or not at all.

"Okay!" A woman with a clipboard appeared in front of them. "We're going to take Sadie, Ryan and James for a quick interview now, if that's okay. Cameron and Mia, why don't you go grab a coffee."

Just three of them?

Sadie made a mock sad face and waved at Mia as they were steered out of the room.

"Just over here," the woman said, gesturing to a sofa surrounded by cameras. "James in the middle, please."

The sofa felt small for three: it wasn't like the old days with hands on knees and arms looped casually across shoulders.

"Hey, guys." A man now, standing beside the camera. "So we're going to talk in a bit more detail about the day when James didn't turn up for that gig."

Sadie frowned. "Haven't we already talked about this? I mean, I have…"

"Let's go through it again," the man said, in the same way that someone who had you held hostage didn't say please. "Why don't you start, Sadie. Take me through it from your point of view. As much detail as you can remember."

Sadie tried to glance at Ryan but James was sitting right in her eye line.

"The show was in the afternoon, right?" the man prompted. "Take me through it from that morning. How were things between the five of you?"

Sadie thought for a moment. "Well, we didn't see James in the morning, but that was normal. He didn't live with us in the band house."

"Why not?"

"I liked my own space," James cut in.

"You didn't think that was strange, Sadie, that James had moved out?" the interviewer asked.

"I…" Sadie paused, thinking back. "Hang on, I thought it was because of the girl you were seeing?"

James shook his head. "I didn't have a girlfriend when we were in the band."

Sadie frowned. "Oh. So why did I… Hmm." She shrugged. "I guess I thought he'd moved in with a girl so no, that didn't seem strange. It seems strange *now*."

She looked at James, but he wouldn't meet her eye.

"So you didn't see James that morning. When *had* you seen him last?"

"The day before, I guess," Sadie said. "I don't remember what we were doing, but we hardly ever got days off so you can pretty much guarantee we all saw each other the day before that show."

"And things were fine with the five of you?"

"Yes. Honestly, I feel like we've been through this already…"

"What about you, Ryan? Did everything seem fine from your point of view?"

Ryan was silent for a moment. "If you're asking whether it was a surprise that James left the band, then yes, it was. But we have to be honest here, right? It wasn't all sunshine and rainbows. We'd been in the studio a lot trying to work out a sound for our new album, and we were doing all these summer shows, and everyone was tired... It was a bit tense, sometimes. Differences of opinion."

"Did James seem unhappy in the band?"

"I mean, he's right here. You could ask him."

"I'm asking you."

Ryan paused again. "Yeah, sometimes."

"Do you know why that was?"

"I don't think this is my story to tell," he said, shifting uncomfortably.

"Did you talk to James about how he was feeling?"

"No," Ryan said, looking away.

"Where were you the day of the gig, James?"

"I was at my flat."

"Did you have any intention of going to that gig?"

"No," James said.

Sadie felt like a deflated balloon.

"But you didn't tell anyone that?"

James sat forward. "Look, I know you want this to be some big drama, but it wasn't, all right? Being in the band felt like a mistake, for me. I didn't like all the things that came with fame. The more successful we got, the more fed up I felt. And I was young; we were all young. You don't handle things very well when you're young. Yeah, in hindsight, it could have all gone a lot better, but I'd come to the end of my journey with the band, and that's all it was."

Being in the band felt like a mistake.

Well that was something that was going to come back to her in the middle of the night.

"What happened at the gig, Sadie? Walk me through it."

"We were supposed to meet James there," she said. "We... He always got a different car. David – our PA – kept saying he was just running late, but he missed the soundcheck altogether. He'd never done that. Sometimes he was late, or not in a very good mood, but he never missed soundcheck."

"You were singing live?"

Sadie nodded. "They let us for those kinds of shows."

"So James missed soundcheck…"

"Yes. And the show started and he still hadn't turned up, but David was still saying everything was fine. We weren't supposed to have our phones, but it didn't feel right: we all tried ringing James but no one could get through to him. We got changed, and we were waiting by the side of the stage, and…" Sadie faltered. "The rest… It's not really my memories, only what people have told me."

She looked to Ryan for back-up, or reassurance, but he just looked strangely sad.

"But you *were* there?" the interviewer asked.

"Yes. But… What I thought happened next wasn't actually what happened, apparently."

"What did you think happened next?"

"I thought we just went home," Sadie said, feeling a weight settle in her stomach.

"Can you elaborate on what *did* happen, Ryan?"

He sighed heavily. "We did the gig. But not the songs we were supposed to do. Sadie was…" He shook his head. "I don't really like talking about this."

"I was what?" Sadie asked.

The expression on Ryan's face was unsettling. She didn't like it. Not one bit.

"You were hysterical," he said. "We couldn't do the set we'd planned. We got them to set the mics up in a line and we did a couple of slower tracks so we didn't have to dance. David made you neck practically a whole plastic cup of vodka to try to calm you down before you went on stage, and Mia sang your parts."

Hysterical?

"You don't remember any of this?" the interviewer asked.

Sadie shook her head.

"That seems strange, doesn't it?" he asked, looking at Ryan. "How was Sadie after the gig?"

"Not good."

"So what happened next?"

A heavy pause.

"I want it on the record that I am not proud of this, okay?" Ryan said. "Don't cut that out."

The interviewer nodded.

"After our set we got straight into the car and…" He shook his head. "I'm so sorry, Sadie. I gave you a couple of pills. I told you they were Valium, but they weren't."

"What were they?"

She felt sick. She didn't want to know.

Ryan looked away. "Roofies."

"Why did you have *roofies*?" Sadie asked, horrified.

"Not for the reason you think, okay."

"What other reason is there for having *roofies*?"

"Come on Sadie, you know I wouldn't do anything like that," Ryan said.

"Well I don't know. You did it to me, you could have been going around date-raping girls the whole time we were in the band."

"I didn't *date rape* you, Sadie," Ryan said, exasperated.

"Is that why I can't remember anything?" Sadie asked, tears springing to her eyes. "Cameron said that we did two more gigs after that, but I don't remember any of it!"

"I didn't know what to do," Ryan said quietly. "David was trying to fix things, and he told me I had to make sure you did those gigs like nothing was wrong. We couldn't have pulled it off if you'd known what was going on."

"So you *drugged me*?"

"No! I didn't. Sadie, I didn't. I just… I needed to keep you level."

"I don't even know what that means," Sadie said, feeling like a hole had opened up in the middle of her.

"Is this really the place to talk about this?" James asked.

"Well maybe, if you'd *handled it* better, we wouldn't even be here right now, talking about this!" Ryan snapped. "Maybe," he said, standing up. "I wouldn't have done something really fucking stupid to my *best friend* to get us all through the absolute *train wreck* you turned our lives into!" He took a step back from both of them, shaking his head. "All this is on you," he said, turning and walking away.

Sadie took a shaky breath. "Can we turn the camera off?"

22

It was a great vantage point. Kitty might go so far as to say that it was the *perfect* view.

The only thing that would perhaps make it more perfect would be if she had some binoculars, so she could really see the expressions on everyone's faces. She leaned against the wooden balcony in satisfaction. She definitely definitely shouldn't have done it, and she was definitely definitely going to return it, but borrowing the key fob from Mabel's lanyard so she could get into the café by the beach – and everywhere, essentially – was turning out to be one of her greater ideas. She'd gone from being hidden away in her cabin to having a front row seat; she was going to watch this on TV knowing she'd had a *better* view than everyone at home.

At the moment all the bands were lined up on the sand, and it looked like they were getting some kind of safety briefing because the cameras weren't filming and everyone looked bored. But Kitty was anything but bored, trying to process the image of her entire adolescence standing awkwardly on a fake beach right in front of her. *Finally* she was getting a taste of what she'd come here for. Never mind barely brushing shoulders with the comeback bands at work, this was truly something else. It was like looking at a memory come to life: all these people had been such a prominent feature of her teens, and now here they were, and here she was, and it felt *insane* that this was even happening. It felt like her brain was struggling to process that she *wasn't* watching it on TV, and that she really was seeing this with her actual eyes.

You could see the stars amongst the crowd from a mile away. It was so obvious who had come from nothing and would be going home the same way. Sure, Adam was cute, but he was just wearing a hoodie. Sadie had a certain amount of charm, but she wasn't exactly dressed to impress either. But Freddie in that shirt with the white t-shirt underneath, Jay in those skinny black jeans with the ripped knees, and George with the remains of his classic boyband baby face still visible, his once-floppy hair now pushed back... Even *James* exuded something mesmerising (if you didn't have to live with him).

And then there was Ryan.

What a sight for sore eyes. It was the first time Kitty had managed to catch a glimpse of him since she'd arrived – the first time she'd seen him with her own eyes for more than ten years, in fact – and it did not disappoint. And it was just mind-blowing, when you thought about it. How was it possible that after all these years they were both in the same place at the same time? This boy who had broken her heart, who she never thought she'd ever see again, now standing just metres away from her. The pictures she'd found of him online really hadn't done him justice, either: time had been incredibly kind to him. And couldn't you just see it? Her and Ryan, walking down a red carpet together, being labelled the hottest power couple in town. Oh she was made for more than a quiet life in a seaside town, she was sure of it. Was this, *finally*, going to be her right-place-at-the-right-time moment?

The safety briefing wrapped up, the cameras started rolling again and the celebs were herded into groups of four, Ryan ending up with Freddie, George, and Nat from Prairie Dogs. Talk about *The A Team*. Jesus Christ. What a collection of chiselled jaws and tousled hair. It was obvious which pedalo was going to be getting all the screen time here. Kitty watched them clamber into the boat: Freddie, George and Nat were all chatting, but Ryan looked distracted and kept glancing towards Sadie's group. Sadie, in a boat with Mia, and two of the five Polar Opposite girls (everyone who wasn't wearing a crop top, basically), almost seemed like she was deliberately looking in the opposite direction, Mia frowning next to her.

Which was interesting, because by all accounts Sadie and Ryan had been best friends during the band. Maybe that hadn't translated so well into real life? Had something happened in the band? Out of the band? Oh how Kitty wished she could get amongst all this. And she should be able to: she was James' girlfriend, for God's sake! She *should* be able to ask him about anything she wanted to, including this, without it being such a big deal. But at the moment she felt like she couldn't even ask him if he'd had a good day, let alone enquire about the reason why Sadie and Ryan looked like they'd fallen out already.

Kitty sighed, looking back across the water to Ryan, offensively radiant in the spring sunshine. Was she absolutely crazy for thinking there might something bigger at stake here; something that could eclipse her limping relationship with James altogether? Because when you thought of the odds of her ever even *bumping into* one of Ryan's former bandmates in real life, let alone ending up *dating* them for four years, and then added it to the odds of someone wanting to make a TV show about the band *during* the time they were dating… Those odds were pretty slim, right? And yet here they were, same place, same time… Surely that *couldn't* mean *nothing*?

She was going to have quite the job even letting him know she was here, though, if the last 24 hours had been anything to go by: it seemed like he was going to be surrounded by this massive group of people – and cameras, oh and her actual boyfriend – almost every minute of every day. She was either going to have to find out where Ryan's cabin was, or maybe see if she could engineer things so she casually ran into James while he was on a break but still with the group; put herself in Ryan's eyeline and see what happened. Tricky, but not impossible, and if the universe had gone to such great lengths to put them both in the same place all these years later, it was really the least she could do.

23

"I'm sorry."

Sadie carried on watching the men drag the pedalos off the beach and into the water as Ryan hovered next to her. She'd managed to avoid speaking to him after the interview as they'd almost immediately been rounded up and split into teams of four for the next activity. Her team hadn't won the pedalo race but it had been a nice distraction, she supposed.

"Are you okay?" he asked.

Sadie shrugged.

"Can I sit?"

She shrugged again.

Ryan nodded, perching awkwardly on the wall.

"I don't know why I said any of that on camera," he said. "That wasn't how you should have found out. It's just… It's really haunted me, ever since. I guess I just needed to get it out."

Sadie didn't want to cry in front of Ryan, she really didn't, but it seemed like speech was going to be virtually impossible without bursting into tears. She was just so thrown by it all: what James had said, what Ryan had said… This was *her story*, and it turned out she hadn't even known how it'd ended.

"Why didn't anyone trust me with what was going on?" she squeaked out, trying to suppress the lump in her throat. "I mean, it's… It's *grotesque*. You had to *drug me* to stop me from making things worse?"

"I know," Ryan said, nodding. "I know. It was an appalling thing to do. I wish I hadn't done it, Sadie, I really do. Literally if I could only take back one single thing in my whole life it would be that."

Sadie dug her bare toes into the sand, watching as the grains tumbled into the holes she left.

"Please," Ryan said, putting his hand over hers. "I am so so sorry. What can I do? I will do *anything*. Please don't hate me forever."

"They're definitely going to show that part on TV, aren't they," she said finally.

Because she couldn't hate him, forever or at all, not even if she wanted to.

"I'm going to look like such an idiot."

"*You're* going to look like an idiot? I'm the one who admitted to having roofies!" Ryan said. "So many potential headlines to choose from. *Sad Admiral guitarist admits drugging former bandmate. I slipped her a couple of roofies, said Ryan "Rohypnol" Malone.*"

"*My date rape drug hell,*" Sadie offered.

"Exactly. The press are going to have field day with me."

"But you didn't date rape me."

"I definitely didn't! I mean, come on, I like to think I don't need Rohypnol to get a shag."

"Eurgh, from me you would," Sadie said. "Pretty funny, isn't it?"

"Is it?"

Sadie paused. "No," she said.

"I really am sorry."

"Did Cameron and Mia know?"

"No. David told them the same as I told you: that James was ill and he was coming back soon. He got me to tell you all that I'd spoken to him on the phone, to back up the story."

"But you hadn't."

"No. I knew he wasn't coming back, though."

Sadie frowned. "You shouldn't have had to deal with that on your own. We were a team."

Ryan shrugged. "I think David was just so thrown by it. It was chaos, Sade, what was happening behind the scenes during that week."

"Do you know more about why James left the band than I do?" she asked. "Not that that's any mean feat seeing as I was basically unconscious for a week after he left."

Ryan sighed. "I don't know. Maybe I do. I mean, it's nothing that I've heard from the horse's mouth, but I think it kind of makes sense."

"What?" Sadie asked, wondering if it was going to be this hard the entire time they were here.

She'd kind of thought they'd all have one big conversation about it at the start and that would be it, but it felt like she was having to crack some kind of secret code every time she wanted an answer to a question. It was more like being on a game show than a reunion show.

"Well I don't know if what he said about not enjoying the fame is bullshit or if it's part of it, but Cameron said he'd found out that James was getting into some pretty heavy shit that didn't seem like a very good idea."

"Drugs?" Sadie asked, frowning. "Really?"

Ryan nodded.

"I can't picture it. It doesn't seem like something he'd do. He was *never* like that, was he? How would he even…"

Ryan shrugged. "We didn't see him a lot, didn't we? We don't know what he was doing in that flat. Who he was hanging out with."

Sadie flicked back through her memories of James, trying to fit this new information into the gaps.

"He was drinking too much anyway, but Cameron was worried he was going to screw everything up for us."

"He was right," Sadie said.

"Yeah, although I don't think that's what he meant. We did talk about whether James should even be in the band…"

"Is that why you said it wasn't your story to tell, in the interview?"

"It's up to him whether he wants to talk about that, isn't it? Although I don't know how he's going to get away with not talking about it. They're just going to keep asking him the same questions until he gives them something."

"I feel like we should have helped him, if he was struggling," Sadie said, none of this sitting right with her.

And, sure, she *knew* this was the kind of thing that happened, and probably in most bands, but not *her* band. They were pick 'n' mix. They were ice cream with sprinkles. It just didn't *fit*.

"Yeah but he cut himself off from us, didn't he? Way before he actually left. Moving out. Never travelling with us. He'd show up for the bare minimum. It wasn't cool. You can't be a band like that. It doesn't work." Ryan shook his head. "It seemed like a shame. Me and him were tight before all that. We were talking about going in a whole different direction with the sound, writing our own stuff, bringing instruments into it. I know he didn't like the manufactured pop stuff but I thought he was really on board with our ideas…"

"I don't know if I really noticed any of that. It didn't seem like such a big deal to me," Sadie said. "I think I would have sung and danced to anything anyone put in front of me. Was I just the worst bandmate ever?"

Ryan smiled, putting an arm around her. "No, you were the best."

Sadie sighed, liking the weight of his arm across her shoulder.

"They want us to fall out, right?" she said. "The TV people."

"Definitely."

She had ten days with Ryan and that could be it. Did she really want to waste it by holding a grudge?

"I'm going to need you to promise not to date rape me again," she said, leaning her head against him.

"I promise."

"Okay. And don't say sorry again. I just want to forget it."

Ryan nodded. "Okay. I'll stop being sorry."

Sadie smiled. "Don't stop *being* sorry, just be sorry quietly, in your own head."

Ryan gave her a squeeze. "Okay. I shall repent silently forever."

"Good," Sadie said. "So what are we supposed to be doing now?"

"Eating," Ryan said. "Which you know is my favourite."

"Well I would hate for you to miss that," Sadie said, putting her shoes back on, the sand gritty between her toes.

Ryan hauled her off the wall and they turned their backs on the lake.

"So I was thinking," Ryan said as they walked, "and I should say that I was thinking this before date-rape-gate so it doesn't seem like I'm just being a creep."

"Noted," Sadie said.

"I'm here for ten days, right, and then… God knows when I'll ever get to spend this much time with you again."

Sadie felt her heart sink a little. In the blink of an eye she was going to be deposited back in Bristol and her normal nine-to-five life, except without a job any more, because not turning up for a couple of days hadn't gone down so well with her manager. Was it going to be even more painful than before, having experienced this? She couldn't bear to think about it.

"It seems crazy to me that we're staying in separate cabins," Ryan continued. "I want that maximum Sadie time, you know? How do you feel about moving into my cabin? It's *pretty luxe.*"

"I bet it's exactly the same as mine," Sadie said, trying to hide her surprise.

The amount of times over the years that she'd tried to make the first move and repair their friendship only to be knocked back, she hadn't expected any of this easy affection from Ryan.

"Yeah, okay, it's the same as yours. You moving in, or not?"

"You don't want to just bunk up with Mia and Cameron?" Sadie asked, playing it cool in the absence of blurting out that it was literally all she wanted from her time here.

"He brings out the worst in me," Ryan said with a smile.

"I really don't like you so much when you're with him," Sadie said, their hands finding each other again.

"Is that a yes?"

"I feel like I should keep you hanging. You know, as penance."

"Yeah but you can't resist my company," Ryan said as they approached the main square.

If only he knew how true that was.

"Fine, you've twisted my arm," Sadie said.

"Excellent," Ryan said, grinning. "Now enough of this tedious friendship stuff. Let's buffet."

They piled a plate with sandwiches from the makeshift canteen and took it back out into the square. Mia and Cameron were sitting with Natasha and Gemma from Polar Opposite, so they headed for an empty bench next to the fountain. There seemed to be a lot more people around than there had been that morning – people she hadn't seen before – as if everyone's families had been released from a holding pen all at once. She saw James sitting across the square with Kitty, talking to Fabian from Granola Fantasy. She was so pretty. Look at her being all super casual in her little floral dress and denim jacket and that amazing hair. Sadie looked down at her own faded sweatshirt and wished they hadn't made them take their fancy clothes off for the pedalo race. Her perfectly beachy hair had got damp and she knew without even looking in a mirror that she just looked frizzy now. Someone had once said to her that her fashion sense was "tomboy chic", but she didn't necessarily think that was a compliment.

"When are we actually going to rehearse?" she asked, picking the tomato out of a chicken sandwich.

"Later, I think," Ryan said.

"Why are you staring at James' girlfriend?"

"The girl with the ginger hair?"

"I'm not sure she'd like *ginger* very much, but yes," Sadie said.

"Why are *you* staring at her?"

"I'm not."

Ryan smiled. "You know we know her, don't you?"

"What do you mean?"

"Well, *I* know her..." Ryan raised an eyebrow.

"Eurgh, what? You have not slept with James' girlfriend!"

"Well not recently."

"What are you talking about?" Sadie asked, putting her sandwich down.

"You don't recognise her?"

"No?"

"She was a fan, Sade. She was my favourite, actually. You met her a bunch of times."

Sadie frowned deeply. "Today is hurting my brain," she said. "Are you sure?"

"Oh yes," Ryan said.

"You are awful. How many other people here have you slept with?"

Ryan started to look around but Sadie held up her hands in protest.

"I was *joking*! Jesus. I don't want to know."

Ryan didn't look particularly ashamed of himself, it had to be said. There were two very different sides to Ryan Malone, and the less she knew about the other one the better.

"You must be thinking of someone else, anyway. Kitty didn't even know James was in a band. She made a whole big thing about it when I was at their house."

"*Really*. Well that *is* interesting," Ryan said, with a wolfish grin.

"Are you sure it's her?"

"There is *no way* that girl didn't know that James was in the band."

Kitty looked up then, as if drawn by their gaze. She locked eyes with Ryan for just a moment, her smirk matching his as she looked away.

"Oh Christ," Sadie said. "So wait, she's pretending that she wasn't a fan of the band James was pretending he was never in? What is the matter with those two? Will you stop telling me things that confuse me?"

"Sorry."

"What *else* do you know that I don't?"

Ryan grinned. "I mean, who knows at this point."

"Now tread carefully, because there's very little I want to know about this subject in general, but she was what, one of your groupie flings?"

"Something like that. I think I owe her an apology, actually," Ryan said.

"Why doesn't that surprise me," Sadie said. "I don't think I like this very much. It's weird."

"Why didn't James tell her he was in the band?" Ryan asked. "How does that work?"

Sadie shrugged. "He didn't seem to think it was a very big deal. And it obviously wasn't, because she already knew… Blurgh. I'm staying out of it." She looked pointedly at Ryan. "You should too."

"I know," he said.

But since when was knowing something the same as doing it.

24

Mabel sat back against the cushions on the sofa, watching the kittens play-fight up and down the coffee table, trying to pretend that she felt relaxed. Wouldn't that be nice, to not feel the constant tension in your shoulders and the churning in your stomach. After what had happened the previous day, she wasn't sure she'd ever feel at ease again.

Adam had left his vigil on the doorstep of her cabin eventually and, true to her word, Kitty had taken James to gather up all the things Mabel needed (and the kittens). Sharing a space with someone else really wasn't as bad as she'd been expecting and although Kitty didn't stop talking, Mabel had to admit that she did actually prefer it when she was around, the effort of making small talk helping to drown out the relentless thoughts of Adam that snuck back in when things were quiet.

She still couldn't really process what had happened in the woods: seeing him so unexpectedly had felt like being ripped in two. There was the version of her that couldn't face him; that didn't want to or answer his questions, or see the way he would look at her now, knowing what he knew about her. This she had expected: the gut-wrenching desire to avoid him at all costs and her good old reliable flight instinct. But what had shaken her the most was the version of her that wanted to run *to* him. To be absolved. To let his goodness absorb the badness in her. To finally allow him to make her feel better, the way that she hadn't let him all those times before. She'd initially thought that her heart had almost jumped out of her chest in *horror*, but actually...

Mabel sighed. She'd replayed the moment over and over. The look on his face... But there was no point entertaining a fantasy where it wasn't too late and she hadn't ruined everything and he still wanted to save her. No point wondering why he had chased after her, and sat on the doorstep of her cabin for three straight hours looking, as Kitty had put it, "really really sad". She knew who she was, and what she was capable of, no matter how deep she tried to bury it. She had already done enough damage and if all she achieved for the rest of her life was not hurting Adam the way she had hurt Freddie, then that was a life well spent. She hadn't come all this way to let her resolve falter at the most important hurdle. She didn't deserve this reunion with him, and he deserved far better than her.

A knock on the front door cut through the quiet and both Mabel and the kittens stopped what they were doing. The kittens tilted their heads curiously as the knock came again. Mabel frowned. Maybe the cleaners?

But she should have known better than that.

Another knock and she was off the sofa and walking towards the door, her brain too slow to identify the shadowy figure behind the rippled glass.

"I heard a rumour," Jay said, regarding her from the doorway as Mabel took a step back in surprise.

"Jay..."

She was 17 again and his swagger filled the room.

"Thought I'd drop in and say hi," he said, moving towards her as she moved back, two poles of a magnet pushing against each other. "What are you doing here, Mabel?"

Malevolent energy surrounded him like an aura and she couldn't look away.

The kittens, however, weren't so perceptive.

"Fuck!" Jay exclaimed, as both kittens launched themselves at his legs in unison, haphazardly scaling them as if they were climbing a tree.

"Oh. They do that," Mabel said.

"Ow! Can you get them off?"

Mabel tried to hide her smile as she knelt down and gently removed the kittens from his jeans.

"It's worse when you're trying to feed them."

"I think I'm bleeding," Jay said, rubbing at his legs. "Funny kind of guard dog."

"Sorry," Mabel said, stepping back from him again, the kittens wriggling away from her and plopping down onto the floor. "They do what they want."

Jay nodded. "I used to know someone like that."

He held her gaze for longer than felt necessary; for longer than was comfortable. Mabel didn't know where to put herself. Her skin felt opaque;

too tight. It was as if, in his presence, everything she had tried to bury was drawn back to the surface by a static charge.

"You left us with a lot of shit to deal with."

Mabel watched the kittens wrestling by her feet.

She was an unstable compound; a reactive element.

"And now here you are."

This was a science experiment just waiting to go wrong.

"I missed you," Jay said.

His words were like a physical jolt. Mabel looked up, curious, but Jay gave her nothing in return, leaving what he'd said hanging there in the space between them, unclaimed.

"Some might say it's not good manners to just disappear. And you telling Fred everything was a bit of a problem for me," Jay said. "I had a better nose before you left."

Mabel frowned, not understanding.

"You really did disappear."

He smelled of smoke and soap, an inexplicably heady combination that took her straight back to the time spent in cramped backstage rooms where she used to wonder how the two things didn't cancel each other out.

"Oh I'm fine, by the way. Thanks for asking," he said. "I don't want to come across as needy but this is all feeling a bit one-sided at the moment."

Mabel smiled weakly.

"I wasn't expecting to see you," she said.

"Ditto," Jay said, looking over to where Mabel's laptop was still open on the coffee table, surrounded by notes. "Am I interrupting something?"

She shook her head, moving over to the table to close the laptop, awkwardly shuffling the notes into a pile. She could feel the push and pull of the magnetic force as he drifted past her and sat down on the other sofa.

"This is very..." Jay gestured to his own clothes. "Not you."

"This is me now," Mabel said, too quickly.

"Is it," he said, looking at her as if he were doing a critical evaluation.

It had always been like this with Jay. There were things you didn't have to say for him to know; things he didn't *want* you to say to him. It was some kind of wordless symbiosis, where you never had to explain anything. But, of course, everything they were doing back then defied explanation. And "I missed you" was not the kind of thing they used to say to each other.

"So you work here? Call it a wild stab in the dark..."

Mabel nodded.

"And you're surprised to see me? Surely you knew we were coming?"

She shrugged, lacking the words to explain, but Jay had never been one for the details.

"You thought I wouldn't seek you out?" Jay asked, leaning back into the sofa. "I had to see it with my own eyes. The girl who destroyed everything."

He said it like it was the tagline for a film. Her heart sank, confirmation – as if she really needed it – that they all blamed her for what had happened to them as much as she blamed herself.

"But I suppose you don't know a whole lot about what happened after you ran away," he mused.

"How did you know I was at this cabin?" Mabel asked, eager to skip the recap. "Does Adam know?"

"Oh, people talk. I worked it out," Jay said. "What's Adam got to do with it?"

Mabel shook her head quickly. "No, nothing."

Because he hadn't, after all, got anything to do with it, to anyone's eyes but hers. Nobody else was there when she realised far too late what had been in front of her the whole time, and what she had spoiled for herself.

"This yours?" he asked, picking up a copy of *Little White Lies* from the coffee table. "Sure you weren't expecting me?"

Mabel shook her head, not following.

"Isn't life full of coincidences," Jay said, flicking through the pages until he found what he was looking for, handing the open magazine to Mabel.

"What am I looking at?" she asked, seeing only the film review she'd already read.

"Oh, only my life's work," Jay said.

She looked more closely and then she saw it: his name at the bottom of the page.

"You wrote this?" she asked, wondering how many times she'd had his words in her head without even realising.

"I had to do something with my time," Jay said. "I couldn't do music any more. Not after you."

He held her gaze again, one out of every three things he said piercing the bullseye dead centre. She wasn't so naïve to think it was accidental, but wasn't this the very least she deserved? She'd been expecting a lot worse.

"This is your job?" she asked.

"I do all sorts," Jay said. "When you end up with a whole lot of nothing, watching other people's stories helps pass the time."

"I never even noticed your name," Mabel said, the similarities between the way they'd both coped with what had happened not lost on her.

Or was *coped* the wrong word entirely?

Jay laughed. "Well it's good to know all the effort is worth it. Here," he said, moving next to her on the sofa and taking the magazine from her again. "I did loads in this one."

Mabel blinked, a swell of flashbacks triggered by his leg suddenly pressing against hers. He was pointing things out to her on the pages like them being in each other's personal space was nothing, her stomach tying itself into a knot as he talked.

"You watch a lot of films?"

She nodded.

"Is there even a cinema around here?" he asked. "I can't smoke in here, can I?"

"No. To both those questions."

"Here's one I rolled earlier," he said, getting up. "Coming?"

He unlocked the patio door and slid it open, stepping outside. Mabel watched the sparks from his lighter fade to nothing in the fresh air.

"What to say to the girl who took everything from you?" He took a long drag on his cigarette. "I never met anyone like you since, you know. Nobody does a good time like we did it."

One out of every three.

"So what does this version of Mabel do for fun?"

"I work," said Mabel, breathing in his second-hand smoke, his mere proximity melting away the years like they'd never passed.

There was no less danger in Jay than there had been before. His confidence and the way you never quite knew what he was going to say next were both mesmerising and terrifying. The glittering calm that belied a ruthless riptide underneath; their horrible, irresistible, *inexplicable* chemistry. Being here with him now was something akin to that feeling when you stepped across the yellow line on a tube platform or peered over the edge of a cliff. The fear and fascination that there were no divine laws stopping you from doing something catastrophic on a whim; the pull of the things you knew you absolutely must not do.

And, just for a second, Mabel wondered what the old Mabel would do, right now.

"You haven't bagged yourself a nice clean-cut husband to accessorise the new you?"

She shook her head.

"No, well, I think me and you both know you're not the settling down type. Dress yourself up in high street office wear all you like. You're not fooling me."

Being with Jay had always been easy. All you had to do was be the worst you could be. There were no limits; no boundaries. It was thrilling, of course, that licence to truly be your worst self. And now it almost felt like a relief to see everything she despised about herself reflected in his opinion of her: a conclusive answer to the question of whether she had been too hard on herself, and proof of the lasting damage she was capable of doing to a person.

"I hate who I was," she said, but somehow it didn't come out the way she'd intended it to. "What we did. It's not something to be proud of."

"Yeah but we had fun," Jay said with a sly smile.

He leaned in closer to her and this time she didn't move away.

"You don't get to choose who you are. It's either in you, or it isn't. And we're the same, you and me."

What would happen, Mabel wondered, if she stepped off that platform again… There was nothing to break here that hadn't already been broken. They'd already ruined each other, after all.

But then Jay pulled his phone out of his pocket and swore under his breath.

"I've got somewhere to be," he said, stubbing out his cigarette on the patio table and heading back indoors.

Mabel followed, feeling dazed, closing the patio door before the kittens could make a break for it.

"It was nice to see you, Mabel," he said, that riptide curling out a hand, beckoning her into the midnight black. "We'll talk again."

"Don't tell anyone that I'm here," she said as Jay stepped onto the path at the front of the cabin.

He turned, a look of smug amusement on his face. "Now why would I want to do that?" he said, sauntering away from her in the same way he always had.

25

He is such a creep, Sadie thought, rolling her eyes all the way back into her head as she watched Ryan wheedle an "introduction" to Kitty from James.

She'd thought Ryan had been right behind her as they'd headed inside with the rest of the bands, but of course he wasn't. He was, instead, several feet away, shaking hands with Kitty and maintaining a really intense eye contact. And then, when James turned to go, Ryan leaned in and said something to Kitty that made her whole face light up.

Sadie shook her head as he returned to her side, looking smug and stupid and like he'd benefit greatly from being hit over the head with a tray.

"What did you say to her?" she asked as they walked through the doors.

"Just that she didn't look like that the last time I saw her," Ryan said, trying – and failing – to control his smirk.

"Urgh."

"She didn't," he said, as if clarification was what was needed here.

"Do you have to be the problem child of this band?"

"Oh am I? I thought that was you," Ryan said.

Sadie shoved him in the side, falling into line with the rest of her bandmates as everyone clustered round Helen, flanked by cameras.

"Good afternoon, ladies and gents!" she said. "Hope you're all enjoying yourselves so far. This afternoon we're going to get to what I know a lot of you have been waiting for: rehearsals!"

A collective whoop.

"But before that, we've enlisted a special guest to lead you through the next segment. I'm sure this will be a blast from the past for the majority of you. Please give a warm welcome to *Maddie Fox*!"

"No way!" Sadie whispered.

Maddie Fox had been the pinnacle of kids' TV presenting back in the day, fronting the most popular Saturday morning TV show and always popping up as the host of ensemble tours and roadshows.

"Oh my God, I loved her so much."

She had been in her early twenties when Sadie had known her: she had had the biggest smile, the shiniest hair and was basically the nicest person in the entire world, on screen and off. Having a tough time backstage? You needed a hug from Maddie Fox. Having the time of your life? Maddie Fox was there for that too. She was like the big sister that everyone wanted.

"I wanted to be her so bad."

"I wanted to be on her," Ryan whispered back.

Sadie made a face. "You didn't..."

"I wish. She wasn't having any of it."

"Good for her."

Yeah, Maddie Fox had class.

"Although maybe if she's single, and I'm single..." Ryan grinned.

"Oh stop," Sadie said, elbowing him again as Maddie Fox walked into the room, surrounded by an ethereal glow, cherubs with trumpets, and unicorns throwing glitter. "Now that's what I call a signature haircut."

She had exactly the same straight golden hair that she'd always had, and the white blouse tucked into cropped jeans with heels seemed like the perfect graduation from the t-shirts, jeans and trainers she'd worn on TV. Here was a woman who wore her late thirties effortlessly.

"I love her," Sadie murmured. "She looks amazing. Do you think she would adopt me?"

Everyone was clapping. If they'd been sitting down Sadie would have led the standing ovation.

"Hi everyone!" Maddie gave them a wave. "Eek, I can't believe I'm here with you all! So many familiar faces! It's like going back in time!"

She looked genuinely thrilled to be there and her infectious enthusiasm was everything Sadie needed to recharge after a thoroughly weird day.

"So I am *very* honoured to be here for this. It's my great pleasure to introduce to you to the one, the only, Indigo Lion!"

"This is a bit elaborate," Sadie muttered to Ryan, as the door opened again and five of the most famous figures in UK pop music sauntered in. "They're only guest stars. This is our show."

"Also, I am super world famous like they are, you know," Ryan said.

Sadie smiled. "You're the pub quiz question everyone would get wrong."

"How dare you."

The five members of Indigo Lion – all chunky high tops, incredibly skinny jeans, white t-shirts, denim jackets and ruffled hair, just barely out of their teens – lined up either side of Maddie in a move so perfectly choreographed that Sadie wondered if they just ran on autopilot most of the time these days.

"I've met them before, actually," Ryan said.

"Have you?"

"We played some shows with them. Hung out. Had a couple of beers."

"You're so fancy, I hate you," Sadie said. "Tell me everything. Later."

"Now, these guys are going to be performing some of your best-loved songs in their own inimitable style, which I, for one, cannot wait for," Maddie said, beaming.

Traitor, Sadie thought idly.

"And I don't know if you all know this, but we've actually put it to the fans to decide which songs they do, and I'm going to be revealing the results of this now! Exciting!" Maddie turned to Theo Monroe, the unofficial but widely acknowledged frontman of Indigo Lion. "You'd have been, what, about eight years' old when most of these guys were making music?"

"Ouch," Ryan muttered.

Theo nodded. "Something like that, I think."

"And, be honest, had you heard of any of these bands before you were told about the show?" Maddie grinned conspiratorially, like she was on their side in all this.

Indigo Lion did, in their defence, attempt to look a bit sheepish that they hadn't, but it was a little too much like laughing *at* them rather than *with* them for Sadie's liking.

You'll be us, one day, she felt like saying. *And the Next Big Thing won't know who you are, either.*

"I believe you each have an envelope?" Maddie asked, Indigo Lion collectively holding them up as confirmation, right on cue. "Great! Josh, we'll start with you. You've got the results of the Polar Opposite vote. If you'd like to reveal which song of theirs you'll be performing…"

Sadie was wondering why this all needed to be on camera until Josh read out the name of Polar Opposite's only Number 1 single to a collective horrified gasp from the band.

"Does that mean Polar Opposite won't get to perform it?" Sadie asked Ryan.

"I guess so."

"But that's so mean! Who's voting, our fans or Indigo Lion fans?" Sadie asked. "And if it's our fans, did they know they were voting to take their favourite song *away* from the bands?"

Ryan just shrugged.

"Oh that's a great song," Maddie said, nodding. "You're going to have fun with that one. Let's go with Connor next. Who have you got?"

"Granola Fantasy," Connor said, looking at the front of the envelope.

"Ooh, this is a big one," Maddie said. "Reveal the song choice, if you will!"

Connor ripped open the top and pulled out a piece of card from inside. "Okay, it says... 'Early Morning Light'."

Maddie frowned. "Oh! I'm not familiar with that one." She looked to where Granola Fantasy were standing. "Was it an album track?"

"B-side!" Freddie called out, nodding.

Granola Fantasy weren't a band Sadie had spent a lot of time with in the past. They'd been a bit rockier in sound than the bubblegum pop of Funk Shui, a little older, and had been edging towards being something of a crossover band, half way between screaming teenage girls and adults who just enjoyed a good quality pop song. They were more *CD:UK* than *SM:TV*; being interviewed on *Popworld* about more than just their favourite farm animal. And, to be honest, they always gave the impression of being too cool for the roadshows and early morning TV appearances that they'd occasionally crossed paths at. She'd never been able to shake the slightly intimidating feeling that they were the mean boys at school who skipped classes and smoked behind the gym at lunch time.

"Wow, okay. A bit of an obscure choice there, fans," Maddie said. "Let's move on to Theo."

"I've got Kingpin," Theo said, opening up the envelope and reading the card inside. "And the winner is... 'Careless'."

"A ballad!" Maddie said approvingly. "Right, let's do Prairie Dogs next. That's you, Jasper. Now, Prairie Dogs are a bit of an anomaly here because they didn't ever actually get to release their songs officially, although they *had* started to build up a bit of an underground following, so we've had to do a bit of digging with their old fans to find out what the favourites were. We didn't put this one to a public vote, instead leaving it to our little focus group to decide which song they'd most like to see Indigo Lion perform. So let's see what they came up with, if you'd like to reveal that, Jasper."

Jasper nodded. "We've got 'Chasing Echoes'."

A ripple of assent from the Prairie Dogs boys, who hadn't seemed particularly phased by anything so far.

"And last, but not least, it's Funk Shui," Maddie said.

Sadie felt her stomach tighten a little bit. She hadn't realised until they'd started reading out song titles quite how much she wanted to perform 'Rise' as a five. They'd recorded it with James, and rehearsed it all together, but they'd never performed it live with him. To have all five of them, up on stage, belting out that amazing song: that was your goosebumps moment right there.

"Rhys, if you'd like to do the honours," Maddie prompted.

Sadie watched Rhys reading the card before he spoke, trying to anticipate the shape his mouth was forming in slow motion, willing him to say anything but 'Rise'.

"It's 'Hello Sunshine'," he said.

Sadie let out an involuntary whoop, covering her mouth with her hand as the rest of her band looked in her direction.

"Sorry." She grinned.

"It's not that good a song," Ryan said, but she felt sure that he knew.

Maddie Fox looked round then, clearly out of script.

"So, I think that's it from me?" she said, pulling an exaggerated pout as Helen stepped back in. "I'm going to stick around for the rest of the day, though – watch some of the rehearsals! So excited to be up on stage with you all in a few days!"

As soon as the cameras were turned off Indigo Lion dropped their TV faces, their entourage stepping back in immediately. Within seconds, Rhys was on his phone, disappearing out through the door with a lighter in his other hand, while Connor, Jasper and Josh gravitated towards the corner of the room. Theo was the only member of the band who broke the fourth wall, going over and introducing himself to Polar Opposite.

"I forgot about your weird staring thing," Ryan said, nudging Sadie.

"I'm not staring," she said. "I'm just trying to imagine… We were doing stuff like that once, and people were watching us, and I never even thought what it might look like from the outside."

"Okay, guys! Your attention for just a second please!" Helen said, addressing the room. "I know these segments are a little choppy, but wait until you see it all put together. We're getting some really good stuff here, so thank you all for that. We're going to have a quick break now while Maddie and Indigo Lion do an interview. Can we all meet in the sports hall in 20 minutes ready to crack on with it? The bags you brought down this morning with your rehearsal gear in are in the changing rooms already."

"Where's the sports hall?" Sadie asked.

Ryan shrugged. "I'm just going to follow everyone else."

People were starting to file back out into the square so they tailed along behind. Sadie had got about half way across when she felt a hand on her arm.

"Hey. Have you got a minute?" James asked, a pensive expression on his face.

"Now?" she asked, watching everyone else meander past her.

James nodded but didn't offer any further explanation.

Sadie looked to Ryan. "I'll catch you up?"

He raised an eyebrow in question but nodded anyway. "See you over there."

"What's up?" she asked, trying to keep it light.

She felt all kinds of awkward being one-on-one with James after the interview that morning. They hadn't spoken since, unless you counted a few brief moments on camera, plus there was all the stuff Ryan had said about his suspected drug use, and the whole bizarre situation with him and Kitty.

"Can we go somewhere?"

"Sure," Sadie said, despite the fact that she would much rather not.

She followed him down to the lake – she could see everyone else walking away from them in the distance – and when he stopped at a bench and sat down, she did the same. They sat in loaded silence for a few minutes as James studied his hands and Sadie watched the ripples on the water. She was about to attempt an ice breaker when he finally spoke.

"What came out in that interview this morning was really shitty," he said. "I wanted to talk to you afterwards but I didn't get a chance. You and Ryan seem… okay, though?"

Sadie shrugged. "I think it's one of those days where you just keep going and think about it later… Like in the middle of the night, which I find a really prime time to freak out."

James nodded.

"Maybe I was naïve to think that we didn't have those kinds of secrets to be uncovered. But still, on *day two*. Bit harsh," Sadie continued. "I'd still rather be here than not, though. Don't they say that anything worth having doesn't come easy?"

"Well, sometimes, I think..." James said. "Look, I didn't think I was going to do this but after this morning I think it's the least I can do."

He paused, and Sadie let the gentle sounds of the water and the wildlife fill the gap.

"I suppose I'm trying to find the right words for the explanation I owe you," he said. "I don't think I can say sorry enough for what I did to you by leaving the band. I never, in a million years, imagined that it would have had such horrible consequences for you all, and at the time I really felt I couldn't stay, but..." He shook his head, looking up at her. "I am so so sorry."

His eyes were glassy and she didn't know what to say.

"I have been such a coward since you came to see me. I thought it was no one's business but mine; my secret to keep." He sighed. "I have filled my life with so many lies. I don't want to talk to the cameras about it but I owe you this much."

"About what?"

"Why I left the band. What was really going on. All of it. The truth this time."

Oh God, this was happening now? Right now? When they were supposed to be starting rehearsals in 10 minutes?

He paused and she waited, not knowing what else to do.

"I was in a jazz orchestra when I was a teenager, did you know that?"

Sadie shook her head.

"I always wanted to be a musician, but jazz isn't so cool when you're an 18-year-old boy. I thought being a pop star was the answer," James said. "It wasn't a lie that I didn't enjoy being famous, but it was more than that. I felt different to the rest of you, like I cared about different things, or saw things differently. I wanted things for the band that didn't fit with what everyone else wanted."

"But we loved you," Sadie said, a lump in her throat. "Didn't you know that?"

James smiled sadly. "It wasn't anything you did or didn't do. I wasn't feeling like myself and I wasn't happy and I blamed the band for that: the fame, the emptiness of the music, the industry as a whole. I don't know that this wouldn't have happened to me anyway, whatever I'd been doing... Sometimes I wonder whether I didn't do this to myself, or make it worse for myself, but hindsight is a tricky beast."

He paused again.

"I felt like I was pretending, every day. It was exhausting. The only time I didn't have to keep up the façade was when I was on my own."

"Is that why you moved out?" Sadie asked.

James nodded. "I thought it would be easier, only having to put on that happy pop music persona a second before I stepped out onto a stage, but it didn't actually make me feel any better. If anything, the more I isolated myself the worse I felt. One day I thought, I wonder what would happen if I didn't make the effort to smile at all during this whole performance. And nothing happened – no one even noticed – and it really went downhill from there."

Sadie frowned. Had she really not noticed? Why had she not questioned any of this when it was happening? Was she really that self-absorbed?

"I felt very weird," James continued. "It's hard to explain. It was like I managed to completely switch off when I was in front of a camera or on a stage. Like I wasn't even in my body. It was frightening, how I could disengage from reality like that. It frightened *me*, like I wasn't in control of myself any more. It felt like it was going to end with me going to bed one night and never getting up again. Not even dead, just not *there*. And feeling like that and also having to deal with being recognised every time I left the house…"

"I can't imagine…" Sadie said, feeling as small as she'd ever felt. "I wish you'd told me… *something*."

She wanted to hold his hand, or link her arm with his, but every gesture felt insignificant and trite.

"Oh Sadie, I wouldn't have even known how," James said. "All the things I thought I was doing to deal with how I felt only made it worse. I was drinking far too much, just trying to drown out how hollow I felt all the time." He looked at her. "I can stop here…"

She shook her head.

"It's not classy," he warned.

"I don't care," Sadie said.

"I got myself in a real mess, by accident, really. It started in such a stupid way and got so out of hand. I cringe when I think about it now."

"I'm not judging," Sadie said.

James nodded. "I don't expect you remember, but just after we got back from doing that magazine feature in Italy I got the most horrendous cold, and for weeks afterwards I had this cough that I just I couldn't shake. I wasn't sleeping well before, but with the cough thrown into the mix it was verging on insomnia. I didn't think I could go on like that much longer, doing what we were doing every day, and then someone said to me that codeine was a cough suppressant, and that you could get it over the counter as co-codamol. I'm just grateful that we weren't running in the kind of circles where someone might have suggested cocaine instead. I was pretty desperate at that point, I'm not entirely sure I could have relied on myself to have made a sensible decision."

It all felt a bit real then, how easily things could have turned out so much worse. Sadie had always felt very secure in the knowledge that they weren't that kind of band, but she hadn't realised that it was owing to serendipity alone that none of them had ever gone down that route.

"Anyway, the co-codamol ticked a lot of boxes for me. It felt like being wrapped up in a warm glow; it softened that scary detached feeling. I slept better than I had in months, and then I worked out that if I combined it with alcohol I could scrape through public appearances that little bit easier. Perks like that made it pretty hard to stop taking them." James shook his head. "It's pathetic, isn't it. Codeine, for Christ's sake. Not very rock and roll."

"How could I not have known this was happening to you?" Sadie whispered, trying to blink away her tears.

"How *could* you have known?" James asked.

It was too kind, and it was more than she deserved, and it didn't help the crying situation at all.

"I can only imagine how awful I was to be around by that point," he continued. "You couldn't have done anything. I was barely there."

"I could have done something before it came to that."

"I really don't think you could have. I wasn't myself for a long time. Being in the band was the wrong thing for me, but I guess there are things you don't know about yourself until you know," James said. "I wasn't intending to leave the band that day. What happened was an accident, at least to start with. I'd got really paranoid about fans finding out where I lived; obsessing about them following me home and breaking in when I was asleep. The night before that roadshow I was so jumpy, I couldn't get to sleep, not even with the painkillers, so I just kept drinking until I finally passed out. I slept right through the show, and when I woke up and realised what I'd done I felt calm for the first time in as long as I could remember. And you know the rest."

"I don't think I do," Sadie said, feeling at a complete loss. "Did David know all this?"

James shook his head. "I don't think so."

"But it was his job to look after us…"

"When you've got a problem like that you get really good at hiding it from everyone," James said. "It's no one's fault, Sadie. I went to see a doctor eventually: my sister-in-law literally delivered me to the door after they worked out what was going on. The doctor said I was depressed and gave me another pack of pills, but that wasn't how I wanted to feel better. It felt like going from one crutch to another. It took a while, but I got there on my own eventually."

"And you're…" Sadie hesitated, unsure of the etiquette surrounding a real conversation about mental health. "Are you better now?"

James' sad smile wasn't the answer she'd been holding her breath for.

"I don't know if you do get *better*," he said. "I manage it."

"How?"

James hesitated. "Don't laugh. It sounds really pretentious."

"I would never."

"I meditate. I can't explain how it works, but it keeps me in a good place if I do it every day. Which has proved a bit more difficult here…"

Sadie frowned, something dawning on her. "Does Kitty know about all this?"

James sighed. "No," he said.

"Not about the meditation, or…"

"Any of it."

I hate everything about your relationship, Sadie wanted to say. *I don't understand it and it makes me feel sad.*

"I know," James said, before she had a chance to respond. "But I can't. Things with me and Kitty are… It's not who she wants me to be."

"But it's a huge thing…"

"It doesn't have to be," James said. "It's not the kind of thing that fits in with what she wants."

"What about what you want?"

"I want her," James said.

Sadie had a horrible feeling that Kitty wasn't worthy of that kind of devotion.

"How do you keep it from her?" she asked.

"I go to a meditation class once a week in the middle of the day. The other days I go home for lunch and do 20 minutes then. I live close to work."

"But don't you need support with this kind of thing?"

"It's under control," James said firmly, and Sadie gathered that they'd reached the extent to which she could express disapproval.

Because where had she been for the last nine years? She'd let him walk away from the band without even asking why, so consumed with what *he'd* done to *her* that it hadn't even crossed her mind how he was. She wasn't much better than Kitty.

"Can I help with anything?" she asked. "Are you doing your meditation?"

James shook his head. "There are always people around. And Kitty's invited this random girl to stay in our cabin. I haven't had a chance."

"But don't you need to do it every day?"

James shrugged. "I'm sure it'll be fine."

"Do you want to use my cabin?"

"No offence, but this isn't the kind of thing I want to share with Mia and Cameron," James said. "Or Ryan."

Sadie nodded. "I won't tell anyone. But… You can talk to me, if you need to. I know you probably wouldn't want to, but I could just listen, if you did want to."

James smiled. "Thanks." He looked at his watch. "We should get going or we'll be in trouble. I didn't mean… This was a quicker conversation in my head."

Sadie wanted to throw the whole show in the lake and just sit with James forever and talk about everything until she was sure she knew it all. To pause time for nine years and make up for all the times she wasn't there for him. She still had so many questions and she didn't want to walk away from this conversation in case she never found the secret door again. She wanted to stay with the version of James who talked to her like a friend and told her the truth, but she could already feel him pulling away.

So she nodded, helplessly, as he stood up.

It was too big, everything he'd just told her, to shake hands and part ways as if nothing had happened. As if her whole perspective hadn't just shifted three feet to the left. She needed another half an hour; half a year.

"Is this… a trigger?" she asked. "Being here."

James shook his head. "I'm fine," he said, but somehow it wasn't quite the reassurance Sadie was looking for.

26

You didn't look like this last time I saw you.

Kitty's insides were doing cartwheels.

Was this a dream? Had he really said that to her? Had he really recognised her after *ten years*, without her having to say a single word to him? This was the kind of thing she daydreamed about; a bedtime story she told herself when she couldn't get to sleep. She'd had high hopes for their reunion but she hadn't expected *this*.

And what exactly *was* happening here? Could she dare to hope that maybe he had been thinking about her all these years like she'd been thinking about him? Was that possible? Would you *really* remember someone who had been in your life so briefly – one of many many girls, she was sure – if they hadn't meant anything to you?

The door to the sports hall swished open and Kitty's heart practically threw itself out of her chest.

Don't look don't look don't look, she urged herself, eyes fixed on the book in her lap that she had failed to read a single word of the entire time she'd been sitting there.

Just whiling away some time, if anyone asked. A complete coincidence that she happened to be doing that outside the building where all the bands were.

Why would she need a book, anyway, when the entertainment was this good: a few moments ago Indigo Lion had walked right past her as if she were completely invisible. She'd watched curiously as they'd milled around outside the building with their entourage, most of them smoking, two of them bickering and one of them standing alone and silent to the side of the group. And wasn't that just pop music all over. Maybe some things just repeated themselves over and over until the end of time.

"Don't tell the fans I smoke," Ryan said, eyes twinkling.

"Hi," she squeaked, hastily trying to recover from the surprise that he could possibly have remembered something he'd once said to her.

It had been their inside joke, and not something *she* was ever likely to forget, but it seemed impossible that he was able to recall such a small detail when *surely* she hadn't been a highlight of his life like he had been in hers. Just how much *did* he remember?

"Blast from the past," Ryan said, not even trying to hide the fact that he was checking her out. "You look incredible."

Kitty tried so hard not to beam back at him, she really did, but honestly resistance was futile.

"You here for Cameron?" he asked, regarding her with a mischievous grin.

"What?"

"You know, get the full set?"

She laughed in surprise. "No!"

Ryan exhaled a stream of smoke out in front of him. He was so effortlessly sexy it was almost painful. If you were to place him in a line of other male celebrities who had survived their pop band break-up, arranged according to their success, by rights he should be top of the pile by now. He was utterly wasted in the background of his new band: he had all the makings of a superstar.

"So you and James, huh? How did that happen?"

"By accident," Kitty said.

Ryan raised an eyebrow.

"Really! We met through work."

"He win you over with his vibrant personality?"

She smirked disloyally. "Yes."

Ryan nodded. "I guess he must have done, because I heard you didn't even know your boyfriend was in a band…"

"A girl can't have secrets?" Kitty smiled coyly.

It wasn't like all she'd done over the last ten years was think about Ryan, but he was always there, lurking in the background. Even when she thought she'd let him go; even when she'd actively *tried* to let him go. Sometimes she had gone for years without thinking about him – years, perhaps, when she had real life boys to daydream about – but he always popped up again at some point, and the more settled she had got in her relationship with James, the louder the thoughts about Ryan had become. Say what you like about the one that got away, but they didn't go very far, figuratively speaking. She couldn't say she'd never imagined the life that hadn't been: the one where her and Ryan had coupled up as teenagers and stayed together forever. Or bumped into each other as adults and picked up where they'd left off…

"Sounds like you've got rather a lot of secrets to me." Ryan grinned. "So what have you been doing with your life? Apart from getting smoking hot."

"Not as much as you've been doing," Kitty said, trying not to trip on that A+ compliment.

"Haven't seen you in the front row of any of my shows lately…"

"You don't play Devon very often."

She was far too not-single to be having this kind of conversation with someone like Ryan and she knew it.

"No, I suppose we don't," Ryan said. "Plus last time I saw you I was a complete shit to you."

Kitty's heart catapulted itself from one side of her chest to the other.

"There's that too," she said, wondering how far she could nudge this conversation. "You don't seriously remember all that?"

How many chances was she going to get to talk to him like this? Time wasn't there to be wasted.

"Course I do," Ryan said. "How could I forget you?"

Yeah, that would do it. That would definitely do it.

"I bet you say that to all the girls," Kitty said, unable to resist fishing a little more.

You did hear those stories, though, didn't you, where people met as teenagers and were drawn back together later on in life…

"I don't tend to run into *all the girls* in such unusual circumstances," Ryan said, jumping up from the bench before she could formulate a comeback. "I've got to go. I only snuck out because Sadie was correcting the choreographer's dance moves, at length. You here for the whole thing?"

Kitty nodded.

"See you around, then," he said, firing one more grin in her direction before ambling back towards the sports hall.

Kitty watched him go, sure of only one thing: Ryan Malone was just as much trouble as he had always been.

27

"I don't know what to do," Adam said, watching the condensation drip down the outside of his pint glass.

In a minute he might liken it to the despair he felt. He might also liken his despair to that lightbulb in the far corner that had gone out. Or the way the tables were too close together to be comfortable, in the style of a badly-planned wedding. Was that a double likening? He could write a whole bloody poem about his utter utter despair and what ordinary household objects it was like if someone would only give him a pencil.

"You know how I feel about her, man. Tell me what to do."

Jonny looked at him quizzically. "Am I allowed to say that this is a bit pathetic?"

Adam sighed "Yes."

Was it still only Tuesday? Time had passed exponentially slowly since Mabel had been catapulted back into his life and then whipped out of it just as fast. Rehearsing that afternoon had been a bloody nightmare. He couldn't get over the look on Mabel's face and Nat wouldn't meet his eye. And now, to further prolong the torture, he was crammed into a faux pub with everyone else, playing a "hilarious getting to know you game" that seemed like it was coming slightly too late when they were two days in already. Ah, show business. The gift that just keeps on giving. Even when you really don't have space for any more gifts and you secretly wish it would just stop.

"She did not go to Alton Towers with the cast of *Friends*."

"What?" Adam peered out of his misery for a moment.

"Two truths and a lie!" Jonny said. "That's the lie."

He raised his beer in the air, calling out his conclusion to the room as Adam hastily rearranged his face into something vaguely resembling a neutral expression, ever-aware of the cameras.

"What's yours?" Jonny asked.

"Huh?"

"Two truths and a lie. Three things that seem equally realistic or ridiculous. They're asking everyone."

"How about, I haven't had a meaningful relationship since I fell in love with someone who apparently doesn't want to talk to me nine years after we last saw each other," Adam said. "My life basically doesn't mean anything without her and there's a very large chance that she doesn't even care. Not doing absolutely everything differently is the biggest regret of my life. There. Three things."

"I don't think that's quite what they had in mind," Jonny said. "And all those things are true. That's not the game."

Adam drained the last of his pint, pulling another full glass towards him. In an unusually proactive move, Jonny had suggested loading up with as many beers as they could fit on the table in case the evening turned out to be excruciating.

"What were you going to do if you found her?" Jonny asked. "Last time. Years ago."

"Well I wasn't exactly going to declare my undying love for her straight away. I thought maybe we'd be friends again first and just see what happened. Or maybe ask her on a date? I don't know, man. I didn't realise it was going to be a one-shot kind of situation." He sighed. "I thought I just wanted to see her; to make sure she was okay."

"But you've seen her now."

"And it's not enough." Adam sighed. "Have I made this into a total melodrama? Am I actually being very creepy?"

Jonny made a face and shrugged.

"Is this not staggeringly romantic?"

"Did you and Mabel ever actually have a thing?"

Adam paused. "No. We were friends. At the start. I don't know what we were at the end."

"Friends and you were secretly in love with her?"

"Yes…"

"Was she secretly in love with you?"

"I don't know. I mean, maybe?"

"Because she was shagging a lot of people, and if you weren't one of those people…"

"Oh fucking hell, have I completely made this up?" Adam ran his hands down his face.

"You might have been expecting a bit much," Jonny said.

"Yeah, like a scene from a fucking rom-com."

"I just don't think you've been cast in the lead role here, man. To continue the analogy," Jonny said. "Shouldn't it be Freddie banging down her door, all heartbroken and shit? What she did, she did to him. I think you came off lightly, to be honest. Like, you were kind of friends and then she didn't send you a postcard after she left? She wasn't shagging your best mate behind your back, you know?"

Adam sunk a little lower in his seat. For Jonny to be making sense it must be bad. Had he really wasted nine years of his life – the bloody majority of his youth, to be specific – on a completely delusional fantasy? He'd just got so fixated on *finding her*, as if that was the only piece of the puzzle that was missing.

"I guess I just wanted to tell her that it's okay. That what she did wasn't as bad as she thinks and that no one cares any more."

"They do care, though."

Adam sighed. "Yeah, I know."

After just one afternoon playing supergroups with Granola Fantasy he was already thoroughly sick of listening to Jay bicker with everyone over set lists and who got which vocals and anything else he could find to pick a fight over. There was a kamikaze vibe surrounding him that made Adam want to be anywhere but in the same room.

"It *was* pretty bad, what she did…"

"You would make a terrible agony aunt," Adam said, defeated.

He *was* delusional, wasn't he. They weren't two ill-fated lovers, battling the odds to make it back to each other, upon which point they'd fall into each other's arms and disappear off into the sunset. They weren't bloody Romeo and Juliet. Why would seeing him again mean anything to Mabel at all?

"I mean, I don't know, maybe I'm wrong…" Jonny mused.

"I need some air," Adam said, glancing towards where the current focus of attention was in the room.

"Wait, you're leaving me to sit here on my own?"

"I'm just a bit of a dick like that," Adam said, clapping Jonny on the shoulder and swiftly making his escape.

It was quiet and dark outside, which was very fitting for his current mood.

He was getting the hang of navigating the site now, enough so that when he took a right rather than a left he couldn't convincingly fool himself that he didn't know exactly where he was going. And sure, he'd made a deal with himself last time he'd been to Mabel's empty cabin that he wouldn't go again, but he really just needed to go one more time, just to make sure, and then perhaps he'd find some way to put this whole sorry mess behind him. Method TBC. He wasn't sure that drinking copious amounts of alcohol was going to help him at this stage. What did sober people do to take their minds off a crisis? Was it craft? Was he going to end up losing himself in knitting, or a really intricate sewing thing? Christ. What had he done with his life.

It was actually pretty creepy out in the forest at night. The roads were lit but the unoccupied cabins were in darkness, and there was something unsettling about walking through the middle of that. Adam paused instead at the top of the road that Nat was staying on. Nat, and all the other people who hadn't completely fucked up their lives and actually had wives and families to bring along. Plenty of lights on there, and Adam was fairly confident that the road ended up in about the same place as the one with all the creepy empty cabins.

Half way down the road the smell of cigarette smoke and the murmur of conversation caught his attention, pulling his gaze to where two people were perched on the front step of a cabin, lit only by the glow of a street lamp and the dim light that spilled from the window behind them. Jay's laugh carried on the still night and when Adam saw who he was with the shock was like a physical jolt, as if he'd walked into a force field and been thrown backwards. He stopped, dipping into the shadow of a tree. Mabel shifted position, her face suddenly illuminated, smiling at Jay in a way he'd seen too many times before. He should be surprised, but more sickening was the realisation of how inevitable this seemed. And how deeply unfair. She'd run from him, when he'd never done anything but try to be her friend, and yet here she was making small talk with the person responsible for the mess she'd got herself into in the first place.

Adam's mind raced ahead. Had Jay known where Mabel was all along? Had they been *together* this whole time? Or worse, not together in an official capacity, but a weekend here and there. He couldn't think about it. He couldn't *watch*. This was his worst nightmare being acted out right in front of him.

Jonny was right: he was pathetic. This was never going to play out in his favour. That just wasn't the story of his life.

Jay nudged Mabel, she smiled again, and Adam turned and walked away from the whole sorry thing.

EIGHT DAYS TO THE LIVE SHOW

28

"So rehearsals are hard," Sadie said, hobbling out of her bedroom, pulling her haphazardly repacked suitcase behind her. "I didn't realise it was possible to pull so many muscles at the same time."

She knew she wasn't exactly *fit*, but her entire body felt like it had simultaneously seized up and was on fire after yesterday's rehearsals. The warm-up exercise alone had almost seen her off; it hadn't occurred to her that she might need to get into better shape before coming on the show. It might have been nice if that had been suggested when they signed up, but perhaps that was the point.

"How did we do it before? We never worked out when we were in the band."

"We were young," Cameron said, stacking their breakfast plates by the sink.

"Well I wish someone had told me how easy being young was," Sadie said. "I feel like I've been run over."

"Youth is wasted on the young."

"I hate that quote," Sadie said. "I hate how right it is."

"You know there are already some things we will never do with our lives?" Cameron said. "There are things we're already too old to do."

"Like what?" Mia asked.

"Loads of things! Olympic gymnast. Professional footballer. Ballet dancer. Figure skater. Probably too late to train for a really decent career, like doctor or lawyer. By the time you've got anywhere it'll be time to retire."

"Oh. I don't want to do any of those things," Mia said. "What about astronaut?"

"You want to be an astronaut?" Cameron asked.

"No, but it's nice to know that I could be if I wanted to."

Suddenly Sadie felt very claustrophobic. The thought that time was running out and her choices in life were getting more and more limited by the day when she didn't even have a life plan made her want to scream.

Had she wasted her youth? Was it really over? What even counted as your youth? She certainly hadn't wasted the years she'd spent in the band, but all those years since it felt like she'd just been waiting around for something magical to happen when apparently she should have been perfecting her figure skating instead. Was that *it*? Gone, just like that? Were those motivational quotes on planks of wood in Dunelm right after all?

Music's moved on without us, George had said, but maybe *life itself* had moved on without *her*. It was probably a little too late to realise that life wasn't going to wait for you to pull yourself together or get a handle on what your actual purpose was. It just kept on rolling by, whether you were making the most of it or not. And it was devastating, wasn't it? When you were in the thick of it you never imagined for a minute that youth was finite. Why didn't they warn you? Why didn't someone sit you down at 16 and tell you that you needed a Plan A, and then a Plan B in case that went wrong, and that you needed to pick a career and train for it, and get on the career ladder early so you had to time to reach the top, and not to spend all your money every month so you didn't find yourself living in a tiny rented flat at the age of 28, consuming fast fashion and fast food as if they were the only small pleasures still available to you.

Oh hang on, didn't that happen at school? Was *that* what that was? Being sat down in a dingy office and being lectured about how your hopes and dreams were wrong and based on your grades you should probably become a dentist instead?

But I've had a call back for this band I auditioned for, she'd said blithely, not listening to a word that they were saying.

Oh God, was she as old as those teachers now? Had *they* felt like she did now, when they were trying to bestow their hard-earned wisdom upon a hoard of teenagers poised to mess up their lives just like they had once upon a time?

She could only hope that something happened to you when you crossed the threshold into your thirties that made you miraculously satisfied with your lot, fondly looking back into your twenties from the comfort of your satisfactory life. But she had a horrible feeling that it wasn't going to be like that and if she didn't do something quickly she was going to enter her thirties still feeling empty and lost.

She didn't *feel* old – didn't *feel* like those teachers she rolled her eyes at when she was 15 – but more and more often the celebrities she assumed were her age turned out to be at least five years younger and that age gap was only widening as more bright young things burst onto the music scene and she drifted further away from it. Was she a *joke*? Were the people watching this show going to be laughing at how washed up and pathetic they all now were? Was this not the second chance she'd been holding out for? Was it all just *too late*?

"Are you okay?" Mia asked, frowning at Sadie. "You've gone pale."

Sadie nodded, feeling a bit fuzzy around the edges. Perhaps she'd focus on "life begins at 30" and take some very deep breaths into a paper bag.

"I wish you weren't going to live with Ryan," Mia said. "I'll miss you."

"I know, I'm sorry. But I'm only going one street over," Sadie said. "And I'll see you all the time when we're filming. I just need to spend some time with him."

And possibly come up with a whole new life plan, she thought.

"I don't see what the point is," Cameron said. "You'll just get all attached again and then be sad when he ditches you to go back to America. You're just a novelty to him while he's here. This whole thing is. He might seem really into it now but you know he won't have time for you when he goes back to his superstar band."

"He might," Sadie said stubbornly.

That wasn't true, was it? Ryan seemed so keen to reconnect with her. She knew he had to go back to his fancy life in America but things would be different this time, wouldn't they? In fact they had to be, because she didn't think she could handle losing him again.

"And I don't know why you let him get off so lightly about the whole roofies thing. That is *messed up* that he did that to you."

"He didn't have a choice," Sadie said, feeling surprisingly defensive. "David told him to do it."

"Yeah okay," Cameron said, not sounding the slightest bit convinced.

"What am I supposed to do? Hold a grudge until the end of time just to make a point? I don't need to fall out with him over it. He said sorry."

And sure, she *did* still feel a bit weird about the whole thing, but she'd brush it aside to be able to spend time with Ryan again. Maybe that was a weird dimension to their friendship but she could live with that. If she could forgive James, she could forgive Ryan.

"Well I guess we'll just pick up the pieces when he abandons you again," Cameron said.

But somehow that didn't sound very reassuring.

"I have to go and take my stuff over before we start filming." Sadie said, trying not to rise to it.

An argument with Cameron was about the last thing she wanted to deal with right now. Even when he *knew* he was wrong he'd fight to the death claiming he was right.

"I'll see you at the… Wherever it is we're meeting for the scavenger hunt."

"Patch of trees in the middle of nowhere," Cameron muttered.

Sadie grimaced apologetically at Mia, mouthing a goodbye as she pulled her suitcase towards the door. She did feel a little bit bad at leaving Mia with Cameron, but actually Mia could handle Cameron much better than she could, being equipped with infinite patience and a much kinder spirit than her, so they'd probably be just fine. She was putting herself first for once, and she wasn't going to feel guilty about it.

Well, maybe just a tiny bit guilty.

Her suitcase bumped along the path as she walked round to Ryan's cabin, feeling excited, feeling nervous, feeling achy and tired; thinking about what James had told her by the lake and what Cameron had said about Ryan, their words piling up against each other and the joy of them all being together again offset by the emotional distance between them all. She didn't know what to do about James: how to carry such a heavy, important secret; how to support him and let him know that she was there for him. She wanted to talk to Mia about it but she couldn't. She wanted to bake him a cake and give him a hug but it didn't seem nearly enough. And *should* she be throwing herself so enthusiastically back into the ring with Ryan? What if Cameron *was* right and he didn't really care about any of this, *or her*, and being dropped from his life a second time was going to hurt much more than the unread WhatsApp messages and forgotten birthdays. Was this all actually the worst idea she'd ever had? Instead of making her feel complete again, was this experience going to leave her in more pieces than she'd been in to start with? Could life not just be simple for once?

She stopped outside Ryan's door, wondering whether to knock or just go in. Once upon a time she would have burst into any room he was in without thinking, but things felt a bit more complicated now. She decided to err on the side of unfamiliarity and knock.

"Yes! You're here!" Ryan beamed at her in the doorway. "Why are you knocking? What am I, your grandmother?"

Sadie shrugged, absorbing Ryan's warmth as she stepped into the cabin.

"Why do you look stressed?" he asked.

"I'm not," Sadie said.

"Er, thank you, I spent four years looking at your stupid face, I know when you're stressed," Ryan said, taking her hands and pulling her into a really tight hug. "Does this help?"

Sadie laughed, face squashed against his chest. "Honestly, I'm fine."

"Coffee, then?" Ryan asked, relinquishing his grasp on her and leading her over to the kitchen area. "Breakfast?"

There was a shiny coffee machine on the counter and a spread of pastries on the table.

"Where did you get all this?" Sadie asked.

"Well this," Ryan pointed to the coffee machine. "I brought with me. Because instant coffee is shit."

Sadie grinned.

"And they bring you this stuff if you ask," Ryan said of the food. "It's a welcome breakfast! For you."

For a moment he looked so eager and hopeful that Sadie wanted to grab him and squeeze him.

"You did this for me?"

"Yes! Well obviously I'm going to eat it as well," Ryan said, pulling out a chair for Sadie. "And it's a sorry breakfast. Another sorry. And I know you said to stop saying it and just quietly repent in my own time, but I really don't feel like I've said it with enough gusto still."

"You don't have to keep saying sorry," Sadie said, sitting down. "It's okay."

"It's just that I've been thinking about it, and it really *wasn't* okay, what I did," Ryan said. "You know, I've managed *not* to think about it for years, and now I *am* thinking about it I realise how horrible it was, and I don't know why I thought it was an okay thing to do. I am *so* sorry, and I'm so glad you still want to hang out with me."

Sadie hastily stuffed a croissant into her mouth to stop herself from getting all teary and embarrassing.

"And, I don't know, do you want to talk about it?"

Sadie shook her head. No she definitely did not. She wanted to put it to the very back of her mind and unpack it again when she was well clear of cameras and TV shows and live televised performances. This was not the place to think about it because she didn't know how she'd end up feeling when she actually did try to process it.

"Do you want to just eat breakfast pastries and talk shit about Indigo Lion?"

She nodded, mouth still full.

"Sweet," Ryan said, looking relieved. "So obviously they hate each other."

"All of them?"

"Well, no, but there's this thing between two of them. Something about a girl."

Tale as old as time, Sadie thought.

"And then one of them is being lined up behind the scenes to go solo."

"Theo?"

"Yeah."

"So obvious."

"You'd think. Not to the rest of the guys, though."

"Maybe it's not possible to see what's really going on in your own band," Sadie mused, thinking back to her conversation with James and everything that *she* had missed. "Maybe you're too close to it."

But it wasn't going to be like that any more, she decided. They may only be playing at being a band again, and it might only be for a handful of days, but she was going to make it her business to notice every last thing about every last one of them. Whether they liked it or not.

29

"I think you're going to find it hard to avoid every other member of your band during a team activity."

"They're not my band," Adam muttered petulantly.

"That's the spirit!" Jonny said, smirking as Adam shoved him in the side.

They were standing in a clearing in the forest with everyone else, waiting for someone to tell them what they were supposed to be doing. The cameras were rolling but the "host" was yet to appear and Adam felt like he'd rather be anywhere else. He had lain awake half the night, not able to get the image of Mabel and Jay out of his head, and the thought of having to buddy up with him now to solve stupid treasure hunt clues was inciting a fury within that he hadn't known he was capable of feeling. But worse than having to interact with Jay was the fact that he hadn't even fucking shown up yet, and the thought of where he might be made Adam feel sick to his stomach.

"I can't be around him. I think I might punch him."

"It would probably be better if you didn't."

Adam let out a low growl in reply.

"Why is this happening? She won't even *talk* to me, but she's…" Adam shook his head to dislodge the image. "With *him*."

"Maybe it's genuine. Maybe they're rekindling."

"Nothing is genuine with him."

"Maybe he missed her," Jonny said, the devil's advocate that Adam could really do without today.

"*I* missed her," he said, knowing how childish he sounded.

But it *wasn't* fair, and he was so over trying to feel differently about it all. Even if Jonny was right and he'd spent the last nine years fabricating a love story in his head, it still felt like his heart had been ripped out of his chest and stomped on.

"Maybe, mate, he feels the same about her as you do and, I don't know, he just got in there first," Jonny said. "Do you hate the idea of them because of *him*, or because *you* want her?"

"I just don't understand what she's doing. He ruined everything for her! She *left* because of him! She could have been happy with Freddie but he had to interfere, and now look where we are: in a fucking *supergroup*."

"But if Jay hadn't got with her then she might *still* be with Freddie and you still couldn't have her anyway."

"Okay well fine, I just want to be her friend, then."

"Can't you do that? Even if she is with Jay?"

Adam kicked at the ground. "No," he muttered crossly. "She won't talk to me anyway, remember?"

He didn't want to be talking to Jonny about all this. He wanted to be talking to *Mabel* about all this. He just wanted to lay all his cards on the table and tell her exactly how he felt because this situation was absolutely bloody ridiculous and he couldn't bear it.

"Supergroup assemble!" Nat said, grinning, ambling over with Harry and Freddie. "We're going to win this, right?"

"For sure," Jonny said. "Probably because there's more of us than anyone else."

"Why can't we just be Prairie Dogs for this bit?" Adam said quietly.

"Because they're probably hoping one of us is going to punch Jay out," Jonny said.

"I wish someone would."

"Where are Jay and Fabs?" Nat asked, looking round.

"Fabs was on the phone to Sara. He's around. Don't know where Jay is. I haven't seen him this morning," Freddie said.

The knife lodged in Adam's heart twisted a little.

"Oh there he is," Nat said, pointing through the trees.

And there he was, sauntering down the path towards them, looking as smug and self-assured as ever. Was that what it was for Mabel? If she had been trying to avoid Jay, would he have cornered her anyway, taking what he wanted from her just like last time? Adam hadn't thought that the world humoured *persistent* men any more, but what did he know.

"Sorry," Jay said. "Had a bit of a late one."

"How do you manage to have a late one somewhere like this?" Nat asked.

"I have my ways," Jay said.

It was the smirk, Adam thought, that he found especially unlikeable. As if Jay had managed to tap into some kind of inner satisfaction at everyone else's expense; like he had absolute confidence that he was better than everyone else in the room in every way. Except he wasn't. He was a dick, and Adam wasn't in the mood.

"You always could find trouble," Fabs said, coming up behind them.

A man of few words, Adam had always found that Fabs had a knack for cutting straight to the truth of a situation. He was entirely affable, until he wasn't, and that's when you had better listen.

"You're not going to fuck this up for us, are you?" Freddie asked, rolling his eyes. "Please don't deal drugs to kids, or anything."

Jay laughed. "There's no trouble," he said. "Don't worry about it."

But Adam had a feeling that that was easier said than done.

"Right then!" Helen said, clapping her hands to get everyone's attention. "Is everyone ready for a scavenger hunt?"

A distinctly unenthusiastic whooping rang out around the group.

Helen smiled. "You'll like it, I promise. Bit of fun before we get back to the serious stuff. You're going to play in your bands for this one. Each team will be given a different set of questions that will lead you to a number of coloured tokens, and you'll be competing against each other to collect all your tokens and be the first team to make it to the final location. There's no set time limit, but if you take too long you'll miss lunch."

"It's like being at school," Adam muttered.

"Okay! Let's do this!" Helen shouted. "Get your envelopes and get going!"

Adam reluctantly took the envelope that was offered to him and opened it up, scanning down the list of five clues.

"*Girls Aloud covered this Pointer Sisters classic,*" he read out, frowning.

"'Jump'!" Nat said.

"Yeah, but how is that a clue?"

Nat shrugged.

"Jump," Adam repeated thoughtfully, watching as several of the other bands took off into the woods. "*Christina Aguilera, Mya, Lil Kim and Pink teamed up on this movie hit,*" he said, reading the next clue. "These clues are easy."

"But what do they mean?" Nat asked.

"I don't get it," Adam said. "And why would they give us all the clues straight away?"

"Oh man, I get it!" Jonny exclaimed suddenly. "We've got to collect these tokens, right? So I bet the answers are something to do with where they're hidden!"

"So *jump* would be…"

"Trampoline?" Freddie offered.

"Oh! Yes. Maybe," Adam said.

He had to grit his teeth very hard when Jay snatched the list off him.

"So here's the plan," Jay said, clicking his fingers. "I'm not running around like some kid playing hide and seek. You lot find the tokens, or whatever, and call me when you know where we're supposed to meet up."

"No," Fabs said. "We're all playing."

"I don't see the point," Jay said, scowling. "It's not going to take seven of us to work out five piss-easy clues."

"We could split up?" Freddie said. "Do it in half the time. Go for a pint."

"I don't think that's the rules, though," Adam said.

"You should try not playing by the rules some time," Jay said. "You might have more fun."

Adam felt his fists clench involuntarily by his sides. He'd never actually punched someone before. Was this how it happened? Jay was still looking at him as if he was challenging him to react, and the rage inside him felt like boiling hot lava. But then he felt Jonny's hand on his arm and he saw the blink of the red lights on the cameras surrounding them and he found himself slowly exhaling instead.

"Splitting up sounds cool!" Jonny said enthusiastically, ever so subtly inserting himself between Adam and Jay.

"Yeah, nice, two teams of three. See you later," Jay said, turning and walking away from the group.

Adam saw the look that passed between Freddie and Fabs – a look they had clearly shared many times before.

"Toss a coin for him," Freddie said, rolling his eyes.

Fabs shook his head. "I'll go."

"Better take a couple more of us so when he ditches you it looks like we're cheating rather than fighting," Freddie said.

"Jonny and Harry?" Fabs suggested.

"Dream team," Freddie agreed, although Adam had a feeling they both knew that they were the least inflammatory choice when it came to spending time with Jay.

"The *A Team*," Jonny said, heading off with Fabs and Harry. "See you later, B Team!"

"Send me a photo of that list!" Fabs shouted back to Adam.

"Right," Freddie said. "I guess we better find a trampoline."

Much as Adam felt the lack of Jay's presence as a relief, he wasn't particularly in the mood for socialising with Mabel's estranged brother and her ex, either. He hadn't spoken to Nat about Mabel since he'd first run into her – God knows what he thought telling him about it then was going to achieve – and he didn't know if Freddie now knew about her being there as well.

"This is like old times!" Nat said, looking genuinely happy about the arrangement.

Yeah, thought Adam, *just like old times when I watched the girl I liked fall in love with someone else – twice? – and didn't do anything about it.*

He had toyed with the idea of asking her out, once upon a time. He'd even spoken to Nat about it and he'd told him to go for it. But he'd lost his nerve more than once and then Freddie had burst onto the scene and it had quickly become obvious that he'd missed his chance. Asking Mabel out when she clearly had Freddie-shaped stars in her eyes had seemed beyond pointless. Better to leave it as mates, he'd thought. Mates would do, he'd thought. Maybe he'd meet someone else anyway, he'd thought. So that had worked out just great for him, hadn't it.

"So where are we going to find a trampoline?" Nat asked.

"A play area?" Adam suggested. "I don't know, not really my area of expertise."

Freddie nodded. "They do have trampolines in play areas: sunk into the ground, that kind of thing."

"Shall we go and have a look?" Nat asked.

Adam shrugged.

"Might as well," Freddie said.

"Are things okay with Jay?" Nat asked as they walked.

"I don't know," Freddie said. "He's distracted by something. Not sure what. It's never good, though, is it."

Nat glanced covertly at Adam and he wished he wouldn't. Clearly Freddie didn't know about Mabel, and Nat had jumped to exactly the right conclusion about Jay, and Adam would rather throw himself into a well than discuss any of this with either of them.

"You don't think he's going to throw the show?" Nat asked, glancing at Adam again.

"Who knows *what* Jay might do at any given moment," Freddie said. "I don't know. Hopefully Fabs can keep him on a short enough leash. He does at least listen to him sometimes."

So Nat wasn't going to tell Freddie about Mabel, then. What did he think was going to happen if Freddie found out Mabel was there? What would happen if Freddie bumped into her, as Adam had done? Would she run from *him*? She clearly hadn't run from Jay… And they weren't going to fight over her again, were they? Freddie was all settled down. He had kids. But what if Mabel had been the love of his life? What if his now girlfriend, much as he loved her, had always been second best? Adam had never managed to overcome his feelings for Mabel to get anywhere near having a serious relationship, but if he *had* settled and then her found her, what exactly *would* happen? Could you really bury feelings that strong? God, where was this going to end? He wished she wasn't here. He really really did. He'd rather spend the rest of his life looking for her and missing her than ever have to feel like *this*.

"Why are you scowling?" Nat asked, shoving Adam in the side.

"Bitter taste in my mouth," Adam muttered.

"What clues did you send Fabs?"

Adam looked at the list he'd inadvertently scrunched up in his hand. He cleared his throat.

"They're going to do the last two. *The music video to this popular Oasis single is shot entirely in black and white and remains one of the most iconic singles on (What's The Story) Morning Glory?*"

"'Wonderwall'," Nat said.

Adam nodded. "And *This Grammy Award winning smash from Seal featured on the Batman Forever soundtrack.*"

"'Kiss from a Rose'," Freddie said. "I hate that song."

"You can't hate 'Kiss from a Rose'," Nat said. "It's a classic."

"And yet, I do hate it."

Was it something do with Mabel, Adam wondered. Or was he just making everything about her, like he always did? Would that stop now his quest to track her down had hit a final dead end? Or would everything always be about her, forever, and he'd have to feel like this for the whole rest of his life?

Sounded like so much fun.

"Trampolines," Freddie said, pointing ahead of them.

"And a token!" Nat said, going over and picking a blue plastic disc off the ground. "Nice. I guess we're the blue team, then. What do we have to find next?"

"Marmalade," Adam said. "Or Lady Marmalade, but I'm assuming it's the jam, not the person."

"Where would they have marmalade?" Nat asked. "A café? Is there a café?"

"I think there's a café," Adam said.

"Could also be in a shop," Freddie suggested.

"Could also be in a shop," Adam agreed.

"Hit up the café? I could do with a coffee," Nat said.

Adam nodded. "Lead the way."

30

"*This band's songs include Barbie Girl and Doctor Jones!*" Sadie said, clapping her hands together in a motivating way. "Okay! Go team! Let's go!"

"Go where?" Cameron asked, regarding her with amusement.

"Aqua!" Sadie exclaimed. "So… I don't know, the lake?"

"The swimming pool?" Mia offered.

"A rusty old outdoor tap?" Cameron suggested.

"Come *on*, I want to win this thing!" Sadie said, bouncing on her toes. "We're so close!"

"I vote swimming pool," Ryan said. "Isn't it called Aqua-something?"

"Okay! Let's go!" Sadie said, leading the charge.

"We're not going to have to actually go *in* the pool, are we?" Mia asked, as they all trailed behind Sadie.

"Who knows! Maybe!"

Oh she was trying, she really was. Trying to bring these people back together. To remind them of what they'd once been. But at the moment it was a bit like trying to coax old Playdoh back to life: it was a bit dried up and gritty around the edges and it just wouldn't smooth out no matter how much she worked it. The whole atmosphere between them all was flat and she could only imagine what it was going to look like on TV. Least charismatic band ever.

"Oh look, a squirrel!" Mia said, pointing just ahead of them.

The squirrel was rooting around in the undergrowth and paid them absolutely no notice as they walked towards it.

"Why isn't it running away?" she asked, looking more interested in the squirrel than Sadie had ever seen her look about anything.

"Probably just really used to people?" she said.

"It's so lovely!"

"We have squirrels at home, you know," Cameron said, moving Mia along the path.

"I have *never* seen a squirrel in Bristol," Sadie said.

Not that they had a garden or access to any kind of green space to have noticed a squirrel. For a moment she couldn't even think whether there were any trees on the street they lived on. When was the last time she'd even noticed a tree? The trees seemed different here, anyway. More regal. Quietly wise.

"I actually think this whole place is banging," Ryan said. "I forgot what peace and quiet sounded like."

"I'll tell you something, it's a lot quieter in our cabin now Sadie's staying in yours," Cameron said.

"Luckily I enjoy a bit of Sadie chaos," Ryan said, winking at her.

"Bringing us all here is certainly one of her most chaotic stunts yet."

"And what a jolly time we are having," Ryan said, grinning.

Another thing she'd barely noticed before: how irritating Cameron was. She'd really settled, hadn't she, with her entire social life revolving around him and Mia. She should probably do something about that when she got home. She should probably do something about a lot of things when she got home. Including noticing the trees.

"Where's your cabin, James?" Mia asked.

"With the Z-listers," Cameron muttered.

"Oh, it's a bit further out than yours," James said, ignoring him. "Plenty of chaos there: everyone's kids are on the same street. It's a good vibe."

"Do you have children?" Mia asked.

"No." James smiled. "Maybe one day."

Hopefully not with Kitty, Sadie thought disingenuously.

She'd love to be proved wrong, but Kitty really didn't strike her as the settling down type.

"Are there lots of children here?" Mia asked. "Is it weird that none of us have children?"

"There are quite a few," James said. "From talking to the other bands it sounds like there'll be more here at the weekend."

"How can people have *school age* children already?" Sadie asked. "Are we really behind on this?"

"Quite a few of my friends have kids," James said. "I don't think it's unusual at our age."

"At *your* age," Cameron said. "We're all still in our twenties."

"Not me," Ryan said, raising his hand. "Rocking the big 3-0 over here."

"Oh no, I missed it!" Sadie said, feeling that hollowness creeping back. "Did you have a big party?"

"A small one," Ryan said, linking his arm with hers. "We'll have a bigger one for your 30th."

"Will you invite all your famous friends?" Sadie asked, smiling at him. "I don't have any."

"Oh all of them. It'll be the event of the year. How long have I got to plan it? Two years, right?"

"Yes," Sadie said. "How do you remember things like that?"

And also, if you know when it is, why did you never send a card, or even a message?

Ryan shrugged. "I just do."

"Do you want children?" Mia asked.

"Me?" Ryan laughed.

"Come on, he's probably got illegitimate children scattered all over the place," Cameron said.

"Well I don't *think* I do…"

"Eurgh," Sadie said.

"I don't know, I wouldn't say never to kids," Ryan said.

"If you can find someone you want to spend more than 30 minutes with," Cameron said.

"Come on, be fair, 45 minutes," Ryan said, grinning.

"I think the last thing the world needs is *more* of you," Sadie said, elbowing him.

"Are you going to have babies with Katie?" Mia asked Cameron.

"I don't know," Cameron said. "It's a bit soon for all that. We've only been together a year."

"We just seem too young to have children," Sadie said. "I can't even imagine it."

"I quite like the idea," Mia said.

"With *Jonah*?"

She smiled. "Maybe."

"Oh my God, are you going to move in with a boy and leave me all on my own?" Sadie asked.

Mia had always been such a constant in her life, she'd never even considered the fact that she would ever go anywhere.

"No, not yet," Mia said gently.

"*But some day?*"

"What, you thought you two were still going to be living together when you're old ladies?" Cameron jeered. "Maybe you should date twins and then you can be one of those weird couples that all live together."

Had she thought that? Somewhere subconsciously? The thought of living on her own made her feel almost panicky. God, what a state she was.

"Well I think we've established that none of us should be having kids any time soon," Ryan said as they approached the pool complex. "What's the plan with this swimming pool?"

"Can we just go in?" Mia asked. "Maybe we should ask at reception."

"We're the only people here, aren't we?" Cameron said. "I think we can go where we want."

"I'll go and ask," Sadie said, feeling like she could probably do with a moment or two without them all. "You just wait here."

She pushed open the glass door, noting another group of scavenger hunters – 50% of the strange Granola Fantasy/Prairie Dogs supergroup – in the far corner by the soft play.

"Hi," she said, leaning on the reception desk. "Can I go into the swimming pool? I'm looking for a yellow token. We're doing a scavenger hunt."

The receptionist nodded, gesturing to a door to the right. Sadie pushed it open and walked down a long corridor, wondering whether she should still have her shoes on as she came into a large changing room. It was probably fine, though: like Cameron said, they were the only ones there. She pushed open a swing door and stepped into the deserted swimming pool. The lights were on and water was whooshing down the slides, but there was no music and not a single person to be seen. It was like stepping into the aftermath of an apocalypse.

"Creepy," she muttered, peering into the water and wondering how she was going to find a small yellow piece of plastic in such a massive space.

She didn't hear the door swing quietly open behind her, or the soft pad of socks on the wet floor. She barely registered the hands on her back as she fell into the water, gasping in shock, chlorine rushing up her nose. She broke the surface, spluttering, and through bleary eyes she saw Ryan on the side of the pool, almost doubled over with laughter.

"What are you doing!" she shrieked, thrashing around, trying to get some purchase on the water.

"Your face!" Ryan exclaimed.

"I thought I was being murdered!" Sadie yelled, wiping a wet hand ineffectively over her eyes.

But Ryan just laughed harder, and then Mia, James and Cameron appeared through the door as well, hands over mouths in surprise and amusement.

"I'm going to kill you! What about the scavenger hunt?"

"Fuck the scavenger hunt!" Ryan shouted, pulling off his t-shirt and jeans, and throwing himself into the pool.

Sadie shrieked as water splashed over her, and then Mia was running towards the edge of the pool too, her dress fanning out like a parachute as she jumped in, closely followed by Cameron, both fully clothed.

James watched them for a moment.

"Fuck it," he muttered, launching himself into the water.

And then they were all in there: five idiots in an empty swimming pool, splashing and laughing, and not a soul around to document it. Jumping into a swimming pool with your clothes on? So very Funk Shui. Maybe there was a shred of charisma left in them after all.

31

"Oh what now," Adam muttered as one of the production minions handed him a clipboard. "I don't want to do any more activities: I just want to go and lie in a dark room on my own."

Unsurprisingly, seeing as they'd technically been cheating, they had won the scavenger hunt, had been rewarded with precisely nothing, had been rushed through lunch – not being allowed to film people when they were eating was boring, clearly – marched into another lacklustre rehearsal, and now this.

"But you sold your soul and now you have to…" Jonny looked at the clipboard. "Specify what song you want to play on guitar at tonight's campfire gathering."

"Kill me," Adam said. "Honestly, put me out of my misery."

"You're a right Negative Nigel this week, aren't you?" Jonny grinned. "This show's really bringing out the best in you."

"Yeah, well. Doesn't feel quite like what I thought I was signing up for." Adam checked the time on his phone. "We've got a bit of time now, right?"

"Yeah, they said we can grab dinner in our cabins and then we're meeting back here at eight," Jonny said, waving the clipboard at him. "After you pick your guitar karaoke song."

"Put me down for 'Hey Jude'."

"I will not, you basic bitch," Jonny said, grimacing.

"'Wonderwall'?" Adam grinned.

"It's 'Take Me Home, Country Roads' or nothing, man."

"'Hotel California' it is. No problem," Adam said, getting up. "I'll catch up with you later, mate. I'm going to find my aunt."

Because of course he *couldn't* leave it alone. He knew full well he was going to keep picking at that scab, over and over, for as long as he was here.

Willpower at this point was down to zero. He had to hear it; had to know if Mabel and Jay had been a thing for longer than the last few days. Had to hear about *her*, from someone who knew who Mabel was now. If he hurried he might just catch his aunt before she left for the day. And if he didn't... Well maybe then he'd *grab dinner in his cabin*. Or maybe he'd just sit and obsess about it for another couple of hours.

There was no one on reception as he pushed through the revolving door so he went round the desk and peered into the office, his heart suddenly beating up around his ears as he realised that he could be about to bump into Mabel... But there didn't seem to be anyone there at all, let alone her.

"Oh! Adam!"

He turned to find Diane in the doorway, smiling at him.

"You scared me to death!"

"Sorry." He grinned sheepishly. "Just lurking. Looking for you, actually."

"Oh good! I was just handing over to the night team. Have you got time for a coffee? Or something stronger?"

"I have, actually. That would be nice," Adam said, trying not to just launch straight in with his Mabel-related interrogation.

"Have you been to The Lounge bar?" Diane asked. "It's only a short walk if we go out the back way."

"Honestly, I couldn't tell you if I had or not," Adam said. "It's all been a bit of a blur."

"I'm sure!" Diane said, ushering Adam out of the office and locking the door behind her. "Is it going well?"

"Hard to tell," Adam said, following her across the foyer and down a short flight of steps. "They've put us in a supergroup with another band that we knew back then, so there's too many people playing the same instruments, and we're having to learn new songs..."

"That sounds interesting, though?" Diane said.

She pushed open a door at the end of the corridor and they stepped outside.

"That's one word for it," Adam said.

"Bit different from your day job."

"That it is."

"So what kind of things have they got you doing?" Diane asked. "The amount of resources they've asked for... I can't even imagine."

"It's like part holiday camp, part boarding school, part... I don't know, a little bit like being in prison?"

Diane laughed. "Surely not as bad as that!"

"Okay no, probably not as bad as prison. We're doing campfire songs later."

"Oh fun!"

Adam raised an eyebrow.

"No, sorry, probably not very *cool*..."

He laughed. "I think we're way past being concerned about what's *cool*. It's just not very spontaneous when you have to write down your song choice in advance," he said. "But no, it's not that bad – I guess it's just a bit of a shock, being filmed all the time and being told where you have to be and when you can eat..."

"Well don't blame me for the catering: I offered our in-house team but they insisted bringing someone else in."

"Yeah the food is *rubbish*."

"What number cabin are you in?"

"71."

"I'll sort you out some decent food."

Adam smiled. "Now you're talking."

They emerged from the forest onto an open grassy area where a large wooden building overlooked the lake, strings of lights twinkling along the balconies.

"Well I definitely haven't been here! What is this place? It looks like a ski lodge."

"This is The Lounge," Diane said. "They asked for it to be staffed so they must be using it for something."

"Where are we in relation to the coffee shop on the lake?" Adam asked as they approached the entrance. "I can't get my bearings. Every path seems to lead to this lake."

"We're about as far away from that café as we can get," Diane said, pointing out over the lake. "It's all the way at the other end, but it bends round, a bit like a kidney bean shape. Haven't you got a map?"

"Oh, yeah, I think so, in all the paperwork they left in the cabin," Adam said. "So where are the pedalos?"

"They're on the main straight. If you followed that edge of the lake round," Diane said, pointing to the left.

"How big is this place?" Adam asked, trying to get his head round where they were and how they'd got there.

"Oh it's pretty big," Diane said. "Come on, let's get a drink."

They went inside, Diane directing him out onto one of the tables on the balcony while she got their drinks.

This feels like a holiday, Adam thought, as he looked out across the lake in the gathering dusk. A place like this would be perfect, wouldn't it, if he'd just bumped into the love of his life who he hadn't seen for nearly a decade. Imagine that, bumping into someone you'd spent so much time physically *yearning* for and being able to have a conversation with them. He should be so lucky.

"Cheers," Diane said, smiling as she set a bottle of lager down in front of him.

"Cheers," Adam said, clinking the bottle against her wine glass.

"So," she said, regarding him from across the table, "what am I missing, Adam?"

Adam sighed, the game clearly up. "How well do you know Mabel?"

Diane paused. "The thing is with Mabel, she's very hard to get to know."

"What do you mean?"

"Well you must know, if you know her? I've worked with her for years and I couldn't tell you a thing about her, apart from that she's fabulous at her job." Diane shrugged. "I'd say at least I know she *enjoys* the job, but to be honest I don't even really know that. I mean, I assume, seeing as she barely leaves the site, but I couldn't tell you for sure."

Adam frowned.

"How did you say you knew her?"

"Oh, er, through the band. We lost touch, a long time ago." He paused. "Doesn't even sound like the same person, to be honest."

"Well maybe it's just work. Maybe she likes to keep her personal life separate."

Maybe, Adam thought, but that brightly shining light of a girl that he'd been drawn to all those years ago certainly hadn't been hard to get to know back then.

"Have you ever seen her with a boyfriend?" he asked, cringing at himself for even asking the question.

"I've never even seen her with a *friend*, Adam, but maybe this is something you should be talking to her about?"

Adam looked away. "She's not exactly pleased to see me."

"I see," Diane said. "And is this something I need to worry about, as her manager?"

"No. Don't worry about it. I am overstepping. Vastly," Adam said, shaking his head. "It's just... Did she know which bands were going to be here? Before we arrived?"

"No, we found out at the same time as everyone else," Diane said. "It was all coded this end until the line-up was announced publicly."

But no one announced us, Adam thought.

So that meant that, although Mabel would have known to expect Granola Fantasy, she might not have known that Prairie Dogs would also be there.

Was it just a shock, thinking she knew what to expect and then seeing him all of a sudden? And if it *was* such a shock, did that mean that seeing him again *did* mean something to her after all? But then how exactly did Jay fit into all this? Adam didn't know where he was going to get any of these answers from.

"She won't let anyone in," Diane said. "Any of us here. And we've tried. She doesn't ever let her guard down. Maybe she needs a friend who already knows her?"

Adam nodded thoughtfully.

"Anyway. While we're here, do you want to eat?" Diane asked. "I hear the chef is rather good."

"Finally, some VIP treatment," Adam said. "Show me a menu."

32

Kitty peered through the trees at the flickering fire, watching the way it illuminated the faces of the pop stars sitting around it as they held marshmallows over the flames. She wasn't invited, of course – strictly celebrities only – but that didn't mean she had to stay in the cabin. It wasn't like anyone was going to notice she was there.

"Are you going to pick them off one by one, or are you just going to burst out and try and take down as many people as you can at once?"

Or maybe they would.

She span round and saw Ryan grinning at her, his face soft in the filtered firelight.

"What?" she asked, unable to help the smile taking over her whole face.

"You look like you're planning an assassination," he said, handing her a warm mug.

She looked at it in surprise.

"Mulled cider," Ryan said. "I think they're trying to loosen us up."

"For me?" Kitty asked, needing to clarify what was happening here.

"Well I don't need two," Ryan said, holding his own drink up.

"Thank you," Kitty said, her heart pounding. "How did you know I was here?"

"Your hair is the same colour as the fire. It's poor camouflage."

"Oh," Kitty squeaked out.

"There anywhere to sit around here?" Ryan asked, looking around them before picking his way through the trees away from the bonfire.

Kitty followed, wondering whether she'd actually fallen asleep and this was all a dream.

"You opposed to the floor?" he asked, stopping in between two tall trees.

Kitty shook her head and he sank down onto the ground, resting his back against one of the trunks. She did the same, sitting opposite him, the glow from the fire stretching lazily through the forest. She folded her fingers around the mug, Ryan's mere presence warming her more than the lukewarm cider. He looked at her thoughtfully for a moment before taking a sip of his drink.

"So," he said.

"So."

"I have to say I find your presence here intriguing."

"Do you?" Kitty asked innocently.

Ryan raised an eyebrow. "Some might say that you being here with James is a bit of a coincidence."

"Coincidences are wild," Kitty said, holding her nerve.

"Aren't they just," Ryan said. "So, what did you do with your life?"

"Oh is it over? I didn't realise."

"Well it probably is if you're planning to stick with James for the long term."

"Maybe," Kitty said, maintaining eye contact despite feeling like her heart was going to beat its way out of her chest. "Maybe not."

"You're bored," Ryan said, a glint in his eye that could have just been the firelight.

"You can't know that."

"I know the look," he said.

Was it a challenge, or a come-on, or… This exchange they were having in the middle of the forest, surrounded by shadows, was so surreal it was hard to get a handle on it. Ryan's words floated around her like smoke, disappearing before she could read between the lines, or even tell whether there was anything between the lines to be read. Was he flirting? Was he drunk? Were either of them actually even there?

"I don't know," Kitty said, shrugging. "Life is…"

"A grand disappointment."

"Something like that."

"Yeah."

"Yours isn't, though?" Kitty asked. "You've got the band, and all that."

"Well, assuming they let me back in the band after this."

"What do you mean?"

"Me being here is… *Contentious*."

"Oh." Kitty frowned. "Wait, you threw away your career for *this show*?"

"I *potentially* threw away my career for..." Ryan paused. "A friend who needed me. Dress up, show up. You know."

Kitty frowned. Was he talking about Sadie? Or *James?* To be honest, who *didn't* need Ryan in their life.

"Are you having a thing with Sadie?" she asked, without really meaning to.

She'd been thinking it, but she didn't actually mean to say it. Stupid magical forest.

Ryan laughed. "No! Why would you think that?"

"Oh, you two just look close, that's all."

All over each other, she'd go as far as to say. Hands and arms and shoulders constantly touching in one form or another whenever she'd managed to catch a glimpse of them. Sadie needed to back off a little bit, in Kitty's personal opinion, because it looked a tiny bit desperate.

"Well yeah, she's the best person I've ever known. Why wouldn't I want to be around that."

Foolish, the little pang of jealously that pinged towards her heart. But just imagine Ryan Malone feeling that way about you...

"Were you two ever... More than friends?"

Ryan smiled. "She'd never have me."

"So you wanted to be?" Kitty asked, trying to conceal her surprise.

It really wasn't an obvious match. And also, *when* exactly? Had she come before, or after?

"Maybe once, a long time ago. Not *now*."

"Did she know?"

"No, I don't think so," Ryan said. "I mean, *maybe*, but we never talked about it. I didn't get that kind of vibe from her so I think I just left it alone."

"Hang on, so Sadie *friend-zoned* you? Teen heartthrob *Ryan Malone?*"

Ryan smiled again, so wide she could see his canines, like the boy who used to laugh with her in the corner of a cheap hotel bar long after everyone else had gone to bed.

"I suppose she did," he said. "Anyway, wow, that was a bit real, wasn't it? Shall we move on?"

"You used to tell me all kinds of real things," Kitty said, almost holding her breath as the words left her mouth.

"I know," Ryan said eventually. "You were..." He trailed off, shaking his head, and Kitty knew instinctively that she would spend the rest of her life wondering what he was going to say.

She waited, creating the space for him to finish his sentence, but he didn't.

"So why is your life so disappointing?" he asked instead. "Apart from the fact that you have to spend it with James."

Kitty smiled involuntarily. "Aren't you supposed to be mates?"

"Me and James?" Ryan shook his head. "Nah, I think that ship's sailed, hasn't it? Probably a bit too much of water under the bridge there."

"He said you were his best friend. Back then."

And if James wouldn't be drawn on the topic maybe Ryan would.

"Yeah, we were," Ryan said thoughtfully. "But when you leave your band high and dry without even having the decency to talk about it beforehand you might as well toss that friendship in the trash. You can't really pick that back up again."

"I guess not."

"And I don't *get* you and James, by the way," he said, raising his eyebrow again.

And, wow, he was gorgeous, and this was unbearable.

"No?"

"No! Because he is… And you are…" Ryan shrugged and laughed. "I don't know. He's punching, let's just leave it at that."

Oh let's not, thought Kitty, but Ryan was already moving onto the next topic of conversation.

"So I was thinking earlier… Last time we were hanging out you told me you were going to change the world: you were going to shut down all the zoos, rescue all the animals, throw a bunch of people in jail, right all the wrongs."

Kitty opened her mouth in surprise.

"Did you do it?"

Good lord, where was he pulling all this from? He was absolutely right: that *had* been her teenage dream, way before he had been. She'd had it all planned out, her whole career path mapped out in front of her, and then she'd discovered pop bands and she'd forgotten all about it, just like that. Like a moth to a flame, Funk Shui – and then Ryan – had become all she could see. But how exactly did *Ryan* remember any of that when she hadn't even thought about it herself in years.

'Oh, no, I didn't," she said, wishing for the first time that she actually *had*; that she had something grand and impressive to tell him.

"No? What did you do instead?"

Nothing, Kitty thought. *Nothing because I was heartbroken over you and I let everything else slide. Nothing, because I didn't get the right GCSE grades and I didn't care about A Levels any more. Nothing, because I threw all my energy into becoming someone who was worthy of being with you, and by the time I felt pretty enough and skinny enough it was all over.*

She shook her head. "Nothing worthwhile. I..." She paused. "I changed my mind. About the animal thing."

Because it hadn't been sexy or glamourous or interesting enough; because nothing had felt like it mattered any more.

"I changed my mind about a lot of things."

"How come?"

"Because of a boy," she said, feeling sick with false bravado.

Ryan frowned. "Me?"

Kitty shrugged. She wasn't going to elaborate. How could he ever understand the effect his stupid teenage choices had had on her. She didn't think *she* even fully understood what had happened to her the day she woke up and found him gone. She didn't realise until years later how much of herself she'd left in that hotel room.

"You gave up on what you wanted to do with your life because of *me?*" Ryan looked genuinely shocked. "Shit."

Kitty shrugged again. "Teenage girls make silly decisions, I guess," she said, inadvertently downplaying the fact that the pain of being rejected by Ryan had essentially derailed her entire life.

But... Had it really? Because here she was, sitting in the woods having a private audience with a much more attractive and mature version of the boy who'd discarded her all those years ago. That was pretty close to all she'd ever wanted, after all.

"I don't like that," Ryan said. "At all."

"It's no big deal."

"It kind of sounds like a big deal."

"I guess I just felt like who I was wasn't good enough for you," Kitty said, feeling bolder with Ryan so visibly remorseful.

"No," he said, looking her in the eye. "I wasn't good enough for *you,* babe, if I made you feel like that."

Jesus Christ, it was like pure electricity coursing through her veins when he said things like that. Was she going to wake up in a minute?

"I think I'd better get back," he said suddenly, standing up. "Before someone misses me. Probably bad form to be caught on camera hanging out in the dark with your bandmate's girlfriend."

He held out his hand to Kitty and she took it, letting him help her up. Then she was standing, but he didn't let go of her hand and his skin felt so soft and his face was so close to hers and his eyes were so blue, even in the darkness, and he looked at her so intensely for just a moment that she thought her knees were going to give way.

"Maybe we'll do this again," he said finally, letting go of her hand.

Kitty nodded, not wanting it to be over.

But it was, and she clutched her mug of mulled cider tightly as she watched him pick his way back through the undergrowth, floored once again by a boy in a band.

SEVEN DAYS TO THE LIVE SHOW

33

"I hate these dance moves," Cameron muttered, trying and failing to match the steps of the choreographer at the front of the room.

"You're moving the wrong arm," Sadie said, looking at his reflection in the mirror. "That's what's throwing you off."

"I'm not moving the wrong arm," Cameron said crossly. "It's right arm up and left arm across."

"No, you're doing it backwards. You're supposed to be mirroring."

"*I am*," Cameron said, gritting his teeth.

"Why don't we take a break?" Ryan suggested.

Cameron exhaled loudly. "I'm not the one doing it wrong."

"Well you might not be, but I think I am," Ryan said. "So why don't we come back to it in ten minutes, or try a different song, or something."

"I don't want to change the song," Sadie said picking her water bottle off the ground. "I love the dance to this song."

It felt like every time they rehearsed the tension between all of them increased, and it was really starting to bother her. After the swimming pool incident the previous day she'd thought they were all going to start getting along, but clearly that was too much to hope for. Even Mia had stopped trying to mediate the situation, and nothing spelled trouble more than the most diplomatic person in the world taking a step back.

"We could change the dance moves?" James suggested. "Just slightly? Make it a bit easier? I don't think I'm quite getting it, either."

"I don't need it to be *easier*," Cameron snapped. "*I'm* doing it right."

"Hey, I'm not saying you're not," James said, holding up his hands. "Just making a suggestion."

Sadie glanced at Ryan and he made a face.

"You always want to change things, don't you. You can never just leave it alone," Cameron said, looking furious. "I think I speak for everyone when I say, what are you even doing here?"

"Woah," Ryan said, stepping in. "You're not speaking for me there, personally. And I think we're all just trying to figure it out, doing our best. It's a tricky dynamic. Lots of unresolved shit, probably. And we are on camera, so perhaps we should table this particular discussion?"

He raised his eyebrows pointedly at Cameron and he got another heavy sigh in return.

"I think I'm just going to take a minute," James said, leaving the room.

"*Why*," Sadie muttered, glaring at Cameron and following James.

He wasn't in the lobby so she went outside, finding him sitting on a low wall opposite the entrance.

"He's not speaking for any of us, you know," she said, sitting down next to him. "I don't know why he has to be like this."

James shrugged. "He thinks I deserve it. Maybe I do."

"I don't think you do."

"I don't know, things could have been a lot different for all of you if I hadn't ever been in the band. If I'd been more honest with myself about what I wanted, right from the start."

"You were great in the band!" Sadie said. "The fans loved you!"

James made a face. "I don't know about that."

"They did! Just ask Kitty!"

He frowned. "Why would I ask Kitty?"

Oh shit, that was stupid.

Oh, just because, er, I think she was doing some research on the band," Sadie stammered, desperately back-pedalling. "Looking at old forums, or something. I'm not sure. But trust me, you were a hit."

James didn't say anything and Sadie wondered whether he'd seen what she had in the light of the campfire the night before, and whose job it was to step in before things got out of hand. Kitty was researching something all right, but it appeared to have very little to do with James. It was creating such a tangle of conflicting emotions in Sadie's brain. Whose side was she supposed to be on? James'? Ryan's? How was she supposed to focus on rebuilding her friendship with Ryan when she was so furious with him for getting involved in something that was none of his business, and how was she supposed to be there for James when she knew so many things about his own life that he didn't know?

"I'm sorry Cameron's being such a pain," she said finally, feeling like everything she had to offer him was going to come up short.

Had she actually lived a charmed life to have never come across such uncomfortable emotions in a friend before? Or had she lived such a *self-centred* life that she'd simply never noticed? How had she got to the age of 28 without having to support someone through a difficult time? She didn't know what to do and it felt absolutely horrible.

"It's not your fault," James said, looking defeated and tired. "It's not like I didn't expect it."

"*I* didn't," Sadie said honestly. "I think I've been a bit stupid."

James smiled kindly. "No," he said. "I don't think it's a lot to ask for two fully grown men to be civil to each other."

"It seems like a lot at the moment."

"Yeah," James nodded. "It does."

Sadie sighed. "I just wanted it to be how it used to be. I thought if I could get everyone here, things would just click back into place," she said. "Have I been really selfish dragging everyone here?"

"We're all here willingly, Sadie."

"Even you?"

James nodded again. "Even me."

"I feel like I've made you more stressed than you needed to be."

"I'm fine," James said, never quite sounding as convincing as Sadie would like. "This is just a tiny snippet of time out of all of our lives. You're not asking too much of anyone. We can pull it back. I'll just stay in my lane and then Cameron won't have anything to complain about."

"I didn't think you were out of your lane."

"No, well." James shrugged.

"I really wanted us all to be friends," Sadie said glumly.

"Friends might be a bit of a stretch," James said, smiling and standing up. "Come on, I think I've had my minute. We've got a dance routine to master. Some of us more than others."

Cameron was laughing with Ryan and Mia when they went back into the rehearsal room, the lights on the cameras forever blinking red. They got back into position and the choreographer started the song again, leading them as they moved from left to right. And just for a moment it seemed like they might all be getting it, in time with the music and each other. The microphone in Sadie's hand felt as natural as it always had, and she grinned at Ryan in the mirror as he stuck his tongue out at her. But when it came to the part where they had to spin and slide, Cameron went the wrong way and slammed into James, his microphone flying out of his hand and smacking into Sadie's arm. She yelped in pain as Cameron glared at James.

"What are you doing?" he demanded.

"What am *I* doing?" James asked. "I'm so sorry, Sadie, are you okay?"

Sadie nodded, rubbing at the sore spot on her arm.

"You went the wrong way!" Cameron exclaimed.

"*You* went the wrong way," James said. "But look, does it really matter? Sadie's hurt."

"Oh don't pretend you care."

"Of course I care!" James sighed in exasperation.

"You think you can just waltz back in here and act like everything's fine; pick up where you left off. It's a joke," Cameron fumed.

"Oh for God's sake," James said. "I didn't *waltz*, I was invited, and I didn't actually *want* to be here–"

"Oh well now we're getting the truth."

"Stop!" Sadie exclaimed, both her arm and her patience feeling bruised. "Will you just stop it! This is the only chance we are ever going to have to be a band again and you are *ruining* it! We all know that James left the band! It happened! We can't change it! And I don't even care any more, because we're all together now and we could make *this* into something amazing, but all we're doing is bickering and falling out! You're embarrassing yourselves! You're embarrassing *me*! And, actually, I know my dance moves, so I'm going to go and put some frozen peas on my arm and the rest of you can stay and work on it until you get it right."

"Sadie…" Ryan started.

"No!" Sadie said crossly, cutting him off. "Learn the dance moves. That's all I need you to do."

And then she turned and stormed out of the room, not entirely sure whether she was cross with them, or herself, or the whole bloody world.

34

"Why do they put up with him? Every single time he does something like this," Adam grumbled to Jonny as they hung around pointlessly at the edge of the rehearsal room. "Why did Freddie forgive him in the first place? Why are they even still mates?"

Jonny gave an expansive shrug. "I don't know the answer to any of your questions, my friend."

They were supposed to be rehearsing their supergroup songs that morning but so far rehearsals had been a non-starter on account of Jay apparently having disappeared into thin air. Freddie and Fabs had gone to look for him, leaving Adam, Jonny, Harry and Nat standing around unsure of exactly what they were supposed to be doing.

"We could just start rehearsing our own song?" Harry suggested.

"Yeah I guess," Adam said, his enthusiasm for life in general seriously waning at this point.

"Do you know where Jay is?" Nat asked him.

"Why would I know where he is?"

"Is he with her?" Nat raised an eyebrow pointedly.

"With who?" Harry asked.

"Mabel's here," Nat said.

"Oh, Jesus."

"Yeah," Nat said, looking just thrilled about it. "*Is* he with her?"

"I don't know!" Adam exclaimed, potentially a little too defensively.

"Why is Mabel here?" Harry asked.

"Why are you both looking at me?" Adam asked. "I don't know why she's here or who she's with. It's nothing to do with me."

"This can't happen," Nat said. "You have to do something about this."

"Why do *I* have to do something? It's none of my business. Can't you just get Fabs to sort Jay out?"

"Fabs will tell Freddie. He can't know she's here. Or about her and Jay." Nat exhaled. "Her timing is really bloody impeccable yet again."

"Why does it matter if Freddie knows or not, anyway?" Adam asked petulantly.

"Oh come on, you know what she does to people," Nat said. "You think your bad mood at the moment isn't obvious?"

"Yeah and she won't even *talk* to him," Jonny said.

"Oh thank you for that," Adam said, rolling his eyes at no one.

At himself. At Mabel. At everything.

"Why won't she talk to you?" Harry asked.

"Because she loves the drama," Nat said

"But were you two even friends?"

"Okay. Great chat, everyone," Adam said briskly. "Maybe I'll get some coffees, or something. Why don't you just call me if you need me to do any drumming."

Being there just got more and more fun, it really did.

There was no one around as he walked down towards the lake, but presumably everyone else was in bands with decent human beings so there was no need to be running around the site looking for them when they were supposed to be rehearsing. The other bands looked like they were having a much better time than he was: obviously he'd opted for the wrong genre and pop was the way to go.

He stepped onto the decking surrounding the cafe and sunk into one of the chairs overlooking the lake with a heavy sigh. Coffee in a minute. First: moping with a view.

"That's where I was going to sit."

Adam looked round in surprise to see a girl standing over him holding a mug with a tower of cream perched on top.

"Oh! Sorry!" he said, making to stand up.

"I'm only joking," she said, smiling. "I think there's probably enough space for both of us out here. Evidently everyone else's bands aren't falling out with each other."

"Yours too, huh?" Adam said, gesturing for her to sit down. "I thought it was just me."

"Ah, displaced band members club," she said, putting her mug on the table without hesitation and pulling out a chair. "Are you the one doing the falling out or the one that's fed up with it?"

Adam made a face. "If only it were that simple," he said. "Adam, by the way. Prairie Dogs."

"Sadie," said the girl, doing a strange little wave. "Funk Shui."

"So you're not currently rehearsing with your band because…"

"Oh they are doing my head in," Sadie said, spooning some of the cream into her mouth. "It's like they are deliberately sabotaging any possibility that we might all be able to be friends again. One of them won't let it go, one of them is attempting to make it all *much* worse, one of them I'm not sure will even make it to the end of the show mentally intact… And why is it my job to hold it all together? I thought we were adults."

"That's a bold assumption," Adam said.

Sadie smiled. "They also suck at the dance moves."

"Forever grateful that I was not in that kind of band," Adam said. "Have you tried letting them fight it out amongst themselves?"

"I'm kind of hoping that's what they're doing right now," Sadie said. "Why are you here?"

"Oh you mean staring morosely out over the lake?" Adam said. "I honestly wouldn't even know where to begin."

"There's a lot of cream on this hot chocolate, I've got a while."

"Well," Adam sighed. "There's a girl…"

"Oh not you too," Sadie interrupted. "What is it with men moping around after girls who don't deserve it?"

Adam smiled in amusement. "Well I kind of think she does deserve it."

"That's what they all say," Sadie said, getting up abruptly. "I'm getting you one of these. I'll be right back."

Adam watched her go back inside. He didn't think he'd ever spoken to Sadie before. Of course he knew who she was: everyone knew who Sadie Dawes was. Even from a distance her confidence was intimidating, but he'd always idly thought she looked like a lot of fun. There was something about how *bouncy* she was that reminded him a bit of Betsy.

"So this girl…" Sadie said, coming back to the table with another mug of cream. "You like cream, right?"

Adam smiled. "Who doesn't like cream?"

"Boring people," Sadie said. "So…"

"Ah yes, I was about to tell my deepest, darkest secrets to a complete stranger."

Sadie grinned. "Sometimes that's the best way. Go on, I won't tell anyone. I don't know your band, anyway. You're too cool for me."

Adam laughed. "I'm not sure I've ever been described as "too cool" before."

"Oh, you know, brooding around with your guitars and your swoopy hair. I bet you like obscure poetry and you hate Eurovision."

Adam choked on a spoonful of cream. "I'd love to say you're wrong but you've just described two members of my supergroup to a tee there," he said. "Eurovision, though. Is there anything greater?"

"Right?" Sadie said gleefully. "Okay so now we've established that we are best friends, tell me about this girl."

Well, what did he really have to lose at this point? Maybe talking to someone truly impartial would help him get it all straight in his head.

"Okay," he said, settling in. "So there once was a girl, and there was a boy who really liked her, but before he could tell her that he liked her, two other boys came along that liked her, and she liked them both, and let's just say that she couldn't decide who she liked best, so they both fought over her."

"Who won?" Sadie asked.

"No one," Adam said. "She left."

"And how did the first boy feel about that?"

Adam paused. "Very sad. Very very sad."

"Did he see her again?" Sadie asked.

"He did," Adam said. "On Monday."

"Oh!"

"Yeah."

"So..." Sadie frowned. "You're the first boy, right?"

"For my sins," Adam said.

God, this drink was sweet.

"Wow, and you haven't seen her for..." Sadie paused. "Let's say *many* years to save me embarrassing myself."

Adam nodded. "Many many years."

"So why is the girl here?"

"She works here. Of all the places in all the world. She was here all along."

"This is huge, isn't it?" Sadie asked, looking captivated. "Like something that would happen in a film! Please tell me it was impossibly romantic when you saw her again?"

"Thank you!" Adam said, feeling oddly validated. "It should have been! But it was not."

"Oh. Why?"

"You know, Sadie, I really could not tell you. Here is the thing," Adam said, wondering just very briefly whether he should be telling her this at all. "Things were not that great for anyone last time I saw her, but I like to think I abided by the "decent man code", and I was a really good friend to her, and I tried to support her the best I could, even though I did not agree at all with the choices she was making, and I didn't project any of my stupid romantic feelings onto our friendship, or make it weird in any way, because obviously it's absolutely fine that she didn't have those kind of feelings for me, and just before she disappeared, not that it's really a big deal now, but she did actually take quite a lot of money from my flat, which I forgive her for, because I know she felt like she needed to get away, but I have now spent quite a substantial part of my life missing her, and trying to find her, and I thought I was okay but actually I'm feeling pretty not okay right now, so it would just be really nice if maybe me and her could talk it out. Is that too much to ask? Because I feel like it isn't, personally."

Sadie silently sipped her hot chocolate, eyes wide.

"This is probably a lot of ground to cover in the space of a five-minute conversation," Adam said apologetically, feeling like a bit of a tit.

"No no, I'm caught up," Sadie said. "So you haven't talked to her?"

"I've tried."

"She won't talk to you?"

He shook his head.

"But you don't know why?"

"No."

"And you can't find out, because she won't talk to you."

"Right."

"And she didn't leave because of you?"

"No."

"So when you saw each other again, it should have been like a running into each other's arms and crying happy tears kind of thing?"

Adam smiled ruefully. "I don't think that's actually what I expected, but I thought she'd at least be pleased to see me? I didn't expect her to have just… put it all behind her and moved on. Like to the point where she wouldn't even want to have a *conversation* with me. I mean, does that make sense to you?"

Sadie frowned. "Not if you two were really good friends once. I mean, unless you *thought* you were a really good friend but really you were one of those "friends" who was lowkey hitting on her the whole time and making her feel really uncomfortable and turning the whole thing really awkward."

"I'm pretty sure I was a gentleman throughout our entire friendship." Adam paused. "I mean, I think? You're making me doubt myself now."

"Did you ever hit on her in any way?"

"No, I'm far too spineless."

"Did you regularly bring up that time you accidentally had a bit of a drunken fumble and make "casual" lewd comments about it?"

"Jesus, no," Adam said. "There wasn't ever any drunken fumbling to comment on."

"You wish there had been, though?"

"Yeah, all right, Jeremy Kyle, but not in a gross, sleazy way," Adam said. "That's not the kind of thing I ever wanted from her."

"Because you love her."

Adam shifted uncomfortably. "Yeah," he said. "Because I'm pathetic, clearly."

"I don't think it's pathetic," Sadie said.

"The thing is, I don't even want to tell her how I feel about her, or any of that. I just want to…" Adam paused. "I don't know. Catch up? See if we can be friends? Start again, even?"

"I don't know why she wouldn't want that," Sadie said thoughtfully. "I mean, you seem quite nice."

"Thank you, I am nice," Adam said.

"There must be something else going on. I think you definitely need to talk to her."

"How do I do that, though? She doesn't *want* to talk to me."

Sadie frowned. "I'm just trying to imagine what would make me react like that to a friend that I hadn't seen for a long time. You definitely didn't fall out?"

"No," Adam said. "I mean, the night before she left she was at my house. She was really upset about…" He paused. "Well, something I didn't know about yet, and she kind of… There was a moment where she tried to kiss me."

"Details I did not know about!" Sadie exclaimed. "How am I meant to agony aunt you if you're holding back all the good stuff. That is what we're doing, right? It's £20 an hour, perhaps I should have mentioned that."

Adam smiled, despite himself.

"So, what happened?" Sadie pressed.

"I…" Adam faltered. "I stepped away, from the situation."

"You didn't kiss her."

"No."

Sadie raised an eyebrow. "So, she's embarrassed?"

"After all this time?"

"Oh God yeah. I still have flashbacks to awkward things I did when I was at *school*. Totally possible that she still feels embarrassed about being knocked back. Especially if she actually does have feelings for you."

"I didn't *knock her back*. Jesus, Sadie, if you knew how much I wanted to kiss her in the moment."

And sometimes he wondered, if he'd known that was the last time he was going to see her, would he have still pushed her away or would he have allowed himself just a moment of glorious delusion? And would he have felt more or less empty afterwards when he woke up and found she was gone?

"And what do you mean if she actually has feelings for me? Please don't say that if I'd kissed her then we'd have lived happily ever after."

"Weren't there two other guys involved at that point?"

"Yeah, kind of."

"I don't think living happily ever after was on the cards then," Sadie said. "Maybe she's not embarrassed because you rejected her, but because she did something that she didn't really mean to do and put a weird vibe on your friendship? Or maybe she was worried she gave you the wrong impression and then seeing you again would just be horribly awkward because she'd have to explain that she doesn't actually have feelings for you after all, and that might hurt *your* feelings…"

"Is this all from personal experience or are you just making it up as you go along?"

Sadie smiled coyly. "Bit of both."

"You really think she ran away from me because she's embarrassed about something that happened that long ago? She's *that* embarrassed she felt the need to literally sprint away from me?"

"Wait, she *ran away from you*? Physically ran away?"

Adam nodded.

"Wow. I should have charged you my premium rate," Sadie said. "I think you need to try harder to talk to her. Risk a bit of embarrassment on your part, maybe. I don't think we can figure this out without more information."

"I'm not sure that's premium rate kind of advice," Adam said. "I might just stay here and mope into copious hot chocolates."

"No, I think we've both done enough moping today. I keep forgetting that being here was supposed to be fun."

"Yeah, me too," Adam muttered.

Sadie looked thoughtful for a moment.

"Do you want to do something stupid?" she asked.

"Yeah, I think I do, actually."

Sadie grinned. "Follow me."

35

"Well, this is certainly stupid. Potentially life threatening."

Sadie grinned. Oh she liked Adam. Where had he been all her life? She was so on board with coming out of this show with more friends than she'd gone in with.

"Don't you need a life jacket for this kind of thing?"

"No! Can't you swim?"

"I feel like that's something you maybe should have asked me before I climbed to the top of an incredibly high water slide holding a giant inflatable doughnut."

Sadie laughed. "I think you'll be fine."

"You think?"

"Are you going to wimp out on me?"

"No!" Adam said indignantly. "I am fully on board with this possibly illegal activity."

"Why would they leave the water on if they didn't want us to use the slides?" Sadie said, nudging Adam towards the entrance.

At least she wasn't fully clothed this time. Adam had done a marvellous job of distracting the girl at the desk while she swiped them a pair of swimming costumes and two inflatables.

"Are we taking it in turns or leaping to our death together?" he asked as Sadie set her unicorn swim ring on the water.

"Oh together, definitely," she said, lowering herself into it. "You better be right behind me! Give me a push!"

He did as she asked and she whooshed away, shrieking and laughing as she hurtled down the tunnel, almost falling out of the ring several times and clinging on for dear life as it got very dark and very fast towards the bottom. She burst out of the end of the slide with a huge splash, the impact pushing her under the shallow water as she tried to find her feet. She just got out of the way in time as Adam came flying out after her, his doughnut ring following leisurely behind him.

"I wasn't expecting it to be that fast!" she exclaimed, wiping the water out of her eyes. "Did you fall out of the doughnut?"

"It got away from me on that last really fast corner. I bashed my elbow," Adam said, rubbing at his skin. "Are these supposed to be for children? That was brutal!"

"Fancy the lazy river?" Sadie asked.

"How lazy is it?"

"Very," Sadie said. "Haven't you been to a holiday park before?"

"I literally never have," Adam said, following her as she waded towards the main swimming pool. "Have you?"

"Sometimes, when I was younger," Sadie said. "Not like this. Just, Haven, and stuff."

"What's Haven?" Adam asked.

"Oh dear," Sadie said, grinning. "Were you very poor?"

Adam laughed. "Yes! We were, actually! What's Haven?"

"It's just a fancy caravan park, really. With a pool and entertainment in the evening. They have them all over the place."

"Sounds like someone had very unimaginative parents."

She grinned some more. "What can I say, Adam? I'm as basic as they come."

They dragged their swim rings into the lazy river, the gentle current pulling them slowly along the short loop as they dangled their hands into the warm water.

"That's more like it," Sadie said, leaning back to look at the domed ceiling. "I am so comfy."

"If only we had some beers," Adam said, his ring bumping against the side.

"Now that would be something," Sadie said. "Can you see the big clock?"

"Nope," Adam said.

"Do you think we're in trouble?" Sadie asked, wondering whether the rest of her band had actually managed to pull it together enough to rehearse.

"Probably," Adam said. "Although half my band wasn't even at our rehearsal so I doubt I'm missing much. Don't know what we're supposed to be doing afterwards."

"Bowling," Sadie said. "Well, later. Bowling and food."

"Hmm. I like both of those things."

"Me too," Sadie smiled, finding the sound of the water lapping against a giant plastic unicorn surprisingly soothing.

Maybe she would just come here every day and leave the aggro to everyone else.

"How do you connect with someone who doesn't want to be connected with?" she asked Adam.

"In your band?" he asked.

Sadie hesitated.

"Hey, giant doughnut code, remember? You don't spill my secrets and I don't spill yours."

"Giant Doughnut Gang," Sadie said. "Crew? Gang?"

"I feel like we could come up with something cooler?"

"No," she said contentedly, "that's definitely what we are."

"If you insist," Adam said. "So who doesn't want to connect with you?"

"Well– Wait, should we be using code names?"

"Nah. It's all covered by the giant doughnut code."

"Okay. It's James," Sadie said. "The one who left. He– Do you know about my band?"

Adam shook his head. "Not really."

"Oh. Well James left, and then the band broke up. We all spent a really long time being cross with him, but it turns out that it wasn't really his fault. Just... life stuff."

Adam nodded.

"Every time I talk to him it's like talking to someone I don't know. Like we're starting again from scratch except with one person holding back the whole time."

"What do you want from him?"

"Just to be best friends! I don't think that's too much to ask?" Sadie smiled. "No, I don't know. He's been through some stuff, and I want to help? Or, just be his friend? Like, be able to ask him whether he's okay and he tells me the truth so I can stop worrying about him all the time?"

"Oh well join the club, mate," Adam said.

"I don't want to *marry* him, though," Sadie said, flicking water towards Adam.

"I don't want to *marry* Mabel."

"Yes you do."

"I'd take vague Facebook friends at this point," Adam said. "But seriously, I think that kind of bond and trust takes a bit of time. He's talking to you, right?"

"Yes. Half-heartedly."

Adam shrugged. "Maybe just stick with it? Maybe a half-hearted friendship is what he needs at the moment?"

"I see what you're saying, but I am much more of a fan of instant trust and bonding and all the oversharing that comes with that."

Adam smiled. "Don't take this the wrong way, but is it possible that your enthusiasm for being his best friend could be a bit… much?"

"You're saying *I'm* a bit much?" Sadie asked, in mock-horror.

"No, I–"

"You're saying I need to back right off?"

Adam laughed. "Not exactly, but sometimes if you're just *there* for people, and you let them know that, one day they'll come to you."

"But that's not what you're doing with Mabel?"

"That's what I *did* with Mabel," Adam said.

"Did it work?"

"Yes. For a while."

Sadie waited for him to elaborate but his face had clouded over and he looked… kind of hopeless, to be honest. What must it be like, she wondered, to be that caught up over someone. To have found a love that could weather years of being apart even with no guarantee of reconciliation. Not something that she had an awful lot of experience of. She felt like she'd been so distracted by the fact that she didn't have a career any more that she'd totally forgotten to worry about finding the love of her life. So now she didn't have a career *or* a boyfriend. Well wasn't that just something. Once again, her life choices were turning out to be impeccable. Although, was anyone here really doing any better with theirs? The collective tally of skeletons in closets seemed to be running fairly high at this point and there didn't seem to be a great deal of difference between the people running from their past and those clinging onto it for dear life. Was being famous a curse? Or was it just too far a height to fall from and be able to pick yourself up again afterwards?

"Can you do it again?" she asked, thinking that she might as well add Adam to the list of people whose lives she was going to try to sort out.

"Hmm?"

"With Mabel. The whole letting her know you're there for her and then just waiting thing. Can you do that again now?" Sadie asked. "I mean, I guess it's either that, or really fight for her?"

Adam sighed. "I feel like one of those is going to end up being the wrong call. Or both of them."

"Or they could *both* be the *right* call?"

"Do we think that's incredibly unlikely, with my track record?" Adam asked.

"Shall I come with you to talk to her?"

"Oh I'm sure that would go down really well."

Sadie grinned. "Hello Mabel, I have thoroughly vetted this young man by spending at least two hours with him this afternoon and I can reassure you he is definitely not a creep and his intentions are probably very noble."

"You jest, but it probably wouldn't be any worse than how things have gone so far."

"How *have* things gone so far?" Sadie asked, pushing herself further away from the edge of the pool with her foot. "How close have you got to talking to her?"

"Well let's see. I did a lot of wailing outside the door of her cabin. Then she moved cabins, I can only assume to get away from the man wailing outside. Then I saw her talking to…" He paused. "Someone she used to be involved with, and, well, that's that, isn't it. She's clearly made her choice already."

"So basically you've seen her face-to-face a grand total of zero times? You've done some lurking and then given up?"

"No," Adam said sulkily.

"What's she chosen out of? Did you throw your hat into the ring?"

"I didn't get a chance!"

"Oh my lord, men are hopeless," Sadie said. "What's she supposed to do, read your mind?"

"But–"

"Your sulking is invalid until you've actually told her how you feel and she's flat-out rejected you to your face."

"Rejection to my face sounds like a riot," Adam muttered.

"Do you want to go home not having talked to her and be sad forever and always wonder whether you could have done more?"

"No."

"Going to have to put your big boy pants on, then."

"I can't just loiter and mope?" Adam asked.

"Not now you've dragged me into this sorry state of affairs," Sadie said, grinning at him. "Welcome to Team Sadie. Buckle up, bitch."

36

"What now?"

Adam looked at Sadie, wet hair hanging around her face; a growing damp patch around the neckline of her sweatshirt. They'd finally called it a day in the pool when their fingers started to resemble prunes, and were currently standing outside the pool complex contemplating their next move.

"Unsure," he said.

"Have we missed lunch?"

"I would assume so."

"It's not time for bowling?"

"No."

Sadie looked at her phone.

"I'm so hungry," she said, tapping at the screen. "I'll find out what everyone else is doing, hang on."

Her phone buzzed almost instantly in reply.

"We are in trouble," she said, nodding. "*Our absence has been noted.*"

"Nice to be missed, I guess."

"They're currently holding owls." She looked at Adam. "Do you want to hold an owl?"

He frowned. "I don't think so? Do you want to hold an owl?"

"I'd rather eat an owl."

Adam laughed out loud. "Is that something that happens? Is this another one of your childhood holiday tales? *Every year we went to Haven and ate an owl.*"

"No!" Sadie said, laughing too. "But I am *starving*. Can we get food outside of official meal times? Honestly, are we actually adults, or have we been shipped off to boarding school by our awful parents and all this is some kind of deluded coping mechanism?"

"I know where we can get some food," Adam said.

"Thank God."

"I don't know if I can actually *find* it…"

"I have a map, if that helps?" Sadie asked, pulling a folded piece of paper out of her back pocket.

"You legend," Adam said, taking it from her and trying work out where they were. "Ah, okay, so here's the swimming pool." He pointed to the middle of the map. "Oh we're not too far away. This is where we need to go."

"The Lounge," Sadie read. "What is it? I don't think I've even been over that side."

"It's a really nice bar. With food. My aunt works here; she took me there yesterday."

"What!" Sadie exclaimed. "Is that even allowed? Isn't that nepotism? Or conflict of interest, or something?"

"I didn't realise we were working for the council," Adam said, grinning.

"What other cool stuff do you know about that I don't?"

"I literally only spent an hour with her yesterday. This is the only insider knowledge I have to offer you."

"Well I'll take it," Sadie said. "So how do we get there?"

"Head for the lake and follow it round, I guess?"

"Or we could go *across* the lake," Sadie said, a wild glint in her eye.

"I don't know if I want to ask," Adam said. "Does everything involve some kind of water-based peril with you?"

"Oh no," Sadie said. "There'll be land-based peril too."

"Can't wait," Adam said dryly.

She took the map from him and he followed her as she cut through the trees along a scrappy little path, eventually coming out opposite the beach. The pedalos bobbed gently in the water and Sadie looked pointedly at him.

"What are your pedalo skills like?"

"About on a par with my water slide skills," Adam said. "Is this like carjacking? Are we going to end up being chased by a police speedboat and hauled off to jail?"

"You know what I think?" Sadie asked.

"What?"

"I think we can do whatever we like," she whispered, grinning mischievously. "For we are former celebrities! Come on."

They walked along the wooden jetty and Sadie stepped gingerly into the pedalo moored on the end of the row. It lurched in the water and she almost went head first over the other side.

"I think you're supposed to hold it for me!" she said, sliding down into her seat.

"Hey, I'm not the one who decided to do this without supervision," Adam said, joining her in the boat. "I can't really call myself a former celebrity, anyway."

"Why not?" Sadie asked.

"I wasn't ever famous," Adam said unhooking the pedalo from the jetty.

"So what are you doing here, then?" Sadie asked, as they drifted slowly along. "I have to admit, none of you looked familiar, but I just assumed maybe you came slightly after my time."

"Honestly, I don't really know *what* we're doing here," Adam said. "The more I think about it, the more I think it's completely bizarre that we were invited to be on the show."

"But you're in a supergroup with Granola Fantasy?"

"Yeah, we're here because of them," Adam said. "They signed us to their label, we put down some tracks, drank a lot, pissed about at some festivals, and then Granola Fantasy split up and it all went poof, as if it had never happened in the first place."

"Did your band split up?" Sadie asked, her feet moving with the pedals even though Adam was fairly sure he was doing the majority of the legwork.

"No, but it didn't really work after that. It didn't feel the same. I wasn't bothered so much, but Nat had got a taste of the big time and that was all he wanted. It stopped being about the music and just the sheer joy of playing a gig. He was constantly chasing a way back in."

"Why did Granola Fantasy split up?" Sadie asked.

Adam paused. "Well, *because of Mabel*, is the official line within the band, but it wasn't because of Mabel. It was because Jay showed himself up as the snake he really is, and Freddie couldn't get past that. Rightly so. But they all blame her, and so does Nat. So it's a bit difficult, her being here."

"Those *two other boys*, in your story…"

Adam nodded. "Freddie and Jay." He smiled ruefully. "This guy didn't stand a chance."

"Did you say you saw her talking to one of them?"

"Yeah. Jay. On Tuesday night. And then he turned up late to the scavenger hunt yesterday claiming he'd had a late night, or something." He sighed.

"You think he was with Mabel?"

Adam shrugged. "Huge coincidence, no?"

"Is Jay a bad guy?" Sadie asked.

"Yes," Adam said. "He's the worst."

"Still?"

"Hell yeah."

"Was he a bad guy to Mabel?"

Adam shrugged. "I think so, but I guess the only people who really know what went on is the two of them."

"Is she the type of person who'd go back to something even though she knew it was bad for her?"

"I don't think I even know *what* type of person she is any more," Adam said. "It turns out she actually works *for* my aunt, if you can believe that coincidence, but when I was asking her about Mabel yesterday it's like she was talking about a completely different person. She said she was hard to get to know; that she never lets anyone in."

"And your Mabel was…"

"She was tremendous. Like a full moon in a pitch black sky."

Sadie smiled. "You know, I think if someone was describing me like that I'd want to know about it."

Adam sighed. "I just… I wish I knew what had happened to her between then and now. If she didn't look exactly the same I wouldn't have even known it was her. How can someone change so much?"

"I feel like that about James," Sadie said. "He's *so* different, like his trauma reaches to depths that I don't even *have*."

"Yeah," Adam said. "Are we the lucky ones?"

"I don't know," Sadie said.

Adam nodded thoughtfully, slowing down his pedalling and leaning back into the seat.

They were in the middle of the lake and not making a huge amount of progress towards their destination, it had to be said. There seemed to be a lot more water now they were actually on it. His gaze drifted along the shoreline, taking in the rippling water, the ducks, the blonde girl walking along the path…

"Oh Christ," he muttered.

Because of course this would happen now. Of course this would be the next time he would see her, when he was sitting in a pedalo in the middle of a lake with a girl in a rainbow-coloured jumper.

"Does this look romantic?" he asked, hoping that perhaps some kind of weird trick of the light thing would make them invisible from the shore.

"What, *this*?" Sadie gestured around the boat.

"Yeah."

"No?"

Sadie turned to look in the direction he was looking at the precise moment that Mabel looked over at them. Adam saw the expression on her face change as if in slow motion: the deepening of a frown, her eyes widening in surprise.

"Is that Mabel?" Sadie hissed.

"Yes," Adam whispered back.

"Shit."

He felt their eyes meet across the water, and it was just about the most intense and heart-wrenching moment of his entire life, because this time she didn't run, she just looked at him, and her expression didn't change, and he didn't know what to do, so he just smiled hopefully and raised his hand in futile greeting. And she looked for just a moment longer, her expression unchanged, and Adam's breath caught in his throat and his heart fell right out of his chest and plunged into the water, and his whole body was simultaneously set on fire and turned to stone, one hand still pointlessly raised in the air. But the boat continued to drift and although Adam turned his head slightly to try to maintain eye contact, Mabel looked away, and then she was gone.

Adam blinked: stunned, wounded.

"That didn't look like someone who had already made her choice," Sadie said.

"Oh don't," he said, looking back towards her. "Don't get my hopes up like that."

"Why not?"

"It's the hope that kills you, isn't that what they say?"

"Who says that?"

"Incredibly pessimistic yet realistic people?" Adam said. "Jonny thinks I've fabricated this entire thing. Like some kind of deluded weirdo."

"Jonny didn't just see *that*," Sadie said.

"I don't know what any of this even is," Adam said hopelessly.

"She didn't run away this time."

"No, she didn't," Adam said. "But then I am quite safely on a boat in the middle of the lake so it probably didn't seem necessary."

"You are going to talk to her, aren't you?" Sadie asked. "When you're not on a boat in the middle of the lake."

"I'll *try*, but..."

Sadie nodded. "Just try."

"Let's just go and eat, shall we?" Adam said, trying to shake off the image of Mabel watching him from the shore. "I'm sick of hearing myself talk about it."

"Well, Adam, I'd love to, but..." Sadie gestured at the water surrounding them.

"I think, *Sadie*, this particular mode of transport was not my idea, actually," he said, smiling. "And, just a tip, but you might want to try actually peddling? Instead of pretending to and letting me do all the work?"

"I am pedalling!" Sadie protested.

"Sure."

"I am!"

"Hey, I believe you! Just, you know, I'm going for my life here and we don't seem to be getting very far..."

"Any minute now I'm going to start pedalling so hard you're going to be thrown from your seat. And then you'll be sorry."

"Well, I can't wait."

Sadie grinned. "Fine, I wasn't pedalling."

"Mmm-hmm."

"But I am now."

"I can tell. Very impressive. We might even make it there before sundown."

"At the very least before midnight."

And, he thought, if it weren't for the traumatic eye contact exchange with Mabel, some might say that the day hadn't turned out all that badly after all.

37

"I am so full," Sadie said, leaning back in her chair. "You know like on *I'm A Celebrity* when they sometimes get extra food and it's like the best thing ever because they're usually so hungry? That's what this was like."

Adam laughed. "Happy to say I have never watched a single episode of that show."

"Why? Because you're a boy?" Sadie asked.

Had she really just spent the majority of a day with this complete stranger? She felt like she'd known him for a lifetime. Wasn't it strange, the way sometimes you met someone and just instantly clicked? It was like pure magic when that happened.

"No! It's just… not my thing."

"What is your thing? iPlayer reruns of 1985 Glastonbury?"

"You are so catty, you know that?" Adam said, grinning. "That's the last time I bring you to a secret bar."

"I'm only teasing. You are very sensitive," Sadie said, making a face at him. "*Is* this place a secret, or can I bring other people here?"

Adam shrugged. "My aunt seemed to think it was going to be used for something at some point so I don't think it's a secret," he said. "Unless it's supposed to be something that's going to be revealed to us with a big grand flourish as a reward for good behaviour."

"I would love it if that was happening right now and we're both just sat here as they reveal it," Sadie said. "Like, hiiiiii."

"And talking of the TV show we're supposed to be filming…"

"Time to go back?"

"Probably better had before they send out a search party."

"Or assume we're secretly shagging and edit the whole of the show around something that's not actually happening," Sadie said, getting up and tucking her chair back under the table.

"Well yes, or that," Adam agreed, doing the same.

"This was a nice holiday from our bands, though."

"It was."

They left through the doors at the front, picking their way down the wooden steps, the afternoon wine hitting Sadie at the same time as the fresh air.

"I don't have to do a rehearsal or an interview now, do I?" she asked. "I think I'm capable of neither."

"No, don't worry, it's just throwing a really heavy ball in a straight line," Adam said. "Piece of cake after half a bottle of wine."

"And I drunk-bowl all the time, so…"

Adam looked at her as they walked. "Really?"

"No!" Sadie chuckled. "I haven't actually been bowling for years. Mainly due to the fact that I'm not 15 years old."

Adam smiled. "You are not what I thought you would be like, you know."

"Me?"

"You."

Sadie eyed him in surprise. "How do you mean? We didn't know each other before today!"

"I knew *of* you," Adam said. "You're a *former celebrity*, remember? You were on TV when I was slumming it in my band, playing dingy pubs to five people at a time. Which was our minimum baseline for a successful gig, by the way, just to put it into context. And you played a roadshow with Granola Fantasy once – I was there with them."

"*Were* you!"

"Yep, just, you know, wasting my own time."

"So what did you think I'd be like?" Sadie asked, interest piqued.

"So much cooler," Adam said, grinning, and Sadie let out an involuntary guffaw of laughter. "No, but seriously, I thought you'd be much more like the popular mean girls at secondary school. Unapproachable. *Sneery*."

"*Me?*" Sadie smirked in surprise.

Surprised that anyone would mistake her for a popular mean girl; surprised that anyone was ever thinking anything about her at all.

"Yeah, you know, like, scary as hell."

"*Really?*" Sadie asked. "In *this* sweatshirt?"

Adam laughed. "It's a work of art, mate."

"Damn right it is," Sadie said. "So are you horribly disappointed that I'm not actually cool?"

"Sadie," Adam said, smiling at her. "You are right up my street."

She grinned. "Why did you think I'd be cool?"

"I don't know, it's just the vibe you give off," Adam said. "You're so confident, and colourful, and you always seem to burst into the room. You're very bouncy."

Sadie nodded, processing Adam's string of compliments. That was pretty nice, wasn't it? Being known for bursting into a room. And she would never have imagined that anyone would have described her as *confident*. Or *bouncy*, but that was much more of a niche compliment.

"I thought you'd be more serious," she said. "The bad kind of cool, you know?"

"Yeah, I know the type."

"But you're not. You're the good kind," she said, elbowing him affectionately.

"Oh well there you are!" said Ryan loudly, appearing literally as if from nowhere, with Mia.

"Where have you *been* all day?" Mia asked.

"Oh hi!" Sadie exclaimed. "I've been with Adam!"

"Have you now," Ryan said, raising an eyebrow at both of them

"Sir, I know that look, and I assure you I haven't laid a finger on her," Adam said.

"Adam thinks I'm cool," Sadie said, as Ryan fell into step next to her.

"Well Adam is wrong," Ryan said.

She giggled and he slipped his hand into hers, like he always used to; like she had come to think he never would again.

"This is Mia and Ryan!" Sadie said to Adam. "From my band. They're the best ones."

"True," Ryan said.

"Adam is from Prairie Dogs but it turns out he's the good kind of cool," Sadie said, the lovely warm feeling she always got around Ryan combining with the wine to make her feel wonderfully tipsy.

"Have you two been boozing in the middle of the day?" Ryan asked. "Christ, we haven't even been here a week yet."

Sadie grinned. "We turned a bad day into a good day. Right?" She looked to Adam. "Oh, with a short bad bit in the middle."

"Just a brief interlude," Adam said, nodding.

"How was holding owls?" Sadie asked.

"Yeah well we held owls, and then all of us who weren't skiving got awarded modelling contracts and given a million pounds," Ryan said. "It's a shame you missed it."

"Have Cameron and James murdered each other yet?" Sadie asked, the stress of that morning's rehearsals feeling so far away now.

"They did try quite hard after you left, actually. To learn the dance. Not to murder each other," Mia said. "I think we know it's serious when Sadie storms out of a room."

"I do save all my storming out for very serious situations," Sadie said. "I wish Cameron would stop picking at James, though. It's so unnecessary. Oh and now I feel stressed again."

"Back in the pedalo!" Adam said.

"He's just getting it all out," Ryan said. "He'll settle down."

Sadie wanted to believe him, she really did, but she was more concerned about what Cameron's constant antagonising was doing to James' already fragile situation. If you were already at a low point, and surrounded by your worst triggers, how much more could you really tolerate? Especially when Ryan was also quite blatantly eying up your girlfriend. Yeah, life was definitely simpler out on the lake.

"Do I have time to shower before bowling?" Sadie asked as they reached more familiar territory. "I feel like I've been pickled in chlorine."

"You smell like you've been pickled in *wine*," Ryan said.

"Thank you, friend," Sadie said.

"I will escort you back to our cabin for a shower and I'm also going to make sure you don't lie down at any point because I think we've got a serious nap risk on our hands here," Ryan said.

"Are we all going in the same direction?" Sadie asked.

"Not me," Adam said. "I think my cabin is that way."

"I'll see you at bowling, then?" Sadie said, going in for an unsolicited hug.

She was pleasantly surprised when Adam hugged her back. He smelled like chlorine too.

"You're lovely," she said, without thinking. "Don't give up on her."

He smiled at her, looking thoughtful.

"Nice to meet you, man," Ryan said, shaking his hand.

Adam nodded. "Likewise. See you later."

Ryan cocked his head at Sadie as they walked away from Adam.

"And that was…?"

"That was Adam," Sadie said airily.

"Yes I know *that*," Ryan said. "And you've been running around the site with him all day because…?"

"Why, are you jealous?" Sadie stuck her tongue out at him. "Worried he's better company than you?"

"No," Ryan said, putting his arm around her. "Just keeping an eye on you. You fragile, vulnerable young lady."

Sadie smiled, resting her head against his shoulder.

"Well thank you, but I've managed perfectly fine without you for this long."

"Has she?" Ryan asked Mia.

Mia smiled. "Well I don't think you'd have approved of any of the boys Sadie has brought back to the flat recently…"

"Yeah, that's what I thought."

Sadie sighed, wrapped up in a cosy haze of food and wine and this lovely lovely enduring friendship. "You guys are the worst," she said happily. "I couldn't love you more."

38

"Shouldn't you be tucked up in your cabin watching a rom-com, or something?" Ryan asked, sitting down on the picnic bench next to Kitty as she pretended to be engrossed in the starry sky above them.

She didn't know how much more leaping out of her chest it was possible for her heart to take, but what a way to die.

"Shouldn't you be bowling?" she retorted.

"Thought I'd see if there was anything more interesting happening outside."

"And is there?"

Playing it cool was almost impossible around Ryan but she supposed she had to at least appear like she wasn't hanging on his every word. Although he didn't seem at all surprised to see her sitting outside in the dark on her own so she assumed there was no need to fabricate an elaborate excuse for how she'd ended up there. She knew really that what she was doing now was no different to the evenings she had spent loitering round the back of gig venues and hotels, waiting for Ryan to come out and scoop her up into his glowing inner circle, but the lure of his sparkle was so great that she was more than willing to loosen her self-respect a little for these purposes.

"Hell yeah," he said, passing her a half-empty bottle of something.

"Champagne?" she asked, looking at the label. "Who drinks champagne on a Thursday night?"

"Flash git, aren't I?"

She took a cautious swig, hoping that was the right move, trying not to dwell on her lips and his lips being on the same bottle.

"Not the first time we've drank champagne straight from the bottle, is it?" Ryan said, grinning at her.

She smiled back.

No, it certainly was not.

"Do you remember the time we sat on that fire escape with the contents of the mini bar?" Ryan asked. "David kicked you out of the bar, or something?"

"*There's post-show socialising and then there's post-show taking the piss,*" Kitty said, doing a mighty fine impression of David even if she did say so herself.

"Yes!" Ryan laughed. "*You're only as famous as the amount of sleep you get.*"

"*Here we have a common garden teenager forgetting they have a bedtime,*" Kitty said, giggling.

"Oh man, so many classic lines," Ryan said. "What a guy. He had quite the job, trying to keep us all in check."

"Especially you."

"Oh *especially* me," Ryan said, his eyes meeting hers for a moment.

"Did you keep in touch?" Kitty asked.

"No, not for years! I wish I had. I've got a lot to thank him for. Wish I'd realised that at the time. The vanity of youth, you know?"

Kitty nodded.

"I looked him up once. He's got a bunch of kids now. Crazy. I guess he had the practice for it."

"You didn't get in touch with him then?"

"No. I don't know why. Still too vain, I guess. Maybe I will, though."

Ryan leaned back against the tabletop, his elbow brushing gently against Kitty's arm as he looked up at the night sky. She took a bigger gulp of the champagne and passed the bottle back to him.

"Do you still want to do the zoo inspector thing?" he asked.

"Oh, er, I don't think so?" Kitty said, surprised by the sudden change of subject.

Not a lot of glitter to be found in her neglected hopes and dreams.

"What do you want to do, then?" he asked, turning his head to look straight at her.

"I don't know," she said cautiously, wondering where this line of questioning was going.

"What do you like?"

You. She thought. *You. That's all I like. That's it. That's everything. You, and everything you stand for.*

"I don't know," she said again.

"You don't know what you like?"

"I know something I like," she said boldly, biting her lip, trying to steer things back on course.

But Ryan just smiled and looked away.

"I've been thinking about your disappointing life," he said after a while.

"Why?" Kitty asked.

"Well, because you told me some things I didn't know about actions having consequences. And I'm wondering why you're sitting here with me instead of blanking me entirely, to be honest. I'm not James' biggest fan but I'm assuming he treats you better than I did. So why?"

He looked at her again and she willingly fell headfirst into the swirling galaxy of his eyes. She moved her arm two millimetres closer to his so their skin was just about touching and he didn't pull away. Every fibre of her body was on high alert being this close to him and she couldn't think of a single thing to say.

"And don't just say nice things to inflate my ego," he said, grinning.

Kitty melted a little bit more.

"I like being around you," she said. "You make me feel... important."

There. A snippet of honesty for him to play with.

He nodded slowly, seemingly processing her words.

"James doesn't make you feel important?"

She shook her head.

"More fool him," Ryan said thoughtfully. "Why doesn't he make you feel important?"

Kitty shrugged. "It doesn't really feel like my life," she said, before she'd really thought about it.

"What do you mean?"

"Oh I don't know. It's nothing," she said, trying to brush it off.

"Tell me why it doesn't feel like your life," Ryan said, and something about the tone of his voice made Kitty want to tell him everything she'd ever thought about anything, including all the things she'd never told James.

"It's just..." She hesitated, trying to think how to explain it. "He always has the final say on everything. And it's always no. No to holidays and parties and moonlit walks along the beach, or walks along the beach at all, because he hates sand, so I don't even know why he lives by the sea in the first place. No to drinking too much or jumping on a train to somewhere on a whim or... Buying a Christmas tree without measuring it first," Kitty said, her voice tinged with exasperation.

"Sounds like you're living with your dad," Ryan said.

Kitty looked at him sharply. "My dad?"

"You used to say the same thing to me when we were… How old? 16?"

"You were 18," Kitty said. "Seriously, how do you remember things like that? I thought you were winging it, but…"

"Why would I forget?" Ryan asked. "You weren't like anyone else. Any other fan. Any other… girlfriend."

"But then why did you…" Kitty said, not able to say it.

Ditch me like I was nothing. Move on to the next one so quickly. Fail to fall in love with me.

Ryan shrugged and shook his head. "I don't know, Kit," he said, sighing heavily. "I really don't know."

He fell silent again, looking back towards the stars.

What was I to you, Kitty wanted to say. *Spell it out for me, please! What was I to you then, and what am I to you now?*

She looked at him, not looking at her, his perfect profile lit by the moonlight, and she was gripped with the overwhelming urge to slip her hand into his. It wouldn't take a huge amount of effort: there was his hand and there was hers, only centimetres away from each other already. Could it be that… Because it seemed like he… That just maybe he might…

Her fingers twitched in anticipation and almost simultaneously the door to the entertainment centre swung open, light spilling out onto the slabs. Kitty's hand shrunk back as Sadie marched over to them and Ryan sat up and whatever could have happened vanished up into the stars.

"Hi Kitty," Sadie said.

Kitty barely had time to mumble a greeting before Sadie was pointing at Ryan.

"Absolutely not," she said.

And with that *she* took his hand, pulled him off the picnic bench and they both disappeared back inside without another word.

SIX DAYS TO
THE LIVE SHOW

39

Kitty was having a street party and it seemed in bad taste to Mabel, but what did she know about having a female friend?

It was nearing the end of the first week and the cabins on the street were slowly filling up with husbands and wives and children. Mabel had expressed her reservations to Kitty about effectively turning their street into a huge blinking beacon that everyone would end up gravitating towards, but of course she couldn't quantify it with any real concerns because Kitty didn't know about all the many people she was trying to avoid. And anyway, Kitty had said, everyone would be filming until much later in the day. She'd checked the schedule, she'd assured Mabel, and they didn't even get a break until mid-afternoon.

"It'll be cute! Just the plus-ones! Why can't we have fun too?"

So somehow here she was, clutching an armful of bunting that she honestly couldn't think how Kitty had got hold of without leaving the site, while various other people that Kitty had befriended milled about setting things up.

"Where do you want this?" she asked, holding up the pile of coloured flags.

"Oh! I was thinking between the street lamps! Can we do that?" Kitty asked.

Mabel looked up sceptically.

"It would look so pretty!"

"I could maybe get a ladder…" Mabel said.

"Oh great!" Kitty said. "Have you met Annabel?"

Mabel shook her head, smiling at a very pregnant girl who was holding two giant plastic pinwheels in each hand.

"This is Mabel!" Kitty said. "She works here! She's my man on the inside."

Annabel smiled. "Hi."

"Annabel is a Prairie Dogs plus-one. Nat's wife," Kitty said. "Also Freddie's sister!"

Mabel stiffened.

But of course she was. Of course, because apparently there was literally no version of reality where she was able to avoid things like this happening.

She had never met Annabel when she was with Freddie, but she'd seen photos. She was older than him, and there had been some kind of reason why she hadn't been around. Perhaps she was travelling, or away at university... Mabel couldn't remember now.

She braced herself, looking at Annabel for that awful flicker of recognition, for her to work out who she was, but Kitty – obviously putting two and two together just slightly too late – had already hastily commandeered her attention and was talking about pinwheel placement.

"I'll go and find a ladder," Mabel muttered, turning and almost immediately bumping into Jay.

She flinched as he put his hands out to deflect her, half of the bunting tumbling onto the floor.

"What are you doing here?" she hissed, glancing back at Kitty and Annabel.

"I brought you a sandwich," he said, picking up the trailing bunting and bundling it back on top of the pile.

"Aren't you supposed to be filming?"

"I heard there was a party," he said.

"How?"

Jay shrugged. "On the wind."

"I can't be out here," Mabel said, stamping past Jay and down the road.

She knew he'd follow her whether she wanted him to or not, no pleasantries required. He was like a cat that thought itself the king of the street: if he wanted the roast chicken he was going to come right into your house and take it. She didn't really know why she hadn't already put a stop to the way he'd been hanging around her over the last few days. She *did* know that it was stupid, whatever it was that they were doing. Old habits clinging on to the bitter end, she supposed.

She opened the door of the cabin with her elbow, depositing the bunting just inside the door.

"You're not coming in," she said to Jay, stepping back outside and closing the door behind her.

She didn't like him in her space; didn't like seeing the kittens climbing onto his lap. The orbit needed to be wider than that.

"All right," he said, that arrogant smile playing across his lips. "Lunch al fresco, then."

Mabel nodded slightly, heading round the side of the cabin to the patio.

"Nat's not going to like you hanging out with Annabel," Jay said, throwing two packaged sandwiches down onto the table.

"I'm not *hanging out* with Annabel. I didn't know who she was."

"Sure."

"Does Nat know you're here, because you should probably get permission," Mabel said curtly, not touching the sandwiches.

"I don't give a fuck what Nat thinks. I do what I want."

"Why are you here?" Mabel asked.

"I told you. For lunch. With you."

"I'm not hungry," she muttered.

Jay sat back in his chair. "You can be a bitch to me all you want but I know you don't want me to go," he said. "Why don't you just eat the fucking sandwich and enjoy my company."

Mabel glowered but took a sandwich anyway. She *was* hungry – she couldn't actually remember the last time she'd eaten something. Had she had breakfast? Why couldn't she remember?

"Does Annabel know who I am?" she asked hesitantly.

"Why, are you a celebrity now?"

Mabel sighed. Oh how she hated this.

"I mean…"

"I know what you mean. You want to know if we're all still pondering over *The Mystery of Missing Mabel*. If we get together at barbeques and talk about you over a couple of beers."

He held her gaze and she couldn't say he was wrong.

"*Nobody* is talking about you, love," Jay said. "And no one cares that you're back."

He screwed his sandwich wrapper up and flicked it into the middle of the table.

"Except for me."

"Why do you care?" Mabel asked, her voice smaller than she'd like.

"Unfinished business," Jay said, winking at her.

The sound of footsteps down the side of the cabin made them both turn to look, and Mabel's stomach lurched so much she thought the half a sandwich she'd eaten was going to come straight back up again. She stood up as Nat approached the table, his expression hard.

"A word," he said, looking straight at her. "Fuck off a minute will you, Jay?"

Jay made a mock-horrified face that only Mabel could see, his expression fading back to a smirk as he waved glibly behind Nat's back before disappearing from view.

"What are you playing at?" Nat asked.

Not so much as a hello from the brother she hadn't seen for almost a decade.

"Did you tell Annabel who you are?"

She shook her head.

"You don't talk to her," Nat said, stepping forward into her personal space. "You understand? You're *nothing* to this family."

His anger wrong-footed Mabel and for a moment she forgot that he was trespassing on her territory and not the other way around. She'd expected this kind of reaction from Jay, and Freddie, and even Adam, but not from Nat.

"I don't know what the fuck you think you're playing at but I don't want to see you anywhere near her," Nat said. "And stay away from Freddie, all right? He's happy now. He doesn't need you stirring things up."

And that was it. He turned and walked away without a backwards glance, leaving Mabel stunned, blinking away unexpected tears.

She couldn't take another week of this. She should have left when she had the chance. She started walking away from the cabin, into the forest. She had to get off this site and away from these people.

"Where are you going now?"

Jay's voice, from behind her.

"What did he say to you?"

Mabel didn't stop walking.

"Mabel!"

She heard his footsteps become heavier as he tried to catch up with her; his hand suddenly on her arm as she broke out of the forest onto a dusty path. She stopped, angrily rubbing at her eyes, not wanting him to see her cry.

"Stop bloody running off! What do you think this is, *Hollyoaks*?" Jay said, hand still on her arm as he stood in front of her. "I did warn you about Nat."

"I am not here to stir things up!" Mabel exclaimed in frustration, shaking off his hand. "I was here first: *you* are all in the wrong place!"

"Yeah, okay, I get it," Jay said. "But what are you going to do? Disappear again?"

She looked sullenly down at the ground.

"Yeah, I thought so," Jay said.

"You said no one cared except you!"

"Okay fine, they *do* care. But you know why everyone is so pissed off with you?"

Mabel opened her mouth to speak but Jay cut her off.

"No, you think you know, but you don't. They're pissed off because you left. You made a right mess of things and you opted out of the clean-up. You thought you could just wipe the slate clean and start again? Trash that version of your life that didn't work out and have another go somewhere else? Because none of the rest of us had that luxury."

"No, I…"

"It wasn't *over*, Mabel. You *just left*. You didn't have to make a choice; you didn't have to deal with what you'd done. You think it all went away just because you weren't there?"

Mabel closed her eyes, what was left of her spirit sinking right to the pit of her stomach.

She had thought that, hadn't she?

You stupid girl.

All those miserable years. All the running and the reinventing. All because she'd thought that removing her toxic influence from their lives would give them the space to put things right.

"It made it all *pointless*. Everything *we* did was pointless. What do you think that was to me? You think I'd screw around with a mate's girl just for *fun*? I thought you were going to choose."

And if she'd stayed? Weathered whatever the storm had to throw at her and owned her mistakes? Where she might have ended up couldn't possibly be worse than where she was right now.

"And then after…" Jay shook his head. "You know, I really thought that was it then. I thought there was no way Freddie would have you back and you'd *have* to choose me. But you know what? He would have had you back,

Mabel. And I had to watch him playing the heartbreak card at every opportunity for *months*, like I had no claim to my own bloody feelings. And then I didn't have a band, or a best mate, and I didn't even have you."

He would have had you back.

Well wasn't this just karma at its finest. *This* was justice being served: to see laid out before her everything she could have had were it not for the deluded, cowardly choices she had made. And the act she had thought was the most selfless turned out to have been the most selfish of them all.

"But maybe I can forgive that if you stay now," Jay said, his voice softening.

Mabel looked up in surprise. He seemed to move imperceptibly towards her as his eyes locked with hers.

"I wasn't lying when I said I missed you," he said.

Both his hands were on her arms then and he pulled her towards him before she could even register what was happening, her thoughts still caught on his words. Their lips met and, involuntarily, all the commotion in Mabel's head faded out, just like it always used to.

40

Adam turned on his heel and walked away from the horror show that was Mabel kissing Jay in the middle of the path. Like it was nothing. Like it didn't matter who saw.

Bloody Sadie and her bloody stupid advice.

Lay out your feelings for the world to see! Do not give up until she has physically slapped you around the face and said no thank you!

Well if this wasn't a slap in the face he didn't know what was.

That would teach him, wouldn't it, to take advice from short, vivacious women. To go wandering around in the woods in between filming. To hold out *hope*, against all the evidence in front of him, that they could ever be something to each other again.

Well this was it. No more. He had his answer and now he was done.

41

"No!"

Mabel disentangled herself from Jay, heart pounding, lips tingling as if his were made of sour sherbet.

"No?" Jay said, his face forming into a familiar sneer as she tried to gather herself.

She felt burning hot under his gaze, as if she were a speck of dusk under a magnifying glass and he was the sun.

"Oh what, you think you're too good for this now?" he asked. "You think you're a *changed woman?*"

"This isn't what I want," Mabel whispered, physically shaking.

"Because you've got a husband and 2.4 children at home? You think you can do better than this? You think you *deserve* better than this?"

Jay looked livid and she wanted the ground to swallow her whole and crush her to death. What had she done? All those years of abstinence, of penance, of barely existing under the weight of her guilt and remorse. All of that, for this? To go back in time, right back to the start, right back to the thing she should never have done in the first place?

"No!" Mabel exclaimed, her thoughts like furious wasps swirling around her head. "I don't deserve anything!"

And wasn't that the truth. If she ever needed proof that a life of solitude was the only way for her, here it was in a nutshell. Because Jay. Of all people. And once again this colossal mess was entirely of her own making.

"Oh we're going to be a martyr about it, are we?" Jay said. "Do you need me to go and print off some affirmation cards so you can tell yourself you're *worthy of love* or some such shit?"

Mabel closed her eyes but it wasn't Jay's face she saw. It was Adam's: disapproving, kind, worried, forgiving. Back when she'd been lost in a labyrinth of bad decisions.

You must know you are worth more than this, he'd said, as she'd turned her back on him again and again.

And yet here she was, still proving him wrong all these years later.

"You don't think we'd have fun?" Jay said, the hint of a smirk on his face. "I've learned a few tricks since last time."

"I can't," Mabel said, her voice wavering.

He sighed, irritated. "Oh what are you holding out for? Some white knight to come and whisk you away? You're such a fucking mess, Mabel. Let's face it, I'm the only option you've got. You should be fucking grateful."

And maybe he was right, but if she'd learned anything over the last nine years it was that every mistake you made had a value, and multiple mistakes were a lot heavier than just one.

"No."

She took a deep breath and a step back.

Jay narrowed his eyes but he stayed where he was.

"I'm sorry," she said, carefully picking up the scattered shards of her self-respect.

How different might things have been last time if she'd walked away after making just one mistake instead of one hundred? She had a choice now, just like she'd had a choice back then. But it *wasn't* the same as last time; *she* wasn't the same. She could choose to just make one mistake this time.

She looked at Jay, trying to find the right thing to say to end the conversation – to end everything that had ever been between them, forever – but the words didn't come. So instead she offered him a smile, reset the *Days Since Mistake* timer back to zero, and then turned and walked away.

"Waste of my fucking time!" Jay shouted after her, but she didn't look back.

Nothing good could ever come of being around these people again, she realised now. She wasn't here to make amends and neither were they: that ship had long since sailed. No, her initial instinct to lie low had been the right one. And maybe, if she could just avoid making any more mistakes until they were all gone, then life could go back to some semblance of normal.

42

"Kitty's making friends," James said, looking over to where Kitty and Ryan were sitting with another couple of girls, talking and laughing. "She seems like she's in her element here. I can't believe she organised all this. I thought she'd be bored."

Oh I don't think she'll be bored, Sadie thought, glowering at the back of Ryan's head.

Had James not met Ryan? Was he not aware that he was the pied piper of shameless seduction? Why was he entertaining this? Could he not see what was happening here? She was going to be having a stern word with Ryan later, and she didn't trust Kitty as far as she could throw her either, exceptional street party or no exceptional street party.

They hadn't actually been invited to the party but when they'd gone to check it out in between filming it had become apparent that the plus-ones were having a much better time than they were. It was as if someone had dropped a container full of Pinterest into the street: pastel bunting was strung between street lamps, there were giant pinwheels lining the pavement and the entire road was full of patio tables covered with polka dot table cloths. The children were all leaping around playing with inflatable beach balls and there was a cake stand piled with cupcakes in the centre of each table. And Kitty, apparently, was responsible for the entire thing.

"She's really hit it off with Ryan, hasn't she?" James said. "They look like old friends."

Did it not occur to him to be jealous, or suspicious? Sadie wondered. Was he too naïve, or just too nice?

"She gets this twinkle in her eyes, when she's really happy." He paused, thoughtfully. "I don't think I've seen her like this for a long time."

Sadie didn't know what to say. At this point she knew so many weird things about so many people that she was having trouble keeping track of who knew what.

"Did you ever hear that saying about pinning a butterfly to a board?" James asked.

Sadie shook her head.

"Only when you've pinned a butterfly to a board do you realise that its beauty lies in its freedom," James said. "I think about that, sometimes."

"About you and Kitty?" Sadie asked.

James nodded. "I feel like I kidnapped her, almost. When I first met her she was like this fizzing ball of energy, and I just wanted that in my life, whatever the cost. So I took her, knowing full well that I didn't have enough to offer. She's different these days, and I feel like it's my fault: I tied her to this dreary life that she probably never wanted, and I can't help feeling that the old James would have come a lot closer to matching her spirit."

"Why didn't you tell her about the band?" Sadie asked.

Conversations with James just made her feel sad. He was too decent for all these things to have happened to him.

"I suppose I was trying to prove to myself that the new James had just as much going for him as the famous one. I didn't like who I was in the band; I didn't want anyone else to like him either."

"I liked who you were in the band," Sadie said. "I like this version too, though."

She paused.

"Do you think you would have enjoyed it more if we'd been making a different kind of music? Like, not so pop?"

"Oh I don't think so. I think it was just the fame, and maybe some of us are predisposed to feeling this way, I don't know. I did think we should have started pushing for a less manufactured vibe, though. You had Granola Fantasy coming up behind us doing their pop-rock thing, and they were getting the same kind of fan base as us. I thought we could develop the sound into something really unique, but I know the rest of you guys didn't want to go down the route of song-writing and playing instruments..."

"Yeah, what would Cameron play?" Sadie said, smiling. "I didn't know about that, though. I would have been up for a change. Wasn't Ryan?"

"Apparently not," James said. "Cameron was pretty determined that I should forget the whole idea, and as you know I wasn't in the greatest frame of mind, so I just left it after that."

"Cameron was?" Sadie asked.

James nodded. "He said that you'd talked about it and no one wanted the change in direction and that I was going to ruin it for everyone if I didn't drop it."

"He said that?"

"Ah, yeah, but you guys are still good mates; I shouldn't be bringing this up now. It's irrelevant, isn't it. We'll never know which of our choices would have made us more or less happy."

"Hmm," Sadie said, still not convinced that she'd had much of a hand in any of the choices that had made her unhappy. "I don't think he should have said that. That's not how I felt."

James shrugged. "I don't know, Sadie. It was a pretty bad time for me. Perhaps he didn't mean it the way I took it. Jim was pretty bloody melodramatic."

He smiled but Sadie couldn't quite dispel the lingering echo of discomfort. Something wasn't sitting quite right with Cameron this week: it seemed like the deeper they got into the show, the more belligerent he was becoming. And saying something like that seemed like crossing a line. None of them had known how James had been feeling, but surely that kind of comment wasn't going to help when you were already a bit wobbly. Not to mention that it wasn't based on any kind of general band consensus. Where had Cameron got something like that from?

"Did it…" Sadie wasn't sure what she was trying to ask.

"Sadie, I can't blame Cameron for what happened to me," James said, evidently reading her mind. "I don't."

But can I? Sadie wondered.

They lapsed into silence, James watching Kitty with a resigned look on his face.

"You shouldn't let her talk to Ryan," Sadie said, feeling bad for saying it, but saying it nonetheless.

James sighed. "I just feel like the worst thing you can do when you feel someone pulling away from you is to hold on more tightly."

"I don't think that's true," Sadie said. "I really don't. You can fix this if you want to. You don't have to just give up and wait for her to leave you. If you think she's worth it."

"She is," James said.

Agree to disagree, thought Sadie.

But it wasn't her place to talk him out of a relationship just because she thought his girlfriend was a bit of a dickhead. Give it another six months of renewed friendship, though, and he wasn't going to be getting off this lightly again.

"I think you can be what she wants without having to be someone you're not," she said, trying to be tactful. "Just because being boring is your default state it doesn't have to be all you are."

James smiled. "It's very hard to pick the compliments out of your pep talks."

She matched his smile, standing up. "I'm going to take Ryan out of the equation for you. Go and unpin that butterfly."

She left James at the table, walking over to where Ryan was sitting.

"Hello," she said, standing behind his chair and putting her hands firmly on his shoulders. "We're going for a walk now."

"Are you?"

"*We* are," Sadie said. "Come on, up you come."

"Do I get to ask why?" Ryan said, reluctantly standing up.

"You do not," Sadie said, ignoring his wistful glances in Kitty's direction. "And I think you know why, anyway."

"I didn't even get any cake," Ryan protested as she marched him down the street.

"Well let that be a lesson to you."

"For what?"

"You have to stop encouraging Kitty. You don't know what you're doing."

She was probably walking a little too fast for a casual stroll but it was either that or she was going to strangle Ryan in the middle of the street for being so maddening and so stupid.

"I do know what I'm doing."

"She's James' girlfriend."

"Screw him, he left us," Ryan said, sounding surprisingly bitter.

"And now he's back," Sadie said evenly. "And you cannot steal his girlfriend. You don't even want her!"

"I might do."

"Do you?" Sadie looked at him, trying to slow down her pace.

Ryan shrugged. "It doesn't sound like there's much of a relationship to ruin, anyway."

"That doesn't make it okay."

"Seriously though," Ryan said, lowering his voice slightly as if he'd just remembered that there were other people around and this perhaps wasn't something to broadcast. "She's the one turning it up to 11. I mean, I'm just *there*: she's putting all the work in."

"That doesn't mean you have to encourage it!" Sadie said. "Ry, it was enough effort to put this band back together without you blowing it up again in the first week. It's bad enough that Cameron and James are at each other's throats; I could really do without you guys falling out as well."

"I didn't blow it up the first time," Ryan said stubbornly, kicking at a stick on the path.

"I know you didn't…"

"Look, if it's not me it's going to be someone else."

"Yeah, well I'll take someone else, please," Sadie said, exasperated. "Can't you just back off? For me?"

"It wouldn't stop her."

"I don't doubt it, but I'm just asking you not to make this any worse," Sadie said. "Come on. Please?"

"It's just a bit of fun."

Sadie sighed. "Why are you being such a pain about this?"

"Honestly, it seems a bit weird that you care so much. Why are you and James best friends all of a sudden?"

Sadie paused, not wanting to break her promise to James, but feeling nonetheless that what this conversation really needed was a dose of hard reality. Ryan was acting like a dog in heat that she'd just pulled off a particularly attractive cushion, and this was precisely why she usually steered clear of The Other Ryan.

"James adores her."

"More fool him."

"Ryan!" Sadie protested. "I don't like this version of you! Can't you just be nice?"

"I thought it was an unwritten rule that we don't talk about this kind of thing," he muttered.

Sadie sighed. "I'm worried about James."

"Why?"

She made a face. "I can't really tell you. I said I wouldn't."

"What is it? Something serious?"

Sadie nodded.

"Drugs again?"

Oh and that was another thing.

"Ryan, what you said before… Are you sure Cameron said James was using drugs?"

"Yeah, because I remember being so surprised. It wasn't the kind of thing we did. We laughed about that kind of thing, didn't we? People who took loads of drugs. And vegetarians. But Cameron said he had it on good authority that that was what was going on with James."

Sadie frowned. "But he didn't say exactly how he knew that?"

"I don't think so. But he was pretty sure."

"It isn't true, though, Ry."

"James told you that?"

"Not exactly, but… He told me a lot of things – a lot of really honest things that he didn't have to tell me. I'm *sure* what Cameron told you isn't true."

Ryan shrugged. "Maybe his source wasn't a good one."

"Maybe." Sadie paused. "There's something else."

"If it means you're distracted from my questionable romantic liaisons then I'm all ears."

"We'll come back to that."

"Can't wait."

"Tell me again about you and James working on a new sound for the band," Sadie said.

"I think I told you the full-length version of that very short story last time we talked about this," Ryan said. "We didn't actually get round to writing anything, but we talked about it a bit. About doing something different to all the other stuff that was out there. I thought it could go somewhere, but then he seemed to lose interest and it wasn't something I could do without him. And then there was all that stuff about drugs, so I just thought I'd leave him to it, whatever the issue was."

"So it wasn't you that didn't want to work on new songs?" Sadie asked.

"No way, I was well keen."

Sadie frowned. "Something doesn't add up," she muttered.

"Why don't you ask Cameron about the drugs thing if it's bothering you?"

"I don't want to. He's being especially snarky this week," Sadie said. "I can't be doing with him when he's like this."

"And now you have to put up with me instead," Ryan said, nudging Sadie with his elbow.

"You are just as bad right now."

"Look, if you've got a really good reason why I should refrain from entertaining myself with Kitty then I'll stop."

"Apart from the fact that she's your friend's girlfriend."

Ryan made a face. "Are we saying friend? I think bandmate at a push."

"He's our *friend*," Sadie said. "And I do have a really good reason."

"So let's have it, then."

Sadie paused. "I can't. I promised."

"I really think you're going to have to tell me," Ryan said. "That girl is half an hour away from coming back to mine, I'll be honest. We've covered a lot of ground already."

Forgive me, James: I am doing this for you really.

"Okay fine, but you can't tell Mia or Cameron," Sadie said reluctantly.

And then there were three.

43

"I have to get back. We're supposed to be filming again in five minutes."

Kitty nodded as James stood up.

"This was amazing." He gestured round at the remains of the party, the street almost empty of people now as dusk fell. "You should do it as a job or something."

"Party planning?" Kitty asked.

Now there was an idea. Was that a legitimate career?

"Event planning. You've got so much vision. I'll do your website," he said, smiling. "Anyway. I'll see you later. I don't know what time I'll be done tonight: we have to do something awful like bingo."

I love bingo, Kitty thought, that warm feeling fading as quickly as it had arrived.

She watched him walk away down the street, eventually disappearing out of view. She didn't exactly know how it had happened, but at some point this afternoon her fortune had changed for the worse with Sadie dragging Ryan away from her and James appearing in his place. It had been inevitable, really – she knew James had been watching her with Ryan all afternoon and there would have to be some pushback at some point – but she had been having such a lovely time and it was a real shame it had to end.

Being around Ryan was quite the experience: he was full of glamourous anecdotes and accidental name-dropping, and his flirting was truly expert level. James had replaced him with awkward small talk and some half-hearted attempt at being enthusiastic about a holiday they could maybe go on when the show was over, and the thought that that was all that was waiting for her at home was too depressing to even contemplate.

"Kitty?"

Kitty looked up and gasped, leaping out of her chair.

"Jess? Oh my God!"

"I thought it was you!" The girl laughed as Kitty launched herself into a hug. "I saw you earlier but you looked deep in conversation and I didn't want to interrupt."

Kitty stepped back. "This is…" She shook her head, grinning at the face she hadn't seen in so long. "What are you doing here?"

"Oh, just some bits and pieces for the show," Jess said.

"This is crazy! How long has it been?"

Jess made a face. "I dread to think. All I know is that last time I saw you we weren't old enough to drive a car or have a drink. Well, legally, anyway. And we were spending most of our time hanging around outside arenas and hotels."

"You won't believe how perfect your timing is," Kitty said. "Do you have time to catch up now? My place is just over there."

Jess nodded. "Sure."

"This is too exciting," Kitty said. "Come on, I have wine."

There was no sign of Mabel as she pushed open the front door, directing Jess to the sofas and gathering wine and glasses from the kitchen.

"So you're working on the show? That's so cool!" Kitty said, flopping down on the sofa, the kittens looking at her reproachfully as she shuffled them over to the far side.

"Oh, well, that makes it sound a lot more glamourous than it is," Jess said, taking a glass. "It's donkey work, really. Freelance stuff. But what are *you* doing here?"

"I'm here with Jim, actually," Kitty said, unable to contain her glee.

The glorious serendipity of being face to face with one of her old Funk Shui fan friends was just too delicious: finally she had something interesting to say to someone who would actually get the significance of everything that was going on.

"Or James, as he prefers to be called these days."

"Jim?" Jess asked. "Wait, not *Jim*?"

Kitty nodded emphatically. "Jim! I know! Can you believe it?"

"You two are dating?"

"Yes!"

Jess looked suitably impressed. "Wow. Girl did good."

Kitty beamed. Oh yes, this felt *great*.

"Wait, am I remembering this wrong, though? I thought you and *Ryan* had a thing?"

"Oh, er, just a *brief* thing..." Kitty said airily.

Jess grinned. "You legend! So was it just a hook up, or...?"

"Just a casual thing. It was never really going to go anywhere: he had so much going on with the band, you know."

"But you and him..." Jess raised her eyebrows suggestively.

"Maybe once or twice," Kitty said, coyly.

"I kind of want all the gory details and I also kind of don't."

Kitty laughed, revelling in the limelight despite the blatant lie.

"So now you and Jim? I'm guessing that's more than just a casual thing?"

"We live together, actually."

"Oh! A serious relationship! Are you heading for *Mrs Jim from Funk Shui*?"

Jess nudged her playfully but Kitty involuntarily made a face, immediately clamping her hand over her mouth to hide the smirk.

"Well I'll take that as a no!" Jess said. "Come on, spill! What's wrong with him? Is he awful? A serial killer? A Star Trek nerd? I mean, it must be bad because he is certainly nice to look at."

Kitty paused. No, he wasn't awful, was he? But was not being awful *enough* to sustain a relationship? Was it unfair of her to want more than simply *not awful*?

"A serial killer *and* a Star Trek nerd?"

Kitty laughed. "No, no, he's neither, he's neither."

"But..."

She sighed. "It just doesn't feel like it's going very well at the moment."

"Why, what's going on?" Jess asked, topping up both of their glasses.

"It's a bit of a weird dynamic."

"In what way?"

Kitty couldn't help but love the way that Jess was sitting – literally on the edge of her seat – waiting for her to tell her a tale. When had been the last time that someone had been this interested in what she had to say?

"Well when we met, obviously I knew who he was, but he didn't *know* that I knew who he was."

"Where *did* you meet?" Jess interrupted.

"At work! He's a graphic designer now. I swear I nearly fell off my chair when he walked through the office the first time. I thought I was hallucinating."

"I feel so weird about famous people getting proper jobs," Jess said, wrinkling her nose.

"Handy for them randomly turning up where you work, though."

"Which doesn't tend to happen to most of us," Jess said. "So, sorry, there you were, minding your own business, when suddenly Jim from Funk Shui turns up at your work. And you hit it off right away?"

Yes, Kitty thought, in the version that she told everyone else. In the version that she told herself, even. But had it really, honestly, been anything close to love at first sight? This whirlwind romance, where he had swept her off her feet. *Had* she been swept, or had she pulled out a little step stool, climbed up, and placed herself in his arms? Had the fantasy she'd fallen for propelled her through those first dates, where he seemed kind but a bit reserved and talked a little too much about work? She wasn't sure she could say with complete honesty that she would have ended up moving across the country to be with that guy if he hadn't been *Jim from Funk Shui*.

But then, perhaps he never really was…

"Well we went on a few dates and all the time I was sort of waiting for him to bring up the band so I could say that actually I'd known all along," Kitty said, brushing off her uncomfortable thought. "I thought we'd laugh about it and then he'd tell me all about being in the band, you know. But he never mentioned it."

Jess frowned. "What, not at all?"

"Nope."

"You don't think he just assumed you already knew?"

"No, no, definitely not. Because when Sadie turned up at the house a couple of weeks ago he was all like "Oh I used to be in a band, it's no big deal"."

"They were a huge deal!"

"I know."

"And how long have you been together?"

"Four years.

"Jesus, Kitty!" Jess exclaimed. "That is messed up."

"I know!"

"Four years and he never mentioned that he was in one of the biggest pop bands in the country?"

"Nope."

"But *how* is that even possible?"

Kitty sighed. "I don't know. It sounds so stupid saying it out loud! It just got so weird. Like, I waited too long to tell him that I knew and then it got to the point where it was just too late."

Jess exhaled loudly. "Well this is not the fairy-tale ending I was looking for."

"Me neither," Kitty said.

"And when he did finally tell you?"

"I pretended I'd never heard of Funk Shui," Kitty said with a grimace.

"Wow," Jess said. "I'm sort of disappointed he didn't recognise *you*, to be honest. Nice to know we left no lasting impression whatsoever on these people for all the effort we put in sitting on binbags round the back of arenas."

At least I made an impression on someone, Kitty thought, relishing that warm glow she got whenever she thought about Ryan and their latest encounters.

"So now he knows that you know, can you guys, like, move past it all? I mean, I guess you can't really tell him about being a raging fangirl."

"Not really," Kitty said.

"It's not like he'd find out any other way though, would he? Unless you're still hanging out with people you knew from back then."

"I guess."

"You don't sound convinced?"

"I don't know." Kitty sighed. "It's just been a really weird four years waiting for James to become the person that I thought he was." She shrugged. "Perhaps he's never going to be that person."

"It always seemed, in the band, like he had hidden depths; other things going on. Demons, or something."

"I know. I think I just hoped I would be able to get underneath all that and discover the real him."

"Maybe you did."

Kitty nodded slowly. Yeah, maybe she had. And maybe it was time to properly admit to herself that she didn't like what she'd found.

"And what about *The One That Got Away*?" Jess needled.

"Who?"

"Oh who."

"*Ryan?* He's not the one that got away!" Kitty protested weakly.

"You sure about that? He's quite something these days…"

"I hadn't noticed…"

Jess grinned. "Have you spoken to him?"

"Maybe…"

"And?!"

Kitty bit her lip, trying to stop the smile spreading over her face.

"Oh really," Jess said, eyes lighting up.

"I didn't even say anything!"

"You didn't have to – I know that smile."

Kitty attempted to straighten her face out. "Stop it."

"I certainly will not! What's going on with you and Ryan?"

"Nothing! Yet. Maybe something. I don't know." Kitty paused. "Can I say something that sounds crazy?"

"Definitely."

"I just can't help thinking that maybe all this was supposed to happen. Like, James turning up at my work, and being single, and interested in me – what are the odds of that?"

"Very slim." Jess nodded.

"So maybe this show was always going to happen. Maybe I was always going to run into Ryan here. *Maybe* this whole thing was a really long con by the universe to get me back together with Ryan."

"I mean this in the most respectful way, but your life sounds like fan fiction."

Kitty grinned. How good it felt to be talking to someone who understood. What a relief to be able to voice these secret thoughts.

"The universe couldn't find a quicker way to put you and Ryan in the same room? I mean, four years…" Jess said.

"Worth the wait, though."

"Well sure. I mean, this is *Ryan Malone* we're talking about."

Kitty sighed. "It really feels like it could be something. Being around him again is…" She shrugged. "Honestly, it feels magical. And I'm *sure* it's not my imagination that he keeps seeking me out. He remembers all this stuff about when we were together before. Like you said, I didn't make much of an impression on the rest of them. That has to mean something."

"What about Jim?"

Kitty paused. "I don't know if it can be fixed. Or if I even want to fix it. I just can't help thinking that if I walked away from whatever this is with Ryan I could be putting all my eggs into a broken basket."

"Well, maybe sometimes you need to be the bad guy…"

Kitty nodded. "Maybe sometimes you do."

44

"I cannot believe we didn't win on a single line," Jonny said, pushing the bingo card away from him. "On any of these cards! What a joke."

"Should have worn a skimpier outfit, mate," Adam said, knocking back the last of his pint.

Was it just a coincidence that the girls in low-cut sequinned tops, prone to jumping around and whooping every time they won, had been a lot luckier at bingo than the rest of them?

"No," he said, putting out his hand to stop Sadie as she approached the table. "No I am not taking any more advice from you."

"Why, what's happened?" Sadie asked, ignoring his protest and pulling out a chair next to Jonny.

She wasn't wearing a low-cut sequin top, she was wearing a bright yellow sweatshirt with a big white sunshine emblazoned across the front. It was like the exact opposite of how Adam felt, in fabric form.

"Hi, I'm Sadie."

"So you are," Jonny said. "Apparently you're his new best friend?"

Sadie grinned. "Are you his old best friend?"

"No," Adam said.

"I am," Jonny assured Sadie. "Happy to be replaced, though. It's all getting a bit samey, if I'm honest."

"I am right here," Adam said.

"So what's happened now?" Sadie asked. "Why does he look like that?"

"He saw Mabel kissing Jay."

Sadie gasped. "No! When?"

"This morning," Jonny said sagely. "Right in the middle of the path, by all accounts."

"And then what happened?" Sadie asked.

"And then nothing happened because I left," Adam said.

"In a cloud of misery," Jonny said. "Which is where you find him right now."

"Why are you in a cloud of misery?" Sadie asked.

"Why do you think?" Adam said, slumping further down onto the table.

"This was not the agreement."

"The agreement is invalid!" Adam exclaimed. "She was kissing her ex! I think I have my answer, don't you?"

"You thought you had your answer when she was just talking to him," Sadie pointed out.

"I think this is definitive now," Adam muttered.

"What's your take on all this?" Sadie asked Jonny.

"I think he's being a bit much," Jonny said.

"Can you two pick apart my heartache somewhere else, please?" Adam said.

"No, this is important work," Sadie said. "Why do you think he's being a bit much?"

"I'm just not sure he's got the claim to her he thinks he has." Jonny shrugged. "No offence, mate."

"I am taking unimaginable amounts of offence at both of you right now."

"What I can't get past is the not knowing why she won't talk to him. Even just as a friend," Sadie said.

"What does it even matter now, anyway?" Adam asked. "I think I might just go home."

"You can't go home, you haven't got anywhere to live," Jonny pointed out.

"Oh thanks, mate. That's making me feel loads better."

"Why don't you have anywhere to live?" Sadie asked.

"I'm just *between accommodation* at the moment, that's all," Adam said. "I'm going to stay with Nat, anyway."

"Nat's here, though."

"Well maybe if *I* go home, everyone will have to go home, and no one gets to be with Mabel," Adam said petulantly.

"I'm not sure that's how it works," Sadie said.

"He did say he was going to let it go now," Jonny said.

"Looks like it," Sadie said, trying to suppress a smile. "Look, you've got to find out why she doesn't want to talk to you. You have to know. Otherwise you'll always wonder. You'll never have peace." She paused. "Am I being really wise right now?"

"No," Adam said, resting his head on the table in despair.

"Incredibly wise," Jonny said.

"No Regrets Club!" Sadie said enthusiastically, putting a fist in the air.

"Maybe I like having regrets," Adam said. "Maybe they keep me warm at night."

"What if she's kissing Jay because she thinks she has no other options?"

"No one should be kissing Jay," Adam muttered.

"What about those girls?" Jonny asked.

Adam followed his gaze across the dance floor to the far corner of the pub, where Jay was standing around a high table with several other people, none of whom were in his band and all of whom were female. He leaned in to say something to one of the girls and she smiled flirtatiously. His hand was resting on her back. He did not look like a man who had just been kissing the love of his life in the woods earlier that day. Not that Adam thought Jay was remotely capable of loving anything other than himself, but still.

"Oh *that's* Jay," Sadie said. "What is he doing?"

"Is Mabel here?" Adam asked, quickly averting his eyes in case he saw something he didn't want to see.

"Can't see her," Jonny said.

"Surely he wouldn't be doing that if she was?" Sadie asked. "Or am I just really old fashioned?"

Adam looked up again to see Jay with his arm now around the shoulders of a different girl, cheering as *another* girl appeared with a tray of full shot glasses.

He felt a bit sick. What was happening here?

"Doesn't surprise me," Jonny said. "Coming from Jay."

"Who are those girls?" Sadie asked. "They're not in the bands."

"Maybe they're working on the show?" Jonny suggested.

"One of them was on the reception desk the other day," Adam said.

"Strikes me as kind of unethical?" Sadie said, wrinkling her nose. "Urgh, what a creep. Why are they all letting him touch them like that?"

Adam shook his head. "He can't do this."

It was like going back in time. It was grotesque: his privilege, his arrogance, his greed. The way he treated everyone around him with utter contempt and still managed to get exactly what he wanted whenever he wanted it. It was unfair and it was unbearable.

"*Why* is he doing this?" Sadie said. "I don't get it."

They all watched with a twisted fascination as Jay downed more and more shots, the girls clustering around him like he was some kind of prize.

"Is he going to go home with *all* of them?" Sadie asked.

"Oh, don't. I'm going to throw up," Adam said.

"Wait, am *I* supposed to fancy Jay? Are we all supposed to fancy Jay?" Sadie asked. "He's really not that good looking."

"Isn't it like that sexy scowl thing?" Jonny said. "Don't girls like that?"

"I really don't get the thing with sullen men," Sadie said. "Why would you want that?"

"I'm going to punch him," Adam said, his fists clenching again.

He wanted to haul Jay into the middle of the room and throw him against a wall. He wanted to lift him in the air and hurl him through a window; to put him in his place once and for all. But even if he did have the guts, he knew, as with everything else, that Jay simply wouldn't give a damn.

"No you're not," Jonny said. "Jay would annihilate you in a fight. He's like a stray dog. You'd probably get rabies. Or he'd pull a knife and stab you to death. Wouldn't put it past him."

"Ooh, sexy danger," Sadie said, pulling a face. "Not really. I still don't get it."

"I wish *someone* would punch him," Adam muttered.

"Yeah, don't we all, mate," Jonny said, clapping a hand on his back.

"Maybe we'll leave," Sadie said. "Shall we? Would that be a good idea? They said they were done with filming for the day."

"Yeah. Someone's had enough misery for today," Jonny said, and Adam found himself being pulled to his feet and escorted out into the fresh air.

"I hate him," Adam said.

"I know," Sadie said.

He felt her slip her hand into his as they walked and was horrified to find tears springing to his eyes.

"Coming here has made everything worse," he said, his voice wavering.

"Oh tell me about it," Sadie agreed. "I begged James to come here and now Ryan is trying to steal his girlfriend, so that's fun."

Jonny shook his head. "You two. Drama central."

"I think I was happier when I didn't know where she was."

Was that true? He hadn't *felt* particularly happy before, but this definitely felt like a new low, in a series of already pretty low lows.

"You were happier on the *lake*," Sadie said. "Well, until Mabel actually turned up. Then you were sad for a bit."

"Why were you on the lake?" Jonny asked.

"Oh he didn't tell you? We stole a pedalo!"

"That's where you were yesterday after you disappeared?"

Adam nodded.

"How did you steal a pedalo? I didn't know that was an option," Jonny said.

"We just unhooked it! They're not even locked up," Sadie said.

"Oh man, you guys had all the fun. We had to listen to some guy talk about owls," Jonny said.

"Let's go now!" Sadie suggested.

"Night time pedalo?" Jonny asked.

"Night time pedalo. With *wine*." Sadie grinned, holding up a bottle she must have taken from the table.

Unless she was a magician, which seemed unlikely.

"Yes! Now you're talking!" Jonny said.

"You want to?" Sadie asked Adam. "Life is better on the lake…"

"I don't care where we are as long as Jay isn't there and there's alcohol," he said, finding it incredibly hard to feel enthusiastic about anything that evening. "How much worse can tonight get, anyway?"

"We could all fall in and drown and no one would know we were out on the lake and they might just assume we'd gone home and it would be several weeks before they found our bodies?" Sadie said.

"I look forward to it," Adam said morosely.

"Come on, sad case," Jonny said, clapping him on the back. "Let's get you back on the lake."

FIVE DAYS TO THE LIVE SHOW

45

"What are we supposed to be doing today?" Sadie asked, tying her dressing gown cord in a bow and sitting down on the sofa opposite Ryan.

"What did you just do?" he asked, smirking at her in amusement.

"What?"

"Did you just tie your dressing gown thingy in a bow?"

Sadie looked down. "Yes. Doesn't everyone?"

Ryan burst out laughing. "No! No one does that! Get over here, you loon," he said, shuffling up as Sadie moved onto his sofa. "I'm going to smuggle you home in my luggage. There's not enough Sadie in L.A."

She smiled, resting her head against his shoulder. It had been a late night by the time she'd finally made it home, the newly-formed No Regrets Club having conquered the lake and then finished off several bottles of wine back at Adam's cabin.

"Why didn't me and you ever get together?" Ryan asked, smoothing down her hair with his hand.

"Because I'm not into fuckboys," Sadie said, grinning.

Ryan gasped in mock horror. "I am not a fuckboy!"

"Yes, you are!"

"I'm a catch! I'm premium husband material!"

"You will never settle down," Sadie said. "Too many fish in the sea."

Ryan grinned. "What about when I'm 40 and you're 40…"

Sadie shook her head firmly. "No. Disgusting. Never."

"What about Cameron? You ever hook up with him over the years?"

"Can you not? You're making me feel queasy."

"What about Cameron and *Mia*?"

"No!"

"Hmm. We really weren't the kind of band that shagged each other, were we?" Ryan said thoughtfully. "Do we need to find *you* a boyfriend?"

"No thank you."

"What the deal with this Adam thing?" Ryan asked. "I saw you leave with him last night."

"We're just friends," Sadie said.

"Uh-huh."

"What, because he's male? Men and women can be friends, you know."

"No they can't," Ryan said. "It never ever works. It always either ends in sex, or with some awful torturous unrequited feelings."

"That is absolutely not true."

"Oh come on, someone *always* takes it too far. It's too easy! There's that point where you've got super close and then inevitably someone steps over the line. Or you both do."

"*We* never crossed that line," Sadie pointed out.

"Yeah, well," Ryan muttered. "Just watch yourself with Adam. Didn't anyone tell you that men are despicable human beings?"

"I have become aware of that more recently, yes," Sadie said, giving him a pointed look. "Anyway, Adam is so hung up on this girl that the only person in danger of having unrequited feelings is me. And I'm not. So we're all good."

"Okay, Master of Friendship. If you say so. What about George? Pick up where you left off? Rekindle… I don't know, whatever it was that you two did. Snogging in the corridors during *SM:TV*, probably."

Sadie grinned. "Mostly, yeah."

"I've seen you talking to him…"

"Oh stop, it's nothing! I haven't thought about him for years; we were barely even a thing back then, anyway. We're just catching up!"

"Okay." Ryan raised an eyebrow. "But he's quite cute…"

"He is quite cute," Sadie conceded. "But still no."

"Not even a hot fling in the lazy river under the cover of darkness?"

"I feel like maybe this is something you want more than me?"

Ryan grinned. "Just looking out for your sex life."

"My sex life would like you to mind your own business," Sadie said, elbowing him. "Now seriously, what are we doing today? I don't want to turn up wearing the wrong thing again."

She caught the smirk on Ryan's face before he managed to get a handle on it.

"What are we *actually* doing today, please."

"Oh but I just enjoy embarrassing you so much."

"You are horrible to me. I don't know why I'm even here," she said, smiling nonetheless.

"I know. I love you, though," Ryan said. "I think we're supposed to be doing something with animals?"

"Oh the petting zoo?"

"When you say zoo, I think lions and zebras, but it's not, is it?"

Sadie grinned. "No. More goats and guinea pigs."

"And why do we have to touch them?"

"Because, princess," Sadie said, clocking the time and getting up off the sofa. "Everyone loves a celebrity holding a rabbit."

"Okay, but what will you hold?"

Sadie laughed, throwing a packet of makeup wipes at the back of Ryan's head as she walked towards her bedroom. It was considerably later in the morning than she'd thought it was, but luckily smart girls got up early to shower and do their makeup before losing enthusiasm and giving up on choosing an outfit in favour of staying in their pyjamas for a while longer.

"Do you think James will be there?" Ryan asked, leaning on the doorframe.

"Well considering that he's in our band I think there's a high chance he will be there," Sadie said, slipping off her dressing gown. "Do you mind? I'm trying to get changed here."

"All right, you prude," Ryan said, turning round. "Feeling a bit weird about the whole James thing, I have to be honest."

"Oh, the thing where you tried to sleep with his girlfriend during a televised reunion while he's battling his mental health issues?"

"I'm not saying it's been my finest hour."

"You weren't *actually* going to do it though, were you?" Sadie asked, glancing in Ryan's direction before pulling on a pair of jeans.

"Of course I was," he said.

"Urgh. But you're not now."

"No, I'm staying well clear of that shitshow."

And that was one thing about Ryan, at least: he was a man of his word.

"The whole thing about James and Kitty just makes me feel so sad," Sadie said, sitting down on the edge of the bed to put on some socks. "It all sounds like such a mess."

"You're telling me."

"How can you be in a relationship with someone who doesn't know who you really are?"

"Are we talking about *James* or *Kitty*?" Ryan asked, trailing behind Sadie as she gathered up her phone and lip balm from the dining table and tucked them into her bag.

"Er, James, obviously. What more is there to Kitty?" Sadie looked at the clock on the wall. "Do we need to go?"

"We do," Ryan said, heading towards the front door. "I think it's a two-way street, anyway."

"What, you think Kitty's hard done by in this relationship? James worships her, more fool him. It's not his fault that she's entrapped him in some weird superfan fantasy. The only reason you're Team Kitty is because you want to take her clothes off."

"No. Well yes, but I don't think he's exactly ticking a lot of her boxes, either."

"What, because he's not taking her to celebrity parties and film premieres?" Sadie scoffed. "She's a gold digger, but with fame rather than money. If she's so miserable why doesn't she just leave him?"

"Wow you really don't like her."

"No I don't. I don't know what James sees in her."

Ryan raised an eyebrow.

"Okay, I can see *that*. But he needs her support, and instead she's messing around with you right under his nose!"

"But she doesn't *know*, does she?"

"Well she should know. She should know *him*," Sadie said grumpily. "When he was watching her talk to you yesterday it was like he'd already given up. Like he knew you were going to take her from him and he was just going to *let* you if it would make her happy. It's tragic. Why is he so nice?"

"Maybe she needs him to fight for her," Ryan said.

"Oh what do you know about relationships."

He smiled. "Fine, but I'd bet you my considerable fortune that if they were to have a blazing row where he called her out on this she'd be all over him."

"Is that how you got her into bed the first time?"

Ryan smiled. "I was a pop star, babe: I didn't need to do anything to get her into bed."

Sadie rolled her eyes. Gross.

"What *did* happen with you and Kitty back then? Or don't I want to know?"

"Oh you know, the usual."

"I thought you said she was your favourite?"

Ryan smiled. "She was."

"But you still messed her around the way you messed everyone else around?"

"Not quite the way I'd put it, but yeah, I guess."

"Why, if she was your favourite?"

Ryan shrugged. "I was a kid, wasn't I? Kids do stupid things."

Sadie narrowed her eyes. "Was this going to be something? You and Kitty. Before I told you about James."

"It was going to be *something*..." Ryan said lasciviously.

"You know what I mean," Sadie said.

"Don't be stupid," Ryan said, brushing it off. "She's just some girl I used to know."

"You can't go there."

"I know! I said I wouldn't!"

And he *was* a man of his word, but still...

"I think you two probably deserve each other," Sadie muttered. "Anyway, can you be nice to James today, please? I think it's the least you owe him."

"Can't I just avoid him completely? Go and touch goats next to someone else?"

"Or you could rebuild your friendship one guinea pig at a time?"

"How can I honestly look him in the eye when I know some really personal stuff about him that you weren't supposed to tell me, and when I've also spent a considerable amount of time this week trying to seduce his girlfriend, on purpose."

"You two were such good friends once."

"Once."

"He's really nice," Sadie said. "He's not the *same*, but I really like him."

Ryan shrugged. "You be his best friend, then."

"Okay, you big baby, maybe I will." She laughed. "Didn't you miss him, though?"

Did you miss me, she desperately wanted to ask, but it meant too much and it was too important and she couldn't ask a question like that on the way to a petting zoo.

"Why would I miss him?" Ryan asked gruffly.

"He's just some guy you used to know, right?" Sadie said, raising her eyebrows.

"Right," Ryan said, breaking eye contact.

"Forgot you were made of stone," Sadie said, linking her arm through his as they approached a yard lined with animal pens.

There were cameras all over the place and people milling around but nobody was obviously in charge.

"Oh is this one of those weird ones where they make it look like we've just wandered along of our own free will?" Sadie asked, waving at Mia who was sitting on a hay bale holding a rabbit.

"Does that mean I can wander off of my own free will?" Ryan asked, looking uncomfortable.

"Oh embrace it," Sadie said, peering into a pen full of chickens. "Don't you like animals?

"I mean, I guess, but I'm not five years old."

"Zoos are the new nightclubs," Sadie said, scanning the area for the rest of her band.

"I doubt that, but I will continue to humour you."

"Oh there's James," she said to herself. "Why don't you go and hold rabbits with Mia. I'll be back in a bit."

"I hate you."

"I hate you more." Sadie grinned, heading over to a grassy area where James was leaning on a fence staring intently at a pair of donkeys.

She sidled up next to him, nudging him with her elbow when he didn't seem to notice that she was there. He blinked, and she smiled as he looked at her.

"Sorry, I was miles away," he said.

Did he look more tired than normal? Was the melancholia that sat behind his eyes more pronounced than it had been yesterday? Was he still okay?

"Everything okay?" Sadie asked hesitantly.

James nodded, looking back at the donkeys.

"Have you been down here before?" he asked.

"No. I didn't realise it would be so big. Have you?"

James nodded again. "I found it on the first day. I walked round the whole site, actually. There never seems to be anyone else here. It's... peaceful."

"Is this where you are when I can't find you?"

James smiled. "You weren't supposed to notice."

"I notice everything."

He shrugged. "I can't do the mingling and the small talk like you can. I don't know what to say to anyone. The donkeys don't mind me sitting here in silence."

"They're probably better company than most of the people here," Sadie said. "Was it okay with Kitty yesterday?"

James nodded. "We talked about going on holiday. She seemed keen on the idea. She always wants to go on an adventure. Whatever that means."

Sadie frowned, Ryan's words from earlier echoing in her head. Placating Kitty with the promise of a holiday didn't sound much like fighting for her, but then Sadie didn't think Kitty deserved any kind of effort in that respect so maybe it was irrelevant anyway. It was very confusing trying to support your friend in keeping his girlfriend when you didn't actually want that for him.

"I don't know... Maybe we're too different..." James sighed heavily.

"Maybe you should have left her at home," Sadie said, immediately regretting it. "No, sorry, I shouldn't have said that."

"This is the kind of life she wants, Sadie," James said, gesturing around him. "Well, no, what she wants is her boyfriend in the thick of things, bringing her along for the ride. A shining star in front of the cameras. Not avoiding everyone in favour of farm animals. But..." He shrugged. "I can't be that for her. So I can't compete with the people who can."

"You don't have to compete. Or you shouldn't have to."

James shook his head. "I'm not stupid: when Kitty found out I used to be in a band it was like turning a light on. *Finally* there was something shiny about me."

Sadie cringed inwardly. Oh how she wished she didn't know anyone else's secrets.

"And I just feel like I'm disappointing her all over again because I'm not into it enough."

If only you knew, Sadie thought, forcing the words to stay on the inside of her head.

"It's not your fault you find it hard," she said instead.

"It's not very sexy though, is it," James said.

But was anything, Sadie thought. Up close, and in real life, was anything ever as good as you expected it to be? Maybe sexy only really worked from afar.

"It's brave, though. You being here at all. And selfless. I'd take that over sexy any day," she said. "Maybe Kitty would too, if she knew?"

James smiled, but it was tight and sad and she had to look away.

"I'll leave you to it, anyway," she said, squeezing his arm briefly. "Just checking in."

Was that progress at all? He'd opened up to her a bit, at least. Adam's watch and wait approach didn't really feel as if it was contributing much towards rebuilding their friendship but she supposed it might work out in the long run. And if it didn't then maybe it wouldn't be too late to revert back to being full-on and too much.

Some kind of miniature cockerel ran past her feet – was that supposed to be on the loose? – as she wandered back over to the yard. More people had arrived while she'd been talking to James and the semi-circle of hay bales was full of pop stars being handed various small animals by people in green polo shirts. Mia now had a fluffy yellow chick in a basket and Sadie laughed out loud at the sight of Ryan awkwardly holding a tortoise.

"What is that!" she exclaimed. "That's not very cute and cuddly!"

Ryan made a face. "I don't know, someone just gave it to me! What am I supposed to do with it?"

"Pet it, I guess?" Sadie said, perching on the end of the bale next to Cameron.

"Is it even in there?" he asked, shuffling up and peering into the shell.

Ryan yelped and Cameron jumped as the tortoise's legs moved and its head poked out, and Sadie felt tears coming to her eyes as she doubled over laughing at the horrified look on their faces.

"Okay you pair of wimps, give me that poor creature," she said, taking it from Ryan once she'd caught her breath. "Let's get you to someone who can handle you."

The tortoise looked at her as she stood up and walked over to another cluster of hay bales on the other side of the yard.

"Hello," she said, smiling at George. "Would you like a tortoise?"

46

Adam was horribly hungover and it was turning out to be an unreasonably long day. Why was it that cheap wine always hit harder? Was this what getting old felt like? Would he soon reach that mythical stage of life he'd heard rumours about where he started forgoing drinking altogether, saying that the hangover wasn't worth it? The horror.

"Are you eating that?" Jonny asked, pointing at the sandwich on Adam's plate.

"No," he said, his stomach churning.

"Waste not want not," Jonny said, taking a big bite.

"How are you not feeling as bad as I am right now?" Adam asked.

Jonny shrugged. "I get a lot of practice."

Adam stifled a yawn. He hadn't got much sleep that night, even after all the wine. The image of Jay in the pub surrounded by girls had felt like a scab he couldn't help but pick, so after Sadie and Jonny had left he'd slunk over to Jay's cabin to prove to himself that he couldn't possibly be so despicable as to take some random girl home on the same day he'd been kissing Mabel in the woods. But that was exactly what he'd found, and he'd spent a large proportion of the rest of the night lying awake trying to comprehend how anyone could have Mabel and it still not be enough.

"You think Jay is going to bother coming to any of the rehearsals?" Jonny asked.

"I think Jay is doing what Jay does best," Adam muttered.

It was hardly a surprise that he hadn't shown up to any of the organised fun that morning, but his antisocial whims didn't seem to be going down too well with Freddie and Fabs. There were the rumblings of some kind of intervention, not that Adam thought it would make much of a difference.

"I don't think we're going to make it to the end of the show," Jonny said cheerfully. "That guy's a liability."

"I don't think that would be any great loss," Adam said.

"Are you drinking that coffee?"

Adam shook his head.

"Sweet," Jonny said, knocking it back like it was a pint of water. "I'm well pumped for life drawing. Hope it's a female model."

"It'll probably just be fruit," Adam said, staying where he was as everyone started to get up around him.

"You coming in?" Jonny asked.

"I feel like shit," Adam said. "Think I'll sit this one out. Drawing bananas isn't my forte, fruit or otherwise."

"All right, mate. I'll tell them you're not feeling well if anyone asks," Jonny said. "Don't forget it's a free bar later!"

Adam just nodded, watching the square quickly empty of people like water going down a drain. Apart from Jay, who appeared to be heading in the opposite direction...

Adam frowned. What was he up to now? And did he even want to know?

Oh who was he kidding? At this point finding out what Jay was up to was a compulsion and not subject to any kind of rational thought process. He got up from the bench, making his way quietly across the square after him. He tailed him all the way to the sports hall, where he came to a sudden stop. Adam dipped behind a tree, watching as Jay lit a cigarette and pulled his phone out of his pocket.

"What are we doing?"

Adam jumped clear out of his skin as Sadie appeared next to him out of nowhere.

"Jesus! Are you everywhere?" he hissed.

"Why are you hiding behind a tree?" she hissed back.

"I'm spying on Jay," Adam said, glancing around nervously. "Where did you come from? Is it just you?"

"Just me," Sadie said. "Why are we spying on Jay?"

"Because he's up to something."

"What's he up to?"

"Being a lowlife," Adam muttered. "What are you doing here, anyway? Everyone's supposed to be at life drawing."

"Oh I'm doing a loop," Sadie said, if it were perfectly normal to bump into someone cowering behind a tree; as if she came across people she knew like this all the time. "You weren't at life drawing and James isn't at life drawing so I'm just checking in on everyone."

"It didn't occur to you to just enjoy life drawing?"

"Some things are more important than life drawing, Adam," Sadie said gravely.

He smiled, despite himself. He wasn't sure quite how he'd been taken under Sadie's wing or why exactly he was letting it happen, but he had to say he didn't hate it. He missed Betsy at this time of crisis, and Sadie was a pretty good understudy for someone who didn't actually know him. He had a feeling that Sadie and Betsy would get on like a house on fire. Or perhaps more like an unstoppable *forest* fire…

"Just to be clear, are you going to randomly turn up everywhere I am for the entirely of the time we're here?" he asked.

"Oh probably. Someone once told me that I lack boundaries." Sadie grinned. "Which I think is supposed to be a bad thing, but I'm not so sure. Who's Jay talking to?"

Adam peered round the side of the tree to see what Sadie was seeing.

"I don't know," he said. "She looks familiar… Is she one of the TV people?"

"Aren't they the enemy?" Sadie asked. "Is this coming across as very suspicious to you?"

"Yes," Adam said, frowning. "Don't you need to check on James?"

"I'm still checking on you," Sadie said.

The woman looked at her watch, nodded, and then they were walking away from Adam and Sadie, dipping out of sight round the side of the building.

"Are we—"

"Yes," Adam said, stepping out from behind the tree and heading after them.

"Should I come?" Sadie asked, following close behind him.

"Yes, but be quiet."

They followed Jay and the woman down to the artificial beach, hanging back and watching as they walked up a set of steps and disappeared into a small wooden box of a building that extended over the lake.

Sadie looked to Adam for direction. He shrugged, making a face.

"I wonder if there's a window, or something?"

"It's too high up, isn't it? It's on stilts," Adam pointed out.

"Let's go and look," Sadie said, breaking cover and picking her way down onto the path.

Adam followed and they skirted round the building together, feet sinking into the soft sand as they walked under the decking, the water lapping at the shore a couple of metres away. There were no windows and Adam was about to admit defeat when the boards above them creaked and someone coughed. Sadie looked up in surprise, raising an eyebrow at him. There was the sound of a door opening; feet clipping against the wood.

"Sounds good," Jay said, his voice clear as day above them.

Sadie gave Adam an enthusiastic thumbs up. He nodded, thankful that there were no gaps between the planks so Jay wouldn't look down and see them peering up at him. Sadie sat down on the sand with her back against one of the wide wooden columns holding up the deck and, seeing no other real options, Adam did the same.

"Okay, Jay, do you want to sit down over there with your back to the water?" The woman said. "That's great. Have you got him in shot?"

Shuffling sounds, the scraping of chair legs, and Sadie miming an old-fashioned movie camera, as if they were playing Charades. Adam nodded, making the same assumption that they were filming whatever was happening up there. But *why*?

"Yep. We're rolling. Good to go," a male voice said.

"Great. The floor is yours, Jay."

Jay cleared his throat. "Shall I just..."

"Just go for it. Like we're having a chat. I'll jump in with questions if I need to, but we can edit out whatever we don't need. Let's see where it goes, shall we?"

"Right." Jay paused.

"So there was something you wanted to talk to us about? On camera?"

"Yeah. Right. It's just something I need to get off my chest, really. It's weighing a bit heavy, you know? Mind if I smoke?"

"Not at all."

Some rustling, the flick of a lighter, and then Jay spoke again.

"Something's come up that's been a bit... unexpected," he said. "*Surprising*. I assume you've done your research on us? You know about the split? That there was someone else involved?"

"We do," the woman said evenly.

"Yeah. So, not what we told the press, obviously." He took a heavy drag on his cigarette. "Me and Fred had a bit of a falling out, you probably saw. And I think he feels like we can brush what really happened under the rug, so to speak."

"But you don't think so?"

"I did, at first. Not sure that's going to be possible now."

Adam frowned. He had a horrible feeling that he knew exactly where this conversation was going. What on earth was Jay playing at?

"The rumours were that there was a girl involved in your falling out?" the woman prompted.

"Nat's sister," Jay said. "Mabel."

Sadie's eyes were wide. Adam felt sick. He didn't want to hear this: it was going to have some kind of catastrophic consequence on his mental health, hearing Jay talk about Mabel. He knew the basics of what had happened between them and that had been plenty. To hear it from the horse's mouth was not something he had ever wanted. And yet he stayed where he was, stuck to the sand, a glutton for punishment it seemed.

"She started hanging round with us a lot. Not really sure why. She had a thing for Freddie, and they started hooking up, which was cool, you know. No drama. But, I don't know, maybe she got bored, because she started making eyes at *me*, and, well, I hold my hands up, I didn't exactly discourage it. I mean, you don't really, do you, if a girl like that comes onto you."

Adam's heart sank a little. Was that the truth? That *Mabel* had instigated the whole thing with Jay? He so badly wanted not to believe it; to carry on believing that she had done nothing more than get herself into something that she couldn't find a way out of.

"And this was while she was still with Freddie?"

"Yeah. I'll admit, not my finest hour. I guess you could say I was *not entirely sober* for…" Jay paused. "Well, most of it, really. It was not a good time. Things got a bit messy, you know?"

"Freddie found out?"

"Yeah, Freddie found out, and that was that. We couldn't be in a band together any more: it was too… *volatile*."

"And the girl?"

"Oh, yeah, well she royally screwed us all over. She upped and left. Skipped all the aftermath. Never saw her again." Jay paused. "Well, I say I never saw her again. I *thought* I was never going to see her again."

Oh fuck.

"Turns out she's here!" Jay said. "Talk about coincidence."

"The girl who split your band up is *here*, at the holiday park?"

"Yeah. Saw her myself. *Quite* a shock. And the thing is, yeah, it's not really cool, is it? What she did to us; to the band… I'm man enough to say that she broke *my* heart. I can't speak for Fred, but he wasn't in a good way either, after she left. It's just not on to come and stir things up again when we're trying to get the band back on track. She could ruin everything, you know?"

"Do you know what she's doing here?"

"Well apparently she works here, but I don't know. Hey, maybe you guys could find out?" Jay said innocently, as if the thought had only just occurred to him.

As if this hadn't been his game plan the entire time.

"And you said her name was Mabel?"

"Yeah," Jay said. "Mabel Alexander."

Adam was shaking his head. No no no no no. This was not happening. *How* could he be doing this to Mabel? Adam had *seen* him: talking to her, laughing with her, *kissing* her, and God knows what else. Why would he do all that and then do *this*? He might as well have lit a match during a gas leak.

"Am I missing something?" Sadie whispered. "Did he just set the dogs on Mabel?"

Adam nodded. He didn't think he'd ever frowned such a frown.

"Why would he do that? I thought he was, you know, *with* Mabel?"

"I have absolutely no idea," Adam said.

"What a dick," Sadie said. "Should we… We need to tell Mabel, right?"

"Yes," Adam said. "We do."

47

These are the best people I've ever met, Kitty thought as she watched Annabel touching up her lipstick.

They were at Annabel and Nat's cabin, the gathering spilling out onto the patio as the majority of Granola Fantasy and Prairie Dogs ate and drank and smoked and laughed. Was there a collective noun for boys in bands? There was a dizzying amount of celebrity testosterone swirling around her and it was *everything*. This was *better* than when she'd imagined hanging out with Funk Shui, who were, in the majority, pretty poor imitations of their former selves. *These guys* were the real deal, oozing charisma, the scent of superstardom still lingering on their clothes like cigarette smoke. They held themselves like they were still in a band; like they still had more than an ounce of self-respect left. Even Fabian, older than the rest of them and with that slow Scandinavian calmness about him, gave off an air of having been thoroughly marinaded in the music industry, even if these days it was mostly behind the scenes. *This* felt like what she'd been looking for all along. *This* vibe; *these* people.

The wives and the girlfriends were all so nice. There was no protectiveness or jealousy or bitchiness; it wasn't like hanging around with fans. These were real adults living their real adult lives with these incredibly attractive and charismatic boys and, somehow, she'd managed to become a part of it, welcomed in by Annabel. And, of course, these *were* her people, regardless of the state of her relationship with James or his failure to embrace his pop star heritage. She was a *girlfriend of*, and finally now she was part of the gang.

"Drink?" Annabel asked, handing her a plastic champagne glass.

Kitty smiled, taking it and looking at the glass in Annabel's other hand.

"No-secco, obviously," she said. "Tastes like nothing. Bring on 40 weeks!" She laughed, a hand on her bump.

Well that must have been quite the wedding. Imagine your husband *and* your brother being in a band. She couldn't *be* more surrounded by it. Nat and Freddie seemed like best mates, and it sounded like they saw Jay all the time. Imagine hanging out with Freddie Armstrong and Jay Harper like it was nothing. Jesus. Maybe if it didn't work out with Ryan she'd move to London, somewhere near Annabel, and maybe she could become part of their thing too.

And speaking of Ryan... There'd be no hanging around in the dark hoping he'd find her tonight. It was a free bar and a free-for-all, everyone invited; the cameras turned off for the evening. And there was no chance he wouldn't notice as she swept in as part of the Granola Fantasy entourage. It was going to be quite something, all of them walking from the cabin over to the bar, like a slow-motion scene from a film. Surely the cameras would be rolling for *that*? And there she'd be, part of something, finally, for the whole world to see.

"Is James coming tonight?" Annabel asked. "I haven't met him yet."

"He's not really the partying type," Kitty said, unable to help but imagine what she'd be saying if it was *Ryan* that Annabel was asking after.

Except she wouldn't be asking after him, would she, because he'd already be here, one hand on Kitty's waist as he ate and drank and smoked and laughed with the rest of them. James didn't even know where she was right now and she could only assume that he didn't care.

"No?" Annabel said. "Well we'll look after you! Until nine o' clock when you'll have to look after *me* because I'll be dead on my feet."

Kitty smiled.

"Have you met everyone?" she asked, taking Kitty by the hand and walking through the cabin. "I love this, don't you? I love it when they all get together. It's such a buzz. I just sit back and watch them. It's like this is who they really are. Can you feel it?"

Kitty nodded, soaking it all in. Couldn't she ever.

"Did you spend a lot of time with them when they were in their bands?" she asked.

"No." Annabel shook her head. "I didn't even meet Nat until after the bands broke up. I wish I had known him back then and that my early twenties self had realised how cool it all was rather than being a bit snobby about it. Sounds like a riot. But Fred probably didn't want his big sister hanging around, anyway."

"Not true," Freddie said, appearing beside them.

Annabel smiled. "Well I was terribly busy back then, anyway. And I did think there'd be more time."

"Didn't we all," Freddie said, toasting the air with his bottle of beer.

"I like seeing him like this," Annabel said, smiling conspiratorially at Kitty. "Strutting around, thinking he's cool."

"I am cool," Freddie said, grinning.

"No you're not."

"We are the top-billed band on this show, thank you, Annabel. We're everyone's favourite band who imploded themselves."

"Jay's penis imploded the band," Annabel said, and Kitty almost spat out the sip of prosecco she'd just taken.

"Well there's an image I'll take with me," Freddie said.

"Something about a girl," Annabel said to Kitty. "We don't talk about it."

Kitty forced a smiled, trying to stop *herself* imploding at all this gossip being casually handed to her like she'd always been a part of the group. Was *girlfriend of* just an automatic ticket into the inner circle, no credentials required? She felt like she'd been let under the rope she'd been standing behind for years.

"You know that thing you were saying about not wanting my big sister hanging around..." Freddie said.

"Well who else is going to take you down a peg or two?" Annabel grinned, tilting her head towards the patio. "Jay seems manic."

Freddie shrugged. "Fabs is keeping an eye. I genuinely thought he'd be fine, but..."

"Jay was never going to be fine in a situation like this, surely?"

"Ah, I don't know. He seemed so steady recently."

Kitty followed her gaze to where Jay was talking animatedly to a small audience. She'd noticed him talking to Mabel when they were setting up the street party: she hadn't seemed entirely pleased to see him but she'd disappeared off with him anyway. Kitty hadn't seen much of her since and she was still trying to figure out how it all linked into the Adam thing. Maybe if she hung around with Annabel long enough it would all make sense eventually. And of course it was none of her business, but you didn't turn off a Netflix true crime documentary just because it was nothing to do with you, did you?

"Oh come on," Annabel said. "I've known Jay since he was a skinny teenager. He *always* finds a way to ruin it. It's just what he does. He's chaos personified."

"It'll be all right. If he ever actually shows up for rehearsals," Freddie said. "So I hear Nat's taking in waifs and strays again?" He looked pointedly at Annabel's bump. "Controversial timing."

"Oh Adam?" Annabel smiled.

Kitty's ears pricked up. It was a little bit like being allowed to stay up late when your parents had their friends round: the later it got and the more interesting the conversation got, the harder you tried to make yourself invisible lest you were remembered and got sent to bed. She didn't want Annabel and Freddie to realise that she shouldn't really be a part of conversations like this and shut it down when it was getting so interesting, so the best approach seemed to be just to stand there, quietly sipping her prosecco, smiling and nodding where appropriate.

"I don't mind him staying with us for a bit," Annabel said. "He could do with a bit of mothering. It'll be good practice. Plus I bet he'll do the washing up."

Freddie laughed. "Yeah, I can see that. Right, I'm going to round everyone up or we'll never make it to the bar."

Kitty had been hoping for a little more Adam chat to fill in that picture a little, but Freddie was already weaving away from them across the room.

"Oh hello," Annabel said as Nat appeared, kissing her on the cheek. "I think we're making a move in a minute."

"You're not going to give birth during the show, are you?" he asked, putting a hand on her bump. "This looks bigger every time I see you."

Annabel laughed. "Oh but that was my plan all along," she said, leaning into Nat. "Don't look so stressed. Is Freddie putting too much pressure on? I can have a word?"

"No, no, it's all good," Nat said, waving off her concerns. "We've just got a bit of a motivation disconnect going on. It'll straighten itself out."

"Is Jay being a pain?"

Nat grinned. "Yes. But did we expect any less?"

"I just said the same thing to Freddie."

"Fred is overly optimistic when it comes to Jay," Nat said. "But I get it. You don't clock up that many years of friendship without being able to humour each other's flaws."

"You have a friend like that," Annabel said.

"I do. And he's pissing me off as well."

"Adam is? Why?"

"Oh nothing," Nat said, shaking his head. "It's just this show. It's winding me up. I just really wanted us to come in here and show everyone what we could do, but..." He shrugged. "I don't know if it's going to work out that way."

"You probably can't *win* this kind of show," Annabel said, smiling. "This is Kitty, by the way!"

"James' girlfriend, right?" Nat said.

Kitty nodded.

"He's a man of few words, isn't he? Nice guy, though."

Kitty forced a smile, a sinking feeling in her stomach. There it was again. *A nice guy. Not awful.* She was pretty sure you wouldn't catch anyone talking about James behind his back like they were with Jay.

"Are you sure he won't join us?" Annabel asked. "You don't have to be partying to enjoy a free bar."

But wouldn't it be nice to have a boyfriend she didn't have to make excuses for? Who wasn't too quiet and reserved to fit in with her friends? Who could muddle along with any combination of people on a night out. Someone who just *fitted in*. Someone like Ryan.

"No," she said, her resolve hardening. "It's just not his scene."

With every day she spent here it became clearer and clearer that she was living a life she didn't want. And if she could just avoid Sadie, who seemed intent on ruining things between her and Ryan, as if it was any of her business, maybe tonight she could get one step closer to the life she *did* want.

48

"He did *what?*" Jonny asked. "What a twat."

"It's a good thing in a way, isn't it?" Sadie said, raising her voice to be heard above the music. "Like, now he's done this there's no way Mabel will want to be with him. He's taken himself out of the game. You still have a chance."

Adam exhaled glumly. "I think we've got bigger problems than whether or not I'm still *in the game*."

They'd tried to look for Mabel earlier but she'd been nowhere to be found, and then Sadie had remembered that she was supposed to be looking for James – also nowhere to be found – and then they'd bumped into everyone else on their way to crazy golf and that had been that. She'd exchanged several agonising glances with Adam across the course as he was forced to make nice with Jay for the cameras, but there hadn't been much more she could do for him. James had turned up eventually, claiming he'd had a headache after lunch and that was why he'd missed life drawing. He'd played his obligatory round of golf and she hadn't seen him since. It suddenly felt like there were an awful lot of things slowly spiralling out of her control and she didn't have enough hands to catch them all.

"I think I'm going to go," Adam said. "I'm not really feeling it. Are you sure I can't just go home?"

"Not until you've spoken to Mabel," Sadie said. "And you have a legitimate reason to talk to her now! This is progress!"

"If you say so," Adam said, shrugging his jacket on. "I'll see you tomorrow. I'm assuming you'll just jump out at me from somewhere."

"You betcha," Sadie said. "Don't mope too hard."

"No such thing," Adam said.

Sadie sat back in her chair, her stomach doing a stupid little flip as she watched George pick his way through the crowd towards her.

"Here you go," he said, putting a cocktail in front of her and sitting down. "People are really taking that free bar seriously, aren't they? I felt like a right loser just ordering two drinks."

Sadie smiled. She absolutely one hundred percent was *not* taking Ryan's "advice", but she couldn't deny that George made for very pleasant company.

"Third wheel alert," Jonny said, grinning. "I'll leave you to it, Rainbow. Stay classy."

"Rainbow?" George asked, as Jonny walked away from the table.

Sadie shrugged. "Don't you think it feels like we've been here a really long time, but also like we've only just arrived?" she asked.

"Well I've never been more exhausted in my life," George said. "I thought panto was gruelling but it's got nothing on this."

"So much drama," Sadie said. "So much more than I expected. I didn't know we had so many secrets."

"Tell me about it. There is some serious angry sexual tension going on between Lee and Craig that I don't think any of us had any idea about."

"Lee and *Craig?*" Sadie said, surprised.

"Yes! Right? Maybe they can't believe it either and that's why they're so tetchy, who knows. I'm staying well out of it. Just going to do my embarrassing dance moves and go home with my tail between my legs."

Sadie laughed. "Embarrassing?"

"Oh look, it's fine for you with your swirly hand movements and sexy strutting, but there is an unfortunate amount of pelvic thrusting in our dance moves that I'm just not sure a man in his thirties can get away with doing in public."

"I like the dancing more than the drama," Sadie said, trying not to dwell on *sexy*. "Do you think the TV people knew all this stuff was going come out? Do they know more than we do about our own bands?"

"Oh undoubtably," George said. "I mean, think about all the bands that aren't here. They brought us here because we've got the most skeletons."

"Hmm."

Sadie looked around the room picking out the rest of her band. Ryan sitting with Cameron, who hadn't left his side for more than 30 seconds all night. Mia looking like she was having a lovely time with the Polar Opposite girls, all sparkly and confident in a way that was so unlike her. James missing entirely. Were all their secrets out in the open now or were there still more to come? It was an uncomfortable thought that the people pulling the strings knew more about her friends and her career than she did.

"Have I lost you?" George asked, and Sadie's attention jerked back to his face.

Green eyes – was that quite unusual?

"Sorry. Just thinking about my stupid band," she said, looking at the door as Kitty swept in with a whole bloody entourage made up of Granola Fantasy and Prairie Dogs band members.

She half expected James to be trailing behind but there was no sign of him. Where was he then, if he wasn't with Kitty? And why was she here if he wasn't? She watched as they strutted their way over to the bar. So Kitty was in with them now, was she? The cool kids smoking by the bike sheds. Was Ryan old news already? Even older news than her own bloody boyfriend? She looked over at Ryan, surprised by the expression on his face as he stared at Kitty. And for a moment she wondered whether she should just leave them all to it. Let Ryan and Kitty be whatever they were going to be; allow Kitty to show her true colours and break James' heart. Would that be better in the long run? For James? For everyone? Had anyone actually told her that she was responsible for holding them all together?

"There's a whole soap opera playing out on your face," George said, gently squeezing her wrist and bringing her back to the table. "I knew you'd be good at theatre."

Sadie smiled. "Why did you come here?" she asked.

"To this table, with you? Or the show in general."

"The show."

George thought for a moment. Sadie wished his hand was still on her wrist.

"I don't know, actually. Because it sounded more interesting than what I'd normally be doing? It seemed like it would be fun, which obviously we now know it definitely isn't."

"Yeah."

"Why did *you* come here? I heard you had to track down your elusive fifth member before you could sign up? That sounds like a lot of effort."

"I thought coming here would fix everything that's wrong with my life," Sadie said.

"Oh. Just a small reason then."

"I think I've just wasted the best years of my life not being able to get over being famous. How pathetic is that?"

"It's not, though, is it?" George said. "Because you don't. You can't. You just... do other things instead and you try to pretend it all means something."

"I don't think I've even been doing that," Sadie said. "I've got nothing to show for my life. Nothing at all. If I died tomorrow I wouldn't even leave a dent."

"Well, I don't think I'd be any great loss to the musical theatre world, either."

"I read somewhere that you only get 4000 weeks in your lifetime," Sadie said. "And that's it. 4000 weeks. It doesn't seem like enough. Do you know how many weeks it's been since the band ended?"

"No?"

"Nearly 500," Sadie said. "500! That's an eighth of my 4000 weeks! And do you know what I've achieved in that eighth of my life?"

George grimaced. "I think I can probably guess from what you've already told me."

"Nothing, George," Sadie said glumly. "I've done nothing. *500 weeks.* And I will never get those 500 weeks back." She sighed. "I wish I'd known. I wish I'd known that I was never going to come close to feeling how I felt in the band. I wish we could go back and do it all again, on repeat, forever."

"Yeah. Me too," George said. "But I'd rather have done it and have it end, than never have done it."

"I don't even know if I would rather never have done it in the first place," Sadie said. "Imagine never knowing what it feels like, stepping up on stage and having all those people singing along with you. I'm so tired of chasing that feeling."

"What if," George said gently, his hand back on her wrist again, "you try to find things to fill your life with that make you feel *something*, even if they don't make you feel *everything*."

Sadie frowned thoughtfully.

"Okay, we're going old school," George said, sitting up straighter and pulling out his phone. "You're on Facebook, right?"

"Yes?"

"Okay, I'm finding you, hang on..."

"Okay..."

"Ah, got you." He grinned. "Go on then, accept my friend request!"

"Oh!" Sadie found her phone and did as she was told, pausing on the rather lovely photo of George on his profile.

"Right, here we go, back to the days when everyone posted everything on here..." George said. "Tell me about this."

He held out his phone to her and she looked at the photo on the screen.

"That's me and my brother," Sadie said. "That was... Christmas. My mum got him a watermelon for a present." She smiled. "I can't even remember why, but we almost wet ourselves laughing."

George nodded. "And this?" He showed her a different photo.

"Oh! That was when it snowed and we all went sledging on our lunch break. Like, on trays, and random bits of plastic sheeting, and I think someone actually had a proper sledge in their car. I'd forgotten we did that."

"What about this one?"

"Aw that's my whole family. That must have been my Granny's birthday."

"And this one?"

"Venice!" Sadie said. "With Mia."

"This one?"

"Oh we went to Wales, camping. Me, Mia and Cameron. Just jumped in the car after work on a whim. Took us two hours to put the tent up."

"I don't even know *what* you're doing in this photo."

"New Year's Eve." Sadie smiled. "Best New Year's Eve."

George put his phone away.

"I don't think you wasted your 500 weeks," he said, smiling at her. "I don't think you're going to waste the next 500, either."

"Well I might need a wingman," Sadie said. "Just to make sure I don't."

George nodded. "I can do that."

She looked at him: those lovely eyes, that reassuring optimism...

"Do you want to come back to mine and watch old YouTube videos of our failed careers until we pass out?" she asked.

George grinned. "Hell yes. Let's get out of here."

FOUR DAYS TO THE LIVE SHOW

49

"I don't really do things like this," Mabel said, looking uncomfortable against a backdrop of vintage china.

"But it's Sunday!" Kitty said.

Mabel shrugged. "I'm usually working on Sunday."

"They make you work on a Sunday? That's mean."

"I don't mind," Mabel said. "I don't have anything else to do."

"You do today," Kitty said, smiling at her encouragingly. "Have you been here before? It's so cute!"

Sunday. A morning of rest for the pop stars; a morning of boring for her. No one was around. Everyone was hungover. James had got up super early to "go for a walk", which she hadn't been invited on and wouldn't have wanted to go on anyway. There were no organised activities going on and zero chance of "accidentally" bumping into Ryan. The prospect of staying in the cabin all morning made Kitty want to scream. Something had to give so she'd employed her very best powers of persuasion and convinced Mabel to walk down to the village with her in search of tea and cake.

"I didn't even know this was here," Mabel said. "I only ever really come down here for the charity shops."

"Why?" Kitty asked. "Are you skint?"

"No... I just like looking in them. Don't you?"

"No. Gross. I don't want some granny's old cardigan."

Mabel smiled. "What about eBay?"

"Do I look like I need to sell old baby clothes?" Kitty said. "I mean, sometimes I look on Depop for stuff, but I'd rather get it new."

"What's Depop?" Mabel asked.

"It's like eBay for cool people."

"Oh."

"Are there any actual shops here? We could go shopping afterwards?" Kitty suggested, feeling herself brighten at the prospect of some retail therapy.

Maybe they'd have some quirky independent boutiques, or something. It seemed like that kind of place. Maybe it would also cheer Mabel up, because she seemed to have a permanent frown on her face and Kitty wasn't actually sure she'd been out of her room for the last two days.

"I don't know really," Mabel said. "We could go and have a look?"

"Yes! Great! But cake first." Kitty smiled. "I'm going to get the butterscotch and walnut cake. What do you want?"

"Just tea, please."

"But their cake looks amazing!"

Mabel shrugged. "I'm not really hungry."

"You said that yesterday," Kitty said.

"I'm still not," Mabel said.

"Okay, if you're sure," Kitty said, grabbing her purse and getting up to go to the counter.

Well now Sunday had a purpose: find out what was going on with Mabel. She assumed the thing with Adam was still ongoing, although she hadn't really mentioned him since their daring kitten rescue. Kitty had done her best to extract some useful information out of her new pop star friends last night but nobody really seemed to have much to say about him. So instead she'd danced with Annabel, and she'd danced with Emma, and she'd danced with Freddie – which had felt particularly thrilling – and even Jay had tried it on a couple of times, but Kitty knew where her limits were and he was far too much for her. Ryan was strawberry ice cream in a waffle cone and Jay was a discarded nitrous oxide canister under a park bench. That was *not* somewhere she was interested in going.

And speaking of Ryan, it had been a disappointing turnout overall. Despite giving him plenty of opportunities and throwing out her best effort to look alluring, he'd stayed sitting with Cameron all night. With James back at the cabin with another headache (tiresome) and meddling Sadie leaving with George from Kingpin (intriguing) fairly early on, it would have been the perfect opportunity for them to have made some "progress", but never mind. There was still time.

"Has something happened with Adam?" Kitty asked, putting a cup of tea in front of Mabel and sitting back down.

Mabel shook her head, looking quietly alarmed.

"You seem really sad."

Mabel's expression softened slightly but still she didn't say anything.

"I'm quite a good person to talk to, you know," Kitty said. "I don't know you, or anyone you know. You can just get it all out and then we can never talk about it again?"

"I've done something really stupid and I really wish I hadn't," Mabel said into her cup of tea.

"What did you do?" Kitty asked, unable to help herself. "No judgement, at all. I've done millions of stupid things in my life."

Mabel hesitated.

"Okay, here," Kitty said. "An example. So when I met James I didn't tell him that I knew he used to be in a band, and I also didn't tell him that I was a massive fan of his band in my teens and had met him loads of times before."

"Oh," Mabel said, looking surprised.

"And he still doesn't know," Kitty continued. "It's been five years and now I can never tell him, basically. Is it as stupid as that?"

A small smile. "I don't know. Mine feels like a disaster."

"And it's not to do with Adam?"

Mabel shrugged. "Maybe indirectly." She paused. "It not *just* Adam I'm trying to avoid. It's all of them. It was bad enough when it was just Granola Fantasy on the show, but Prairie Dogs too is… It's a bit too close for comfort."

"Why?"

"Nat's my brother," Mabel said.

Wait, what? Kitty tried to keep her face impassive, but this was a rather big revelation to only just be coming out now.

"Well, step-brother. Kind of. We didn't grow up together, just for a bit when we were teenagers, before he left home."

"Nat from Prairie Dogs? Annabel's husband?" Kitty asked, needing clarification.

Mabel nodded.

"But… Why didn't… I introduced you two? Nobody said anything?"

"No," Mabel said. "I don't think she knows I exist."

Kitty frowned. "How is that possible?"

"I haven't seen Nat for years. I haven't seen any of them for years. The last time I saw them… It wasn't a very good time."

Annabel *had* said that she hadn't known Nat when he was in the band, Kitty thought. But even so…

"You haven't even bumped into Nat at like a family wedding, or anything?" she asked.

Mabel shook her head. "My family… They don't know where I am. Not that I'd be invited to anything, anyway."

"What, you're like a missing person?"

"Oh. No. Not like that. I just… I went away."

"And so Adam is your ex?" Kitty asked, thinking that would make sense.

A bad break-up, or something. Nat, his best friend, on his side and not hers. That urge to leave town and get away from everyone who knew your business. Not that Kitty had thought anyone actually did that, but maybe they did.

Mabel shook her head. "No. I was seeing Freddie, for a while."

"Oh!"

Well that was a curveball. Mabel and Freddie Armstrong. She certainly would not have called that one. Lucky girl.

"I really messed up," Mabel said. "I hurt him. I hurt everyone. I thought if I left it would be better for everyone."

"And now they're all here," Kitty said.

Mabel nodded.

"That's very stressful."

Another nod.

"So who is Adam in all this? If he's not an ex?"

"A friend," Mabel said. "A really great friend. And I was so awful to him."

"It doesn't seem like he's holding it against you," Kitty said. "Not from the way he looked when he was sitting outside your cabin, anyway. You don't want to reconnect with him?"

"I'm not the kind of person he needs in his life," Mabel said.

"What about your brother?"

Mabel shook her head. "He found out I was here. He was so angry. He told me to stay away from everyone."

"That seems a bit harsh?"

"It isn't. He's right."

"So…" Kitty paused, not wanting to lose this fascinating line of enquiry. "What were you going to do? Just stay out of the way until they were gone?"

"I was supposed to," Mabel said, staring into her teacup.

"But Adam knows you're here, and Nat knows you're here…" Kitty paused. "What about Freddie?"

"I don't think so."

"And you don't want to see him?"

Mabel shook her head.

"So why have you been so sad the last couple of days? Something happened, right?" Kitty asked.

Mabel put her face in her hands.

"I don't know why I did it. I don't know why I let him suck me back in. I just… I miss them. I miss being part of it all. I miss Adam. And then Jay kept turning up, and I just thought… Maybe…" She sighed. "It was so stupid, I should never have even talked to him. I'm so *weak*."

"Jay?" Kitty asked.

Mabel nodded. "He was… We were…"

Hold the front page. Mabel and Jay? Mabel and *Jay*? Jesus Christ, what was this girl doing to have all these men falling all over her? You could easily be forgiven for thinking that someone like Jay Harper wouldn't even look twice at someone like Mabel, but here he was, apparently looking twice and three times at her.

"You dated Jay too?" Kitty asked.

"Not exactly," Mabel said, looking embarrassed.

Freddie *and* Jay at the same time? Oh wow. Presumably everyone had found out and that had been the catalyst for Mabel's disappearing act. That must have been quite the show.

"Wait…" Kitty said, the pieces suddenly clicking together.

The sudden implosion of Granola Fantasy. The photos of Freddie and Jay fighting.

"Oh my God," she said. "You're the girl, aren't you? In the rumours about the end of Granola Fantasy they talked about a girl that split up the band. That's you!"

Mabel nodded, hanging her head, but Kitty couldn't help but be impressed. Imagine your claim to fame being that you were so irresistible that you broke up a band. A *famous* band, whose members couldn't continue making music together any more because *you* had come between them. What must that have felt like, to have Freddie *and* Jay falling all over her and then the movie-sized angst that followed. Had she been in love with both of them? With neither of them? Was it socially acceptable to ask Mabel any of these questions?

"So it's all true? What people were saying?"

"Maybe," Mabel said, not looking up. "I don't know what was said."

Kitty was about to rattle it all off, everything she'd read on forums at the time and heard from people in the fandom, but stopped herself. That wasn't the right thing to do, was it? Mabel didn't want that.

"Did you not know they were going to be here? Is that why you were so shocked to see Adam?" she asked instead.

"I knew Granola Fantasy were going to be here." Mabel shook her head. "I should have just made an excuse not to be here and gone somewhere else. I don't know why I didn't."

"We don't look away though, do we? Even when we know we should."

"Yeah," Mabel said, her voice not much more than a defeated whisper.

"Why is it a bad thing that you talked to Jay? Is *he* angry with you?"

Mabel shook her head. "I don't know. Jay is… confusing. But we made such a mess. I can't go back to that."

"Do you *want* to? Kitty asked.

"I want…" Mabel paused. "I want things to have been different. But I can't make that happen."

They weren't really there yet, Kitty realised. Still essentially strangers, she got the feeling Mabel wasn't going to suddenly break down and offer up *all* her secrets. Perhaps not ever, to anyone. She was easy enough to be around, but there was definitely a very big wall there and perhaps no amount of chipping away at it would change that. It was quite the attribute, though, being that mysterious.

"Why don't you want to see Adam?" Kitty asked, unable to resist trying to fill in a little more of the puzzle.

Mabel's tangled history with these two bands was a bit like one of those jigsaws where the picture on the box serves only as a clue to the picture you're actually trying to make. At this point Kitty didn't even know if she had all the corner pieces, let alone any of the edges.

"Because I missed him too much," Mabel said, her composed expression fraying at the edges. "I thought it would stop, eventually, and I'd forget."

"Oh," Kitty said, finally feeling like she had something the offer the conversation. "The thing is, if he was important to you, you never forget. How can you? People leave a mark. The good ones *and* the bad ones. Speaking from experience here."

Mabel nodded.

"But isn't it good that he wants to see you? You could put everything that happened behind you. Start again."

"I can't let him forgive me," Mabel said. "It's the wrong thing to do."

"Why?"

"Because I don't want to hurt anyone again."

"But why would you hurt him?" Kitty asked.

"I hurt everyone. Back then. I destroyed everything. Their careers, their lives. I made terrible, selfish choices. *Horrible* choices that I couldn't see were horrible at the time. I don't want to be that person again. I have to *make sure* that I'm *never* that person again. I never want to hurt Adam the way I hurt Freddie. The only way I can do that is by staying away from him."

"Even if you won't ever stop missing him?" Kitty asked.

Mabel nodded.

"Even if he doesn't want you to stay away from him?"

She nodded again.

Kitty frowned. "How old were you? When all this happened."

"I don't know… 18? 19?"

"How old are you now?"

"28."

"Mabel, that's crazy!" Kitty exclaimed. "Of course you did stupid things when you were a teenager. You're meant to! But that's such a long time ago! You're *not* the same person now. I mean, I'm no scientist but I think it's probably biologically impossible that you'd make the same set of choices as a 28-year-old adult, right? You were a *baby*! You can't *still* be punishing yourself for things that you did back then! So you broke a few hearts? You didn't murder anyone."

"But I broke up the band… Both bands…"

"Yeah, because they were babies too and they couldn't handle their emotions either," Kitty said.

She thought about what Annabel had said about Jay.

He always finds a way to ruin it. It's just what he does.

"Why is it your fault?" Kitty asked.

Mabel looked at her, frowning.

"It takes two," Kitty said. "I don't see Jay exiled for all eternity."

"But I…" Mabel shook her head.

"I was with them last night. Jay, and Freddie, and Nat, and Annabel,"

Kitty said. "I get it. Jay is... an open flame."

Mabel nodded slowly.

"And you really really know that you shouldn't put your hand in that fire, but that glow is so mesmerising," Kitty said. "And I know this because he tried it with me, several times, last night, but I'm an adult and I *know* that's not my kind of thing. But if I didn't know that that wasn't my kind of thing... I mean, you didn't come on to him, right? He initiated all of it? Back then?"

"Well... Yes, but I..."

"Got sucked in by the attention of a *celebrity*," Kitty said. "How many boyfriends had you had before Freddie?"

"None," Mabel said quietly.

"How many famous bands had you hung around with?"

"None," she whispered.

"How were you supposed to make a good decision in that situation?" Kitty asked. "You know who could have made a better decision? Jay. He could have seen his mate having a nice time with a nice girl and just left it at that. Couldn't he?"

Mabel shook her head. "I'm sorry, I can't," she said, standing abruptly and gathering up her cardigan and her bag. "I just can't do this."

Kitty opened her mouth to protest but Mabel was already weaving her way through the tables to the front of the café, barging through the door before Kitty even had a chance to collect her thoughts. She sighed, sitting back in her seat. And she'd thought today was going to be boring...

50

"I didn't have sex with him."

"I know you didn't," Ryan said, putting a coffee down next to Sadie. "You were both asleep on the sofa, fully clothed, when I came in. I don't know whether it was sweet or completely tragic."

Sadie smiled. "Were you alone?" she asked. "When you came in?"

"Of course I bloody was," Ryan said, throwing a packet of custard creams in her direction.

He picked up his own mug and sat down opposite her.

"Why do you look at her like that?" Sadie asked, inhibitions suitably dulled by her lingering hangover and the amount of sugar she'd already consumed.

"Who? Kitty?"

"Of course Kitty."

"Like what?" he asked, dunking a biscuit into his coffee and not making eye contact.

"Like you are literally lovesick," Sadie said. "*A mournful longing.*"

"That's very poetic."

"I watched you last night, when she arrived, staring at her. No, not staring – *gazing.*"

"I'm not allowed to look now?" Ryan asked.

Did you talk to her after I left?"

"No, I didn't."

"Really?"

"Really!" Ryan said. "And I wasn't *gazing*, I was just… Well, I can't help looking, okay? At least give me that."

"You have to leave it alone, though. You know that."

"Yes, I know."

Sadie fished another biscuit out of the packet, watching him.

"But you don't want to," she said.

"No," Ryan said simply. "I don't. But I'm doing what you asked me to do, okay? Or not do. You know what I mean."

"What is it about her?" Sadie asked. "Apart from what she looks like. Or is it just that?"

"No it's not just that, give me some credit."

"So what, then?"

Ryan sighed. "I'm not saying we're soulmates, or anything. She's just... Well we've got history, haven't we? And then she turns up looking like that and..." He shook his head. "No, I'm not talking to you about this."

"No, go on, what?"

"Look, I don't know why she's got in my head, but she has. I just like her! She's funny, and she's got this thirst for life, like she's barely got started..." He shrugged, looking like a hopeless little boy. "Something about her makes me want to go along for that ride. And I get the feeling that I could make her happy, okay? Now stop grilling me about it."

Sadie tried to stifle her laugh but she didn't catch it in time.

"Since when have you cared about making a girl *happy*?" she asked. "Is it just because you know you can't have her? Like, it's safe to go all gooey over her because you don't actually have to commit to a relationship with her?"

"I haven't gone *gooey* over anyone," Ryan protested. "And no, it's not just because I can't have her."

"What if you *could* have her?"

"What kind of a question is that?"

"I mean, would you actually *date* her?"

"Well she'd have to come out to L.A. because some of us have got to get back to our lavish lifestyles."

"Yeah, she'd make a great hanger-oner for your band," Sadie said, sticking out her tongue.

"Oh stop." Ryan threw a biscuit at Sadie's head. "Or I'm going to press you for all the sordid details of your night of passion with George."

"It wasn't like that!" Sadie exclaimed, quietly curious about that nice little feeling that was sitting at the bottom of her stomach. "We just talked, and watched old videos, and it was really nice."

"Really nice *and* you want to rip his clothes off."

"No! It's just nice to talk to someone about the old days," Sadie said. "I like making friends and finding out about people. Swapping stories and feeling like you could go on chatting forever. It's my favourite bit. And maybe there's a little spark there, I don't know."

"Well yeah, that's exactly what it is with Kitty! You reconnect with someone who knew a different version of you and once you've filled in all the bits in between then and now it feels like you knew them the whole time."

"It feels easy," Sadie said, nodding. "Okay fine, I do get it."

"Yeah," Ryan said, "it feels easy. That's what it is. Being with Kitty feels easy."

He looked down at his coffee mug and Sadie felt the tiniest bit sorry for him.

"Sorry you can't have her," she said.

"He doesn't make her happy," Ryan said, not looking up.

"In the nicest possible way, that's not your problem to fix," Sadie said. "Honestly, I'd be thrilled if he ditched her completely. But even then…" She made a face. "It's a grey area."

"Do you think he really cares about any of this, though?" Ryan asked. "We're not a band, are we? Not really. We all know the second we get out of here we're never going to hear from him again."

"Look, if James is going to lose his girlfriend it's going to be on his own merits, not because I guilt-tripped him into doing a TV show that I promised wouldn't be like this, okay? George reckons the TV people know absolutely everything about us, more than we know about ourselves. If you've got any more scandalous secrets in your closet you might want to speak up now. Good time to confess any murders or, you know, unclean thoughts."

She expected to get a laugh from Ryan but none was forthcoming. Was he really that hung up on Kitty? Blurgh. Were men intrinsically stupid? Or awful? She just didn't know. And then she thought about George – the warmth of his arm pressed up next to hers, the intertwined fingers that neither of them acknowledged – and that nice little feeling was back again, and maybe it didn't matter that much whether Kitty was the love of Ryan's life or not.

"Can I ask you something that's probably too personal?" Ryan said.

Sadie cocked her head at him. "Too personal is my specific vibe, is it not?"

He smiled. "I was just wondering how you were feeling. You know, being here. Do you feel better, or…?"

"Compared to what?" Sadie asked, peeling a custard cream apart.

"If you don't want to talk about it that's absolutely fine…"

"Talk about what?"

"Well, it's just that Cameron said about your depression…" Ryan shifted awkwardly.

Sadie frowned, putting the biscuit down. "My what?"

"Yeah, sorry, maybe you don't call it that. He did say depressed, though, so I just assumed…"

She frowned harder. "Hang on, he said *what?*"

"Ah, mate, maybe he wasn't supposed to say anything…"

"*What* are we talking about?" Sadie asked. "Cameron said exactly *what* about me?

"He said you needed some space because you weren't coping well with me being in another band," Ryan said, looking as confused as she felt. "And that talking to me was making you feel worse."

Sadie's mouth hung open, biscuit long forgotten. Frustrated tears came to her eyes as she mentally tried to rearrange the timeline of their languishing friendship.

"When was this?"

"Just after I moved to L.A." Ryan said. "He said you were depressed, Sade. I know he did, because I couldn't believe you hadn't told me about something like that yourself."

"Why would he say that?" she asked, horrified; heartbroken.

"Oh don't," Ryan said, shaking his head. "Please please please don't tell me that wasn't true. That I did *another* awful thing to you. I can't take it. Don't say it."

"It isn't true," Sadie whispered, feeling like something had just been ripped out of her that perhaps she would never get back.

"No, *please*, Sadie," Ryan said, looking distraught. "I missed you like I'd had my fucking arm cut off! Not talking to you felt like the most unnatural thing in the fucking world! But Cameron said it was helping; that you were moving on…"

Sadie clamped a hand over her mouth to stop the sobs escaping.

"I thought you'd dropped me and our friendship meant nothing to you," she choked out. "I thought you were too cool to be my friend any more."

"*Me?* I almost couldn't do it without you!" Ryan said. "I almost gave up and came home! I've been so fucking lonely without you! You can't just make another friend: there's no other version of what we had."

"I thought I'd lost you forever," Sadie said, the devastation giving way to the strangest, warmest feeling of relief, so powerful that she almost laughed.

Everything she thought she'd lost; everything she'd mourned. It had been there all along.

Ryan came at her then, sweeping her into the tightest, most wonderful hug she'd ever had. The relief kept coming, pouring over her until she realised that her tears weren't sad any more, but happy.

"You absolute bloody moron," Ryan said into her shoulder. "I would *never* not want you in my life. I am *so* sorry."

He pulled back and his eyes were wet too, something Sadie didn't think she'd ever seen before.

"So that's why you never replied to any of my messages?"

"I *hated* doing that," Ryan said, rubbing a hand across his eyes. "I felt like such a dick. But I thought I was doing the right thing: I hated the thought that what I was doing with the band was making you feel bad. I hated that more than I hated missing you."

"Ry, I was so proud of you," Sadie said. "And yeah, jealous, but mostly because I thought it had taken you away from me."

Ryan sighed. "You know, I was so gutted when you didn't come to that gig. I kept hoping that you'd show up and I'd come off stage and you'd be there."

"What gig?"

"In London. Last year?"

"What?"

Ryan looked crestfallen. "You didn't know," he said, shaking his head in bemusement. "He didn't tell you."

"Did Cameron go to the gig?" Sadie asked, already knowing the answer.

"Yeah. We had a beer afterwards," Ryan said. "But, Sadie, it wasn't the first time."

"What do you mean?"

"There've been other times when I've seen Cameron. Whenever I've been in England, really. He always got in touch to arrange something," Ryan said. "We had a laugh. It was good. I had no idea that you didn't even know I was back."

"Why wouldn't he tell me? I don't understand! He knew how much I missed you!" Sadie exclaimed, finding it hard to believe that yet another part of her life was actually not what she'd thought it was.

"Are you sure?" Ryan asked. "He didn't genuinely think you were depressed?"

Sadie frowned, thinking about Cameron's initial reluctance to do the show; how negative and difficult he'd been since they'd got there.

"He said I was just a novelty to you," she said. "He said I shouldn't get attached again."

"When did he say that?"

"A couple of days ago. Before I brought my stuff over to your cabin."

"Shit. You know that's not true, don't you?" Ryan asked.

Sadie shrugged, not sure *what* she knew any more.

"Sadie," Ryan said, taking both of her hands in his. "It's not true. Okay? The only reason I did this show was to hang out with you!"

"Do you not tell anyone you were in Funk Shui?" Sadie asked. "Like, cool music people."

"What? Everyone knows I was in a pop band! I regularly get the piss taken out of me for it. You know what my own band call me?"

"What?"

"Britney."

Sadie smiled. "But Cameron said–"

"Oh did he," Ryan said, raising an eyebrow.

Sadie pursed her lips, thinking about it.

"Hang on, what are we actually saying here?" she asked.

"I don't know," Ryan said, looking grave. "But this isn't exactly making me feel all warm and fuzzy inside."

"Me neither." Sadie frowned. "But I don't get it. He's one of my best friends! I spend all my time with him and Mia! Why would he do this?"

"If he *has* done anything," Ryan said cautiously. "Maybe we shouldn't jump to conclusions."

"He didn't want to do the show in the first place…" Sadie said.

"Could just be Cameron being Cameron."

"Or maybe because he knew we'd work it out?" Sadie said. "He's being really hard on James, as well. Is that part of it?"

Ryan exhaled. "This is really not what I want to be doing with a hangover."

"Ryan, what do we do?" Sadie asked.

"I don't know."

"I can't believe…" Sadie shook her head, suddenly feeling overwhelmed, tears coming to her eyes again. "I've missed you so much. Everything has been so bad since you left."

"I know," Ryan said, pulling her in for another hug. "We'll work this out, okay? I promise."

"But how? And what if he *has* done this on purpose? What does that even mean?" Sadie sniffed.

"I don't know, mate," Ryan said. "But we'll get to the bottom of it. Somehow."

51

"You coming or not?" Nat shouted at Adam across the square.

"Not," Adam muttered, getting up anyway and forcing himself to walk towards his stupid band.

He could not be doing with this today. He didn't want to be in a room with everyone pretending everything was fine and he didn't want to be anywhere near Jay. He would dearly love to have the courage to call him out on what he'd done but he knew himself well enough to know that seething in silence was the more likely outcome here. He just felt so on edge, like something horrible was about to happen and there was nothing he could do about it.

"Not supergroup-ing today," Jonny said, giving Adam a sly thumbs up as they filed into the rehearsal room.

"Oh thank God."

"Yeah. Apparently Fabs has put his foot down. Said that Jay needs to put the work in and they need to focus on the Granola Fantasy tracks otherwise there's no point them being here."

Adam wasn't sure there was an awful lot of point to *any* of them being there now Jay had blown everything up. Surely this was not going to sit at all well with Freddie and Fabs, given that their ultimate aim was to relaunch the band.

"You look tense," Jonny said.

"I'm always tense," Adam muttered, picking up his drum sticks and settling himself behind the kit.

It was a vastly better kit than he'd ever used when he was in the band before. Perhaps the only good thing about the show was the fact that they could walk into a room and find all their instruments already set up, tuned, and ready to go. No winding of cables necessary. But really, as the *sole positive thing* about being there it was not enough to negate the rest of the shitshow. As they launched into the song, Adam idly wondered what Indigo Lion were making of having to perform 'Chasing Echoes', a song that in no way lived up to the calibre of the carefully constructed, chart-dominating, pop masterpieces they were used to belting out, by a band that no one had ever heard of. Where had they even found enough "fans" to form a focus group for the purposes of choosing their best song? Or was that just something they said to mask the fact that the only reason Prairie Dogs were there was to make things difficult and awkward for Granola Fantasy? Well, the joke was on them because so far Granola Fantasy were managing to make things difficult and awkward all by themselves. He could only imagine their glee, having that interview with Jay in the bag. A solid gold trump card to play when everyone least expected it...

"Timing, Adam!" Nat shouted from the front.

He shook himself, trying to focus on the song, but his mind kept spinning out in different directions and he couldn't pull it back in. It really didn't help that every time they played this song all he could see was Mabel, nine years ago, standing in the crowd, the very first time she'd seen them play – her very first *gig*, unbelievably – gazing up at them as if her life had just changed forever. Every bloody one of their songs reminded him of her, actually, which was why he never played them at his own gigs now, but this was one of the ones that hurt the most. So honestly it was just a pure delight to have to play it over and over and over again. Perhaps the only thing more awful than rehearsing *this* song, was rehearsing 'Follow You' with Granola Fantasy, a song Adam knew full well that Freddie had written about Mabel.

"Adam!"

Everyone stopped playing.

"Sorry, sorry, I know." He held up his hands in apology.

"What is this, bare minimum o'clock?" Nat asked. "Get with it, will you?"

"Come on, man," Jonny protested. "A little leeway to be shit, please."

"We've only got a few days left to nail this," Nat said. "Be shit on your own time."

Jonny glanced at Adam but he knew Nat wasn't being unreasonable.

"Should we do a different song for a bit?" Harry suggested. "Maybe run through 'Follow You'? So we don't show ourselves up too much when we practice with the others."

Oh yes please, Adam thought. *Let's really hammer that nail into the coffin.*

"Or just play something for fun?"

Jonny laughed. "Play for fun? What's that?"

"Yeah all right, all right," Nat said. "Maybe we'll just take five. Reset. But let's really bring it when we come back, okay? We're the underdogs here: we've got something to prove."

"So much for it being a laugh," Jonny muttered to Adam. "Coming for a smoke?"

Adam nodded, setting his sticks down.

"I don't think I mind being the underdog," Jonny said once they were outside. "Nat's been spending too much time with Freddie. Granola Fantasy wankers."

"Oh he's got a point. I can't get my head in the game today."

"You stressing about the Jay thing?" Jonny asked, lighting up.

"It's like he's set a bloody time bomb off," Adam said, wishing he had a vice that gave him the same satisfaction that nicotine gave Jonny.

Because obsessing about Mabel was his vice, really, wasn't it? And he got absolutely no satisfaction whatsoever from that.

"He's done a stupid thing because that's just what he's like – we've always known he's a bit of a tosser, haven't we? The worst they can do is ask us about it on camera. And Jay's going to get a hell of a lot of stick from Freddie for bringing it up."

"I'm worried about Mabel," Adam said. "She doesn't need this."

"You don't know what she needs, though. You don't know *her*."

"I *did* know her."

"Yeah, when she was a teenager, mate. Am I the same now as I was back then?"

"Yes. Exactly the same. Like you've been cryogenically frozen."

Jonny laughed. "Okay, fair enough. I think you and Rainbow are getting carried away, though."

"Rainbow?" Adam frowned. "You mean Sadie?"

"You could date her instead?" Jonny raised an eyebrow.

"Thank you, I'm not on the *prowl* here."

"I know, I know," Jonny said. "Just relax, okay? If it does all come out they're not going to be asking *you* any questions about it. I reckon we'll know when they're going to bring it up because it'll be Nat and Freddie called into that interview room and they'll leave the rest of us out of it."

Adam shook his head. "I need to find Mabel. I need to do it now while I know where Jay is."

"Every time you come back from trying to find her you look like you're about to throw yourself off a bridge. It's not doing you any good."

"Just one more time," Adam said. "I have to. It's not about me."

"Seems almost exclusively about you from where I'm standing, but okay." Jonny shrugged. "What do you need? I can go and laboriously restring my bass in the interests of "bringing it" – buy you about 20 minutes?"

"Five minutes to talk to her; 15 to drown myself in a river." Adam gave Jonny a wry smile. "*Thank you.*"

Jonny nodded and Adam took off towards the cabin he'd seen Mabel sitting outside in the dark, talking to Jay. He didn't know if she'd be there now but it seemed like his best shot. Funny how that evening had seemed like it was going to be the low point of his time on the show. If only he'd known… But he wasn't going to make this about them, he really wasn't. He just needed to try to intercept whatever nasty stunt Jay was trying to pull before someone got hurt.

As he neared the front door Adam could see movement inside, although he couldn't tell if it was Mabel or someone else. Or multiple people. At least he knew for sure that he wasn't going to find Jay there. He knocked on the door and suddenly there she was, not looking the slightest bit pleased to see him.

Adam took a step back, putting both his hands up in what he hoped was a neutral, pacifying gesture.

"Hi," he said. "Please don't go anywhere."

She just looked at him and Adam's heart continued to attempt to throw itself up his throat and out of his mouth. It really was quite the thing, standing in front of the person you'd been searching for for nine years. And he *knew* that it wasn't going to be the reunion that he'd hoped for and he had to talk to her about things that he didn't want to talk to her about, but still. Quite the thing.

"What are you doing here?" she asked softly.

"I need to talk to you."

It wasn't a great opening line, he had to admit, but he wasn't entirely sure how to get from this to what he needed to say.

"I…" She shook her head. "I can't, I've got to… I need to finish a work thing."

"Please, Mabel. It won't take long. It's important. It's about Jay."

She flinched, managing to look surprised and ashamed at the same time, and Adam caught just a glimpse then of the girl he'd stayed up all night with, skirting around what was really going on as they played all the missions in *Grand Theft Auto* on his PlayStation. *Could* he have done more? Could he have stopped all of this from happening? Or had he really been as inconsequential in Mabel's life as everyone else seemed to think?

"What *about* Jay?" she asked, visibly composing herself.

It was like watching someone draw the curtains on a big window.

"Can I come in?" Adam asked. "Just for a minute? I know you don't want a big heart-to-heart with me – I just need to tell you something and then I'll leave you alone."

Oh it hurt it hurt it hurt to be talking with her like this. To be holding everything back from her, *again*. Would he look back on *this moment* another ten years from now and wonder again whether he could have done more?

Mabel hesitated and Adam felt like he was holding his breath. But then she nodded, still frowning, and stepped aside for him to enter the cabin.

It wasn't much of a welcome. She stayed standing and so did he.

He cleared his throat awkwardly, trying so hard not to heave the weight of reunion onto the situation and just do what he'd come to do. But he could barely process it: her standing in front of him like this, for real, after all this time. He felt light-headed, or sick, or every kind of not quite right all at once. All he really wanted to do was hug her, tell her how much he'd missed her, find out everything that had happened to her since he last saw her, and make sure she was okay.

"Look, I know you're having a thing with Jay," He held up a hand to stop her as Mabel tried to interrupt. "But I just overheard him talking to a camera crew about you and I thought you needed to know."

"About me?" She looked surprised.

"Yeah. About everything that happened. Your links to Nat, to Freddie... He gave them your name and he told them that you're here."

"Oh God," she whispered.

"It wasn't good," Adam said. "He made it sound like he'd only just found out that you were here. Like he hadn't spoken to you, or anything. He said you were here to stir things up and suggested they track you down to find out what was going on."

Mabel closed her eyes, looking forlorn.

"They're going to come after you, I know they are. This show is all about the big drama and Jay has dropped you right in it." He paused. "What can I do? How can I help?"

He didn't know what he'd been expecting but it certainly wasn't to be immediately dismissed.

"Nothing," Mabel said, not making eye contact. "Thanks, but you should go. I've got things to do. I'm sure you have too."

And he *had* done what he'd told himself he was here to do, but had he ever really thought that he was capable of being this close to her and not saying any of *the things*?

He sighed. "Mabel, come on, what is this? I'm not an ex – we used to be such good friends. I don't know why you would need to avoid me? You know, you run into an old friend in any other situation and at the very least you make polite small talk for a few minutes; fire off some empty promises about catching up another time…" He sighed. "What did I *do*?"

Her frown deepened but she didn't say anything, and he knew then that he wasn't going to tell her how much he'd missed her, or how long he'd spent looking for her after she'd disappeared. He certainly wasn't going to tell her that he'd sat and drank tea with her grandmother so he could search the birthday cards on the mantelpiece for the familiar scrawl that would tell him she was at least still *alive*; that he'd jettisoned his whole fucking life for this friendship that apparently hadn't meant a thing to her in the first place.

"It was a really long time ago, Adam."

"No it wasn't," he said, finding the idea that she was fobbing him off truly unbearable. "Not for me."

"Please don't," she said, shaking her head. "I can't have this conversation with you now."

"Why *not*?"

"I *can't*, Adam. This has already gone too far."

"*What* has? You disappear without even saying goodbye and then suddenly you're here and you won't even bloody *talk* to me, and you won't tell me why! What are you even doing here?"

He was getting agitated and this wasn't how this was supposed to go but it was all just too much.

"What are *you* doing here?" Mabel exclaimed. "This was never supposed to happen! You weren't supposed to be here! You weren't supposed to find me!"

"But *why*?"

A hard stare. Tears in her eyes.

"You know, I wasn't going to say this, but actually I am," Adam said. "*Jay*. Of all people. What the bloody hell are you doing with him?"

"It's none of your business," Mabel said quietly, looking away.

"I know it isn't, it really isn't, and it never has been, but that doesn't stop me having an opinion about what a complete disaster he is," Adam said, exasperated now.

"I don't want to talk about this."

"No, *I* don't want to either, but you know what? I've spent enough time not calling you out on Jay. Maybe people do change, but he hasn't: he was bad news then and he's still bad news now. He gave the TV people *your name*, for God's sake, Mabel! He's going to screw you over without a second thought and I can't just sit back and watch it happen!"

"So don't watch," she said icily, her expression hardening.

He held her gaze, painfully, her words hitting him like a physical blow to the stomach.

"Fine," he said, nodding, his poor battered heart finally signalling to his brain that enough was enough. "Fine. I won't."

He turned and let himself out of the front door, walking morosely down the front path, pointlessly kicking at the dirt as he went. That was it, wasn't it? He had his answer now. There would be no grand reunion; no wonderful reigniting of lost friendship. Nine years lost in a maze and it turned out that the middle was just another dead end. Wasn't life just a barrel of laughs.

52

Sadie stared fixedly at the double doors to the rehearsal rooms, willing her band not to emerge. She could still hear a glorious megamix of old pop songs coming from inside, so presumably she had a little bit more time to pull herself together before she had to face anyone. Or, more specifically, Cameron. As much as Ryan had begged her, she hadn't been able to face the thought of rehearsals that afternoon. How could she, though, when potentially she'd just uncovered the world's greatest betrayal? It wasn't just the hangover that was making her feel sick. They'd gone round and round in circles talking about it that morning and were still no closer to making a decision about what they should do. In the end, Ryan had had to leave and that had been that. Let it sit, he'd said. See what happens. So here she was, letting it sit.

At the moment it was sitting right in the pit of her stomach as a hot little ball of fury and heartbreak, and underneath all of that was the strange sensation of not having to actively miss Ryan any more. Of no longer having to spend any mental energy on wondering *why*. Of not having to deal with that sting of regret whenever his name was mentioned or she came across a photo of his new band online. So much sadness, effectively erased in the time it took to say a sentence. She'd looked for that gaping hole inside her that his friendship had left and realised it wasn't there any more. Not even the faintest scar. Wishing she was still friends with Ryan was something she was never going to have to do again. She probably needed to let that sit for a while too.

"Hello."

Sadie was startled out of her staring contest with the door by Adam sitting down next to her. She frowned as she took in the look on his face.

"Oh no."

He sighed heavily. "Oh no, indeed."

"Tell me."

"I have just been to see Mabel," Adam said. "And it did not go very well."

"What happened?"

"I told her about Jay. I offered to help. And she just... sent me away. Like she didn't even care."

Sadie frowned. "What did she say?"

"Oh only that I never meant anything to her in the first place," Adam said. "No big deal. I'll just go back in time and realign my priorities for the last nine years."

"Did she actually say that?" Sadie asked. "She said you didn't mean anything to her?"

Adam sighed. "No. But that's what it felt like. She just fobbed me off; made out like it was such a long time ago that it was all irrelevant now. I asked her what I'd done and why she won't talk to me, and she just said she can't. That was it."

"She said she *can't*?"

Adam nodded.

"Like, she *wants to* but she can't?" Sadie asked.

Adam paused. "That's not really how it sounded."

"What else did she say?"

"She said it had already gone too far. That I wasn't supposed to find her."

"*You* weren't supposed to find her? You personally?"

Adam shrugged. "I guess? I don't know. She was so defensive. She wouldn't answer any of my questions directly." He sighed. "I just don't understand how her being here could be worse than spending nine years not knowing where she was. How does that make sense?"

"I'm sorry," Sadie said. "Today sucks."

"Maybe Jonny's right and I just need to let this go," Adam said. "Find something else to waste my life on."

"Can you let it go?"

He smiled ruefully and shook his head. "No."

"Do you want to give up on her and just walk away?"

"No. Because I still don't know, do I, why she's *being like this*."

"Well no, *exactly*. And it feels like there's something she's not telling you, right?" Sadie paused. "Wait. I'm just going to have to insert a quick reality check in here. Are we harassing her?"

Adam frowned. "No?"

"You just made me think, that's all. If I ran into someone that I didn't want to talk to, for whatever reason, that's my right, isn't it? Is this the same as that?"

"Oh Christ," Adam said. "I don't want to *harass* her."

"No, and obviously your intentions are super noble. I'm just worried now that I've given you bad advice."

"Oh, great."

Sadie made a face. Where was the line here? Would *she* actually like it if some guy she used to know kept showing up trying to talk to her about a load of stuff from the past that she didn't want to talk about?

"I think maybe you do actually need to back off a little bit."

Adam groaned.

"I'm not saying give up! But maybe the only thing you can do now is create the opportunity for her to come to you. If she wants to."

"Sadie, you've made me feel worse," Adam said, his head in his hands.

"Sorry! Sorry. I didn't mean to!" Sadie said. "I just… You're such a nice person! I don't want you to end up with a restraining order or something because I told you to keep trying to talk to her."

"Maybe I will just go home…" Adam muttered.

They both looked up as the door swung open and Jonny emerged. He narrowed his eyes at the two of them.

"Why are *you* here?" Jonny asked Sadie.

"I'm skiving rehearsals."

Adam looked at her, surprised. "Are you? Why?"

Sadie shook her head. "I'll tell you later," she said, not sure she had the energy to explain it to someone else at the moment.

"Am I interrupting something?" Jonny asked. "It's just I'm really scraping the bottom of the barrel covering for you now."

"We were just trying to decide whether Adam is harassing Mabel."

"You are," Jonny said flatly. "Are you coming back in, or what?"

Adam rolled his eyes and got up from the bench.

"Are *you* okay?" he asked, frowning at Sadie.

She nodded, waving him away. How many people here, she wondered, had found out this week that things weren't as they seemed? Was there anything else lurking round the corner waiting to jump out at her?

She didn't know how long she sat there for but eventually the music faded out and people started to emerge from the building in front of her. Everyone looked worn out; there was no joviality here this afternoon.

Yeah, she thought. *Same.*

"Feeling better?"

Sadie looked up at Ryan.

"We've been summoned to interview," he said. "They said you can't skive it even if you were genuinely ill."

"Oh yuck," Sadie said, pulling a face. "Did they say what it was about?"

"No idea," Ryan said. "Nothing good, though, surely."

"They don't know, do they, about what's going on?" Sadie asked. "They *can't*, right? You don't think they've got secret cameras in the cabins, or something?"

"I don't think they can do that," Ryan said. "Maybe they've noticed that something's a bit off, though? We don't know how closely they're watching us. I think we're going to have to be really careful. Don't show any signs of weakness."

"What, like, just pretend everything's okay with Cameron?" Sadie made a face.

"More than okay," Ryan said. "We're going to have to be seamless in making it look like we're all getting on like a house on fire. Until we figure out what we're going to do, anyway. Which means no more flaking out on rehearsals."

"It was literally just this one time," Sadie said.

"Just don't rise to it, okay? No matter what he does or says. Smooth waters, right?"

"I will *try*."

"You have to," Ryan said, looking surprisingly serious.

"Okay, okay, I will," Sadie said, feeling very tired. "How was it in there? With Cameron."

"Nothing to report," Ryan said. "He's still being a dick to James; nice as pie to me." He shrugged. "Who knows what's going on."

Sadie sighed. "When's the interview?"

"Now."

"Wait, aren't we supposed to be doing the Segway thing now?"

"No Segway for Sadie," Ryan said. "You have to come and talk about your feelings instead."

"This is escalating, isn't it?"

Ryan nodded sagely. "It is. Hey, before we go in," he said, looking at her earnestly. "I've been thinking."

"Oh yeah?"

"Why don't you come back to L.A. with me?" Ryan asked. "When we finish filming. Just... get on a plane and come home with me."

"For real?" Sadie asked, her stomach doing a little squiggly hopeful thing.

"Yeah! I'll pay for your ticket; you can stay at mine... I only just got you back. Ten days isn't long enough."

"What about George?" Sadie asked.

"I don't care about George! *He's* not your best friend, *I* am," Ryan said. "Please? Don't make me beg. I mean, I will, but I'd rather not."

Sadie smiled. "Do you have a pool?"

"Er, yeah, of course I have a pool. What do you think I am, some second-rate rock star?"

"What would I do all day?"

"Swim in my pool? Look at beautiful people? Remember what sunshine is like?"

"I don't know, sounds kind of boring," Sadie said airily. "Are you going to ditch me when you have to go and do cool band stuff?"

"No way, you can come with! I'm in the market for a groupie, anyway. It'll help my street cred," Ryan said, his smile matching hers. "I honestly think you'd love it, Sade. There's so much going on. Having you there would be epic."

She nodded fervently. "Yes please."

"Really?"

"Yeah. A million percent yes. Oh my God! So exciting! We're going to be roomies again!" Sadie squealed. "What if I like it so much I don't want to go home?"

Ryan shrugged. "Then don't."

Well. Perhaps things were looking up after all.

"What if I don't have all the right stuff?" Sadie asked as they went inside.

"I'll buy you all the right stuff."

"Is it hot over there? Where *is* L.A.? I don't think I actually know that. Do you live by a beach?"

"You'll find out when you get there, won't you?"

"Are you really really rich?"

Ryan laughed. "No. But I can buy you a couple of t-shirts to wear."

He led her into a small side room that looked suspiciously like a squash court, James, Mia and Cameron looking up from where they were already awkwardly arranged on chairs.

"Found her!" Ryan said cheerfully.

Sadie felt herself physically stiffen when she saw Cameron but she pasted on a smile and carefully took a seat.

"Are you okay?" Mia asked, a hand on her arm.

"Yeah, sorry. Just a bit of a stomach thing. Didn't feel up to dancing."

"Are you feeling better now?"

Sadie nodded as the door was flung open and a girl they hadn't seen before walked into the room holding another ominous clipboard.

"Hi guys!" She beamed at them. "I'm Harmony! Sorry to drag you away from the fun! We won't keep you long. Just a quick one."

She sat down in front of them, nodding to the camera crew.

"Okay, let's see… So, how's it all going with you guys?"

"Er, good?" Ryan said, when no one else offered a response.

"Once more with feeling?" Harmony smiled. "So we've noticed that you guys perhaps aren't *gelling* as well as some of the other bands? What's it like being back together as a five?"

Sadie looked at the floor. No one said anything.

"Okay… You're going to have to give me a little something here, guys. I can't put out a completely silent interview," Harmony said, her mask slipping slightly.

Who was really calling the shots here, Sadie thought. If they flat-out refused to talk on camera was there anything they could *actually* to make them? They *could* drop them from the show, but that seemed like it would take an awful lot of editing when they'd come this far…

"Yeah, sorry, I think we're all just a bit shattered," Ryan said, nudging Sadie. "These rehearsals are surprisingly tough!"

"Is it fair to say that some of you are finding it harder than others?" Harmony asked.

"The dance moves or the reunion?" Sadie asked, reluctantly forcing her on-camera persona back out.

She'd never had to do this before: not once during the band had she not been in the mood to do an interview. But all the stuff with Cameron, plus what George had said about the TV people knowing all their secrets, had put a bit of a bad vibe on everything. Was this how James had felt when he was trying to force himself to do the pop star thing when he really didn't want to?

It was unpleasant and unnatural.

"Well, take it however you like," Harmony said.

"I'm finding the dance moves tricky," Mia said. "Cameron, I think you were too?"

"I think some of us are putting more effort in than others," Cameron said.

"We're all *trying*," Sadie said. "It is hard, though! We're all old and unfit now. Even I'm messing up and I thought I still knew all the moves."

"Do you think there's been a bit of a division of loyalties within the band? Perhaps a bit of a split here?" Harmony asked.

"Between who?" Ryan asked.

"It might have been mentioned that you and Sadie seem particularly close."

Ryan laughed. "By who? I can assure you there is no secret shagging in this band."

"Someone said they saw you holding hands…"

"Because we're best mates, babe," Ryan said, looping an arm round Sadie and pulling her in for an exaggerated hug. "And we missed each other."

"Aw, that's a precious moment for the camera," Sadie said, smirking.

"Isn't it," Ryan said. "Any other ludicrous rumours you'd like us to address?"

"Quite a lot of the other bands seem to be spending more time together than you all have been," Harmony said. "Is there a reason for that?"

"We're just catching up with everyone, aren't we?" Ryan said.

"I live with Mia, and we see Cameron all the time, so if we were all going to stick to hanging out with each other we might as well be at home," Sadie said. "I haven't seen any of the other people here for years. It's fun to catch up."

"What about you, James?" Harmony asked. "You haven't been seen socialising much with anyone."

"Well, I'm used to a much quieter life these days," James said. "You'll have to forgive me for not being the life and soul of the party."

"You wouldn't say there've been any disagreements between the five of you?"

"Maybe a little bit of bickering," Ryan said. "Nothing serious. It's like when you have to work with any group of people to do anything: you're not all going to agree with each other all the time."

"And has the experience of reuniting the band been what you expected?"

"No," Sadie said, before she could stop herself.

"No, not really," Ryan said, nodding in agreement, although Sadie couldn't tell if it was genuine or not. "You know, we've all lived a lot of life since the band split up. It's not quite as simple as just slotting the pieces back together. We're not the same shape any more."

"Physically or figuratively?" Mia asked.

Ryan grinned. "Well I didn't like to say anything but you lot have all really let yourselves go, haven't you? Whereas *I* am in peak physical fitness."

"I don't think you're allowed to say things like that any more!" Sadie laughed.

"I'm sorry, I'm sorry, you all look fabulous," Ryan said. "Just, obviously, I am the most fabulous."

"And the one with the biggest ego," Cameron said.

"I've got the biggest everything," Ryan said, doing an exaggerated wink at the camera.

"Urgh, I just did a sick in my mouth," Sadie said, as everyone dissolved into laughter around her.

"Okay, well, I think we'll leave it there for now," Harmony said, smirking. "Perhaps we'll have a bit more of a chat another time."

"You know where to find us," Ryan said, getting up.

"That seemed pointless," James said as they filed out of the room. "I didn't realise being antisocial was illegal."

"Well, it is, and you really should have known that," Ryan said.

It was a comment that was so very close to their "usual" kind of banter that if it weren't for the fact that Ryan was pining over James' girlfriend, James was miserable and Cameron inexplicably hated them all it would have warmed Sadie's heart a little bit.

"I think we successfully defused that particular line of questioning, anyway."

"Are we too late for Segway?" Mia asked.

"I don't know, shall we go and see?" Sadie suggested, welcoming the fresh air after the weird oppressiveness of the interview room/squash court. "Are you guys coming?"

"I suppose so," James said, without much enthusiasm.

"Count me out," Cameron said. "I've had enough of this circus today. Fancy a pint?"

"Never say no to a late afternoon pint," Ryan said, hitting Sadie with a look that she could only interpret as "I am taking one for the team but I will not be enjoying it".

Well, fine. If that was the approach he wanted to take, so be it. But she certainly wasn't going to be going for a casual drink with Cameron any time soon.

"Oh! What are you doing here?" she asked, clocking George sitting on a wall just outside the building.

He stood up, smiling at her, and there was that nice little feeling again.

"Heard you were having a difficult interview."

"We were having a *weird* interview," Sadie said. "They were digging for something. Don't think any of us were in the mood. Is the Segway thing still going on? We were going to walk over."

"Not sure. I was going to ask you if you wanted to grab a coffee?"

"Oh..." Sadie looked to Mia. "Well I was going to head over there with Mia..."

"It's okay!" Mia jumped in, smiling a very knowing smile at Sadie. "James will come with me. Won't you?"

"Oh. Yes. I love Segways," James said unconvincingly.

Sadie smiled at George. "Okay then. Where's coffee?"

"My cabin?"

She narrowed her eyes at him. "Coffee, or *coffee*?"

George burst out laughing. "Actual coffee! Wow, what do you take me for? What, you think I'm just going in cold, in the middle of the day, no messing around here?"

"Just checking!" Sadie said, as they headed away from the sports hall towards the cabins.

"I promise there will be actual coffee."

"Okay then. I like coffee," Sadie said, feeling strangely awkward as she walked next to him.

Was it going to be *just* coffee? Was this a *date*? Is that what she wanted? It really wasn't the day to be having to decide things like this. Maybe she'd just go with it and let whatever happened happen. Even if it was just coffee.

"Oh hey, guess what?" she said, trying to put herself back in the moment.

"What?"

"Real life just got exciting again: Ryan asked me to go to L.A. with him!"

"Love it when real life gets exciting." George grinned. "I wish I had an estranged bandmate who lived somewhere cool. I don't really fancy going to stay with Craig in Swindon."

"Craig lives in Swindon? That's not that far from where I live!"

"Maybe I will go and stay with Craig in Swindon... Except that you'll be in L.A."

"Not forever."

"You might never come back," George said, smiling and raising an eyebrow at her.

"Well I might," Sadie said, "if there was something to come back for."

Their arms jostled against each other as they walked and it was like a series of miniature electric shocks to the heart. This was so absolutely not what she had come here for but she definitely wasn't hating it.

"I also have a *hey guess what*," George said. "But it is highly highly top secret."

"Ooh, tell me! Can you tell me?"

"Not supposed to... You'll have to swear on the lives of several family pets that you won't tell anyone yet."

"Well I don't like to blow my own trumpet but I have become a legendary keeper of secrets recently."

"We've been offered a deal," George said cryptically.

"Who? What kind of a deal?"

"The band. The kind of deal that involves tour dates and a wad of cash..."

Sadie gasped, stopping in her tracks to look at him. "Oh my God! Are you serious?"

George was beaming. "Just four dates. But big ones. And maybe more, if it sells."

"Oh my God!" Sadie shrieked, flinging her arms around his neck and squeezing him tightly. "You're going on tour! You're a band again! I'm so happy for you!"

He squeezed her back and then — it was hard to say exactly how it happened — he kissed her. And, wow, it was quite some kiss, like doubling the saturation on a photograph and tinging everything with a luminous glow.

She pulled back to look at him and there was something just so lovely about his face that she couldn't help but smile. They'd had moments like this before, backstage at roadshows and in TV show dressing rooms when they'd thought no one was looking (although, in hindsight, they probably had been), but she'd never in a million years considered that they'd be having those moments again, ten years later. She still felt that same rush she'd felt back then when his lips were on hers.

"We don't do this any more…" she said coyly.

"I know," he said, hands lingering on her waist, "but I was thinking that maybe we should…"

THREE DAYS TO THE LIVE SHOW

53

Kitty studied herself in the mirror, smoothing her hair down before checking the time on her phone.

Today was the day.

It had to be, really, because she was running out of time.

Ryan had managed to continually evade her over the last few days and she hadn't actually seen him since the street party. Well, she'd *seen* him, and she'd kept putting herself in all the places where she knew he'd be, but where he'd seemed to constantly seek her out before, now she was getting nothing. Perhaps she was imagining it – perhaps she was imaging everything – but she *had* to know, once and for all, whether there was something there. She couldn't let him go back to L.A. without getting an answer – she knew if she didn't get one she would always wonder, and that would probably feel pretty unbearable for 60-odd years.

Everyone was supposed to be doing yoga in a building near the lake that morning before heading to the sports hall for more rehearsals. James had seemed surprisingly enthusiastic about the yoga when she'd mentioned it over breakfast, but she'd bet money on that fact that she'd be more likely to find Ryan smoking outside than doing a downward dog. She didn't have a plan exactly – she figured she just needed to get him somewhere secluded and then give him enough of a physical signal that she was interested and, knowing Ryan, he'd surely do the rest.

As she approached the lake she didn't know whether the goosebumps on her arms were from the anticipation or because she'd forgotten to pick up her jacket on the way out. She got a full body shiver when, as predicted, she saw Ryan leaning against the outside of the building, cigarette in hand. There really was no way to make it look like she was just passing, so she stepped out into the courtyard and headed straight towards him, trying to temper her grin into something reasonably indifferent. He frowned when he saw her, stubbing out his cigarette on the wall.

"Not into getting all sweaty on a yoga mat?" she asked.

"It's not quite the same when you've done it on a beach at sunrise."

"No, I guess not."

There was a pause where Kitty waited for Ryan to insert some kind of vaguely smutty comment, but he didn't say anything. Which was weird, because up to this point the flirty banter between them had been relentless.

"So," Kitty said, trying to move things along, "if you're not doing yoga do you fancy coming for a walk? The lake looks pretty this morning."

"I can't," he said, looking awkward. "I've got to get back in."

"I'm sure they won't miss you. I think you'd have more fun with me…"

Ryan chuckled. "Oh I don't doubt that. But trust me when I say I really can't."

Kitty pouted. "You can't come for a walk with a friend?"

He raised an eyebrow at her. "I can go for a walk with a *friend*, but I can't go for a walk with *you*. Sadly."

"Why not?" Kitty asked.

Ryan paused, looking like he was deliberating something.

"I think we both know where this is going," he said finally, "and I think we *also* both know that it's a really bad idea."

"But…"

Ryan sighed. "It pains me to do this, honestly, but I can't get involved. It's not right." He shook his head. "And you really need to talk to your boyfriend."

"Wait, can we…" Kitty stumbled over her words, flustered.

"I've got to go, Kitty," Ryan said, not meeting her eye. "It was good seeing you again. Really."

And then he just walked away without so much as a backwards glance, leaving her with nothing to do but watch him leave.

So all those stolen moments they'd had over the last few days, they'd meant *nothing*?

Embarrassment ignited within her like a red hot flare and tears sprung to her eyes. He'd done it again, hadn't he? He'd sucked her in with his flirting and flattery, toyed with her for a bit and then discarded her like she was nothing. And she'd fallen for it, *again*, all these years later, lapping up the attention like the pathetic fangirl she'd always be. As if Ryan Malone was ever going to run off into the sunset with *her*. As if Ryan Malone was ever going to change.

It felt like a slap round the face; like she'd been toppled from the stupid happy cloud of make-believe she'd been floating around on and had hit the ground really really hard. The pain of rejection throbbed across her body like a physical injury as she turned around and walked slowly back through the forest.

Was she a joke to him? Would he laugh with Sadie about how pathetic she was for believing any of the things he'd said to her? Would anyone tell *James*? She just wanted to go home and never see any of them ever again. Way to ruin an already ruined teenage dream.

Back at the cabin she let herself in through the front door, jumping out of her skin as James stood up from the sofa.

"Oh my God, you scared me to death!" she exclaimed, rubbing at the mascara that had inevitably smudged all under her eyes and hoping she didn't look too red in the face. "What are you doing here? Aren't you supposed to be doing yoga?"

James' expression was stony.

"Are you okay?" she asked uncertainly.

"Who did you talk to?" he asked her.

She frowned. "What?"

He held out his phone and she took it from him, peering at the screen in confusion. And then she read the headline of the article and it was like the entire world fell away around her with a great big *whoosh!* and she was left standing on one single square of solid ground, surrounded by nothingness.

THE SURPRISING LOVE TRIANGLE BEHIND THE SCENES OF VILLAGE OF POP

She saw her name, and James', and Ryan's, and then Jess' in the byline, and in the bizarre twilight moment of something irreversible happening it felt like time froze, long enough for her to wonder how it was possible for there not to be an undo button for emergency use when you really really needed it.

She didn't know what to do. Should she keep reading? Should she start to explain? *Could* she explain?

She glanced up at James and the look on his face was such that she decided she'd rather read the article if it meant she could delay having to talk to him for a few more minutes. Not that she couldn't guess exactly what it said. She'd told Jess *everything* and it seemed unlikely she'd have left out the really juicy bits. How could she have been so stupid to think that someone from her teens would walk back into her life for a catch-up with no ulterior motive? They hadn't even been very good friends in the first place and Jess had been firmly in the camp of girls that had unceremoniously ditched her after things with Ryan had fizzled out.

First Ryan and now Jess: was she really so much of a pushover that she couldn't see people for who they really were?

Sure enough the article recounted the majority of her conversation with Jess in explicit detail, including a fair bit of speculation about why James was lying about his past and the secrets he was trying to keep hidden. They'd taken the photo of Kitty and Ryan that she'd so boldly put up on Instagram after the street party, one of her and James lifted from Facebook – because of course Kitty had added Jess as a friend and given her unbridled access to all the photos she'd ever uploaded – and even one of Kitty as a teenager, likely dug out of Jess' own teenage photo albums.

What struck Kitty most of all was the bitterness and malice that came through from behind the words. She imagined the other girls that had been so jealous of her back then reading the article and laughing; messaging each other to gloat about how the mighty had fallen.

"Where to start," James said, his face grave.

It didn't seem like a question, and Kitty didn't know what to say.

"Is it all true?"

Kitty nodded, closing her eyes.

"You'll have to give me a second to catch my breath here. I've found out quite a lot about you in the last half an hour."

Humiliation surged through Kitty like waves of heat.

"So you've spent four years waiting for some kind of insider gossip about your favourite band. That must have been pretty frustrating."

"James, no…"

"I'm sorry I couldn't give you that. I mean, I feel pretty stupid now, because obviously I thought you were with me for a different reason."

"There are lots of reasons to be with you," Kitty said quietly.

"How many reasons are there to be with Ryan?" James asked.

His tone was so cold and his face so emotionless. She'd never seen this side of him before. It was completely horrible and everything she deserved. How much could she really protest? He knew everything and she didn't have a leg to stand on.

"I'm sorry," she whispered. "Nothing happened."

"Does he know how you feel about him?"

Kitty shook her head.

"But he remembers who you are?"

"Yes."

"I suppose someone could admire your patience. You stuck out this relationship for a long time in the hope it would lead you back to him," James said. "It probably would have been quicker to have gone back to your roots and accosted him round the back of a gig venue."

"That's not what I was doing," Kitty said. "I was with you because I wanted to be with you!"

"But you're bored of that now."

"No!"

"Explain to me how it's possible to feel like you're emotionally connected to someone you haven't seen since you were a teenager; someone who you never really knew in the first place, and who certainly never gave a damn about you," James said. "Give it to me in layman's terms, because I'm struggling here."

"It's not like that," Kitty said.

Except it was. It just was. Sometimes there was just no way to truly let go of something – or someone – that once meant so much to you, even if you meant nothing to them.

"So what *is* it like, Kitty?" James asked. "Because it pretty much says in black and white here that you'd trade me in for Ryan without a second thought if you got the chance. And I guess I get it – he's Ryan Malone, right? All the glitz and glamour of someone who's *still* famous, rather than an aging has-been who – more fool him – didn't realise he needed to play the ex-celebrity card to find someone who wanted to share their life with him."

Kitty looked down at the ground.

"Maybe I'm the fool here but I guess I had hoped that after four years we were past the point where someone else would catch your eye and I'd lose you." James took a shaky breath. "But then four years is a long time to love someone knowing that they won't ever truly feel the same way about you."

"Well maybe four years is a long time to live with someone who's living a lie!" Kitty retorted, hurt, and angry, and completely wrongfooted by all of this. "It's like living with a ghost! What's there to love?"

She'd gone too far and she instantly regretted it. The expression on James' face was unreadable now.

He nodded. "Okay. Well, consider me told. I'm going to need a bit of time. Maybe that will be real enough for you."

And before Kitty could offer to leave he'd walked past her and out of the front door.

54

"This has already gone too far."

Adam squeezed his eyes tightly shut and tried to focus on his drumming.

"You weren't supposed to find me!"

Thinking about drumming and nothing else. Just staying in time with the rest of the band and not pissing everyone off.

"Are we harassing her?"

Oh who was he kidding?

"Stop, sorry, I know, I'm not getting it, I'm sorry," he said, resting his sticks on top of one of the drums.

"Adam, I don't think I have ever witnessed you being so shit at drums in my entire life," Nat said. "If this was ten years ago I would not have you in my band."

"Yeah, I wouldn't blame you." Adam shook his head. "I hate this song, though. I hate the timing of it."

"It's a Fabs thing, isn't it," Jonny said. "He's all about the fancy footwork."

"Can I just sit this one out?" Adam asked, running a hand across his forehead. "I cannot drum along with him to this one. It's going to be fucking embarrassing."

"Yeah, for *all* of us," Nat said. "But we *have* to nail this one! Jay's been talking shit about us to Freddie, which is such a dick move because he knows full well Fred's going to tell me about it. I don't want to give him the satisfaction of being as shit as he thinks we are."

"Aren't you all supposed to be *best friends forever*?" Adam asked.

"What do you think we're doing, having sleepovers and braiding each other's hair? Jay's a fucking mess. I spend as little time with him as humanly possible. Honestly, I'm all for pretending we're mates, but if he's going to start trash-talking us then I'm done with all that. That's not what I came here for."

And of course Nat could say all this because, funnily enough, there were no cameras in the room for Prairie Dogs rehearsals. There would be no footage of them hashing out their greatest songs, or preparing for their once-in-a-lifetime reunion performance. Adam wondered how much they were going to feature at all on this stupid little show.

He looked at Nat, debating whether to tell him about what Jay had done. Did the fact that they weren't best mates after all change things? It seemed like it could go either way. Really Nat *should* care about what Jay had done to his sister, but in reality he probably wouldn't.

Adam had not slept well. Thanks to Sadie's latest take on the situation he'd gone from really depressed to really bothered by the thought that it might look like he was harassing Mabel. He was not the bad guy here, he was sure of it. A bad guy did things like talk to a TV show about you. He was trying to *help* Mabel, but if his persistence was going to *upset* her then that went against everything he stood for. So, sure, he would step away if that was truly the right thing to do, but there was something really niggling at him and he just couldn't shake it.

Their exchange yesterday had just felt so familiar, like the dance they used to do back in the bad old days whenever he would suggest that perhaps she needed a bit of space from Jay, or when he'd ever so gently question her life choices. She would get angry and defensive but the look in her eyes wouldn't match the words she was throwing at him, as if she'd needed his support but couldn't bring herself to let him in. *Was* there a way to get through to her? Some way he could bypass that massive barbed wire fence she liked to wrap around herself? Was it worth just one more blow to his poor broken heart?

"Freddie said that Jay was trying to get him to swap 'Follow You' for something else. He thinks it's in bad taste." Nat said.

"*Jay* was worried about something being in bad taste? That's a good joke," Adam scoffed.

"He said it had a *negative message*."

"Didn't Freddie write that song while Jay was banging Mabel?" Jonny asked, chock full of tact as always.

Adam cringed.

"You wouldn't think either of them would want to play a song that reminded them of Mabel, really," Harry said.

"Aren't *all* their songs about Mabel?" Jonny said.

"Can we *please* not talk about Mabel," Nat said, rolling his eyes. "Fred isn't budging, anyway. So unfortunately you're going to have to keep murdering the drum part, Ad."

And then Adam knew what he needed to do to get through to her. A message. A memory. One last chance. But it was not going to be an easy sell.

He coughed twice and Jonny immediately looked round. Clearly you never forget a secret signal. He discreetly mimed smoking a cigarette and Jonny nodded.

"Any chance of a quick smoke break?" he asked casually. "I could do with five minutes off from being exceptional at playing my instrument."

"Ha ha ha," Adam said, gratefully playing along.

"You know, if we ever did anything other than *take a five minute break* we might actually stand a chance of getting our shit together," Nat grumbled. "Fine, fine, whatever."

"Thanks, Dad!" Jonny said, pointing at Adam, and then the door.

They left the room quickly, before Harry and Nat had had a chance to detach themselves from their guitars.

"You pressed the panic button," Jonny said, scrabbling around his pockets for an elusive filter. "What's up?"

"We need to change our song," Adam said.

"What, 'Follow You'? I don't think that's something I can help you with."

"No, *our* song."

"Why?"

"I think it's a way I can get through to Mabel."

"Oh this again!" Jonny exclaimed. "I'm just going to throw it out there, but I never really got the Mabel thing, for you, or for Freddie. And I think you said it was going to be the last time about two times ago."

"I know, I know. But can you just play along?" Adam asked, glancing towards the door. "And I will owe you, like, a lifetime of pints."

"I think you do already," Jonny said. "Are you ever going to let this go?"

"Probably not."

"Seems like a waste of a life to me, but what do I know," he said, sighing. "Yeah, all right, what do I have to do?"

"Just agree with everything I say."

Jonny rolled his eyes, but nodded all the same, trouping back into the rehearsal room with Adam once he'd finished his cigarette.

"Can we try something different?" Adam said, trying to keep his voice even.

"Like what?" Nat asked.

"Like a different song."

Nat frowned, turning to look at him. "A different song?"

"Yeah."

"What are you talking about? We can't do a *different song*: we've been practicing this one for a solid week and we're still shit at it."

"What's the song?" Jonny piped up.

"I want to do 'Disney Eyes'," Adam said.

Nat looked unimpressed. "We've never performed 'Disney Eyes'. It's an album track. If that."

"Oh man, I love that song!" Jonny exclaimed. "What a classic."

Adam wasn't sure whether he was grateful of the support or whether he thought Jonny should perhaps scale it back a little.

"It's a ballad! You barely play on it."

"I want to do vocals," Adam said, the adrenaline surge drowning out the knowledge that Nat had every reason to laugh him out of the room.

Nat put his guitar down. "Are you joking?"

"No. I want to do the vocals on it. Give me a guitar and I'll play it too, or you can play the guitar part, I don't care. We don't need the drums."

"Have you completely lost the plot?" Nat asked. "Ad, we get to do *one song* on our own: it's our only chance to make an impression and show people the band we should have been. We can't stick you up there with just a guitar and a mic to sing a bloody nothing balled!"

"I don't care about the band we should have been," Adam said. "This is more important. It has to be this song and I have to sing it."

"But *why?*"

Adam paused.

Because it's her favourite, he thought. *Because we sat in my bedroom until the early hours of the morning tweaking it until it was perfect.*

And although he'd never said it he was sure she knew, deep down, that he'd written it about her.

"Alexander and Anderson, the next great song-writing duo," he'd said once he'd played their final version back to her. "Move over Benny and Bjorn."

She'd nodded, and yawned, and demanded a cut of the royalties when it was a number one hit, and he'd put his guitar down, and cleared the crumpled pieces of paper off the bed, and the last thing he'd seen before he closed his eyes was her smiling at him.

That tiny insignificant moment had always felt like one of their *most* significant, and this was the final thing he had up his sleeve when it came to getting through to Mabel now. If he could just sing it to her again maybe she would remember who they were and what they'd had, once upon a time. Maybe she would take down those walls and let him in, even if all it ever came to was some polite small talk and some empty promises about catching up another time.

But he couldn't say any of that to Nat so instead he just shrugged.

"It's the only good thing I've ever written. I just want to sing it on a proper stage, for once in my life."

He knew it was a poor reason, but what else could he say? Mentioning Mabel would only ensure an immediate veto from Nat.

"We've all got songs like that, mate. This is about the band," Nat said.

"Could be a real curveball, though," Jonny said. "Something they'd never expect from us. Might make people really sit up and listen."

Nat made a face as if everyone around him had turned into raving lunatics.

"It's a *ditty*," he said, bewildered.

"I don't know, man. I'd love to see that up on stage. Can't you just picture it?" Jonny said. "It's a real gentle song, isn't it? Really classy. It could be something special."

"Yeah, well, okay, it's a nice enough song, I guess, but couldn't you just sing it at one of your own gigs?"

"It wouldn't be the same," Adam said.

"Couldn't we at least do it in the rehearsal?" Jonny asked. "Do them both?"

Nat frowned. "How would that work?"

"We could say we've been working on two songs, and we can't decide which works best live so we want to try them both out? The rehearsal's all day, anyway – we're not going to be short on time."

Adam nodded. The rehearsal could work. All he'd have to do was find a way to make sure Mabel was there.

"Come on, you love that song. Everyone loves that song!" Jonny said. "He's had a hard couple of years. Let him have this."

Nat sighed, eyeing Adam suspiciously. "Okay, I suppose, if it's that important to you. We'll all have to play on it, though. It can't just be you."

Adam smiled grimly. "Sure, fine."

"Let's get on with it then."

So Plan E it was. In for a penny, in for a pound.

55

"I still didn't sleep with him," Sadie said, turning her back on the camera crew that were trying – and failing – to look casual on the other side of the room.

"Millions wouldn't believe you," Ryan said. "Me being one of them."

Sadie smiled, that nice little feeling having turned into a full-on glow since The Kissing Incident with George. That certainly was not what she'd been expecting to get out of doing the show. Not that it *was* anything. There wasn't a chance for it to be anything, really. He was going on tour. She was going to L.A. It was terrible timing, just like the last time they'd done this. But the thought of maybe having something to come back to after she'd exhausted all the possibilities in L.A. definitely wasn't a bad thing.

"Honestly," Sadie said, "that's not my kind of thing. There was a bit of unexpected kissing. Then we had coffee on his sofa. That was it."

"*Coffee* on his sofa."

"Just coffee!"

"You are precious," Ryan said.

"I'm still coming to L.A."

"I should bloody hope so!"

"So what are you sulking about?" Sadie asked, throwing a glance at Mia and Cameron who were engrossed in something on Cameron's phone.

"I'm not sulking."

"You are sulking. It's a bit like when you were pining, but more gloomy."

"Why do you think," Ryan muttered grumpily.

"Is it… *dealt with*?" Sadie asked covertly.

"To be honest, I was just going to keep trying to avoid her, but she cornered me outside yoga. Asked if I wanted to go for a walk. And it was pretty bloody obvious what kind of walk she had in mind."

Sadie rolled her eyes. "Oh she is the worst."

"Yeah, well, I told her I couldn't get involved with her like that. And it did not feel good, okay? It gave me a pain here," Ryan put his hand to his chest and then his stomach, "and here."

"Did it actually?"

"Yes, it did. It was very unpleasant."

"Aww," Sadie patted him on the arm. "I wish you'd feel like that about someone you could actually have."

"You and me both, mate."

"Why do you two look like you're plotting?" Cameron asked, coming over with Mia.

"I guess we're just shifty-looking people," Ryan said, shrugging.

It wasn't getting any easier, having to fraternise with Cameron. Every little thing he said was putting her back up and she honestly didn't know how much longer she was going to be able to play nice. Ryan had said he'd tried to do some digging when they'd gone for a pint the previous day, playing along with the "Sadie hates my fame" story line and asking Cameron how he thought she was coping with everything. Apparently he'd said she was finding it hard. Oh she was finding it hard, all right: hard to contain her rage when he said things like that. And he was going to find out just how hard she was finding it in the form of a punch in the face if he wasn't careful.

"How late is James now?" she asked.

"20 minutes," Mia said.

Sadie sighed. "Where *is* he? Do you think he's forgotten?"

"Maybe he got held up," Mia said. "I'm sure he'll be here soon."

Sadie tried calling his mobile again but it was still switched off. The similarities between today and the day he left the band were making her feel uneasy.

"When did you last see him?" she asked.

"Oh this again," Cameron said. "Hello déjà vu."

Sadie ignored him, patience level all the way down to zero by this point.

"He was at the sports hall this morning. He was on the phone, and then I think he actually left before yoga started," Mia said.

Sadie frowned, casting a glance towards the camera crew.

"Are you worried this is… The Thing?" Ryan muttered, leaning in closer to Sadie so he couldn't be overheard so easily.

She nodded.

"I thought you said he seemed fine, though?"

"Yeah he did seem fine. But he *seemed fine* last time, didn't he."

"I guess."

"Look I know you don't care, but–"

"I do care," Ryan said, interrupting her. "I do care. If I didn't care I'd be *having a walk* right now, wouldn't I?"

"I thought you only did that because I nagged you to."

"It's a complicated ball of stuff, okay?"

"Okay," Sadie said, shrugging. "I can't just sit here and wait for James to not turn up, though. I've done that once already."

"You want to go look for him?"

"Yeah but I don't want *them* tailing me," Sadie said, tilting her head towards the camera crew, who were obviously trying to eavesdrop to see whether anything juicy was going on. "You know, I really did not expect that trying to hold this band together for ten days would be this exhausting."

"I think we're 90% duct tape at this point, babe."

"Yeah, it feels like it," Sadie said. "How am I going to get out of here?"

"Leave it with me," Ryan said confidently.

She watched him walk over to the two men behind the cameras, saying something to them that elicited a flurry of nodding in response.

"Right, well, shall we get started?" he said to the room. "Those of us that aren't slacking off, anyway. I'm sure we can manage without James. Not like we haven't done it before."

"Might get through a whole song without being tripped up," Cameron said, as Mia started the music.

"Go," Ryan said, leaning into Sadie. "I'll hold the fort."

"What did you say to them?"

"I said you'd left your tampons in the cabin."

She clamped a hand over her mouth to hide her smile.

"Get out of here," Ryan said, winking at her.

She slipped out of the room without looking back, the music becoming muffled as she stepped outside. She knew James wasn't coming to the rehearsal – she could just *feel* it – and she had a hunch where she might find him.

The petting zoo was deserted when she got there. Apart from James, who was sitting on a hay bale staring at the donkeys. He looked up as she approached, not appearing remotely surprised to see her.

"Didn't think I'd get away with it," he said.

Sadie frowned. "Are you okay?"

"Sorry, I know we're supposed to be rehearsing. I couldn't face it today."

"That's okay…" Sadie trailed off, noticing the bottle in his hand.

He saw her see it, and he didn't try to hide it. Sadie felt her heart plummet.

"It's been a long time since I've felt the need to numb anything. This was the best the shop could do, unfortunately," he said, holding up the vodka. "Somewhat lacking in sophistication, but needs must."

James shuffled along on the bale and Sadie sat down carefully next to him, absolutely no idea what to do or say. Where was a grown up when you needed one?

"They've got a really poor selection of painkillers in the shop," James continued. "I had thought that addictive over-the-counter medicine might have come on a bit in the last few years. Maybe I need to pop into Boots, have a *browse*."

Sadie thought her heart might break. The deep sadness of this lovely man – and the feeling of utter powerlessness on her part – was unbearable.

"We can stop…" She said, flailing and useless. "If you need to. Don't do this for me."

The thing that was even harder to swallow was the thought that *she* was responsible for this. All her stupid, selfish whining about how soulless her life was. How boring, how meaningless. She'd dragged them all here and not once had she thought that anyone might be going through anything worse than she was. She knew now with absolute certainty that she'd walk away from it all if it meant that James would be okay.

James' hand found hers and she squeezed it tightly.

"I can handle it," he said.

"I don't want it to make you feel like this," Sadie said, her voice wavering.

He didn't reply, but his hand stayed in hers and they sat in silence staring at the donkeys together.

"What do you know about Ryan and Kitty?" James asked eventually.

Oh crap.

Sadie made a face. "I know it's over," she said, "and that nothing actually happened. Ryan told her where to go."

"Doesn't sound like Ryan," James said.

"He knows where his loyalties lie."

"Not with me, surely?"

"Well, with me, then," Sadie said.

James nodded thoughtfully. "Do you remember Kitty, from before?" he asked. "Did you recognise her?"

"No."

"Me neither," James said. "I keep thinking back and I still can't place her at all, but I suppose I wasn't paying much attention to who was following Ryan around back then."

"Did something happen?" Sadie asked, not wanting to drop herself in it by assuming he knew everything if he actually didn't.

"You could say that," James said, sliding his phone out of his pocket. "I got a message from a friend," he continued, pulling something up on the screen. "He asked if I was okay; sent me this link."

He handed the phone to her.

"Oh no…" Sadie murmured, scanning down the article in horror. "Oh my God."

It was horrendous: there was no other word for it. It read like a work of pure fiction, except Sadie could fully believe that it was all true. It was mortifying for everyone involved but especially James. What a way to find out that your girlfriend was a piece of work.

"Why would she do this?" Sadie asked. "James, I'm so sorry. I knew she'd been coming onto Ryan and that they had some kind of history. I didn't know *this*."

James shrugged. "I didn't give her much of a chance to explain the logistics."

"Oh James…"

"I feel so… *humiliated*," he said, his voice cracking. "What a fool I look."

"No! *She* should be the one who's embarrassed! She sounds like a crazy person! If anything, you come off looking like the victim."

"*Am* I the victim?" James asked. "I lied to her first."

"You didn't lie, you just… didn't tell her something that you didn't think was relevant," Sadie said. "That's not you any more, is it? And there's all that trauma attached to it. It's so personal. Why *would* you tell her? James, why wouldn't *she tell you* that she knew anyway. That's the bigger question here."

James shrugged. "*Could* she have told me? Massive fan of your old band, oh and by the way I used to be Ryan's little plaything…"

Sadie cringed. "She could have told you," she said. "What she's done is worse, and so much weirder. And anyway, it's not even about what she didn't tell you! It's about what she's actually *done*, isn't it?"

"Is this all my fault, though? If I'd just mentioned the band in the first place…"

"She'd still have bumped into Ryan, though, wouldn't she," Sadie said gently. "If she thinks she's got these feelings for him she'd still have gone after him."

"But would we have been happier? Would it have been enough? Would *I* have been enough?"

"For what it's worth, I can't see how you could ever not be enough for anyone," Sadie said. "But some people just can't see what they've got."

James was silent for a moment.

"Wasn't this show supposed to be about you?" he asked eventually.

"About me?"

"We're all here for you, aren't we? Because we've all let you down and this is how we make up for it. But you seem to be spending most of your time holding everyone else together."

Sadie frowned. "You haven't all let me down."

"Yes we have," James said. "And we're still doing it."

Sadie shook her head. "You're not. *I'm* sorry for dragging you here. For putting you through this. If it hadn't been for me…"

"I don't want to quit, Sadie. I took so much from you – to assuage my own guilt, if nothing else, this is something I need to give back to you. But I hate that this is what I've reverted back to," he said, looking sadly at the bottle in his hand, "and I don't know how I'm going to sit in front of a camera and talk about this bloody article."

Sadie looked down at her knees. What could she say to him? How could she make this better? He *couldn't* carry on with the show, could he? She should be talking him out of it, right? She really didn't feel capable of making any of these decisions. Whose bright idea was it to let her do adulthood without a chaperone?

"Do you ever feel like we shouldn't be doing this without David?" she asked.

James looked at her curiously. "I have to say I haven't really thought about it."

"He used to take care of everything for us, didn't he? Scandals, break-ups, hormonal outbursts… Why did we think we could come here and do this again without him?"

The tiniest hint of a smile.

"What did he used to say when we had bad press, or there was some embarrassing story going around?"

"Face it head on," James said, nodding.

"Yeah. Get in front of it. Bring it up before they do," Sadie said. "It always worked, didn't it?"

"*The media is fuelled by shame.*"

"Exactly."

James looked thoughtful.

"*I* talk to *them* about it," he said. "Rather than waiting for them to bring it up."

"I think that's what he'd say."

He exhaled. "That would take some guts."

"Going through what you've been through takes some guts," Sadie said. "Coming back here to do it all over again took some guts."

He nodded.

"Or we could just quit?" Sadie suggested. "Walk away and pretend none of this ever happened?"

He shook his head. "David wouldn't let us quit."

"No, he wouldn't," Sadie agreed.

James shrugged. "So we don't quit."

"Okay," Sadie said. "But he'd take that off you as well."

"Yeah. He would," James said, handing the bottle to Sadie.

She set it carefully on the ground, trying not to think about the fact that it was more than half empty.

"Do you want to hear something horrible?" she asked, watching the donkeys as they meandered towards the fence.

"No?"

She smiled. "Did you know that me and Ryan weren't really friends any more before he came back for this show?"

"I *didn't* know that," James said. "You were always so close – I just assumed that carried on."

"It should have done," Sadie said, feeling that hot little ball still heavy in her stomach. "I spent years wondering why he'd ditched me. Years missing him. Turns out, Cameron told Ryan that I couldn't handle his success and it was best for me if he left me alone. He's *still* telling Ryan that, actually. And I would never have known if it wasn't for this show."

"I'm glad some good has come of us being here, at least."

"You don't seem very surprised?"

"Well, I'm not really," James said. "Surprised about how low he'd stoop, maybe. But he's always been a bit like this. He meddles; I've seen him do it, back in the band days. Just little things like getting David to put him and Ryan in a car together instead of you and Ryan. He did the same when we were split into groups for press interviews. Not every time, but often enough."

Sadie frowned. "Why would he do that?"

James shrugged. "I always assumed jealousy? You and Ryan had a kind of sibling closeness that you can't really..." He cast about for the word. "*Manufacture*, I guess. I don't think Cameron had many friends outside of the band."

"So he tried to *take* mine and Ryan's friendship?"

"Maybe."

"What if he did it to you and Ryan too?" Sadie asked, several of the puzzle pieces clicking together all of sudden.

"What do you mean?"

"You said that Cameron warned you off developing the band's sound with Ryan, right?"

"Yeah."

"So you and Ryan were talking about writing your own songs, with actual instruments. And then *Cameron* told you that none of us wanted to go down that route. But what did *Ryan* say to you about it?"

James shrugged. "He didn't. He just didn't seem interested any more. And I think it all clashed with me not doing so well, and then I wasn't really thinking about anything other than how bad I felt."

"Cameron told Ryan that you were getting into drugs and drinking too much, and that you were going to take the rest of us down with you if you stayed in the band," Sadie said.

"Well..." James gestured around him. "Was he wrong?"

"Yeah, but I think this was before... *the painkillers*," Sadie said. "Cameron said all that to Ryan when it *wasn't* true. He got in between you and Ryan. I mean, maybe he got in between all of us and you. I don't know. But he was either trying to separate you and Ryan, or–"

"Push me out of the band," James said, nodding.

"Or both?"

"Or both," James said, letting it sink in.

"And you pulled away, and Ryan pulled away, and then when you were actually in trouble and you needed us we weren't there for you," Sadie said. "You know, it took me until just a couple of weeks ago to realise how weird it was that none of us ever tried to get in touch with you after you left. We just let you go." She shook her head. "I'm so sorry."

"Don't be," James said. "We got there eventually, didn't we."

Sadie sighed. "None of this really makes any sense to me, though. Why would Cameron ruin what you and Ryan had, and then go after *me* and Ryan? The band was over by then; Ryan was living in a completely different country. What did Cameron have to gain by doing that? And I mean, he ruined *his own career* already. Why keep going?" She blinked. "Oh God. Did Cameron split up the band? Do I have to deal with that *as well?*"

"I thought *I* split up the band," James said.

Sadie smiled. "Oh maybe we all split up the band. What are we going to do about all this, though? This is a bigger mess than it was *before* we came here."

"What would David say?" James asked.

Sadie smiled. "He'd probably tell us to stop being a bunch of wet wipes."

"I'm pretty sure he did actually say that to me once."

"How was it he always knew what to do?" Sadie said wistfully. "We messed up all the time and he always sorted it out. I don't know how to sort any of this out."

"Is this something you need to fix?" James asked. "It's almost over. You've patched things up with Ryan. With me, I hope?"

"It's not just the stuff with Cameron that needs fixing," Sadie said, looking pointedly at the vodka bottle.

"Sadie, you can't fix me," James said gently. "I'll be okay. At some point. I think."

She looked at him: hands clasped, shoulders sagging under the weight of everything that was still dragging him down. Did she have to stand for this? Her band – *her friends* – fragmented and wounded? Where had *putting up with it* got her over the last nine years? Perhaps it was time to be more David. Fake it till you make it, right?

"I can fix *something*," Sadie said, taking James' hand and pulling him to his feet. "Come on. You're coming with me."

56

People leave a mark.

Mabel sighed, watching the water rippling in the breeze.

You could say that again.

What a mess. Just when it reached that moment where she thought it couldn't possibly get any worse, it did. Why couldn't Adam just leave it alone? Why couldn't he leave *her* alone? Why did he have to keep on being the same kind, earnest, forgiving person he always had been and make it all so hard? It had made her feel sick, not correcting him about Jay. It made her feel even worse that he'd seen her with him at all.

How can I help? What did I do? What are you doing here? What are you doing with him?

It was all so unbearable that she just wanted to rip the page out, scrunch it up and start all over again. She'd said too much to Adam as it was. She should have said nothing, just like she should have stayed far away from this stupid TV show. She'd said too much to *Kitty*, even. God, what was she doing?

We don't look away though, do we? Even when we know we should.

Kitty had been right about that but Mabel wasn't so sure about the rest. Was simply being young a good enough excuse for doing appalling things? It seemed almost too easy to let herself off on those grounds, like a get-out clause that was too good to be true. And how could it all have been Jay's fault when *she* did the things they did, too. Willingly, and without coercion. Kitty had been trying to make out that she was a *victim* but that wasn't it at all: she was a mermaid luring sailors to their death, and she always would be.

Mabel rubbed a hand across her face. Her eyes felt dry and tight, and the dull ache behind them wouldn't budge. She needed to get some things from the office but she was still trying to avoid having the "So how do you know

Adam?" conversation with Diane. God knows what he'd even told her. Perhaps she already knew everything. Perhaps she'd already told another colleague who had in turn told someone else. Perhaps everyone that she'd worked so hard to command respect from now knew all her shameful secrets.

What an absolutely horrendous thought.

As she walked the round the outskirts of the site it occurred to her that, now Adam obviously knew where she was staying and seemed to have got past the sitting outside the door thing, maybe she could move back into *her* cabin. And, not that she was expecting to see him again anyway, but it did come with the added benefit of *Jay* not knowing where she was. Maybe she could leave the bloody kittens with Kitty too.

Mabel clicked the front door closed behind her. She'd been hoping to have the place to herself but no such luck. Kitty was in the living room sitting with her back to her. She looked up as Mabel walked past, her face blotchy and her eyes swollen.

Mabel frowned in concern.

"Are you okay?"

Kitty shook her head. "Everything's gone wrong," she said, tears coming to her eyes.

"What happened?" Mabel asked, sitting down cautiously on the sofa next to Kitty.

This was not their prescribed dynamic, and comforting someone in distress was not something Mabel was at all used to doing. If she found her own emotions uncomfortable, she found other people's even harder to bear.

Kitty sniffed, holding out her phone to Mabel, the screen illuminated with some kind of article. Mabel looked at it in surprise, but as she read the first couple of lines she soon realised why it was relevant. Apparently she wasn't the only one making questionable decisions around musicians.

"Oh," she said. "Gosh."

"It's awful," Kitty said, covering her eyes with her hands. "It's so embarrassing! And James is…" She shook her head. "I don't even know *what* James is. And it's all completely pointless anyway, because Ryan isn't even interested! He said so this morning. As if I thought we could actually *be* something! I am such an *idiot*!"

Well that answered Mabel's next question: it *was* all true, then. What a horribly public revelation.

"How did they get all this information?" she asked.

"My friend wrote the article," Kitty said, tearfully. "Well, I thought she was my friend. Obviously turns out she isn't."

"Did you tell her all of this?"

Kitty nodded.

"But you didn't know she was going to write about it?"

"I didn't know she was a journalist at all!" Kitty said.

"But that's awful!" Mabel said. "Why would she do that?"

"It's a good story, isn't it." Kitty shrugged. "I deserve it, I guess."

"No you don't," Mabel said. "This is horrible. It's your private business. No one deserves this."

"Well James doesn't," Kitty said. "And he won't forgive something like this, I know he won't."

"Have you talked to him?"

"Only for long enough for me to say something really stupid. Then he left."

"What did you say?"

"That it's hard to love someone who's living a lie." Kitty sighed. "As if any of this is his fault! I wish I hadn't said it. I just felt cornered; I panicked. I wish I hadn't done *any* of this! I wish I could have just been happy with my nice pointless little life and not felt the need to mess it all up!"

Mabel didn't know what to say. She knew all too well how easy it was to ruin something that had never been broken in the first place; how it felt to like two very different people at the same time for very different reasons. But she was envious, just for a moment, that Kitty's ending had come so much earlier on in the story than her own had.

"I just got so carried away," Kitty continued. "I wanted to show Ryan that he'd made the wrong choice all those years ago. That he shouldn't have discarded me like he did. That I was worth more than that. I wanted to make him regret what he did! But then..." She sighed. "But then it wasn't like that... Or at least, it didn't *seem* like it was like that. The things he said... And the way he was being with me... It was like being 16 again. And I loved it." She looked down at her hands. "I loved it."

Mabel just nodded. Was that why she'd slipped so easily back into her destructive little dance with Jay? Because he reminded her of a time before everything had gone wrong, when it had all seemed so vibrant and so thrilling? Or was it simply because they'd already done all the damage together that could possibly be done?

"I mean, did I imagine it all? I don't *think* I did, but… Was he just being friendly and I span it into some kind of ludicrous fairy-tale?" Kitty shook her head. "Does anyone anywhere ever *get* a fairy-tale? Like, where did all those Disney films even come from if that kind of thing never happens? Why can't I want more than the height of romance being a bottle of prosecco on a Friday night? Is that supposed to be enough?" she asked. "It's not enough. It's not."

Mabel made what she hoped was a sympathetic face, but she wasn't sure Kitty actually needed her input at this point. She wondered what it would be like, getting home from work and sitting down with a person she'd chosen to spend her life with. To be *able* to commit to spending her life with someone without messing it all up. To actually *have* a life with someone. Or a life at all. Would prosecco on a Friday night be enough for *her*? She was inclined to think that actually maybe it would be.

"I guess I literally haven't learned anything in the last nine years, have I? He fooled me last time and I've just let him do it again. And every time *I'm* the loser. *I'm* the one who loses something. Every time he makes me feel like shit – every time *I let him* make me feel like shit – I come out of it without my friends, or my boyfriend…" Kitty wailed, her face pink. "Is it me? Am I awful? Have I thrown away something really good for nothing? The look on James' face, Mabel… And I did that to him. I always thought having someone look at you look that would feel dramatic and a little bit sexy, like it is on the TV, but it isn't like that, is it? It felt like being stabbed with a million tiny little knives."

Mabel knew that look all too well. It was the same look that had been on Freddie's face as he brandished a piece of paper at her and pleaded with her to talk to him; to explain. It was dramatic all right, if you were watching from a distance and weren't the person who had just blown their life up. Up close it was haunting, and not something you were likely to forget.

"Oh, God, did I just split up a band? Do I have to go and live in the hills and be a hermit for the next ten years?" Kitty asked. "Sorry, I didn't mean to– I'm not making light of what happened to you. I know that was much worse than this."

"I know," Mabel said. "It's okay."

"I don't know what's going to happen now," Kitty said. "Do I just go home, or…? Do I even *have* a home now? It's James' house: he could just kick me out! What am I going to do?"

"What do you *want* to happen now?" Mabel asked.

Kitty paused. "I don't know. I don't know how I feel about anything any more," she said, looking hopeless. "What did you want to happen after Freddie found out about Jay?"

"I can't really remember," Mabel said, surprised by the question. "There was so much other horrible stuff going on at the same time: it's all a bit of a blur. I just wanted a reset button, I suppose."

"Where would you reset to?"

"Back to the start," she said softly. "When Adam picked me up from the station."

"You wouldn't reset to never having met him at all?"

"No."

And she really wouldn't. Because the only thing that had kept her on the right track since she left had been the thought of Adam, and how much she had let him down, and how much she needed to redeem herself in his eyes. And if the side of herself that she hated – this *rot* – had always been and would always be within her, then God only knew where she might have ended up if she had got herself into a similar situation without ever having known him.

"Please tell me you've talked to him and you spent all evening catching up and you're best friends again and everything is great?" Kitty sniffed. "I need one of us to not be miserable. I can live vicariously through your fairy-tale instead."

Mabel looked away. "It's not a fairy-tale," she said quietly.

"Did you talk to him *at all*?"

"Yes." She sighed. "It's complicated."

"Why is it complicated? If you still miss him after nine years that means something. That means you *had* something."

"And if I can fall for Jay's little stunt after nine years that means something too," Mabel said. "It means I was right. It means I'm still right."

"What stunt?" Kitty asked.

Mabel shook her head. "It doesn't matter."

Because the thing was that she wasn't *sure* whether Jay's persistence to force his way back into her life *had* been a quest for revenge all along, or whether this was all happening now because she had told him no. But she deserved it either way, so it really *didn't* matter.

"If things get bad again, Adam needs to be as far away from me as possible," she said. "It's the best thing I can do for him."

It *was* what was best. Kitty was floaty and romantic and what she'd got herself into was exactly that: a silver-spun web of fireflies and daydreams. She'd written herself a bedtime story and hadn't got very far. It was so very different to what Mabel had done. She hadn't spent years daydreaming about Jay. She hadn't yearned for him to sweep her off her feet. She'd dipped a toe into the forbidden and the taboo and then she'd willingly waded in so far that her head was barely above the water. She'd discovered a part of herself she'd not previously known; she'd abused passion like it was a drug. Her web was one of darkness and deceit, and she could not let Adam come close enough to get caught up in it.

"Don't you think you've punished yourself enough?" Kitty asked.

"No," Mabel said firmly, not sure how they'd gone from dissecting Kitty's woes to hers.

"I do," Kitty said.

Mabel looked down at the fringe on the rug.

"It just seems like you haven't lived any kind of a life for almost ten years. Like you've just shut yourself away. What you've done to yourself is *far* worse than what you think you did to anyone else. And I think you've served your sentence by now, anyway."

Mabel just shook her head.

"How would you feel if you never saw Adam again?" Kitty pressed.

"Relieved."

"No you wouldn't."

"How would you feel if you never saw Ryan again?"

It was mean and she knew it, but she'd already bared far more of her soul than she wanted to. She couldn't have this conversation with Kitty, with Adam, with anyone.

Kitty shrugged. "He's not real, is he? He's just a daydream."

"I'm sorry," Mabel said, backing down.

She couldn't do it. She couldn't be mean. That was half the problem.

"I feel like a shattered windscreen," Kitty said quietly.

"I know," Mabel said. "Me too."

"Will it all go away now? This stupid unresolved yearning for Ryan? Now he's knocked me back a second time? Will I ever actually be able to let him go?" Kitty asked.

"What do you think?" Mabel asked.

"I think he could break my heart a hundred times and I'd still look up as he walked past," Kitty said sadly.

Mabel nodded. "Yeah."

"Why do we do it? What is it about these stupid boys in their stupid bands?" She sighed.

"I wish I knew."

"You came all this way to get away from them and they found you anyway."

Mabel nodded again.

"Like a boyband of boomerangs."

"That is a horrible image."

Kitty smiled.

"You should talk to James," Mabel said. "Even if it can't be fixed. Say everything you need to say to each other. Just get it out."

"And what about you?" Kitty asked pointedly.

Mabel shrugged. "I'm a sinking ship."

"You're not," Kitty said. "And it's not over for you until everyone's gone home."

Well yes, thought Mabel. *That's exactly what I'm afraid of.*

57

"Shit," Ryan said, handing the phone back to Sadie.

"Yeah," she said.

"And James has seen this?"

"He has."

"Shit," Ryan said again. "So what is this? End of the band? End of the show? No one ever talks to me again?"

"No, he wants to see you," Sadie said.

"Why would he want to see me? After *this*."

"Well technically you didn't do anything wrong…"

"We both know that I did."

"Okay, you didn't do anything *appalling*."

"I wanted to," Ryan said.

"Yeah, perhaps don't lead with that," Sadie said. "It's time, okay, for you two to make amends. Just like you and I have done."

"I don't think those two situations are really comparable," Ryan said, looking highly skeptical.

"What if Cameron did the same thing to you and James that he did to us?" Sadie asked. "Does that change things?"

Ryan frowned. "What are you saying?"

"I'm saying that Cameron got between you and James. He made you think that James was going to derail the band with a drug problem that he did not have."

"But I thought…"

"Well, yes, *now* he has one. But he didn't then. That was a lie, on purpose, just like he lied to you about me needing space."

"But why?"

"I'm still trying to figure that out, but the point is that you and James *think* you fell out, but you didn't. It was a fluke that what Cameron told you about James kind of came true. And by then we all felt so disconnected from him that we didn't help him when he needed us."

'And now I've gone and tried to shag his girlfriend," Ryan said. "Fucking hell. I'm doing really well at the moment, aren't I?"

"I don't think he's mad at you," Sadie said. "I think he's *very* mad at Kitty."

"That article heavily fingers me as an accessory," Ryan said. "He must be in a very forgiving mood."

"He does want to talk to you," Sadie said. "Honestly."

"Has he been heavily coerced?" Ryan asked suspiciously.

She smiled. "*Minimally* coerced. Will you come?"

"It's going to be excruciatingly awkward."

Sadie made a face. "Do you think you kind of deserve that a little bit?"

"Yes, okay," Ryan said. "Can't I just never talk to him again instead? That sounds less painful."

"Didn't you miss him?" Sadie asked. "*I* miss what you two had. I miss being around it."

Ryan looked away. "Yeah I missed him," he said quietly. "Easier to tell myself that I didn't, though. Easier to be angry."

"I know," Sadie said.

Ryan nodded. "Where is he?"

"At our cabin."

"Okay. Just... Can you give me a minute?"

"Of course," Sadie said. "I'll see you in a bit."

She felt hopeful as she walked away. Sure, a large proportion of the life she had been living was currently on fire, and it did seem ludicrously optimistic that this, of all things, could bring Ryan and James back together, but she had to try, and everyone's secrets being out in the open seemed like a good time for a fresh start.

James was on the sofa when she got back to the cabin.

"Did you *lock me in?*" he asked.

"Yes," Sadie said. "You're a flight risk."

"I feel like I'm under house arrest here."

She shrugged. "You are."

"And you are keeping me locked up... indefinitely?"

"I'm looking after you," Sadie said, clearing coffee cups and other detritus off the dining table.

"Oh that's what this is."

Sadie smiled. "Yes. It's called friendship."

"Ah. I'm assuming I'll get used to it?"

"It'll be more like a grudging acceptance," Sadie said. "Ryan will be here in a minute."

James nodded, looking grave. "I don't know what I'm going to say to him."

"That makes two of you," Sadie said. "Look, you just need to talk. If we're not going to quit the show you guys need to clear at least some of the air. Even if it's an argument, or whatever. We can't go and do another rehearsal with things how they are. It's too messy."

"Yeah."

"We also need to decide what to do about Cameron, and it would be really nice to be able to do that as a united front."

"Well, let's not expect miracles."

Sadie grimaced. "Are you okay?"

"I'm sober enough to have this conversation with Ryan," James said, which wasn't quite what she was asking but close enough.

"It's going to be more awkward for him."

"We'll see."

"At least he knows the real reason you left the band so you don't have to rehash the whole thing again."

"Yes, thank you so much for breaking my confidence and telling Ryan about my private issues," James said, but his tone was light.

"I'll make coffee," Sadie said, squeezing him on the shoulder.

The kettle had just boiled when Ryan came through the door.

"I was going to knock," he said. "But then I remembered this was my cabin…"

James stood up. Sadie held her breath.

"Hi," Ryan said awkwardly.

"Hi."

"So I don't really know how to deliver a grovelling apology on the scale that is required here…" he said. "I think I have multiple things to apologise for, actually, and I'll be honest, I don't know where to start."

"It's okay," James said. "I'm not looking for an apology."

"Well, thank you, that's incredibly magnanimous of you, but you are going to get one and it's going to be horribly awkward for both of us, as it should be," Ryan said. "Can we sit? I feel like I'm auditioning for a really bad play here."

James nodded, and Ryan sat down on the sofa opposite him. Sadie finished making the coffees but stayed where she was: it didn't seem like quite the right moment for refreshments.

"So I guess I'll address the largest elephant in the room first," Ryan said. "I promise that absolutely nothing happened between me and Kitty, but I will hold my hands up because I didn't discourage it and I should have done. I could have *easily* done, but I didn't, and there's no excuse for that. It was a really dick move, and I don't actually know what I was playing at."

Sadie accidentally dropped a teaspoon and they both looked over at her.

"Don't mind me," she whispered, wishing herself invisible.

"That hot mess over there told me about why you left the band and what it appears that Cameron has done to all of us," Ryan continued. "And, mate, I am *so sorry* for letting you down. I knew something bad was going on with you but I let Cameron get right in my head and I should have known better. I should have *done something*. We were more than that, weren't we?"

James nodded.

"Yeah, well," Ryan shook his head. "I don't know what to say, really. I feel awful. We were supposed to be a team and I just let you go."

"There wasn't much you could have done," James said.

"Yes, mate, there was. *You* meant more to me than the bloody band! You both did! And I'd have walked away from the band *with you* if that's what needed to be done. Without looking back."

Sadie nodded. "Me too."

James shook his head, looking surprised. "I would never have expected you to do that."

"You were my brother," Ryan said, looking earnestly at James. "I should never have lost sight of that."

Sadie swallowed, her throat suddenly feeling tight.

"And I don't even really know how to process any of this. I mean, what I thought I knew about everything... Well it's all wrong, isn't it? Never mind all the Cameron shit – I can't get my head round everything *you've* been through. It sounds fucking awful, I'll be honest. How you're even here I don't know."

"You and me both," James said. "Not the easiest thing I've ever done."

"No, I bet," Ryan said. "Did you have any idea what Cameron was doing?"

"No, not really." James looked thoughtful. "Once or twice I got the feeling he was trying to edge me out, but I was really paranoid about a lot of things back then."

"I'm gutted we never got to work on that new sound," Ryan said. "Really think that could have worked."

"Me too," James said, nodding.

"Guess we'll never know."

"Shall we start a new band?" Sadie asked, deciding now was a good time to hand out lukewarm coffees. "Just us three?"

"Well *some of us* are still in a band, actually," Ryan said.

"Yeah, and I think I'll stick to my quiet life, thanks."

"Oof, so much rejection this week," Sadie said.

"Not from *everybody*," Ryan said with a wink.

She smiled. "Hey, so, Kingpin have got a deal out of this already. They're doing a tour!" She clamped a hand over her mouth. "Oh wait, no, that's a secret."

Ryan laughed. "Christ, I hope you don't know any of my secrets."

"You know I couldn't do something like that, if they offered it to us…" James said, looking worried.

"I know. I wouldn't want you to," Sadie said. "I mean, I came here wanting that. *Obsessed* with that. But what I actually got is much nicer. Or could be much nicer. It depends how much you two make up. And we'll just have to be that band that no one could sign, no matter how much they begged."

"Sadie, we're still mortal enemies. We're going to fight to the death in a minute," Ryan said.

"After I've finished my coffee," James agreed.

Sadie smiled hopefully. Had she done it? Had she put her band back together? Talk about out of the ashes…

"So me and James have got half a plan," she said. "It needs a second opinion."

"What's your plan?" Ryan asked, relaxing into the sofa for the first time.

"We don't quit," Sadie said.

James nodded in solidarity.

"And?"

"That's it."

"That's barely a plan," Ryan said. "I mean, what are we going to *do* about everything?"

"Revenge?" Sadie suggested.

"Like what?"

"Like... I don't know, kicking Cameron out of the band so I don't have to see his stupid smug face any more?"

It was funny how actually having the facts could make you reframe how you saw a person. She could kind of see now how much of Cameron she'd had to take with a pinch of salt to make his negativity and his unkind jibes more palatable. Why had she humoured him for so long? Was it because he'd been one of her last remaining links to the band? Or because for some reason she'd thought that she'd *needed* his poor excuse for a friendship and that there wasn't anything better out there for her?

"Do you know what's the best revenge?" Ryan asked.

"Violence?" Sadie suggested.

"Rising above it," Ryan said.

"Doesn't sound very satisfying."

"Yeah, but think about what Cameron wants. He wants us divided, right? How's it going to feel if he sees us all getting along, despite his best efforts?"

"Like a theoretical punch in the face," Sadie said, nodding.

"There's no point making a scene, is there?" Ryan said. "What are we, teenagers?"

"Yes," Sadie said, smiling.

"Well you might be, but I don't think Old Father Time over there is going to be much use in a fight," Ryan said, raising an eyebrow at James as if he were inviting a retort.

"I think– Is it too soon to be taking the piss out of me?" James said, smiling. "I do agree though, about not making a scene. The damage was done a long time ago."

"I was going to say that he could even have changed, but he hasn't, has he? Even I can see that."

"Are we not going to ask him *why*?" Sadie said.

"Does it really matter?"

She scrunched up her nose. "Kind of."

"I don't know about all this *closure* thing," James said. "It feels like too trendy a concept to actually mean anything."

"You really could just let it go?" Sadie asked. "Everything he put you through?"

James looked thoughtful. "I might choose instead to focus on what I've ended up with *despite* everything he did."

"I just don't know if I can get over what he took from me that easily," Sadie said. "It still makes me feel funny just thinking about it."

"What would David say?" James asked.

"It's our new religion," Sadie explained, seeing Ryan's confused look. "WWDS. And he'd say *it's all just a beautiful game*, and then we'd tell him that that was football and he'd say that the sentiment remained."

"Have you gone full-on imaginary friend here?" Ryan asked, looking amused.

"Try making every decision based on what David would advise and tell me it doesn't make sense," Sadie said.

"I think David would also say that Ryan is right about rising above it," James said. "Or he'd veto the violence, at least."

"Maybe Ryan is embodying the spirit of David," Sadie said.

"Well I'd have a job seeing as he's not dead, but I'll take that as a compliment, I guess?"

"Should we vote?" Sadie asked. "On what we're going to do?"

"Why isn't Mia here?" James asked. "Shouldn't she be part of this too?"

Sadie made a face. While everything else seemed to be starting to line up nicely, Mia was becoming a bit of a grey area. For Sadie's entire adult life, Mia had been her only real confidant: she'd gone to her with the good things, the bad things, and everything in between. They'd virtually lived in each other's pockets and now Sadie felt like she hadn't even really *seen* her over the last couple of days, let alone told her any of the huge stuff that had been going on. But she'd told Ryan, hadn't she – she'd gone to *Ryan* with all the big stuff – and now she was wondering whether she'd accidentally been a bit of a dick to her oldest friend by ditching her for a stupid boy. It was all making her feel a bit icky and she wasn't sure how to put it right, or when she was even going to get a chance to in amongst dealing with everything else.

"I don't know," she said, feeling guilty. "Mia and Cameron are pretty close."

"You think she'd be on his side?" Ryan asked. "She's not stupid."

"I think she'd give him the benefit of the doubt."

"Should *we* be giving him the benefit of the doubt?" James asked.

"No, we're past that," Ryan said. "I think we know what he's done."

"All those in favour of not rocking the boat..." James said, raising a hand.

Ryan also raised his and Sadie rolled her eyes.

"Two more days, that's all," Ryan said nudging her. "We smash that live show and we go out on a high, and then we can forget this ever happened."

"Except I live down the road from Cameron," Sadie said.

"Not for a while you won't," Ryan said, smiling at her.

She pictured walking through the airport with him. Getting on a plane. Stepping into *his* life. She pictured waking up every morning knowing that nothing was ever going to come between the two of them ever again.

She smiled back at him.

"Two days. Okay. I'll do my best."

TWO DAYS TO THE LIVE SHOW

58

Kitty stopped at the foot of the path, her hand clamped to her chest. Was she going to be sick? Or was this just abject terror?

She closed her eyes and tried to take some *nice deep calming breaths*, but it was not as easy as social media made it out to be. Maybe she'd just go back. Could she do that? Maybe she'd just go *home*; spend a couple of days trying to fool herself that none of this had ever happened. Oh that sounded nice, was that an option? She didn't even feel the tiniest bit prepared for the conversation she was about to attempt to have.

She looked towards the cabin, trying to catch a glimpse of what was happening inside. It was a good job that no one was trying to assassinate any of these celebrities because it really didn't take much effort at all to find out where they were at any given moment. She knew he was in there. She didn't know *why* he was in there, of *all* the places, but she knew that he was. And she knew really that they had to have this conversation, and that it had to be now.

She forced herself up the path, a reluctant fist knocking on the door. When the boy with the blue eyes opened it her heart contracted so painfully that she almost gasped.

Ryan looked at her in surprise, a whole cacophony of emotions flashing across his face too fast for Kitty to grasp any of them. It felt like she was seeing him for the very last time and it seemed, for just a moment, like the whole world paused around her as their eyes locked. And then, a movement over his shoulder, Kitty's stomach lurching as Ryan turned away from her.

"It's for you, mate," he said, melting away into the cabin as James replaced him in the doorway.

"Hi," he said, his expression pensive.

"Hi," she said, not knowing where to look. "I didn't know if I should come... I can go, if you want me to."

"No, it's okay," he said. "I've got a bit of time. We should talk."

The way he said it was so ominous that Kitty felt her heart sink. She'd done something really really stupid here, hadn't she? And what happened next wasn't even up to her.

"Shall we walk?" he asked, slipping his shoes on.

Kitty nodded, wondering how it had come to be that James was at Ryan's cabin. Had he been there all night? It was surely the last place that it made sense for him to be. But this was what she'd wanted, wasn't it? James actually interacting with his old bandmates? A vague semblance of friendship? For them to be *part of something interesting*? It wasn't exactly a family barbeque but it was something. And now it was absolutely none of her business.

"I don't really know what to say..." Kitty said hesitantly, as they walked along the road to some unknown destination.

The physical space between them felt awkward and jarring. Not that they'd been the kind of couple who sat on each other's laps, but at least when he'd been hers they were tethered together invisibly. Now everything felt too loose, as if he could step away from her and keep on walking and there'd be nothing to pull them back together. *Was* he still hers? Did *anyone* want her now?

"We find ourselves in a bit of a strange situation," James said. "I think it's fair to say that there's some key things I didn't know about you."

Kitty cringed.

"But there's also a lot you don't know about me," James continued. "Maybe it's not really that much of a surprise that things have gone the way they have, given the secrets we've both been carrying around."

Kitty nodded, but she didn't really know what he meant. What didn't she know about him? It wasn't Funk Shui, because he knew now that she'd known about that all along. How big a secret could he have possibly been keeping that she wouldn't have noticed? Maybe she did already know and he thought she didn't. Unless they were talking secret wife and child, in which case she was surely off the hook with her particular indiscretions.

"I've been wondering whether things would have been different if I'd been honest with you to start with; f you'd known the kind of person I really was rather than who I was pretending to be," James said. "Maybe if I'd laid all my cards on the table from the start; if you'd known the kind of life you'd be getting with me... Well, I have a feeling we'd never have made it this far, anyway."

Kitty frowned. What was he talking about? *Was* he actually a secret serial killer?

James sighed. "From the moment I walked into your office, all I could see was you. You were… *radiant.*" He shook his head. "You still are. You know, I was only supposed to be visiting for the day. It was just going to be one meeting and then I'd work on the project remotely. I invented the whole "getting to know your company" thing on the spot. So I could get to know you."

Kitty kept her eyes on the ground.

"There's no one like you in the world. Do you know that?" James said. "I felt like I couldn't walk out of that office without you. But I also knew that who I was would never be enough for someone like you. So I put on a *grand show*, and I got what I wanted, but there was a cost, of course. The price I paid, for you, was a constant sense of unease that told me I wasn't enough, and that I could never be enough… Perversely I think that pulled me away from you more than anything. I felt like I would never be able to live up to your expectations so there was no point even trying."

Kitty swallowed hard. Wasn't this the dream? For someone to feel this desperately about her? For someone to agonise over her; to be torn apart by the sheer strength of their feelings for her? This was pure romance, right? Real life angst! Wasn't she happy now?

"I think what I did to you was really cruel, actually," James said.

"You didn't do anything to me!" Kitty protested, her voice thick.

He was looking at her with heart-breaking remorse and it was all wrong! *She* was the bad guy! *She* was the one who had done something awful! He was supposed to be angry with her! Shouting at her! Not *this*.

"I did," James said. "I wasn't honest with you. I sold you a performance I was never going to be able to keep up long-term. I asked you to change your whole life for me *knowing* I would never be able to make you happy. That wasn't fair on you. Part of me thinks I brought all of this on myself. And it's not an excuse – I refuse to use it as an excuse – but I need to explain where all this stems from."

Kitty didn't say anything. This sudden realness from James was disorientating and confusing. This wasn't what she'd thought they were going to talk about.

"I was not in a good place before I left the band," James said. "I was struggling, and I was drinking too much just to get through the day, and I got myself into a real mess."

Oh Jesus, Kitty thought. *We're doing this now?* This *is how I find out why he really left the band?*

She tried to grasp the enormity of what he was saying but it felt like his words were slipping through her fingers as she scrabbled around trying to gather them back up. This moment, that had come out of absolutely nowhere, was *so important*. She wanted him to repeat what he'd just said so she could try to absorb it properly.

We knew it, she thought. *We knew he was struggling.*

But *drinking too much*? She'd always imagined his inner torment as a deep, introspected sadness, not a generic problem with alcohol. Wasn't *everyone* drinking too much back then?

"I hate telling you about this just as much as I imagined I would," James said, looking at his hands. "I did think about it, sometimes. Telling you. But admitting this kind of weakness…" He sighed. "I don't even recognise who I was back then."

Kitty frowned. What exactly was he saying here? How much of a "mess" had he got himself into?

"Things got really dark," James said. "How I was feeling went from miserable to frightening really fast. I just wanted a moment's relief from it all, and unfortunately I found that a certain amount of codeine did the job reasonably well."

"What's codeine?" Kitty asked, finding her voice.

"It's a painkiller. Not generally recommended for psychological pain, though," James said. "It was a really slippery slope from there."

"*Painkillers?*" Kitty said. "Like when film stars get addicted to painkillers and have to go to rehab?"

"Well I don't think they're getting their opiates from Boots, but it's not a million miles away," James said.

She frowned. "I can't even imagine you doing something like that. You're so… *sensible*. Like, you weigh up everything you do before you do it."

"Yeah, well, that's a whole other issue, isn't it?" James said. "I wasn't always like that. I don't think, anyway. I used to be… lighter. More free."

Yeah, Kitty thought, *you did*.

"Did you go to rehab?" she asked.

Such a strange sensation, having a proper open conversation with James about his past; to finally be able to ask questions and get answers.

"No, nothing as glamourous as that. I got *help*, eventually, but…" James shrugged. "It wasn't easy, picking myself back up."

"But… You're okay now, aren't you? You got better, right?" Kitty asked, something really horrible dawning on her.

They were talking about a *past* version of him, weren't they? This didn't apply to their current lives, did it?

"I wish I could say that I was," James said, "but it's never really left me. That feeling. I think maybe it's just who I am. Some days are better than others. Being here is… *a challenge*."

"But you never said…?" Kitty said, taken aback. "I mean, we do normal things. You're a normal person…"

James smiled ruefully. "I manage it okay most of the time. I'm not an *addict*. Most days I can go out for a drink or two and go home a bit merry like anyone else."

"What about here?" Kitty asked, an empty feeling opening up in her stomach.

James swallowed. "Not so much, it seems."

Kitty opened her mouth to say something but nothing came out.

"I don't want to be this person," James said. "And certainly not with *you*. And talking about the band… It's so tangled up with how I was feeling back then that I can't separate it out. Every time I think about it it's like I can see that black hole opening up again; I still feel like I'm standing too close to it. And that's not what you signed up for, was it? When you started dating someone who used to be in a band."

"I didn't start dating *someone who used to be in a band*," Kitty said, tears in her eyes. "I started dating *you*. And I expected too much. I always expect too much. You're always telling me that."

"But that's the point, Kitty. I *shouldn't* be telling you that. *No one* should be telling you that! You deserve more than someone who constantly tells you to lower your expectations."

"You don't," Kitty said quietly, but she knew that wasn't true.

Wasn't that what she had been complaining to Ryan about? Wasn't that one of the things she said she disliked the most about James?

"I don't blame you for wanting more. Because what can I offer you, really? So many times I thought about playing the pop band card," James said, rubbing a hand roughly over his face. "I knew it would make me seem like more of the man I'd presented myself to you as. But I couldn't, Kitty. I just couldn't."

Kitty put her hand to her mouth, her mascara running in grey streaks down her face. How awful she had been to this man. How fickle she was to have turned her back on him because her life wasn't "exciting" enough, when all the time he'd been beating himself up about not being able to give her the life she deserved, as if she was anything special at all. After everything he had been through, there she was, still demanding more.

"I wish you hadn't hidden so much of yourself," Kitty whispered. "I would have taken all of it. All of you."

She saw it all now: the void they'd built their life around. It wasn't made up of James' reticence to acknowledge the band – it was all the other things he'd left out. The more important things: the scorch marks and scars that made you human. And she had tried so hard to be pristine and perfect too, worthy of something fabulous, her hopes and dreams borrowed from books and films, when the one thing that had been missing all along, in *both* of them, was the *depth* that came from being who you really were.

"All I ever wanted was to know everything about you. For you to let me in," she said.

James nodded, his expression so pained that Kitty felt sick.

"I'm sorry," he said.

"Why are *you* sorry?" Kitty asked, shaking her head.

"Because this was doomed from the start, and that's on me."

"But..."

"I really don't want to talk about this business with Ryan," James said, cutting her off. "Honestly, if it had to be someone, I really really wish it hadn't been him, but it's done now, isn't it." He paused. "The things is, Kitty, I don't think I can spend another four years of my life feeling like I'm not enough for you." He looked at her with tears in his eyes and she felt her remaining hopes plummet. "Even though I wish I could. I just... I don't know what that would do to me."

She pressed her lips together tightly and nodded. He was ending it and she couldn't do a thing about it. What could she possibly say when she had treated him so badly when he'd needed her the most? She had no right to protest, even if she could have found the words.

James cleared his throat. "I, er... I'm going to stay with Sadie and Ryan for the last couple of nights. You should stay and watch the show, okay? For your inner fangirl." He managed a small smile. "No one needs to make a dramatic exit."

Kitty nodded again.

"I'll see you afterwards. Then we can go home; sort it all out. We don't have to do it here."

"Okay," she whispered.

James sighed, looking at her sadly.

"I hate seeing you cry," he said.

Kitty tried to force a smile, shaking her head.

"It's okay, I'm..." She took a deep breath. "I'm okay. You should get back to your band."

He reached out and took her hand, squeezing it tightly before letting it drop again. He looked at her one final time before nodding and walking away.

Kitty put two shaking hands over her eyes, trying not to completely lose it on the street outside someone else's cabin. She realised she didn't even know where she was, having paid no attention to the route they'd taken, and it all looked the same as everywhere else. Honestly, this holiday park – they couldn't have colour-coded the different zones, or something? She exhaled hopelessly, slumping down onto a nearby bench, trying to process what had just happened and everything James had told her. What could they have had if only they'd just been themselves from the start? What a stupid stupid waste. Was *this* fate? Was *this* the long con? A really long-winded and horrible way of teaching her that *you cannot bloody have it all*? And why did James have to be so kind, and so decent, and make her feel this awful? He could have shouted at her and it would have felt less devastating than what actually happened.

"Are you okay?"

A voice she didn't recognise: a soft Northern lilt.

She looked up, hastily wiping her tears away, and found herself staring straight into the eyes of Theo Monroe from Indigo Lion.

She blanched in surprise.

"No, not really," she said, knowing that her heart had taken a serious hit when the sight of a mega celebrity standing over her didn't so much as take the edge off the pain. "My boyfriend just broke up with me."

"Oh fuck. Me too," Theo said. "Can I sit?" he asked, gesturing at the bench.

"Of course!" Kitty said, wondering why on earth he would want to. "Oh God, do I look like a panda? My makeup is all over my face, isn't it?"

Theo smiled. "A little bit."

"Well as if my day could get any worse," Kitty said morosely. "Maybe they'll get me on camera as I do the walk of shame back to my cabin, really finish things off."

"We can get you fixed up," Theo said, looking around him. "All we need is a key to one of these cabins, or someone who knows how to pick a lock."

"Oh!" Kitty said, feeling in her pocket for the teardrop shaped piece of black plastic that she'd never quite got round to returning to Mabel. "I actually do have a key. To everywhere."

"A magician! Well what are we waiting for?" Theo asked, gesturing grandly. "Pick a cabin, any cabin."

Kitty looked at him curiously. "You are actually here, right? I haven't started hallucinating pop stars?"

"No, I'm here. As far as I'm aware. I'm Theo, by the way."

She smiled. "I know who you are."

"Well I don't like to assume."

"I'm Kitty," she said, taking his proffered hand and shaking it, trying not to think about the fact that she just touched *Theo bloody Monroe*. "And don't feel you have to…" She gestured at her assumed disaster of a face. "I can manage."

"I'm afraid my sister has drilled it into me that you don't walk past a crying girl, so I'm going to have to see this one through."

"She sounds very wise."

"She is. Very wise and very annoying," Theo said. "So which one? Pick a number."

Kitty looked at the three closest cabins.

"I don't know… Do you think that one in the middle?"

"Only one way to find out."

Was this surreal situation better than sitting on a bench being sad on her own? Probably, Kitty thought as she walked up a path with the biggest pop star in the country. Another thing ticked off her *Village of Pop* bucket list that didn't feel half as thrilling as it was supposed to. But what else was she going to do, anyway? She had two whole days ahead of her which were basically just going to consist of sitting in the cabin on her own, trying to be as far away from James and Ryan as possible, with another silent four hour car journey to look forward to at the end of it. And then… Well, she could only assume that then she'd be packing her bags and leaving James to it, the great unknown stretching out ahead of her. So, yeah, right now she'd rather talk about nothing with an insanely famous stranger than have to be alone with all the unpleasantly heavy thoughts that were filling up her head.

"Who'd live in a house like this?" Theo said, as Kitty unlocked the door with the key fob and cautiously opened it.

It was identical in layout to her own cabin, the remains of breakfast piled in the sink and various items of clothing strewn about the place.

"Girls' shoes," Theo said, pointing at the floor. "We could be onto a winner."

"Do you often break into people's houses with crying girls?" Kitty asked, feeling strange walking uninvited amongst someone else's life.

"Only if I think my sister would approve."

Kitty quickly found the bathroom, and with it a mirror and face wipes. She was surprised when Theo followed her in, trying to focus on her own face and not watch his reflection in the mirror as she attempted to repair the damage to her makeup.

"I didn't think they'd let you wander around on your own," she said, dabbing at the grey streaks of mascara. "Shouldn't you have a bodyguard or something?"

"Oh I gave him the slip," Theo said. "I needed a second of not being a celebrity and just being a person. Which, believe it or not, I still am."

Kitty nodded, deciding that the damage to her foundation was too great and she was going to have to take the whole lot off.

Who was there to look good for now, anyway? Theo Monroe wasn't going to care about a few open pores.

"So is it common knowledge?" she asked cautiously. "The boyfriend thing?"

"Ah *the boyfriend thing*," Theo said, smiling mischievously. "I like to tell people sometimes. Keeps management on their toes."

"What if I told someone?" Kitty asked, getting another wipe out of the packet. "What if I was actually a journalist?"

"Are you?"

"No," she said.

"Well that's good, because otherwise I'd have to pretend to stumble out of a club with Jeanie again and I really can't be bothered."

"Jeanie Foster?" Kitty asked, realising she'd actually seen those photos, of a boy holding a girl's hand, both of them looking dead behind the eyes and like they'd rather be anywhere else.

"If it gets really bad they make me go on holiday with her, which is a total waste of everyone's time, but still." Theo rolled his eyes. "It gets "dealt with", one way or another."

"I would never have known," Kitty said, trying to play it cool in the face of this world class exclusive gossip.

"Seems like it's already being dealt with quite well, huh?" Theo said dryly.

"So what does she get out of it?"

"Oh it's all very cynical. We go on a lot more "dates" when her TV show isn't getting the ratings."

Kitty wrinkled her nose in distaste. "That's just barbaric. As if you're the only gay person in pop music."

Theo shrugged. "I make a lot of money for a lot of people."

"I really thought the world was more open-minded these days."

"If only."

"I'm sorry," Kitty said. "That must be really shit."

"The price we pay," Theo said. "Sold my soul to the devil, Austin said."

"Austin was your boyfriend?" Kitty asked.

Theo nodded.

"Why did he break up with you?"

"Well who would want all of this nonsense? He wants me to stumble out of a club holding *his* hand. And can you blame him?" Theo said. "Why did your boyfriend break up with you?"

"Because I deserved it," Kitty said frankly.

Theo smiled. "Someone's always got to be the dickhead."

Kitty nodded. "Yeah. This time it was me," she said. "Where are the rest of your band?"

"Oh they're holed up in the apartments. I want to get in there, be a part of it all, but they don't. And *I* can't do anything without *them*, because then you get the inevitable rumours about me pulling away from the group and laying the groundwork for my impending solo career, which is such bollocks but it pisses them off no end."

"That's not true?"

Theo shook his head. "Not yet."

"So you're all staying on site? People were talking about how they hadn't seen you; that you hadn't been at any of the group activities."

"You know, I would *love* to do some group activities. Crazy golf? Sign me up," Theo said.

"So why aren't you?"

"We're not allowed. It not the story the producers want. We're not supposed to be mixing with "ex-celebs": we're the *stars*, you see. Too good for crazy golf!" He sighed. "I hate it. It's the same everywhere. And it's not who I am. But your charmed life comes at a cost – got to play the part. Maybe I did sell my soul."

"Maybe one day you'll be having your own reunion and then you can play all the crazy golf you like."

"Well, Kitty, that's the dream."

"I'm all done," she said, putting the pile of used wipes into the bin. "Should we go?"

"Oh I don't know, I kind of like it here," Theo said, walking back out into the living area. "Feels so *normal*."

"How long before they put out a national alert and the SWAT team come bursting in through the windows and take you back?"

Theo looked at his watch. "At least another 15 minutes."

"Just enough time for a nice normal coffee, then," Kitty said, going over to the kettle. "Apart from the breaking and entering part."

"Crime refreshments," Theo said, pulling out a chair at the dining table.

"That could be your next band name."

"It could," Theo nodded.

Kitty hesitated, her back to him as she watched the water bubbling up the inside of the kettle.

Should she say it? Did it really matter, and would it make any difference?

"You know they think it'll last forever?" she said. "Your fans."

"I don't think I know *what* the fans think," Theo said, as she handed him a mug and sat down at the head of the table. "Apart from that they seem to be able to work out where I'm going to be before I even know."

"They think about you every second of every day. In ways you can't even imagine."

Theo raised an eyebrow and Kitty smiled.

"Not just those ways," she said. "Can I give you some unsolicited advice, as a wounded veteran fangirl?"

"I am all ears. Genuinely."

"Don't underestimate your influence on your fans. The really diehard ones. The way you treat them now might stay with them for the rest of their lives. You might never meet these people but you're literally shaping who they'll become."

Theo looked thoughtful. "That's a very big responsibility."

"In all seriousness, it really is. And I know you don't have control over most of what you do, but where you can tread carefully you should. And be generous," Kitty said, a thought suddenly occurring to her. "Do you fancy making someone's day in your last few moments of freedom?"

"Always," Theo said.

She smiled. "Okay. One sec."

She pulled her phone out of her pocket and opened up WhatsApp, hitting video call on her group chat with the Indigo Lion fans she'd met at the gate earlier in the week. One by one their faces appeared in little boxes on the screen, and as she tilted the phone towards Theo their shrieks could be heard all the way across the site.

59

"I don't like it," Sadie said, checking the time on her phone again.

"You don't like what?" Ryan asked. "James talking to his girlfriend?"

"She's no good for him," Sadie said. "And he's fragile! What if she upsets him? What if he goes off and gets drunk again?"

"Then we'll pick him back up," Ryan said gently, a reassuring hand on Sadie's arm. "We've got him. Okay? And it's not like he's *sober*. One drink isn't back to square one. It's a different thing."

"He said he's been drinking vodka from a water bottle all week."

Ryan frowned. "Well I hate that."

"Me too."

"Look, it's not going to be like before," Ryan said. "But you can't fix something like this all in one go. Even if he's not okay after talking to Kitty, we're here, and we'll–" He screwed up his face. "I don't know, what's a more manly word for looking after someone?"

Sadie smiled. There had been something approaching harmony in the cabin by the time they'd finally called it a night yesterday evening. James had stayed over, which had been surprising and delightful and, sure, it had been mainly because he didn't have anywhere else to go, but that didn't change how nice it had been, sitting up with him and Ryan, talking and eating biscuits (in lieu of wine). It was still tentative, and it was still awkward, and Sadie had a feeling that Kitty wasn't going to be an easy thing to get over – for either of them – but there had been banter that morning over breakfast – actual proper banter, like the good old days – and it had made her heart feel so full.

"What do you think he's going to do? About Kitty?" Sadie asked.

Ryan shrugged. "The man has the luxury of making that decision."

"You want him to break up with her, though."

"Sade, I can't go there now, can I?" he asked. "Not if I want something with James."

"Do you want that more than you want her?" Sadie asked, surprised.

"Yes. I do."

"Wow. Are we calling you a *changed man* or…?"

Ryan rolled his eyes. "Come on, we need to leave. And James might miss pottery painting and it'll still be okay," he said, steering Sadie towards the door. "I promise."

"Can I ask you a question?" she asked as they walked down the front path.

"If it's about Kitty you cannot," Ryan said. "Otherwise you can."

"It's kind of a bit of both."

"Go on then. I feel like you're going to ask me either way."

"You know the article about Kitty…"

"Yes."

"You know what she said about me and you?"

Ryan cringed. "Yes," he said, through gritted teeth.

"Is that true?"

"And there I was thinking that I'd had all the embarrassing conversations there were to have this week."

"*Is* it?"

"I told Kitty that, yes. In confidence, I might add, but whatever, I guess."

"Does that mean… you *liked* me?"

"I don't know, Sadie, it was ages ago," Ryan said, avoiding eye contact.

"Do you… *still* like me?"

"No, don't be disgusting. I've moved onto other people I can't have, haven't I?"

Sadie smiled. "Is this making you feeling uncomfortable?" she asked, nudging him in the side.

"You know it is," he grumbled.

"So did you actually fancy me? That is so hilarious."

"Maybe very briefly. Before I got to know you, obviously."

She grinned. "Oh my God, am I the one that got away?"

"No you are bloody well *not* the one who got away! Jesus Christ, woman."

"Did you lie awake on the tour bus pining for me?"

"No I did not!"

"Did you think I was your soulmate?" Sadie asked gleefully. "Did you have sexy thoughts about me?"

"Fuck my life," Ryan muttered.

"Maybe we should address this on camera, do you think?" Sadie asked. "I mean, I wouldn't want anyone to get the wrong idea."

Ryan just shoved her in reply and she laughed as she stumbled over a rogue tree branch.

"I think it's healthy to talk about our feelings!" she said.

"Why don't you go and tell them all about your feelings for George, then."

"Maybe I will!" Sadie paused. "Wait, you're not *jealous*, are you?"

"Oh my God," Ryan muttered, shaking his head in despair.

They walked down the slope to the square, Sadie scanning the crowd for her people. Her relief at seeing James walking towards them was quickly tempered by the expression on his face. Sad, definitely sad. Sadie sighed. This was exactly what she'd thought was going to happen.

"Hello," she said, hoping for a reassuring smile, but James just nodded tightly at her.

She prickled when she saw Cameron talking to Mia, her disgust an actual physical sensation in her stomach. Could she really do this? Could she really keep the peace with him after everything she'd found out? It wasn't exactly her thing, keeping her thoughts to herself.

"Funk Shui! Over here for a minute, please!"

Sadie looked round at the man who was summoning them. He was holding a clipboard so that could only mean one thing. Those bloody clipboards. She was sure they were going to pop up in some kind of recurring nightmare after they left this place. Probably with arms and legs and a weapon. She glanced at Ryan and he grimaced back at her as Mia and Cameron drifted over.

"Okay, that's all of you. Great! I think we've got some things to discuss, haven't we?" Clipboard Guy said, looking smug.

"I'll take this one, actually," James said, stepping in front of the group. "I can think of a few things to say."

Ryan raised his eyebrows pointedly at Sadie. That was a good sign, right? That was James facing things head on; doing all the things they'd talked about.

"He's going to be okay, isn't he?" she murmured to Ryan as they followed the rest of the bands inside.

"Eventually," he said, squeezing her hand.

"Don't make me sit with Cameron."

He nodded, leaving her side and steering Cameron to a table by the window while she sat down at the back with Mia.

"Hello you," Mia said, smiling at her. "Where did Ryan and Cameron go?"

"Oh I don't know, maybe they got put on a different table," Sadie said airily, pulling a paint pallete towards her and picking up a brush. "What are we supposed to be doing with these?"

"I think they're going to auction off the plates for charity," Mia said.

"Or put them in the bin."

"They'll probably put the really bad ones in the bin."

Sadie smiled. "I can't believe it's almost over," she said. "All this."

"It's been quite a week."

"I feel like I haven't really spent much time with you. Apart from all the rehearsing," Sadie said. "Did I abandon you to hang out with boys? Am I an awful friend?"

"You could never be an awful friend," Mia said. "You spend all your time with me at home. It's good for you to be with other people."

"You always said that," Sadie said.

"And was I right?"

Sadie smiled. "Yeah. But these are my people. It's easy here."

"You might be surprised," Mia said. "People have all kinds of sides to them. And I think there's a little bit more to life than hanging out with me all the time."

Sadie nodded. "Will you be okay when I go to America with Ryan?" she asked.

"Sadie," Mia said, and it was like being fondly scolded by your nan. "I've watched you come back to life here. You've been so sad for so long. I don't need you to stay at home with me. Go and find what makes you happy."

"Don't elope with Jonah before I get back, will you?"

"I will be right where you left me when you get back," Mia said.

"No," Sadie said, feeling for the first time that loosening the slack a little on the things she had so fervently depended on might be okay. "Don't wait for me. I'll find you."

Mia nodded. "Okay."

"I mean, don't change your number and move to Antarctica. Make it easy for me to find you."

"I don't think Antarctica is on the cards."

"It'll be really weird not seeing you every day," Sadie said.

"Ditto," Mia said. "But it's time, isn't it?"

Sadie nodded. "Yeah. I *can* do this, right?"

Mia smiled. "You definitely can do this."

"What if I hate it and want to come home?"

"Then you can come home."

"What about the flat? I can't give you any rent while I'm away: I don't have a job any more…"

"Jonah's going to move in," Mia said, "until you get back."

Sadie smiled. "Oh! That's a good idea." She paused. "What if you prefer living with him and you don't want to live with me again?"

Mia smiled. "Why don't you just go to America and see what happens?"

"You don't think I'll come back."

"I think there'll always be a place for you to come back to," Mia said, "if you want to."

"I might want to come back for George."

Mia nodded. "You might."

"Yeah." Sadie smiled.

She watched Mia carefully painting flowers around the edge of her plate. It was an unnerving thought that – whatever happened next – life was going to look different after this, in ways she had never even imagined. Was it the end of an era, or the start of a new chapter, or neither of those things? Would she be happier, or just dissatisfied in brand new ways? Would they actually get to tie up their complicated ending before she got her new beginning?

"We need to talk about Cameron," she said, lowering her voice. "And James. Not here, though. Will you come to Ryan's cabin later? Don't tell Cameron."

Mia nodded, frowning slightly. "Okay."

"Did you see the article about Ryan and Kitty?"

"I think everyone has."

"Oh. Poor James," Sadie said.

"Is he okay?"

"No," Sadie said. "Not really. He went off with Kitty this morning, I assume to talk about what a catastrophic mess she's made. I haven't spoken to him since, though."

"Why did he go and do that interview without us?"

"He's talking about why he left the band. What actually happened," Sadie said. "I will tell you everything later, I promise."

"Okay. I'll be patient," Mia said. "Your plate looks nice. I don't think they'll put that one in the bin."

"Maybe this is my new talent." Sadie smiled. "I'm just going to nip to the loo. I'll be back."

She got up and walked into the foyer, glancing out of the glass doors as she passed them.

She stopped. Did a double take. Felt a lump in her throat as she pushed open the door and stepped outside.

"You're not here," she said, shaking her head in astonishment as she walked towards the man sitting on the wall. "How can you be here?"

"Heard you couldn't do it without me," David said, standing up.

"Oh my God," Sadie whispered. "How did you…? What…?"

She laughed, flinging her arms around him, rogue tears of relief soaking into his shoulder.

"But what are you doing here?" she asked. "How did you know we were here?"

"Ryan got in touch. He told me everything," David said. "I'm here to help."

60

It was when there were too many cameras in the room that Adam knew it was going to be a Bad Day. They were supposed to be rehearsing all afternoon – a final push before the big dress rehearsal on stage the next day – so there should only have been a couple of cameras in an empty room, if that. But instead there were two camera crews and an ominous semi-circle of chairs set up in the corner. And, like the harbinger of doom, Lewis was standing in the middle of the room when they all traipsed in, looking incredibly pleased with himself.

"Morning guys! Just got a quick interview to do with you before we let you get started with rehearsals. If you wouldn't mind doing the honours…" Lewis gestured towards the chairs.

Adam tried to catch Jonny's eye but he wasn't looking in his direction. No one else looked worried but then they didn't know what Adam knew.

Lewis stood in front of them, just back from the cameras, and Adam felt himself tense up with what was surely coming.

"Okay guys," Lewis said. "Who's Mabel?"

Silence.

Absolute silence.

Adam daren't even blink lest this be seized upon as compliance with Lewis' line of questioning.

"No one want to talk about her?" Lewis asked, nodding. "Okay, what about the baby?"

And that's when Freddie got up and walked out of the room.

61

"Mabel?"

She looked up from the email she'd been reading on her phone, not expecting to see a camera crew standing in front of her.

Right in front of her. Blocking her path down to the square, in fact.

She frowned at the blinking red light. Were they *filming* her?

"Oh I work here," she said, forcing a smile. "I think you must have the wrong person."

She tried to walk past them but they moved with her, the camera trained on her the whole time.

"Mabel Alexander?"

"Sorry, I think this is a mistake," she said, Adam's words echoing in her head as a wave of panic gripped her.

This was it, wasn't it? What Adam had tried to warn her about; what he'd tried to *help* her with. Funny how the thing you were dreading so often turned out to not even be the worst of it.

"We just wondered whether you wanted to comment on your involvement in the Granola Fantasy split? Whether you had anything to say about that."

She pressed on, head down, not knowing what else to do. Still they flanked her like a pack of wolves as she reached the square.

"We'd like to hear your side of the story, Mabel. About your relationship with Jay Harper. And the baby."

Mabel stopped dead.

"I don't know what you're talking about," she whispered, a prickly heat coursing through her body.

The door to the building ahead of her burst open and Freddie stormed out, followed a moment later by Adam. Freddie looked from her to the cameras and started to approach them. Mabel wished she could just fold right into herself; cower in the corner like a frightened dog. She could not have this out with Freddie with an audience, and certainly not when the audience included Adam.

But when he spoke, it wasn't to her but the camera crew.

"I would stop filming if I were you," he said, looking murderous. "I really would."

The two men looked at each other before lowering the camera.

"You don't come near her with a camera, do you understand?"

The younger of the two shrugged noncommittally.

Freddie nodded. "Now fuck off."

They hesitated, as if weighing up which was worse – the wrath of their boss at abandoning a story, or of Freddie, who was an untested force – and eventually admitted defeat, retreating across the square, Freddie not taking his eyes off them until they were out of sight.

Then he turned to Mabel.

"You okay?"

She nodded, stunned, watching Adam slink back into the building.

Freddie shook his head slightly. "Of all the places, Mabel."

"I'm not here because of you," she said quickly; desperately. "Or any of this. I didn't want… I work here. I should have left when I found out you were coming, but I…"

But Freddie didn't look angry any more.

"Do you want to go inside?" he asked.

She shook her head.

If Freddie and Adam had been in that building, there was no doubt that the rest of them would be too: she couldn't think of anywhere she wanted to be less.

"I need to get back to my cabin," she said.

Or much further away. Forever.

Freddie nodded. "I'll walk you back."

"Oh, no, you don't have to. I'll be fine."

He looked behind him in the direction that the camera crew had gone.

"Please," he said. "They could be anywhere. I don't want them to ambush you again."

Mabel paused, considering whether making small talk with Freddie for ten minutes would be more or less agonising than being hounded by a camera crew, and if more or less accusations would be thrown at her this way.

"Okay," she said. "Thank you."

They walked up the path towards the forest in a silence for a few minutes, Mabel keeping her eyes firmly fixed ahead of her.

Freddie cleared his throat.

"Does anyone else know you're here?"

"Yes," Mabel said. "By accident. I was trying to stay out of your way."

Freddie paused. "Does Jay know?"

"Yes," Mabel said again, watching her feet scuff along the path, hoping Freddie wasn't looking at her.

"They had no right to do that to you," he said. "To drag you into all this. I don't know what's going on today. It hasn't been like this until now."

Mabel frowned, his words so much gentler than expected.

"I can't believe how long it's been," he said. "Have you been here all this time?"

Mabel shook her head. "Not the whole time."

"I never thought I'd see you again…" He glanced across at her, a curious expression on his face.

She couldn't see the grown-up version of him. All she could see was the boy with the wild hair who'd made her feel so special and whose heart she'd broken so spectacularly.

"But I hoped that maybe I would. I had all these things I was going to say to you… I can't remember any of them now." He shook his head. "Nine years?"

"Yes."

"Nearly a decade."

Mabel nodded.

"Have you been happy?" Freddie asked.

She frowned in surprise.

"Me?"

Freddie smiled. "I don't see any other people around here who I haven't seen for nine years."

Mabel felt herself well up. He wanted her to be *happy*? What the bloody hell was this?

"I…" She trailed off, not even knowing where to start. "Have you?"

"I have. For the most part."

"I'm so sorry," Mabel said, her voice coming out as nothing more than a whisper. "For everything. I wish I could have said that to you. I know that what I did was unforgiveable—"

"No," Freddie said. "Not unforgiveable."

"But I—"

"You made a mistake," Freddie said gently. "*Nine years ago*. And trust me, Mabel, I've thought about this a lot."

She didn't say anything, her feet crunching along next to his.

"Can you honestly tell me that what you did was malicious? That you set out to hurt me, and break up the band, on purpose?" he asked.

"No, I would never... I didn't mean..." Mabel sighed. "But that doesn't make it okay."

"Mabel, if I can forgive Jay, I can forgive you."

She forced herself to meet his gaze and she didn't see anything of what she anticipated in his expression. *Forgiveness*? Could it really be as simple as that? She looked away again, lost for words.

"This was what I didn't want," Freddie said, "from this show. Digging up the past. It's so pointless. It was momentary, in the grand scheme of things. It's impossible to feel the same about things now as we did back then. I don't see the use in talking about any of it."

Mabel nodded, but didn't say anything.

"Jay doesn't speak for all of us, you know," he said, and Mabel's stomach lurched. "I mean, I don't know what he's said to you, but I can guess."

Can you? Mabel thought ruefully. *I bet you can't guess all of it.*

"I thought about you for a long time afterwards. I can't honestly say I don't still, every now and then. But only ever with sadness, Mabel. A melancholy, perhaps, these days. Never with hatred, or bitterness. Because what happened happened, and we are where we are now because of it. And I like where I am."

"But the band..." Mabel said. "You should have had the chance to do so much more. I took that from you."

Freddie shook his head. "We are where we are," he said again. "I will make sure that no one asks you about all this again. Whatever I have to do. *I'm* so sorry that they managed to find out something so personal, and that they had the bad grace to corner you about it. It's no one's business but yours."

Mabel steeled herself, knowing this could be the only chance she was ever going to get to vocalise something she had barely even allowed herself to acknowledge.

"It didn't happen how you think," she said in a rush, her voice wavering. "I lost the baby. I didn't…" She swallowed. "I didn't have an abortion."

As soon as she'd said it she wanted to leave; to run through the forest without looking back. But she forced herself to keep putting one foot in front of the other. To be brave, for once.

"But I found that appointment letter…" Freddie said.

"I panicked," Mabel said. "I didn't know what to do. But on the day… I didn't go to the appointment. But it wasn't… It didn't…"

Freddie was quiet and she hardly dared breathe, the rustling of the trees around them the only accompanying soundtrack.

"Why did you let me think that?" he asked finally.

"I wanted you to hate me," Mabel said. "For everything that I'd done, or thought about doing. I hated myself. It seemed… right, somehow."

"If I'd have known…" Freddie left the sentence hanging between them.

And perhaps things could have been different. Perhaps she did leave before the end. But she had watched Freddie that weekend, playing with three delighted children on the street outside the cabin, his girlfriend laughing and drinking tea with Annabel. He *did* look happy, like he was exactly where he was supposed to be. So perhaps all she was ever meant to be was a bump in the road.

"It is what it is, Mabel," Freddie said, "but you didn't make the mess you think you did. I wanted to tell you that for the longest time."

"Thank you," she whispered.

They walked up the path to Kitty's cabin, Mabel hesitating on the threshold as the door swung open.

"Do you want to come in?" she asked, not needing the answer to be anything, for the first time in as long as she could remember.

"Another time," he said, and she felt that they both knew there wouldn't be another time.

He smiled, and she smiled back, and after she'd watched him walk away without a backwards glance, she closed her eyes and felt all the regret and tension she'd carried around for so long evaporating up into the sky like droplets of dew in the sunlight.

62

No one had moved since Freddie left the room. Adam didn't know why they were all still sitting there. He didn't know why *he* was still sitting there, but where else was he going to go? He had *tried* to leave, but the sight of Freddie talking to Mabel outside had been way too much for him to deal with and he'd slunk back in with his tail between his legs. Apart from a few hushed whispers between Nat and Fabs the room had been mostly silent, with Lewis and the camera crew still standing awkwardly in the corner.

"Fuck," Jonny whispered to Adam, summing up the entire situation in four letters.

He jumped as the door burst open and Freddie stormed in looking furious.

"Turn those off," he said, pointing at the cameras. "Get out."

They did as they were told, dropping everything and heading out of the room, the door swinging closed behind them.

Freddie turned to look at his assembled bandmates.

"What the fuck is going on?" he demanded. "Who did this?"

"Who do you think?" Adam muttered, unable to help himself.

"Oh fuck off, Adam," Jay piped up. "Don't get all pissy just because she never even looked twice at you."

Jonny made a face at him as Adam dug his fingernails into the palm of his hand.

"Was this you?" Freddie asked.

Jay just shrugged and Freddie took a very deep breath.

"Why?"

Jay shrugged again. "For a laugh," he said, his tone deadpan.

"You are such a fucking prick," Freddie said, shaking his head. "How could you do that to her?"

"Can you hear yourself?" Jay sneered. "Because she fucking deserved it, that's how!"

"Do *I* deserve it? Because what you've done is shine a spotlight on something that, honestly, I'd rather forget. Never mind that I thought we'd agreed what we've come here to do, it's not your place to talk about it! Do you know whose business it is? *No one's.*"

"I reckon it's about as much my business as it is yours," Jay said, raising an eyebrow.

And, as if anyone really needed it, there you had indisputable proof that Freddie was a better man than all of them, because Adam was pretty sure anyone else would have smacked Jay in the face for that comment.

"Why do you have to be like this?" Freddie sighed. "This isn't a fucking witch hunt."

"It's not my fault she's here."

"It's not her fault, either! I'm assuming you all knew she was here?" Freddie addressed the rest of them.

He got a collective avoidance of eye contact in return.

"Right, yeah, of course you did," he said, nodding. "And you let me be completely blindsided by it. Thanks for that."

"We didn't want to throw you off," Nat said, looking sheepish.

"You know you've just blown our big chance at a comeback, right?" Freddie asked, turning back to Jay. "You've sabotaged *your own career* by doing this?"

"Nah, we'll get way more screen time for this," Jay said.

"I don't *want* more screen time for this! I don't want to talk about it! You knew that! I *told* you that!" Freddie exclaimed in frustration.

"I just did what I felt needed to be done," Jay said sullenly. "Justice."

Freddie groaned. "I am *so sick* of this "Mabel ruined everything" rhetoric."

"She *did* ruin everything. She took everything *from* us."

"No! She didn't! *We* ruined it!" Freddie said. "Do you know how fucking incredible we were? We could have been interstellar! We had it all and we threw it away!" He shook his head. "I'm not doing this. I'm not going to sit in front of a camera and talk about a load of personal shit that no one was supposed to know about. You are going to sort this out with whoever it is you talked to or I'm pulling us out of the show."

"You can't do that," Jay said.

"Last time I checked there were only three people in this band and it's going to be a pretty fucking dismal show without a lead singer or guitarist," Freddie said.

"I don't believe you'd do that," Jay said. "You want this too much."

"I am going to say this one last time, so make sure you're listening," Freddie said, his expression stony. "I am *not* talking about this on camera. So either you fix this fucking mess you've got us into or we're all going home."

"And you wondered why she looked elsewhere," Jay muttered, which even coming from him was a surprisingly low blow.

Adam felt deeply uncomfortable watching any of this. He fiddled with the note in his pocket that he'd written earlier, asking Mabel to come to the dress rehearsal so he could make his final grand gesture. He had been planning to slip it under her door once it got dark, but now… Maybe Jonny *was* right. She didn't need it, did she? She didn't need to be reminded about any of this. She'd made a clean break and all he was doing was trying to force his neediness onto her, despite her repeated requests to be left alone. It had never been any of his business and he couldn't change that, no matter how much he might want to.

"Right. I think we're going to need the room," Freddie said.

Adam could not have got up faster from his seat.

"Do you think he's going to kill him?" Jonny whispered as they left the room. "Like, actually full-on murder him?"

"Let's hope so," Adam said. "A fitting end to a waste of everyone's time."

"I don't think it's been a waste of time. It's been good to hang out, man."

Adam smiled. "Yeah, you're right. Sorry. I didn't mean that."

"It's all good. The way I see it, there's been plenty of free booze, I haven't had to do a food shop this week, and even though no one's really sure why we're here we're still getting paid. That's a win in my book."

"How much *are* we getting paid?" Adam asked as they stepped out into the weak sunshine.

Jonny shrugged. "No idea. Nat signed the contract, didn't he? I didn't ask."

"You really are just here minding your own business and living in the moment, aren't you?"

"Too right, mate! Who else's business is there to mind?"

Adam nodded. "I think I need to be more Jonny."

"Nah, you're all right, man," Jonny said, clapping a hand around his shoulders. "The world needs a bit of Adam as well."

Adam looked back at the building they'd just come out of. He could hear the raised voices from outside.

"We could be going home tomorrow," he mused. "That could be it. Over in the blink of an eye."

"Time to make your big move on Mabel, then."

Adam looked down at his feet. "No, I don't think I am, actually," he said, the words catching slightly in his throat as he said them. "I think I'm going to leave it. Like you said, it's all a bit much, isn't it? Me. I'm a bit much. Time I took the hint."

"What about the song?" Jonny asked. "It's about her, right?"

"It's…" Adam shook his head, defeated. "It's about friendship. We wrote it together and I thought…" He sighed. "Well it probably doesn't matter what I thought. This whole thing has turned so nasty; I don't want to make it worse. I'm just going to leave her alone now, like she wants."

"How were you going to get her to come to the rehearsal?" Jonny asked.

"I was going to give her this," Adam said, plucking the piece of paper from his pocket.

Jonny took it and read it, nodded and gave it back.

"I can't force her to let me back in, can I?" Adam said, folding the note and putting it back in his pocket. "What kind of a friendship would that be, anyway?"

"I'd take you back," Jonny said.

Adam smiled. "Thanks, man."

"Want to go and piss away our pay check?" Jonny asked. "One for the road and all that?"

"Doesn't look like we've got anywhere else to be," Adam said. "First round's on me."

63

"Well," David said, leaning back against the sofa cushions, "that's quite a story."

Sadie frowned. "You don't think he's done this on purpose?"

It had been the longest, most agonising afternoon of fulfilling their televised obligations, humouring Cameron and biting her tongue, all the while knowing that David was out there waiting for them. She'd barely had time to exchange pleasantries before Ryan had appeared and slipped David his cabin key, hustling Sadie back inside. By the time all four of them had managed to shake off Cameron and make their way to the cabin it had started to get dark.

"I don't know, Sadie," David said, looking thoughtful. "It's a pretty big accusation."

"You didn't notice it? In the band? James said that Cameron used to fix it so me and Ryan didn't travel together, that kind of thing." She looked to James for validation and he nodded.

David made a face. "Honestly, it might as well have been 40 years ago with the amount that's happened since. I don't know if I really remember when Cameron may or may not have stood next to Ryan instead of James, etc etc."

"What did you do for the last ten years that made it feel like 40?" Ryan asked.

"I've got four children, mate," David said. "You have no idea what I've been through."

"I really don't think we're wrong," Sadie said, slightly disappointed that David wasn't immediately on their side.

"The thing is, Sadie, I'm just not sure there's any need for a big confrontation at this point in the show, regardless of what Cameron's done or not done. You're so close to the end. You could just put up with him for another couple of days, collect your big fat cheque and go home."

"I don't like your advice so far," Sadie said petulantly.

David smiled. "Well what's new? Look, I'm not here to tell you what to do, I'm just trying to make sure that you don't do yourselves out of all the opportunities that are going to be available to you if you make it through this show in one piece."

"We can't reform, though," Sadie said. "James isn't…"

"Up for it," Ryan said. "He's got far better things to do with his time."

"I was going to go with *emotionally stable*, but that works too," James said.

They had told David just about everything, although Sadie had glossed over the part where James had a full-on mental breakdown and none of them noticed. It didn't really feel like her place to tell that particular branch of the story: she didn't want to speak on James' behalf and get it wrong, or somehow trivialise everything he'd been through. Maybe, if there was time, James would tell David himself, or maybe he wouldn't, and that was fine too.

"It's not just reforming the band, though," David said. "There'll be other offers, especially if you play well with the general public."

"You mean offers for Sadie," Ryan said.

"I do," David said. "No offence to the rest of you."

"What do you mean?" Sadie asked, frowning.

"He means you're a star through and through," Ryan said.

Mia and James were nodding but she still didn't really understand.

"And, assuming you've worn your heart on your sleeve and been way too honest in your interviews, the public are going to love you."

"Me?" Sadie asked.

"She doesn't know," Ryan said, smiling fondly at her.

"No, I know," David said. "But that's part of the reason why, isn't it?"

"You do realise you're the frontman of this band?" Ryan asked, looking amused.

"No? Don't be stupid! We're all equal."

"I really thought you would have worked it out by now," David said. "That was just something we told you so you didn't get a big head."

Sadie looked at everyone smiling at her and she didn't really know what to do with herself. Had they all gone completely mad?

"You're the favourite," Ryan said. "You idiot."

"*You're* the favourite," Sadie said.

Ryan shook his head. "No. It's always been you. Fan favourite. And band favourite."

More nodding from Mia and James.

"But…"

"And after I've stopped you from jeopardising your future career, I'm also supposed to be making sure Ryan has a band to go back to," David said.

"What do you mean *now*?" Sadie asked, feeling like she was in need of some kind of on-screen subtitle to translate all these cryptic riddles.

If she really was the leader of the band then why didn't she have a bloody clue what any of them were going on about?

"He's not supposed to be here, are you, mate?" David said.

"No I am not," Ryan said, matter-of-factly.

"What? Why not?" Sadie asked.

"Don't worry about it," Ryan said. "Just a small disagreement within the band."

"But you said they wouldn't even notice you were gone!"

"Yeah, well. I didn't want to ruin our reunion."

Sadie looked around in bewilderment.

"Is there anyone else who wants to tell me something massively important that I don't already know?"

"It's no big deal! Honestly! David's going to sort it."

"David is going to agree a less favourable contract for you as a grovelling apology, if that's what you mean," David said dryly.

"Have I accidentally walked into a parallel universe where everything seems like it's the same but it's actually just slightly different?" Sadie asked. "It is too late in the game for these kinds of revelations!"

Ryan put his arm around her, giving her a reassuring squeeze. "It's all good," he said. "Nothing that can't be fixed."

"And with that in mind, I really do think the best course of action here is to do nothing," David said. "Just leave Cameron to it, whatever it is he's doing, or has done, or hasn't done. There are bigger things at stake."

Sadie was just about to respectfully disagree when there was a sound from outside. Everyone looked towards the door as Cameron burst into the room.

"Oh I see," he said. "This is where you've been holding the secret meetings."

David stood up, very much like a lioness protecting her cubs.

"Hello, mate," he said evenly.

"What are you doing here?" Cameron asked.

"Just sorting out a few things for Ryan. Catching up with old friends."

"I don't fall under that category, then?" Cameron said.

"Of course you do," David said. "Come and sit down."

But Cameron shook his head, regarding them all suspiciously.

"You must think I'm really stupid," he said. "You think I haven't seen you all whispering behind my back? And now, what, you've brought in reinforcements?"

"I think you've got the wrong end of the stick, mate," David said. "We're just catching up."

"And you all just *happened* to be in the same cabin at the same time?"

"I've only just got here, really. We were just about to give you a call, see where you were."

Sadie watched their exchange curiously. David was flat-out lying to Cameron, trying to placate him as if he were some spiralling drunk they'd been cornered by in a pub. And Cameron seemed *really mad*. None of that really added up to him having done nothing wrong, in her opinion.

"We're all going to pretend we're best friends, are we?" Cameron shook his head.

"We're not *pretending* anything," Sadie said, not able to hold her tongue any longer.

"Sadie..." Ryan said quietly, but she ignored his warning tone.

"We're all trying to rebuild what we used to have. The only person who doesn't seem to want that is you."

Cameron narrowed his eyes at her as she held his gaze.

"Why would I want that?" he growled. "It's a joke, the way you've just let *him* back in, no questions asked. And *Ryan*. Who in this room has actually been there for you? Who's picked you up every time something went wrong? Who's had to listen to you *moaning* and *whinging* about not being famous any more *every bloody day* for the last *ten years*? Me, and Mia. But it's not enough for you, is it? We're not *exciting* enough. You've got to have more."

Sadie's face fell and tears pricked at her eyes. What to say to that complete character assassination? It was only a moment ago everyone was trying to convince her how great she was.

"No," Ryan said, standing up and stepping in front of Sadie so she could no longer see Cameron. "That's enough. You don't talk to her like that."

"Oh what are you doing getting involved? You love it, don't you? Stepping in, being the hero, saving the day."

"Mate, say what you need to say," Ryan said, holding up his hands in surrender. "I've got no issue with you having a good old rant at me. But you leave Sadie out of it or we're going to have a problem, okay? She's never done anything to you. None of us have, as far as I can see. We're all just trying to have a nice time here."

"Do you want to sit down, have a drink with us?" David asked calmly, standing beside Ryan.

"No I don't want to have a fucking *drink* with you!" Cameron exclaimed. "What is this, some kind of *intervention* or something? You're all going to try and convince me how great James is so we can get back to playing happy families?"

James just rolled his eyes but Sadie couldn't do it, she couldn't sit there and listen to it any more.

"James *is* great," she said, standing up and pushing through the David-Ryan wall in front of her.

"Oh here we go," Cameron said mockingly.

"I don't know what your problem is!" Sadie exclaimed. "James has come here when he didn't want to, and he did that for me; for friendship."

"Oh come on, *none* of us want to be here," Cameron scoffed.

"Not true," Ryan said, raising a hand.

"James has a *really* good reason for not wanting to come," Sadie said. "The only reason *you* didn't want to come was because you didn't want us all back together again. You didn't want us to figure it out."

"Oh what are you talking about."

"I know what you've done," Sadie said, looking him square in the eye, her heart pounding wildly. "We all know what you've done."

"I haven't *done* anything!" Cameron exclaimed. "He was going to *ruin the band* and I was the only one who could see it! All that talk of playing instruments and writing songs! That wasn't the band I joined! The fans didn't want that! Nobody wanted that!" He pointed at David. "You could have stopped him! You could have stopped all of it! Nobody was doing *anything*!"

"The only person who ruined the band was you!" Sadie shouted. "And all that time you let us think that James was to blame!"

"What was I supposed to do? He was trying to push me out! There was no place for me in a band like that!"

Sadie shook her head. "Do you really think we would have let that happen?"

"If it benefitted *you*? Absolutely," Cameron said bitterly.

Sadie swallowed hard. "And me and Ryan? What was that going to ruin?"

"Oh honestly, you were a fucking mess after he left. He was supposed to be concentrating on his new life rather than worrying about who he left behind."

"But he didn't *want* that!" Sadie said, his words smarting.

"It was what he *needed*."

She looked at Cameron in disbelief, the conviction in his words so strong. Did he truly believe that he'd done the right thing?

"You took my *best friend* from me."

"Yeah, well, you would only have dragged him down."

"Stop," Mia said quietly, standing up. "I can't let you do this any more. I've stood by and watched while you put down every idea she ever had, while you discouraged her and kept her small, because you knew what she could do if we let her go. And I always tried to smooth things over and make excuses for you because I know that isn't who you really are. But *you* are dragging *us all* down now and it's time to stop."

Cameron gritted his teeth, looking at Mia. "This stupid fucking show," he muttered. "I knew I should have just told them we weren't interested."

And it took Sadie a moment, then, to realise exactly what he meant.

"Oh my God," she said slowly. "It was *you*. It was you they got in touch with about doing the show! I can't *believe* this! You didn't do enough damage first time round? You almost ruined everything *again*!"

"This *show* has ruined everything!" Cameron shouted. "We were *fine* as we were! Everything was *fine*!"

"I wasn't fine," Sadie said.

"I wasn't fine," Ryan said, putting a hand on Sadie's back.

Finally James stood up. "I wasn't fine," he said quietly.

Cameron stared at them, his expression one of hatred and rage.

"Okay," David said, stepping out of the group towards Cameron. "Let's give everyone a bit of space, shall we? Time to go, mate."

"With pleasure," Cameron spat, turning his back on them.

David followed him to the door, clicking it shut behind him as footsteps echoed down the path outside.

"Well," he said, surveying the remaining four, "that's quite a story."

64

He found her on the beach, the water gently lapping just inches away from her feet.

"You sent out the distress signal," Adam said, sitting down on the sand next to Sadie.

"I need some lake time," Sadie said, staring out over the dark water. "Didn't want to go out on my own, though. You know, in case I silently drowned."

"Seems wise," Adam said. "Come on, then."

He stood up and took her hand, pulling her up next to him, trying to keep his balance as his feet sunk into the soft sand.

"Were you busy?" Sadie asked as they walked along the jetty.

"Not really," Adam said, helping her into the pedalo with a distinct lack of finesse. "Just hanging out with Jonny. Always up for some lake time with you."

"Are you drunk?"

"No! *Merry*. Well, not literally. That would make a change, wouldn't it?" he said, holding tightly to the edge of the pedalo as he attempted not to fall head first into the water. "We had a bit of unexpected free time this afternoon while our supergroup crumpled into a pathetic little heap."

"Oh no, did it happen?"

"It happened."

"Was it bad?"

He sighed. "Worse. I don't know if it came from Jay, but they managed to find out something really awful about Mabel and they asked the entire group about it, on camera. And then it looks like they went after Mabel too."

"What did they find out?"

Adam hesitated. It was absolutely his least favourite fact about the entire sorry thing: the thought that Mabel had had to go through something like that in the midst of everything else that had been going on made his toes curl.

"You don't have to tell me," Sadie said, her earnest expression illuminated by the waning moon.

Adam shook his head. "It's not even my trauma, I don't know why I'm..." He paused. "It was the thing that unravelled everything, in the end. Obviously the version I heard was just gossip – it's not like I had a big heart to heart with Freddie about it. I wondered how much of it was true, but..." He trailed off, watching silver slivers of light ripple across the water.

"Don't tell me," Sadie said, her hand briefly on top of his. "It's none of my business."

"Freddie said it's none of *anyone's* business. Which is right. But I don't think I've ever seen him look so... *ruffled* before. Like, he was furious, obviously, but he looked *upset*. And it just made me think..." He shook his head. "Jonny said all along that I was never the main character when it came to Mabel. I can see it now."

"So that means what?"

"I'm done, Sadie," Adam said. "I'm really done. This just isn't my storyline. I really thought it was, but... It's not Mabel's fault that I've misunderstood the last ten years of my life, is it?"

"It doesn't mean your feelings for her aren't valid, though," Sadie said. "You're allowed to love whoever you want."

"Yeah I know," Adam said sadly. "But none of the rest of what I've done since we've been here has been okay, really, has it?"

"You had to try," Sadie said.

"I was going to do what you said: create the opportunity for her to come to me, if she wanted to. There's a song... I thought it might mean something to her. I managed to convince Nat to let me sing it at the rehearsal tomorrow. One final *grand gesture*," he said wryly. "I was going to put this under her door..." He felt in his pocket for the note that he'd shown Jonny earlier. "Oh wait," He frowned, trying all his other pockets plus his jacket for good measure, but that single piece of white paper, folded and refolded and folded again, was nowhere to be found. "Maybe I dropped it. Good job I didn't put our names on it. Well there you go: fate."

"Will you still sing the song?"

Adam shrugged. "I don't know if we're even going to make it to that point. Freddie may well have literally murdered Jay by now. He chucked us all out of the room after Jay seemed adamant about continuing to be an absolute dickhead right to the bitter end. He said he was going to pull us all out of the show if Jay didn't fix things."

"You couldn't stay if they went home?" Sadie asked. "Your band, I mean. Do your own thing?"

"Oh we're nothing to this show without bloody Granola Fantasy. We were *never* anything without them. Not in anyone else's eyes, anyway."

"What about in your eyes?"

"I loved our shit local band. I loved hanging out playing music with my best mates in the town we grew up in. We should have just left it at that," he said. "But there you are. Time to go home; find some kind of alternative life to the one I thought I was chasing. Time to *let it go*."

"So what does that look like?"

Adam sighed. "I really don't know. I mean, I don't have anywhere to go back to, and obviously I'm supposed to be staying with Nat for a bit, but... It just feels a bit too..."

"Mabel-y."

"Yeah."

"Do you have a job?"

"Nope. I didn't have enough leave to cover doing the show so I had to quit."

"Same. Well, no, I actually got fired for very briefly disappearing to go and find James, not that it matters anyway with me going to L.A. now."

"Why are you going to L.A.?"

"Oh, didn't I tell you? Maybe I told George and thought I'd told you," Sadie said.

"*Who's George?*"

"He's..." Sadie paused. "A boy that I kissed."

"Here?" Adam asked, looking at her with interest.

"Yes." She smirked. "He's in Kingpin."

"The guy with the hair? Looks about 10 years younger than he actually is?"

"Yep."

"Well okay! That is quite a celebrity pairing. How did this happen?"

"We used to have a bit of a thing, back in the day. So we're kind of having a thing again now, I think? I don't know, I haven't really seen him since. There's a lot of stuff going on."

"Hence the lake," Adam said. "And L.A.?"

"I'm going home with Ryan!" Sadie said, her face brightening again.

"But not in a romantic way?"

"No! Gross! Although, did you see what Kitty said in that article?"

"What article?"

"Are you on the same show as me?" Sadie asked. "The article about Kitty, James and Ryan?"

"Nope, I've got no idea what you're talking about," Adam said.

"Well can you please try a bit harder to stay up to date with my life?" Sadie asked. "Quite a lot has happened since I last saw you."

Adam smiled. "Do me a *"previously on"*."

Sadie thought for a moment. "Okay, well – when did I last see you?"

"You were skiving rehearsals. I was going to try to catch up with you afterwards to check you were okay, actually, but I didn't see you."

"Oh, yeah, that was a bad day. And then yesterday was worse. And today was… Even worse than that, actually."

"Shit. Are you trying to give me a run for my money in the *"Worst Time at Village of Pop"* stakes?"

"I wish I wasn't," Sadie said. "So I told you about Kitty and Ryan, right?"

Adam nodded. "James' girlfriend trying to be Ryan's girlfriend."

"Yeah. Well she talked to a journalist about it, so now *everyone* knows."

"Apart from me."

"Because you clearly exist on some sort of higher plane."

"Right."

"So James is a mess, but – saving grace – Ryan didn't actually *do* anything with Kitty so he comes out of this looking okay, ish, and I *think* that it's actually *going* to be okay, like they've talked and Ryan's apologised, and luckily James is incredibly nice so I think he's kind of forgiven Ryan?"

"Which sounds good?"

"Yes. But we also found out that Cameron deliberately tried to push James out of the band, which ultimately split up the band, and even after that he tried to break up me and Ryan, and *then* he tried to stop us coming on this show. And none of us had any idea what he was doing until we started talking to each other, which is obviously what he wanted to avoid happening."

"Wow."

"And then…" Sadie looked at Adam, her expression changing. "Am I the lead singer of my band?"

"Well, you stand in the middle?"

"Everyone was talking about me being the *fan favourite* and the *opportunities* that were going to be available to me after the show, and I just..." Sadie threw up her hands. "*Nothing* makes sense now. I came into this show thinking one thing about my band – and my *friends* – and now I feel like I didn't know *anything* about *anyone*! I mean, in what universe am I the *fan favourite*? If anyone's the fan favourite it's Ryan! *Ryan* got all the opportunities when the band ended! I got nothing! Why would there be opportunities now when there wasn't before?"

"How do you know there *weren't* any opportunities?" Adam asked, musing at the differences between the Sadie that he could physically see and the Sadie that came out of her mouth.

"Because there weren't!"

"That you heard of."

Sadie frowned, looking at Adam.

"Not that I want to throw another spanner into your bag, but if Cameron did all that stuff to you guys then what's to say he didn't do more shitty things that you don't know about yet?"

Sadie's frown deepened.

Adam smiled at Sadie. "You are, undoubtedly, the lead singer of your band, mate. You are pretty much the biggest deal celebrity here, apart from maybe Freddie and – as much as I loathe to say it – Jay. There are cameras on you when there aren't cameras on other people. You're at the front of all the group photos. I knew your face when you were on the cover of magazines and on posters in the HMV window. I've seen your band play. You, out of everyone here, should have been the one who made it. It doesn't make any sense that you didn't. And if *you* didn't turn down the opportunities that came up at the end of the band, maybe someone else did?"

It was time, Adam thought, that someone got a happy ending out of all this.

"I will say it, because I have had a few beers, but nothing about you makes sense, actually," he continued. "It's not just that you're different to what I was expecting, it's that who you think you are and who you *obviously* are seem to be two different people."

"I don't know if I like slightly drunk Adam," Sadie said quietly.

But he just smiled.

"You are not who you think you are," Adam said. "And I know it seems like I'm making a habit lately of telling women that they're wrong about themselves, but I genuinely think that how you see yourself is not who you are. Because you're great! You are just so great and you don't see it! You don't believe in yourself, at all. You act like you think you're nothing. But you're a superstar, Sadie. And everyone here knows it except you."

She started crying then and Adam briefly panicked, wondering if he'd done it wrong when he was just trying to do a nice thing.

"I'm not going to take it back, no matter how much you cry," he said kindly, squeezing her arm. "Regardless of who or what or how, you're going to leave this place in a stream of light riding a unicorn along a rainbow. As is befitting of someone of your status."

"Does the unicorn have wings?" Sadie sniffed.

"Yes."

"I think that's actually an alicorn."

"I don't care what it is, you're riding it," Adam said. "Seriously though, mate. You're the whole package. Even *I'm* starstruck and I know how much of a melon you are."

Sadie smiled, wiping away the tears. "Oh stop it."

"I will not! I'm going to get a banner made, maybe hire a billboard, perhaps do a TV ad, just to make sure you don't forget what a force you are."

"Cameron doesn't think I'm a force."

"Cameron *clearly* thinks you're a force or he wouldn't have tried to screw you over so comprehensively."

Sadie still looked sceptical. "It's so messy, though, isn't it? And how do I even know that I know everything now? Things *keep* coming up and surprising me. We're almost at the end and everything is still all wrong."

"Maybe," Adam said, "the end is just the beginning."

Sadie burst out laughing then, the moonlight sparkling in her eyes as well as on the water.

"I wish I believed that," she said.

"Yeah," Adam said, "me too. But hey, at least we'll always have the lake."

"Pedalo Club!" Sadie said, grinning at him.

"Sure," Adam said, nodding. "Pedalo Club forever."

65

Mabel watched Adam smile at the girl next to him in the boat, both of them illuminated as if the moon were a spotlight and the lake a stage. Were they *together*? It was hard to tell. Why were they out on the lake in the middle of the night? But then, why was *she* out in the *woods* in the middle of the night? And why should she care? Maybe Adam already had a girlfriend before coming on the show; maybe he'd found true love during filming. It didn't matter, did it? If she didn't want him…

She'd been watching them for longer than she should have been, perched on a damp bench on the hill by the sports centre, an artificial mound of grass constructed of goodness knows what underneath. In the shade of the trees there was no danger of them seeing her and she found she just couldn't look away. Everything felt different now after talking to Freddie. *She* felt different: the tightness that she had assumed was just a part of who she was now wasn't there any more. Gone, just like that, by the incredible power of saying sorry and being forgiven. Not unforgivable, *just a mistake*, like Kitty had said all along.

Adam was laughing now, out on the lake, and the ache of missing him spread from Mabel's stomach down to her feet. *Could* she be in his life without hurting him? Just the tiniest tiniest corner of his life? A birthday WhatsApp message, the occasional liking of a photo on Facebook, not even ever seeing him or speaking to him in person but just knowing he was *there*, part of the fabric of her world. Could she do that without causing any harm?

She heard footsteps crunching on the path behind her, the atmosphere changing with the presence of another.

"Swear not by the moon," Fabs said, sitting down next to her.

Mabel smiled. "Hello, Fabian."

"What are you doing here, Mabel?" he asked, in that gentle way of his.

Fabs, the backbone of the band, eternally sitting in the shadows observing the mess everyone else was making of their lives, only occasionally offering up his opinion. Mabel had always had a feeling that he'd known everything that had been going on with her, Freddie and Jay, and his silent disappointment had been so much worse than open disapproval.

"Trying to live a quiet life," she said.

"And yet here we all are."

"Here you all are." Mabel nodded.

She was aware of him following her gaze out towards the lake; she had no doubt that he knew who she was watching and why, even if she didn't really know herself.

"I think I've messed it all up again," she said.

"Oh it's a mess all right, but not of your making."

Mabel frowned. "I don't think I need to do anything more than *be* somewhere to mess things up."

"You can't control how people react to you being somewhere," Fabs said.

"I could have sent Jay away."

"Yes, you could have," Fabs said, "but do you think that would have made a difference?"

"Maybe not."

Fabs nodded. "Maybe not."

Adam was right in the middle of the lake now, dipping in and out of view as the moon slid behind clouds. His back was to her and she couldn't see his face any more.

"Is Freddie okay?" Mabel asked, looking at something else instead.

"He will be now."

"Now?"

"He needed the closure. I think you did too?"

Mabel nodded.

"We all got stuck," Fabs said. "It's like snagging a scarf on a thorn. If you don't untangle it you can put all the time and distance in the world between you and the thorn but that thread will still be attached all the same. Maybe you don't even notice the thread but it's still there, all the time unravelling."

"What if you just cut it?" Mabel asked.

"You can't cut it," Fabs said. "It's too much of you to leave behind snagged on a thorn."

Mabel felt goosebumps crawl up her arms. The moonlight, the darkness;

his words.

"We're all here for a reason. The universe will always try to correct itself," he continued. "It had to happen, Mabel. It had to be resolved, whether it had been ten years ago or in another ten years' time. These things don't go away, they just lay dormant, festering, unravelling. You *had* to talk to Freddie; you *had* to talk to Jay." His gaze moved pointedly back to the lake. "You *have* to talk to Adam."

She looked up at him in surprise but his expression was unflinching.

"Sometimes you have to go back to move forward," he said.

"Are you actually human or are you channelling some kind of ethereal Norse God?" Mabel asked.

He smiled at her. "Painfully human," he said. "And now I have to go. Make sure you see it through this time. I don't want to have to do this again when I'm in my forties. Trying to live a quiet life, you know?"

Mabel watched him go, his outline becoming nothing more than a shadow as he disappeared into the night. She shivered, feeling the pull of warmth and home, wherever that even was. She looked back at Adam, still drifting on the lake. The fear, the shame, the constant yearning "what if". Was that what it would take to unhook that snagged thread? Adam smiled again and she could suddenly feel it, that thread, winding back through time and everywhere she'd been in the last ten years, connecting her to him. And here, where she'd walked the same paths over and over, the thread was now so tangled that she was tripping over it everywhere she turned. Maybe it would be nice to be able to walk down a path without worrying she was going to fall. Maybe it would be nice to be able to *breathe*.

The moon disappeared behind a bank of cloud and she could barely see her hand in front of her face.

Okay, Fabs, she thought. *Okay. Time to let it go.*

ONE DAY TO THE LIVE SHOW

66

"I don't feel very zen," Sadie said, squinting at Ryan, Mia and James as sweat dripped into her eye.

"How about now?" James asked, pouring another ladle of water onto the hot coals.

"Struggling to get past the fact that it looks like you're tipping water over an old-fashioned electric fire, so no, not really."

She tugged her swimming costume up a bit, feeling strangely self-conscious in this hot wooden box she was packed in so tightly with her bandmates, sweaty arms and legs awkwardly, accidentally, touching.

"Am I too booby in this? I think I left my robe outside the last room we were in. Which bits of this are they filming?"

"Too much of it," James said.

"Too much of *us*," Sadie agreed, gesturing around at all the bare flesh. "Does this feel way too intimate?"

"We're an intimate kind of band," Ryan said, looking strangely at ease lying on the top bunk of the sauna.

How he managed to look so comfortable Sadie didn't know. She was too hot and she was too sweaty and the hard wooden slats were digging into her back.

"I really think I could have lived without seeing you two in your pants this week," she said. "Eurgh, I am so hot."

"I think that's kind of the point, babe," Ryan said, his eyes closed now, a picture of inexplicable relaxation.

"I like it," Mia said, her cheeks flushed. "It's like being in a really hot bath."

"I think I've had enough sauna," Sadie said, fidgeting uncomfortably. "I feel like I'm suffocating."

"Yeah, this isn't for me either," James said, standing up.

"Maybe there's a room where they wrap you in blankets and feed you cake," Sadie said, trying to brush the sweat from her arms and legs. "*That* would be relaxing."

She opened the door and cool air flooded into the space, wrapping itself around her hot skin. She definitely had left her robe somewhere else and was massively regretting her skimpy "girls in Tenerife" attire. She missed the sensible swimming costume she'd stolen to go swimming with Adam.

"I don't really understand spas," Sadie said to James, closing the door behind them. "I'm so *damp*. How is that relaxing? We walked past a room of waterbeds when we came in – am I supposed to use those *before* I get all damp? Or just lie there feeling soggy? And how are we supposed to go out in the zen garden without shoes on? We'd be all *gritty*."

James laughed. "And to think this was supposed to be a treat."

"Yeah, a treat *or* they're hoping to elicit some last-minute drama by cramming us all into tiny rooms and making us too hot," Sadie said.

"We seem to have managed that without their help," James said, filling up a plastic cup at the water fountain.

"I don't think he's here, is he?" Sadie asked, peering into another hot-looking room. "What's a laconium?"

"More dry heat, I suspect," James said, handing her a cup of water. "Something to do with the Romans. And no, I don't think he is."

"There's no quantity of water that can replace the amount of liquid I lost in the sauna," Sadie said. "I'm pretty sure Ryan's sweat dripped onto my face at one point. Honestly, spas are so gross."

"At least they can't film us in the hot rooms," James said, gesturing subtly at a camera crew panning past a group of people bobbing around the outdoor pool.

"That's a good point," Sadie said. "Very keen to not be on camera looking like this. Are there any slightly less hot rooms?"

"I think saunas are the hottest, so it can only get better from here," James said. "How about alpine steam?"

"That sounds wet," Sadie said suspiciously.

"And very hard for cameras to film," James said, ushering her into a glowing green room as the camera crew started to approach.

Sadie blinked as the wet heat hit her. "Is it just us in here?" she whispered, trying to make out the space through the steam.

"Think so," James said, sitting down as Sadie suspiciously lowered herself onto the tiled bench.

"Well it's not as hot," she said, "but I'm still damp."

"I think that's par for the course here, unfortunately."

Sadie nodded, trying to work out how to breathe when the air was saturated with water droplets. She did feel slightly less uncomfortable, though, mainly owing to the fact that she could hardly even see James and no one's sweaty skin was touching hers.

"Are you okay, after yesterday?" James asked after a moment.

"Am *I* okay? Are *you* okay?"

James paused. "Assuming there's no point pretending I am, with you?"

"Not really," Sadie said, the sudden honesty from James giving her goosebumps, despite the heat of the room.

That was what she really thrived on, she'd come to realise: that glorious overfamiliarity where your friends make assumptions about you, and say what they really think, and casually give you nicknames you didn't ask for. Never mind a sauna – that kind of thing made her glow from the inside out.

"Well. Not really, then," James said. "But it's only about 36 hours until they turn the cameras off, so there's that."

"And what happens when they turn the cameras off?" Sadie asked. "For you."

"I go home," James said.

"With Kitty?"

"Yes."

"As boyfriend and girlfriend?" Sadie asked hesitantly, still feeling like there was a point with James that you couldn't pry past, despite how frankly he'd spoken about his demons and how much she now knew about him.

James paused. "No," he said quietly. "I don't think so."

And she was sorry for him, she really was, but *thank God*.

"Are you staying in our cabin until we go home?" she asked, deciding not to push it.

"Yes."

"Good," Sadie said. "I like having you there."

She thought she saw him nod through the steam but he didn't say anything, and seeing as they couldn't see each other's faces and it felt a bit like a dream and it was almost all over and she might not get a moment like this with him ever again, she decided that now was the time to say it.

"I love you," she said simply. "I missed you. I like this a lot."

When James squeezed her hand it felt like more than words, and it was quite hard to tell whether she was crying or just very sweaty.

They sat there in damp harmonious silence, still holding hands – could have been ten minutes, could have been an hour. Eventually the door opened, hazy figures emerged through the steam and they quickly slipped out, Sadie guiltily swiping someone else's robe from a hook on the wall. She wrapped it gratefully around her as they wandered the corridors, coming across Mia and Ryan curled up on oversized egg chairs in a dimly lit room.

"Hello," Sadie whispered, nudging Ryan over to sit down next to him.

"You're very wet," Ryan said, touching her hair.

"I've steamed myself," Sadie said, "like a piece of broccoli. What did you guys do?"

"Stayed in the sauna until we almost passed out, then went for a touch of hypothermia in the ice bath," Ryan said.

"Sounds awful."

"It's almost lunch time," Mia said. "I think we've got to leave soon."

"Time to get our fancy pants on," Ryan said.

Sadie frowned. "How are we supposed to do a full dress rehearsal with Cameron after last night?"

"Well he had the good sense not to show up this morning, so maybe we won't have to," Ryan said.

"But what will we say if he *doesn't* turn up?" Sadie asked, feeling any suggestion of zen drain right out of her in an instant.

"We'll say he's ill. As per the classic time-honoured tradition when something shady is going on in a band."

"But we'll still have to do the *show* with him." Sadie said. "In front of an actual audience. I don't know what's worse – seeing him for dress rehearsals or having to get up on a stage with him when we haven't had a proper practice."

Ryan put an arm around her, squeezing her against him. "Mate. Let David sort it out, okay? That's what he's here for, right? He was going to go and talk to Cameron this morning. We'll find out soon enough what the deal is."

"Shall we go and get changed?" Mia asked.

"Yes please," Sadie said. "I'm all spa-ed out."

They all walked together to the changing rooms, Ryan and James going through one door and Mia and Sadie through the other. Sadie unbuckled the key on her wrist, pulling her things out of the locker and dropping them onto the bench. Mia did the same, quietly getting dry and dressed next to her. Sadie rubbed a towel all over her bare skin which seemed to have zero effect. It was as if she was now more than 100% water and would never be dry again. She didn't want to put her leggings on, or her bra, or anything else that required being pulled tight against her sticky damp skin. She felt drained, like she'd sweated all her spirit out in the sauna. She was going to need an awful lot of coffee to get up on stage and do a dress rehearsal later.

"Sadie."

She looked up from rubbing at her legs and saw Mia frowning at her.

"I wanted to say… I'm sorry that it took me so long to stand up to Cameron. I gave him the benefit of the doubt for too long. I think I maybe haven't been a very good friend to you."

"Yes you have," Sadie said. "You don't have to apologise for seeing the best in people."

"But maybe I could have done something…"

"Did you know what he'd done?" Sadie asked, desperately hoping the answer would be no. "To James? To me and Ryan? Did you know he was meeting up with Ryan behind my back?"

"No. I wouldn't have let that happen if I'd known, I promise," Mia said, standing up and pulling on a cardigan. "Ryan was right, you know. You shine much brighter than the rest of us. And you need to fly now. It's time."

"That sounds very final," Sadie said, trying to brush off Mia's earnestness.

"No," Mia said, "it's the beginning."

Sadie nodded, feeling that familiar lump in her throat.

"You go on," she said, gesturing at the towel still wrapped round her, "I'm going to be ages. I'll see you outside?"

Mia smiled. "Okay."

The door swished shut behind her and Sadie went back to rubbing at her skin. She wasn't sure what was more damp now, her or the towel. Giving up on the hope of ever being able to get her leggings back on she pulled her dungaree dress over her striped shirt and shoved her feet into her peach high tops. She stood in front of the mirror, staring at the person she thought she knew.

The beginning.

It was cropping up a lot lately. Adam had said it to her last night, and now Mia. She thought of both James' and George's surprise that she wasn't working in music any more, the fact that a lot of people here were still doing something while she was doing nothing; the way her entire life had felt wrong for the last nine years. There'd been a lot of things in question when she'd come into this show but her sense of self hadn't been one of them. Was it really possible that other people knew more about who she was than she did?

She frowned at her reflection.

And did she dare believe them?

She half closed her eyes, trying to see what everyone else claimed they saw. What was more real, the person she was to other people or the person she felt like inside? Could she be both, or did she need to choose a side?

"The beginning of what?" she asked the girl in the mirror, but she didn't seem to know either.

Sadie sighed, going back over to the bench and bundling her wet things into her bag. Being alone with her thoughts probably wasn't the best idea at the moment: there were too many of them and they were too confusing. She needed to find her people, and do a dress rehearsal, and maybe at some point someone would tell her what to think about all this. She left the changing room and wandered through the reception area towards where her band were loitering outside, wishing she had persevered with her leggings as the cold air hit her.

"Was it this cold when we went into the spa?" she asked, dumping her bag on the floor next to Ryan. "I think being in there has changed my perception of everything and I liked it better before."

"Nobody buy Sadie a spa voucher for her birthday, for the love of God," Ryan said.

"Are we going to get lunch?"

"We're waiting for David. He said he'd meet us here after he'd spoken to Cameron."

"Oh," Sadie felt her stomach do an unpleasant little skip.

"It'll be okay," Ryan said. "He'll sort it out. Whatever *it* is. He'll tell us what to do next. That's his job."

"It kind of isn't any more," Sadie pointed out.

"Old habits die hard," Ryan said. "Honestly. He'll make the right call. You just have to go with it now, okay? Whatever happens."

Sadie nodded, but that sounded a hell of a lot easier said than done.

The automatic doors slid open behind them and another group of damp, dazed pop stars emerged.

"Hey," Adam said, appearing next to Sadie. "You okay?"

She shrugged. "Waiting for news of whether we still have a band."

"Ah. David talking to Cameron?"

She nodded. "How's your band?"

"Tense," Adam said. "By all accounts Jay is still alive, against the odds, not that any of us have actually seen him since yesterday. And Freddie is currently performing some kind of complicated negotiation to convince the producers that they don't actually want to include the biggest piece of pop gossip ever in their show."

"Good luck with that," Sadie said.

"Right. Seems like quite an ask. Unless he's got something better up his sleeve to trade. Who knows, maybe he has. So, I don't know. Maybe we're doing a rehearsal later, maybe we're all going home."

"Don't go without saying goodbye," Sadie said. "Whether it's today or tomorrow."

"I wouldn't dare."

The doors opened again and this time it was George who appeared next to Sadie, Ryan subtly stepping away to create a space for him.

"Hey. You okay?" he asked.

There was a split second of awkwardness where they looked at each other and realised they didn't quite know now how to greet each other in a public space. Then George leaned in and kissed her on the cheek, his hand sliding round her waist to the small of her back.

"I was going to full-on kiss you but I didn't know if you wanted this on camera," he whispered to her, before pulling away.

"This?" Sadie asked.

"Us." He smiled sheepishly. "I mean, if there is an us? There doesn't have to be an us. If you don't want."

"Are you saying you can take me or leave me?" Sadie teased.

"No," George said, staring so deep into her eyes that it felt like he could see into her brain, "I'm not."

And then he put a hand on each side of her face and pulled her towards him and he really did full-on kiss her, in front of everyone and probably a bunch of cameras too. There was a ripple of surprise from the gathered crowd, but for once Sadie didn't care what anyone else thought of her, and she didn't even care what *she* thought of her, because for one glorious minute all there was was George. And it was really really good.

They pulled apart to a smattering of applause and the red blink of a camera in the corner of her eye. Sadie felt the heat in her cheeks and George's hand slip into hers, and she saw Ryan rolling his eyes affectionately, and James and Mia smiling, and Adam on the other side of her, and she felt the push and pull of everything she'd lost and everything she'd gained slowly settle and smooth out. Because this was it, wasn't it? This was the point of it all: of coming here, of digging up the past, of everything she'd put everyone else through and everything they'd done to her. These people were all that mattered. She'd found her village and she knew — suddenly, and with absolute clarity — that she was never going to feel lost ever again.

"What a tart, honestly," Adam said, grinning at her.

But as quickly as it had come — because, really, adulthood was truly the worst — that feeling of contentment spiralled away and the smile froze on her face as David came round the corner. *He* wasn't smiling and she knew, she just knew, that whatever he had to say wasn't going to be what she wanted to hear.

"We having some kind of party out here?" David asked, standing in front of their little group.

"No, just Sadie cementing herself as star of this show by brazenly snogging George in front of the cameras," Ryan said.

"I was not!" Sadie protested. "Well, not the star of the show thing."

"I see," David said, raising an eyebrow in George's direction. "We're going to talk about *that* later."

"Thanks a lot, you traitor," Sadie hissed at Ryan.

"Can I tear you away from your school disco to somewhere with less cameras?" David asked. "Funk Shui only. Come on, let's walk."

The four of them fell into step behind him, neither one of them wanting to start this conversation before they had to. Sadie exchanged an anguished glance with Mia and tried to do the same with Ryan, but he just shrugged.

"Right," David said, stopping by a picnic bench. "Sit."

They dutifully filed onto the bench — Mia next to James, and Ryan with Sadie — and looked up at David, who did not sit. There was a moment of silence, and Sadie squeezed her hands together tightly in her lap. She should have known, shouldn't she? That brief moment of tranquillity was far too out of character for her life, and here was the thing that was going to balance it back out again.

"Cameron will not be finishing the show," David said finally.

"Did you speak to him?" Ryan asked, as Sadie stared dismally at the wood grain on the tabletop.

"I did, and we agreed that it was best for everyone if he left."

"*You* asked him to leave?" Sadie asked, looking up in surprise.

"Yes, and he agreed."

"So he's gone?" Mia asked.

"He's gone. I escorted him to his car."

"That doesn't sound very mutual," Ryan said.

"It was, to a point, but I wanted to be sure that he left," David said.

James frowned. "You think he'd try to sabotage the rest of the show?"

"I think he's got some complex issues going on that he needs to work through and this show isn't the place to do it," David said. "I'm not saying that he'd *do* anything, but I felt that the best thing for the rest of you was to remove him from the equation for now."

"What about his contract?" James asked.

"Not something you need to worry about," David said. "I can handle that. Now, we can spin this however you want, but it is something you all need to agree on and you'll have to be sure you can uphold it under questioning. And there will be questioning. It's up to you how much of that you want to deal with."

"You mean family emergency, sudden illness, that kind of thing?" Ryan asked.

David nodded. "That's one option."

"Doesn't lying just make it more complicated?" Mia asked. "There's been so much lying already."

"It's a tricky one," David said, "because it's a right old can of worms, isn't it? You tell everything you know and everything you think you know to a camera then they're going to want to go after Cameron to verify, and we can't control what he says in response to that. Obviously "no comment" and for him to completely distance himself from the whole situation would be the best-case scenario, but this is a big show and if he feels like you're slandering him this could get really messy."

"What did he say to you?" Ryan asked. "Did he actually admit to anything?"

"No, he wouldn't talk about it."

"Which is clever, because now *we* can't talk about it," James said.

"And we wouldn't usually, would we?" David said. "As far as everyone else would be concerned, he suddenly took ill and couldn't continue. At most there'd be some kind of minor hospital admission for low iron levels, or something like that. But this isn't ten years ago. You're adults now. You don't have record contracts or management contracts or anyone else's careers riding on what you do. You get to choose; make your own decisions. And this is a scandal that could potentially catapult you to the top of the bill with considerably more screen time… It could set a lot of things up, if that's what you want."

"But how would we do that without making everything messy?" Mia asked.

"We could talk about what we don't know," James said.

David nodded. "You could. If you wanted to."

"Why are you all looking at me?" Sadie asked.

"Because this is about you," David said, "and what happens to you next."

"I just… I don't understand how he can be *gone*!" she wailed. "How can you all be so calm? We're supposed to be rehearsing this afternoon! We're supposed to be doing a show tomorrow! An actual show! In front of actual people! On television! What are we going to do?"

"Well, I haven't spoken to anyone yet because I wanted to check in with you all first, but I can't see any reason why you can't finish the show without Cameron."

"As a *four*?" Sadie asked sceptically.

"As a four."

"But nobody wanted us as a four!" she exclaimed.

"Sadie," Ryan said, a hand on her arm.

"No! We can't be a four! Four was where it all went wrong last time!"

"Sadie."

"No one wants a four!"

"Sadie. Honestly, Sadie."

She looked at Ryan with tears in her eyes.

"It's the right four this time," he said. "Okay? Trust me. This is the right four."

67

The letter was brief and unsigned, but there was no doubt in Mabel's mind who it was from. She'd know that scrawl anywhere: exactly the same as it had been back when he'd been asking her to read through song lyrics in his bedroom. She read it for the hundredth time, toying with the edge of the paper, thinking about the way Jonny had furtively pressed it into her hand that morning.

"Don't make me regret this," he'd said, not meeting her eye, retreating as suddenly as he'd appeared.

And right now she didn't know if that was a promise she could keep.

"Do you want one of these?" Kitty asked, rifling through a box of chocolate biscuits. "I think I might eat them all."

"Are you okay?" Mabel asked, regarding her curiously.

Kitty was, as usual, a welcome distraction from all the noise in her head.

"I don't know," Kitty said, mouth full of biscuit. "I feel a bit sick all the time. You know like when you forget for a minute that something really bad is happening and then that wave of doom comes back and sits right here?" She patted her stomach.

Mabel nodded.

"I'm not enjoying that very much."

"No," Mabel agreed, being somewhat of an expert in that particular feeling.

"How can I make it go away?" Kitty asked. "Biscuits take the edge off but it's still there."

Mabel paused for a moment, looking for that feeling in her own body. But it wasn't there this time. The turmoil she was feeling now was only in her head.

"You say sorry," she said thoughtfully, her mind returning to that gentle forgiveness from Freddie that had felt like the world shifting back into focus. "It's probably not as simple as that, though."

But she wondered – *was it?*

"Are you going to go?" Kitty asked, her finger nudging the letter from Adam. "Because it's almost time."

"I know," Mabel said, so aware of the minutes ticking by.

"You might burn a hole in it if you stare at it for much longer."

"I know," Mabel said again.

Did she dare, though? It was a simple enough request: a time, a place, an invitation to watch their set at the rehearsal. Nothing more. But, despite her conversation with Freddie and her weird ethereal exchange with Fabs the previous night (which she wasn't entirely sure she hadn't imagined), it still felt like too much.

"I don't think I'm brave enough," Mabel said.

"Yes you are. He wants you there."

"But why?"

"I guess you'll find out when you go," Kitty said pointedly. "Freddie forgave you. Adam will too. You just have to let him."

"Jay didn't," Mabel said petulantly.

"Jay's opinion is invalid. He's doing his own thing."

"But what about the girl Adam was with on the lake?"

"Well are you planning to jump straight into bed with him?"

"No!" Mabel said, horrified at the thought of jumping into bed with anyone. "That isn't what this is."

"So why does it matter if he was with a girl?" Kitty asked. "Fabs gave you permission to sort all this out."

"I'm not sure Fabs is anything to do with Adam," Mabel said, aware she was just scrabbling around making bad excuses now.

Because she *did* want to go. She did. And if she'd bumped into Adam the previous night after Fabs had left, maybe she would have felt up to talking to him, but overnight her courage had waned and now she didn't want to talk to anyone about anything. She knew she was being a coward – and maybe that was all she'd ever been – but being a coward felt a lot safer than being brave.

"Another ten years and it might be too late," Kitty said. "It isn't too late now."

Mabel sighed.

"Do you want me to come with you?" Kitty asked. "We could be really ninja about it. Sneak in the back way? They wouldn't have to know you're there."

Mabel went to automatically turn her down – to push her away too – but then she stopped.

How was it that this girl, whose life she had literally stumbled into, was turning out to be the friend she never knew she needed?

"Yes," she said. "Okay."

"We need to leave now," Kitty said, shoving another biscuit into her mouth and standing up.

But Mabel hesitated. "Wait, what's the weather doing? Do I need a coat?"

"Come on," Kitty said, grabbing her hand and forcibly moving her out of the cabin.

She didn't need a coat: the weather wasn't really doing anything. As they walked down the front path Mabel could already hear the faint sounds of bands rehearsing. It made her feel queasy, nerves and excitement intertwined with the memory of everything she had loved so much and so briefly. The lights that illuminated the stage and the crowd; the surrounding darkness making you feel like the only two things that existed were you and the band. It had been longer than she could remember since she'd so much as put the radio on, let alone been around something like this.

"Oh God," Kitty said, clutching her stomach as they approached the field from the back.

"What?" Mabel asked, feeling so jittery she wondered whether she might dissolve into a pile of dust before Adam even made it onto the stage.

"They're doing my favourite song," Kitty said, looking at the band currently up there.

Their dance moves were just slightly out of sync and they were beaming at each other as if they were having the time of their lives.

"Is this James' band?" Mabel asked as they came to a stop next to the sound tent.

The last thing she wanted was to get close enough to make eye contact with anyone.

"Yeah." Kitty frowned. "Wait, why are there only four of them?"

"How many are there supposed to be?"

"Five," Kitty said. "Where's Cameron?"

Mabel assumed that was a rhetorical question seeing as she had no idea who Cameron was. She watched Kitty watching the stage, a picture of delighted hopelessness.

"He put his chin stud back in," Kitty said forlornly. "What have I done?" She sighed, eyes still locked on James. "I loved them all so much. Nothing about being an adult has ever come close to how it felt to be a fan of that stupid band."

Mabel just nodded, watching as Funk Shui finished their set, arms around each other and laughing as they took an elaborate bow.

She took a slow, deep breath as the presenter announced that the next act was a supergroup put together especially for the show, and then there they were, sauntering onto the stage like they had never been off it.

"There are too many in your band," Kitty said.

She wasn't wrong. Jay had talked about the supergroup briefly – how unimpressed he was with the idea, mostly – but she hadn't really been able to picture it until now. Was this what Adam wanted her to see?

Freddie muttered a few words into the microphone and the first strains of a song she'd once known so well snaked across the grass towards her, twisting around her body like a wraith. It was more painful than she'd been expecting, seeing them up on stage again: everything she'd loved about the people and the music was still there, despite the passing of time. None of them played quite as well as they once had done, fuelled by adrenaline, youth and pure, urgent passion. But then, none of them had been in a band with three guitarists, two bass players and two drummers before. Freddie was smiling but he looked preoccupied. Jay was scowling at the edge of the group. She couldn't see Adam's face.

"So you didn't ruin *everything*," Kitty said into her ear.

Mabel turned to look at her.

"You said you'd ruined everything for them. But if you'd ruined *everything* they wouldn't all be up there now."

The song finished to cheers from the audience, Freddie, Jay and Fabs swiftly exiting into the wings leaving just Nat, Harry, Jonny and Adam. Nat stepped up to the microphone.

"So we're going to need some audience participation here," he said. "We reached a bit of a stalemate in rehearsals over which song to do in the live show, so we're going to do them both for you now and, I don't know, maybe we'll have a show of hands afterwards."

Mabel watched as Jonny set down his guitar and picked up a tambourine instead, and Adam got out from behind the drum kit and came right to the front of the stage, stopping behind the microphone Nat had just used.

She frowned. This wasn't the Prairie Dogs she'd known.

Adam didn't say a word, nodding to Nat and fixing his expression somewhere beyond where Mabel was standing. He wasn't holding an instrument; he seemed uneasy being centre stage. And then Nat and Harry started to play and the breath caught in Mabel's throat.

She stood, staring transfixed at the stage, watching Adam bring to life a song she'd heard a hundred times in one night and then never again after that. His hands were shaking as he cupped the microphone and she looked down to find that hers were too.

"I guess we know why he wanted you here," Kitty said.

Mabel frowned, pulled from her reverie. "What?"

"Mabel, this song is about you."

"What? No. It's… No, it's not."

It *wasn't*, was it? She thought back to that night, one of the good ones, when life had still felt just about within her control. Adam had presented her with a song he couldn't finish, asking for her opinion. He didn't like the bridge and he couldn't quite get the final verse right so they'd taken it apart and put it back together again, scouring online thesaurus websites for those elusive lyrics and laughing at the results of random word generators. If someone were to put their friendship in a museum, this song would be the final artefact of the collection. But it wasn't about her. It couldn't be about her.

"Oh please," Kitty said, "I've spent most of my life wishing someone would write a song like this about me: I like to think I know my angsty song lyrics. This is classic "guy pines for a girl who's pushing him away". Isn't that what's been happening this week?"

"No," Mabel whispered, so quietly she wasn't entirely sure she'd said it at all, and she knew it was a lie anyway.

She closed her eyes and imagined Adam writing these lyrics down; writing them about her. Could that be true? Did she *want* it to be true?

"I don't think that letter was the invitation. I think *this* is the invitation," Kitty continued. "Just putting it out there. I mean, I'd love to be able to mind my own business but it's never really been my thing."

But so what if it was about her, right? Even if it had been, once, all those years ago, what did it mean now? It was a nice memory and that was it. It was impossible to think that there could be any more to it than that. Impossible.

"This could have been written yesterday," Kitty said. "Did you know he felt like this about you?"

Did she? They'd become friends from the off, clicking together with such ease. And then they were what had felt like *best* friends, albeit within the vacuum of the band, and not that she'd ever had one before to know. And then… Then she lost sight of him, distracted by shinier things, and then much darker things, and when she looked back for him it was like having been swept out to sea, stealing a glimpse of the beach as you pushed yourself up out of the water before succumbing once more to the waves. Occasionally she'd hear him call out to her, telling her to come back in and that the water was dangerous that far out, but she couldn't admit to him that she knew she'd gone too far or that she didn't know how to get back. So she'd kept drifting until she was washed up on the shore, bedraggled and broken, and by then it felt like everything had changed.

She thought about where this song fitted into the timeline of everything. Would it have changed anything if she'd known how he felt? Or would she have drifted out to sea anyway on the foolishness of youth?

"I'm just going to translate what is happening here for you, because this is a romantic gesture on a scale that most people never get to experience and I just get the feeling that you're missing the point," Kitty said matter-of-factly. "This is a song about how Adam felt about you back then. And I'm pretty sure he's singing it to you now because he *still* feels like that about you and he's hoping you feel the same."

Mabel felt like she'd drifted again recently. Perhaps not out to sea this time but into the middle of a deep lake, ominous blackness and swaying shadows hanging beneath her feet. Had Adam seen it happening? There was no way he could have reached her last time – the current had swept her out so fast – but the waters were calmer here and she was closer to the shore…

"Is he wrong?" Kitty asked. "Because if he is you should probably put him out of his misery."

Mabel didn't know what to say, her fingers grazing the edge of the lifebelt that Adam had flung out into the water. Again. Despite everything.

Did she dare?

"Maybe it's time to let Adam make a few mistakes of his own? Not that I think you're a mistake. But what I mean is, it's time to let *Adam* decide what's good for him. Stop trying to control everything so tightly. Let go a little and see what happens."

"I don't think I can," Mabel said weakly.

"Yeah you can," Kitty said. "Start by saying sorry."

68

"I think that was okay," Harry said, setting his guitar down in the tent behind the stage.

"I think we could do better," Nat said.

"Nah, that was a riot!" Jonny said, grinning. "I'd forgotten how good it feels! Why are there no beers back here? Let's go get a drink to celebrate!"

"I don't know, I think there are a few things we need to work on before tomorrow," Nat said.

"Nope!" Jonny said, clapping an arm around his shoulders. "It's beer o'clock."

"I'll catch you up," Adam said, intending to do nothing of the sort.

"You better! I'll come back for you!" Jonny said, leading Nat and Harry away.

Adam sighed heavily, considering the scrappy grass beneath his feet for a moment as their chatter faded into the distance. That had been none of the things he'd wanted it to be. He hadn't even given the bloody letter to Mabel, but Jonny had told him he couldn't back out of doing the song considering the amount of effort that had gone into getting Nat to agree to it in the first place. It had felt hollow and pointless, knowing she wasn't there; knowing that he had to let her go now, like he'd told Sadie he was going to. Knowing it was the *right* thing, but *not* knowing how it was actually possible to just let go of something that you'd built the last ten years of your life around. And he didn't have a life to go back to – he didn't even have a home. The end of this show felt like staring into a void, and he really didn't *want* to stare into a void. He didn't want this to be all his life had amounted to, and he didn't want to let her go.

"Adam?"

He looked up and there she was, right in front of him, hovering uncertainly by a stack of metal barriers.

Had he got to the point where he was actually hallucinating her or was this real?

"Are you busy?" she asked.

"No! No," he said, finding his voice. "Hi."

A tentative smile; her expression and her stance so different to the last time they'd spoken.

"Which song won?" she asked.

"What?"

"The vote?"

Adam frowned. "You watched our set?"

"Yeah, I..." Mabel looked uncertain. "Jonny gave me a note asking me to come? I thought it was from you?"

"Jonny gave it to you," Adam said, nodding as he put the pieces together. "Well that explains a lot."

"Is it okay that I'm here?" Mabel asked. "I can go?"

"No, don't, please," Adam said, not know what to do with his hands or his face or any other part of him that was being controlled by his flailing brain right now.

"So which song won?" Mabel asked again.

"Oh..." Adam shuffled on the spot, debating how honest to be. "There was no vote. Or, there was a vote, but we didn't... It didn't count. We were always going to do the other song for the live show." He shrugged. "'Disney Eyes' was for you."

And she didn't retreat, or run, or even frown.

"I love that song," she said simply.

"Me too."

She looked at him, and he looked at her, and they stood there, suspended, for just a moment.

Adam laughed awkwardly, suddenly self-conscious. "Sorry, I..." He shook his head. "It's really nice to see you."

She smiled, and it looked genuine, and he didn't know what the hell was happening here but he liked it a lot.

"I don't know how to say any of the things I need to say to you," she said, her words coming out almost as a whisper.

Adam shook his head. "You don't need to say anything. We don't have to talk about any of it. We can talk about something stupid instead. Just...

don't go. I mean, you *can* go, if you have somewhere you need to be, but… We don't have to talk about any of the stuff. I don't care. About any of it. Can we just… Can we talk about something stupid?"

And yeah, sure, this wasn't what letting her go was supposed to look like. But she was *right here*, finally — what was he meant to do, just let her walk away?

Mabel smiled again, but it was a different smile, a sadder smile, an "Adam you're very sweet, but" kind of smile.

"Fabs said something to me yesterday. About closure," she said, and Adam felt his stomach tense.

Because he didn't want closure. He wanted the opposite of closure. He wanted to open everything back up and start again. If she had come to him now only to close the chapter he wasn't sure he was going to handle it very well. If he could freeze them both in time, standing in silence together forever, he would do it without a second thought.

"He said that the mistakes we make, the things we can't get over, it's like… What was it? *Snagging a scarf on a thorn.* And you think you're moving on, or you're trying to move on, but all the time you're still caught on the thorn and your scarf is unravelling. And the only way you can break free from it is to go back to where you snagged it in the first place and untangle it."

Adam frowned, letting that sink in.

"Can't you cut it?" he asked.

"That's what I said," Mabel said, with another, different, more open smile. *The many smiles of Mabel Alexander.*

"What happens when you've untangled it?" Adam asked. "You just walk away, carefree, and never have to think about it again?"

"If you want to," Mabel said carefully.

"What if you don't want to?"

Mabel paused and Adam tried to take it all in, the very sight of her standing here before him, in case this really was the last time.

"Maybe you get a chance to do better; to make better decisions. To try again?" she said.

"I think I would want that. You know, hypothetically, if I'd gone back and untangled my scarf. I think I would want to try again."

"Me too," Mabel said, finally meeting his eye.

Adam nodded, feeling like he was exhaling properly for the first time in years.

"Okay," he said. "Well that's... That's good." He smiled. "That's good."

"Do you... I mean... Is there somewhere you need to be?" Mabel asked, tripping over her words.

"No," Adam said. "Do you?"

Mabel shook her head but she didn't say anything.

"Shall we..." Adam started, feeling like perhaps the opportunity was here but he was going to have to be the one to take it. "Do you want to go somewhere we can talk? Somewhere quieter?"

"Do you have time?" Mabel asked.

"I have time," Adam said, not knowing at all whether that was actually true, but not caring one single bit. "Where do you want to go? Where would be quiet right now?"

"Maybe The Lounge?" Mabel suggested.

"Oh the ski lodge? Yeah, I like that," Adam said, thinking of the twinkling lights and the balcony overlooking the lake.

"The ski lodge?"

"You don't think it looks like a ski lodge?"

A fourth smile.

This was going well, right? This was good. Well, apart from the fact that his racing heart might give out any second. But apart from that. Very good.

"Lead the way," Adam said, "because I have no idea where I am or where I'm going at any given moment."

Mabel nodded and off they went, walking beside each other in awkward silence. It wasn't really the kind of thing you could casually dive into whilst walking around a lake, was it? Almost ten years of missing pieces and all the weighty emotion that came with it. And, honestly, he didn't care if they *never* got into it. Because he'd stared right into the prospect of letting her go for good and absolutely *nothing* could be as bleak as that. So he embraced the glorious silence and the simple act of walking somewhere *with Mabel*, and he waited, patiently, for this to play out however it was going to.

"Here we are," Mabel said, the wooden building looming before them.

"Here we are," Adam agreed.

He followed her up the steps and through the double doors, hanging back slightly as she spoke to one of the staff.

"I said we're having a meeting and not to disturb us," she said, coming back over to him.

"Well yeah," Adam said, quietly impressed with how important Mabel obviously was around here, "wouldn't want anyone to trip over all this wool. It's a public health hazard."

Smile number five was a tight smile, and Adam deduced that perhaps they weren't quite at the joking stage yet. The trouble was it felt too natural walking into a bar with her, sitting with her, talking to her. It was like no time at all had passed since they'd last done something like this, in the same way that it had *never* felt right that they hadn't been in each other's lives over the last ten years. It was hard to remember that they were here to have some kind of "difficult conversation" when all he wanted to do was ask her about her day and talk about nothing long into the night as if they'd only seen each other yesterday.

He followed her out onto the balcony to a small table next to the wooden railings.

"Here?" she asked.

He nodded, resisting the urge to pull out her chair for her.

"I need to say some things," she said, her hands clasped in her lap.

"Okay." Adam nodded. "I'm listening."

"I've been really horrible to you since you've been here," she started.

"You haven't," Adam jumped in, unable to help himself.

"Adam, you know I have."

"No, I pushed it," Adam said. "You didn't want to talk to me and I just kept turning up. I should have given you the space you wanted."

"I did want to talk to you," Mabel said quietly. "You were the *only* person I wanted to talk to." She smiled sadly. "For ten years you were the only person I wanted to talk to."

And that was bittersweet, it really was. That was all he had ever wanted to hear, but what a colossal waste of time the last ten years had been if they'd been miles apart feeling exactly the same. Where could they have been now if they'd had those years? What could they have done with that time, together instead of apart?

"Me too," Adam said, trying to maintain the painful and wonderful eye contact they had going on.

"But..." Mabel shook her head. "I don't understand any of this. Jay hates me. Nat told me to stay away from everyone. *That* I understand. That I expected. But Freddie, and Fabs, and *you*... After everything I did... To *you*; to everyone else. I was *awful* to you. I took all that *money* from you."

"Mabel, there was nothing you could have done that would have hurt more than you not being there," Adam said, his voice wavering. "*Nothing.*"

She didn't say anything, her eyes now firmly fixed on the table in front of her.

"I tried to find you after you left," Adam said. "I looked for you for a really long time. Too long, probably."

"Why?" Mabel's voice was more like a whisper.

Adam shrugged. "Because I didn't know whether you'd left because you were sick of us or because you were punishing yourself. Because, selfishly, I missed you, and I didn't like my life much without you in it."

She didn't say anything.

"Why did you stay away, Mabel?" Adam asked. "All I ever wanted to do was make sure you were okay."

Mabel looked up at him then, her eyes shiny with tears.

"*This* is why," she said. "Because you're nice to me when I don't deserve it. Because you would have forgiven every awful thing I ever did. Because I can't be the person that you need me to be, and I can't bear seeing your disappointment when I let you down."

"It's not like that," Adam tried to interject.

"It is! I am a mess, Adam! I keep trying to do the right thing and getting it wrong. I'll probably always get it wrong because that's just who I am. I am *not* a good person – *you* are a good person! And I can't watch you hope that one day I will be able to be one. I'm so tired of trying so hard to be better; I don't think I can do it any more. I don't think I can *be* any more than this. So this is just me. This is all I can be. And you can take it or leave it."

He looked at her anguished expression, the tears slipping down her cheeks.

"I'll take it," he said gently. "I'll take it. All of it. All of you. Exactly how you are."

"I'll let you down," Mabel said.

"Okay."

"I'll hurt you."

"Okay," Adam said again, nodding.

"You shouldn't let me back in," she whispered.

Adam shook his head. "Mabel, you never left," he said, putting a hand to his heart. "Here. You never left."

Her hands had knitted themselves into a tight ball on the tabletop. Hesitantly Adam reached out and rested his hand over hers. He felt the knot soften and she didn't pull away.

"There were so many things I wanted to say to you…" she said. "It's been such a long time…"

Adam nodded. "I know."

"I don't think I know how to do this."

"Well, how about we make polite small talk for a few minutes and take it from there?" he suggested.

And that sixth smile… Well that sixth smile felt like coming home.

69

So here they were, *The Right Four*, waiting to be interrogated about how they managed to lose a member *during* a reunion show, which was surely some kind of world record – or a new low, depending on how you chose to look at it.

"Are you sure he's sorted it?" Sadie asked Ryan anxiously.

"Yes, he's sorted it."

"And everything's okay? You are going back to the band?"

"Yes."

"Are you *sure*? You're not going to have to come and live with me and Mia and work in Asda?"

"Sadie, I'm not going to be working in bloody *Asda*," Ryan said. "It was a really minor thing and it's all sorted now. I didn't want to tell you about it because I knew you would freak out, but it's fine. *It's* fine, and everything is fine."

"Apart from this," Sadie said, gesturing at the sofa and the TV cameras.

"This is also fine," James said, nudging her, surprisingly chirpy by his standards.

"We'll see," Sadie muttered.

Although she had to say, the four of them crammed onto a bright pink sofa in boy-girl boy-girl formation… It didn't feel exactly wrong.

"Why did you do it?" she asked Ryan. "Why did you risk losing your band for me?"

He smiled at her like she'd just asked him the most stupid question in the world.

"I'd do anything for you," he said simply.

The door swung open and everyone else turned to look at the people strolling into the room, but Sadie was still looking at Ryan.

"Thanks for being here, guys. I know you're keen to get to the party," Helen said.

"Oh they've sent in the big guns," James muttered.

"Now, off the record, I've spoken to your manager and obviously it's absolutely fine for you to carry on and finish the show as a four piece."

"*Manager*," Ryan said under his breath, elbowing Sadie.

"We wouldn't dream of cutting you out, so there's nothing to worry about there. *Obviously* we need to have a bit of a chat about it on camera, for continuity. I think we last had footage of Cameron yesterday afternoon, so just a quick recap, *an update*, on what's happened would be great. Appreciate it's all a bit of a shock to you so just do what you can, see how we go. We'll be catching up with everyone again tomorrow morning, anyway."

Sadie could practically see the pound signs in her eyes, fully aware that anything they said now was going to heavily feature in the advertising campaign for the show.

"We're paying off her mortgage, aren't we?" she whispered to Ryan.

"Oh for sure," he said.

"Ready?" Helen asked, and everyone nodded reluctantly. "Let's get started! So, Funk Shui! We've just seen you up on stage rehearsing, but you seem to be one member short? What's going on there? Is Cameron not well?"

They all exchanged a glance and Sadie imagined they were all momentarily considering changing the plan and taking the easy route through all this. Helen had lined it right up for them, as if she was offering them an out. But it wasn't what they'd agreed; it wasn't the way this had to end.

"Cameron is fine, as far as we're aware," Ryan said, "but he is no longer part of the band."

"Wow, okay. Can you tell us a bit about what happened?"

"Well it's not been the easiest reunion for us," James said. "I'm sure you've seen there's been a few disagreements throughout this process; bits and pieces of tension."

"And was that because of Cameron?"

James paused for a moment. "I think it was because of all of us, really. Would you agree?" He looked to Sadie, and she nodded.

"Apart from Mia," she said.

James smiled. "Apart from Mia."

"I think my problem was that I came into this with the wrong expectations," Sadie said. "I practically bullied everyone into doing the show, hoping that we'd fall back into being one big happy family if I could just get everyone in the same place at the same time."

"And that didn't happen?" Helen asked.

Sadie laughed. "No, it didn't. But I got something much more real instead. Not a happy family or a happy ending. Something better. I thought I needed the band to fix all the things that were wrong with my life. But I don't. I think I can do that myself."

Ryan squeezed her knee. "Yeah you can," he said.

"I think some people might have been surprised to see you and James up on stage together," Helen said, addressing Ryan, "given the rumours flying around at the moment."

Ryan cleared his throat. "Well, I think we're saying quite a firm no comment to that, aren't we, mate?"

James nodded sagely.

"But I will say that, luckily for me, James is one of the most decent blokes around so my perfect face has been preserved."

"Your perfect face," Sadie scoffed. "Your *stupid* face."

"And how does Cameron leaving the band relate to the issues James has so candidly spoken about recently?" Helen asked.

"It doesn't," James said. "My struggles are entirely my own."

"But you *have* clashed with Cameron in rehearsals."

"We've all clashed in rehearsals," Ryan said. "Mainly because we're horribly unfit and can't remember how to be pop stars."

"It's been strange coming back together after so much time apart," Mia said. "None of us are the same as we were first time around and it's taken a while to work out how to relate to each other as we are now, rather than who we were back then. Sometimes it's been hard to see past who we *thought* we were to who we actually are now. Things came up along the way but we've managed to work through everything and it feels like we're stronger than ever where we are at this point."

"What she said," Sadie agreed.

"Stronger than ever, but with one member missing," Helen said. "So are you saying you're stronger *because* Cameron isn't with you?"

"No," Ryan said, "not at all. I think we're very lucky that the bond we've reforged over the last ten days means that we can withstand something like this happening. It would have been the same regardless of who was here or not here."

A blatant lie, Sadie thought, but it sounded convincing.

This was what they'd agreed: to overshare their own truths (to a point) to deflect the white lies they were telling about Cameron. Did she really think she could fix all the things that were wrong with her life by herself? Of course not. But could she do it surrounded by people like Ryan and George and Adam? Well, the odds felt a little more in her favour there. And yes, okay, she was absolutely not addressing this whole weird "you're the star of the band" thing, or the fact that David kept talking about "options" and "what happens next for you", but maybe she was done with yearning and what ifs and unrealistic expectations for now. Maybe going to the pub every Sunday with Ryan and Mia and James and Adam and George didn't sound so depressing after all. Maybe it really wasn't the *place* but the *people* who made life okay; who made the crap bits and the dreary bits and the boring bits more bearable and carried you through to the next good bit. And plus, she knew exactly what was going to happen next for her: one hell of a lot of lying in the sun drinking elaborate cocktails, that was what.

"Is there any bitterness there about Cameron leaving you in the lurch just before the live show? How did it feel being up on stage without him?" Helen asked.

"It felt like a bit of a shame after all the work we've done together this week," Ryan said. "It would have been good to have all crossed the finish line together and brought it to its natural end. But I think what I've realised, coming back together for a second time, is that the needs of the band doesn't supersede the needs of us as individuals. There's no contract, there's no record label; we've all got to do what is right for each of us, and if that's being in the band, then great. And if it's not…" He shrugged. "You do you, right?"

"Speaking as someone who has left this band before," James said, "it's never an easy decision to make. But like Ryan said, it's got to be right for everyone."

"And does four feel right?" Helen asked. "Because you were very briefly a four before and I think the general consensus was that it didn't work?"

"Well, look," Ryan said, doing his diplomatic sigh, "we're all such different people now. We were kids back then and it wasn't us pulling the strings, either. We've all somehow emerged as pretty level-headed adults, and to be honest I think we could probably handle it even as a three."

"Oh, well, if you don't need me…" James grinned, half getting up from the sofa. "No, I think we did pretty well with what we had during the dress rehearsal. Like Ryan said, nobody's panicking about it; we're still going up there intending to enjoy every minute and give the fans what they want. Assuming we still have fans? I'm not entirely clear on that."

"I also wondered about the fans," Sadie said. "*Do* we still have fans?"

"You do still have fans," Helen assured them.

"I didn't really think about that, actually," Sadie said thoughtfully. "I wasn't really thinking of this as like a last hurrah for anybody but us. But maybe the fans need this too?" She paused. "Are you *sure* about the fans thing?"

"I think you'd be surprised," Helen said.

"Maybe we should have a quick extra practice tomorrow morning…" Mia said.

"Should I be shirtless for this?" Ryan asked. "I mean, if we're *giving the fans what they want*."

"I'm pretty sure the fans want you to keep your clothes on," Sadie said.

"Well that's not my experience of it, but okay," Ryan said, doing an exaggerated wink.

"So do you think you *can* give the fans what they want, going up there as a four?" Helen asked.

"Yes," Sadie said.

"Yes," Mia said, smiling at her.

"Yes," James said. "Unless I have a moment of pure paralysing fear and forget all the words and the dance moves. Could happen."

"You know what, I think we did great," Ryan said, smiling. "In fact, I'm going to go out on a limb and say we did better than great. And I'm going to stop just short of saying we smashed it out of the park."

"We're saving that for the live show," Sadie said.

It *had* been better than great, though – Ryan was right. Without Cameron there had been no one to curb the good feeling bouncing between the four of them: there was so much genuine joy and excitement and enthusiasm, and at no point did anyone try to sour it with a negative comment or make them feel stupid for enjoying it so much. There hadn't been any less magic with one less member. It hadn't felt any less special.

"Maybe we should change our name to *Four* Shui," Sadie said.

"That would be a horrible decision."

"That is definitely not what is best for us *or* the band."

"Maybe we can take it in turns to leave…" she mused.

"I will happily take the next slot if we change our name to bloody *Four Shui*," Ryan said, raising his hand.

Sadie laughed, and she realised that somewhere along the way this interview had stopped feeling forced and awkward and it had turned into just them, just four friends, vibing off each other like they always used to. Laughing and joking, hands on knees and arms looped casually across shoulders, just happy to be in each other's presence. And even though it was all ending and this was their last interview, their last rehearsal, their last performance, she couldn't help but feel that little flicker of contentment, like the determined match that refuses to be extinguished by the gust of wind just as you are about to light the birthday candles.

Enough, she thought. *This is enough.*

Maybe the end was the beginning, after all.

"And do you want to talk about your rather public display of affection with George from Kingpin this morning?" Helen asked.

Sadie grinned. "I do not."

"Fair enough," Helen said. "So, the end of the show is approaching. Is this it for Funk Shui? Are we saying goodbye to you up on that stage?"

They all looked at each other then, caught off guard by such a final question, none of them wanting to be the one to condemn this incredible thing they'd once shared to the archives.

When the silence went on for too long Sadie opened her mouth to speak, to finish it for good on behalf of all of them, but James put a hand on her knee, stopping her.

"Well," he said, nodding at her, "you'll have to wait and see. Let's say, watch this space."

70

Show me where you live, he'd said. And stupidly, without thinking, caught up in this fictional world where she could hang out with Adam again without any of the Bad Feelings, she'd taken him back to her actual house. The damp lanes had looked dreary in the gloom of the afternoon, the village somehow less picturesque than normal, and now they were standing outside her front door and it all felt like a terrible mistake.

"I haven't been back here for a while," Mabel said, stalling for time. "You know, because of the show."

"Okay," Adam said.

"It's not even my house. I just rent it."

"Okay."

"It'll probably be really cold. It takes ages to heat up."

Adam smiled. "Mabel, I don't care."

She nodded, more to settle her own nerves than anything else. She put the key in the lock but paused again. She knew why he'd wanted to come here. He wanted to see who she was now; discover another piece of the puzzle by looking at the things she had and the way she lived. But he was only going to be disappointed, because no one lived in this house. A ghost of a person lived in this house. And the only thing he was going to discover was just how empty a shell she was.

She turned and looked at him.

"I never come back here," she said. "When I moved in there was already furniture so I just used what was here. I don't have... *things*. I don't... I'm not..."

"Are there 25 pop stars inside?"

"No."

"Do you own two mugs and a kettle?"

"I… Yes," Mabel said, not actually knowing whether she owned two mugs, but thinking that she surely must do, because didn't most basic mugs come in packs of four?

"I think it'll be just fine," Adam said, smiling encouragingly.

"Adam, I stopped," Mabel said, still not able to bring herself to turn the key. "I stopped being a person. After I left, I just… stopped. There isn't anything of me inside this house. There isn't anything of me anywhere."

"Well I don't even have a house," Adam said. "Before the show I lost the place I was living and all of my *things* are in the back of the van that's parked in the car park back at the site. Is that who I am? Is that *all* that I am?"

Mabel shook her head.

"I would sit in any kitchen, on any sofa, lean against the wall, sit on the floor, anything, anywhere, if it meant catching up with you," Adam said earnestly. "I'm not here to nose through all your stuff. I just wanted to get away from all the drama; all the chaos. Get some peace. Find some space."

Don't we all, Mabel thought, steeling herself and finally opening the door.

"I do have a sofa," she said, stepping awkwardly inside.

"Then we're all set," Adam said, following her in.

She watched as he kicked his shoes off by the door, something she'd never even thought to do. She did the same and then paused to turn the heating on, radiators and pipes clicking and clanking as she caught up with Adam in the kitchen.

"I found your two mugs," he said, holding them up. "What do you drink these days?"

"Oh, er, tea," Mabel said, trying to process the sight of Adam in her kitchen casually making a cup of tea.

What this real? Had any of the last few hours been real? It was so far beyond anything she had ever thought could happen. And it was so very very nice.

The kitchen was narrow and there wasn't a lot of space for them to both be making drinks so Mabel sat down at the small table in the corner, just watching as Adam lit up the entire space with his warmth and his smile and his energy.

"Sugar?" he asked.

"No."

"Ah, a proper grown-up," he said, putting a mug down in front of her and sliding the milk back into the fridge. "I cannot drink tea with less than three sugars in it."

"*Three?*"

He nodded, sitting down opposite her. "Three." He smiled. "So."

"So," Mabel said, busying herself with her scalding hot tea.

"I like it," Adam said. "Your house. It's cosy."

Mabel looked around at the cold empty house that usually felt anything but *cosy*. Adam had turned on every light he'd walked past and a yellow glow spilled out through the French doors onto the neglected patio. Steam still floated up from the recently boiled kettle. The cupboard door was ajar and there was a wet teaspoon on the counter. *Things* were out of place and there was a variable in her small closed-off little space that hadn't been there before. The room felt lived-in for the first time and all of a sudden it *did* feel cosy. Just the right amount of space for two, in fact. Fancy that.

"Do you ever light the fire?" Adam asked.

"No," Mabel said. "I wouldn't know how."

"I know how," Adam said, raising an eyebrow.

"It's April."

"Yeah but it's *cold* for April, right?"

"You want to light the fire?" Mabel asked sceptically.

"I do want to light the fire! Love an open fire! Reminds me of my mum's house," Adam said, putting his mug down on the table and standing up.

"How are we going to light the fire?" Mabel asked, watching him curiously.

Was it just her or was there something strangely intimate about seeing someone in socks instead of shoes?

"We're going to find something to burn," Adam said, trying the handle on the patio doors. "Oh. Have you got a key for this?"

Mabel frowned. "I… actually don't know."

"You've been out in the garden, right?"

"Um… I'm not sure. Maybe once?"

"How long have you lived here?"

Mabel paused, trying to work it out. "Five years? I don't… I'm not really a garden kind of person."

"First we find the key, then we find something to burn," Adam said, moving around the kitchen, opening drawers and cupboards. "Well this looks promising," he said, plucking a small key from a drawer that Mabel didn't ever use.

She didn't even think she'd ever seen that key before. Was that possible?

"Here we go!" Adam said, slotting the key into the lock and turning it. "Success! Shoes," he said, disappearing out of the room.

Mabel stepped towards the open patio door, the air outside not much colder than inside, and she realised she really had never been out there. She didn't even know *what* was out there.

The downstairs bathroom window faced the garden but the glass was obscured, and from the patio doors all you could see was the scruffy paving and next door's fence. She couldn't remember ever really looking out of the upstairs windows: on the rare occasion she had actually slept there she'd usually left so early that she didn't bother opening the curtains.

But how could she not have wanted to know what was out there?

She'd been so focussed for so long on making her world smaller and more tightly controlled that she'd stopped noticing anything outside of the tiny circle she existed in. But Adam had stepped right into the circle with what he'd said to her earlier and he was already stretching it out with his elbows, making space where space had seemed impossible – and terrifying – before.

"Here," he said, placing her shoes next to her feet.

His arm brushed against hers and the breath caught in her throat. This was the point that she would usually run. When anyone got too close. When things started to get overfamiliar. But she didn't want to run this time. She wanted to step out into that garden with Adam and see what was out there. She wanted to step out into *the world* with Adam and see what was out there.

He waited for her while she slipped her shoes on, hanging back so she could be the first one to see it, ever the gentleman. And it wasn't a life-changing moment. It wasn't The Secret Garden out there. There wasn't even a lawn. It was as long and narrow as the house was, scrappy like the patio and overgrown with brambles, with just a few stubborn primroses clustered around the shady edges.

"Did you know there's a stream back here?" Adam asked, leaning over the back wall.

"No?" Mabel said, picking her way over to him and putting her hands against the uneven stones.

"There's no traffic noise out here at all. You could just sit and listen to that stream, and the birds, and just nothing else."

And for all that inviting Adam back to her house had seemed like such a big, daunting step, standing here next to him now felt like nothing at all. Because that was the thing she'd forgotten about Adam: when you were with him, he demanded nothing more than that you simply exist in his presence. And it turned out that simply existing next to Adam was the easiest thing in the world to do.

"Oh," he said suddenly, digging in his pocket and looking at his phone. "Why is Freddie ringing me?"

Mabel watched him straighten up and step away from her as he answered the call, meandering in a zigzag towards the house with his back to her. She tried not to listen, feeling herself shrinking back to her former size. How stupid she had been to momentarily imagine that the two of them could just stay in this garden together and forget about everything else. This was, of course, nothing more than a brief one-off before he went back to whatever he was doing before he landed on her doorstep.

"Hmmm," Adam said, coming back over with a frown on his face. "Don't quite know what to make of that."

"What?" Mabel asked quietly, wanting to know and not wanting to know all at once.

"He kind of offered me a job."

"Oh."

"Yeah, something about a promotor in the audience of the rehearsal who wants to take Granola Fantasy out on the road again. *Big* tour by the sound of it, but Fabs isn't keen so Freddie asked if I wanted to step in."

"Oh," Mabel said again, the thought of Freddie and Jay and Adam all in the same band making her feel a little bit sick. "Superstardom awaits, then."

"Well. I don't know if it's really my scene…"

"Fame and fortune isn't your scene?"

Adam looked at her thoughtfully and smiled. "No. I reckon it's not. Plus," he said, "I don't know if I've really got time. I've got a fire to build, you know?"

And Mabel didn't know what this was, or what this could be, but she knew right then that she was going to trust the goosebumps on her arms, and the sound of the trickling stream, and the yellow glow coming from the house, and this man in her garden who had complete and utter faith in himself that he could build a fire with absolutely no supplies, and maybe – just maybe – that could be enough for now.

THE LIVE SHOW

71

"Are you ready for this?"

"No," Sadie grinned, her hands shaking as she gripped the microphone tightly.

"Sadie Dawes, this is the moment you've been waiting for your whole life," Ryan said, grinning back at her, the energy at the side of the stage overwhelmingly infectious.

"Bit of an exaggeration."

"Is it, though?"

Sadie closed her eyes and tried to anchor herself to the moment, to stop it flashing past in hyper speed before she'd had a second to soak it all up. The glare of the lights, the boom of the music, the screams – screams! – from the crowd as Kingpin finished up their set. The weight of the microphone in her hand. The heat of everything. Her three best friends standing in a huddle around her, visibly fizzing with nervous exhilaration. David watching from the sidelines. And if not her *whole* life, she had been waiting a bloody long time for this.

"What about you, grandad?" Ryan asked, nudging James. "You ready?"

"Oh absolutely not. I think I'm going to throw up."

"What if I faint on stage?" Mia asked, managing to look simultaneously terrified and excited.

"We'll just roll you to the back and carry on," Ryan said. "Happens all the time in my band. I don't know if guys are aware, but I'm kind of a big deal? I'm not familiar with this thing you call *nerves*."

"Oh sure, hotshot," Sadie said.

"Yeah, okay, I'm bricking it, all right? What if I forget the words? We spent most of our time in the band miming – now we have to remember lyrics *and* dance moves?"

"I don't think we've rehearsed enough," Mia said. "Can we go back and do some more?"

Sadie just smiled, peering past them to watch Kingpin bowing theatrically for the crowd, radiating happiness and delightedly jostling each other as they exited on the other side of the stage. George turned and met her gaze, blowing her a kiss as he disappeared into the wings.

"Good luck!" Maddie Fox whispered, stepping out past them to do her intro piece.

It was like an out of body experience, hearing her say their band name as the crowd's screams intensified. It was far beyond anything Sadie had felt first time around, back when she'd thought it would all last forever; back when she didn't know what it was like to lose it.

Maddie swept back past them, the lights went down and suddenly it was time: *the moment.*

The end, the beginning, the everything.

Sadie linked arms with James, took a deep breath and stepped out onto the stage, weightless at last.

ABOUT THE AUTHOR

Chloe Banyard spent her teenage years holed up in her bedroom writing stories about boybands and 20 years on nothing much has changed. She lives in the Forest of Dean with her husband and two children, and when she's not writing or parenting she can mostly be found trying to learn the names of constellations, putting together elaborate grazing platters, creating Pinterest boards for home improvement projects she'll never get round to starting and ordering unreasonable quantities of pick & mix.

You can follow Chloe on Instagram @chloebanyardwrites